HER PATRIOTIC DUTY

Esme Colborne is about to marry Richard
Trevannion. When she finds out she is
adopted — from a working class family
— she cannot allow Richard to marry so far
beneath his station. Fleeing the life she knew,
she starts working as a decoy woman, testing
British undercover operatives who may
otherwise reveal secrets in a moment of
weakness. However, she still has feelings for
Richard. Will she be brave enough to risk
having her heart broken all over again?

ROSIE MEDDON

HER PATRIOTIC DUTY

Complete and Unabridged

MAGNA
Leicester

First published in Great Britain in 2020

First Ulverscroft Edition
published 2021

The moral right of the author has been asserted

A catalogue record for this book is available from the British Library.

ISBN 978–0–7505–4853–3

Published by
Ulverscroft Limited
Anstey, Leicestershire

Set by Words & Graphics Ltd.
Anstey, Leicestershire
Printed and bound in Great Britain by
TJ Books Ltd., Padstow, Cornwall

This book is printed on acid-free paper

Clarence Square, London

May 1940

1

Family

'Lou, you would tell me, wouldn't you, if you thought I was being hasty?'

'Being hasty?'

'In marrying Richard so soon. Only, I get the impression some people think we're rushing into it.'

Twiddling the stem of her empty sherry glass while she waited for her cousin to reply, Esme Colborne glanced about the guest-filled drawing room. Where *was* Richard anyway? She did hope he hadn't got cornered by Great Aunt Diana. Or worse still, by Grandpa Hugh.

Beside her, her own glass of sherry barely touched, Lou Channer frowned. 'Not sure I'm the right person to answer that. I mean, what do I know about —'

'It's not that anyone has said anything,' Esme went on, her voice lowered so as not to be overheard. 'And if they've said anything to Richard then he hasn't mentioned it. But I'm convinced that his mother, for one, thinks we've become swept up in some sort of war fever. I can tell from the way she looks at me.'

Lou continued to frown. 'Well, how long have you known him?'

Recalling the moment she'd met Richard Trevannion made Esme smile. 'Just before

3

Christmas, I went to a party with a friend. Bowling into the kitchen in search of olives for a Gin & It, I smacked straight into him.' He'd looked, she remembered thinking at the time, like a younger version of Cary Grant: dark hair; mischievous eyes; nice smile. Impeccable manners, too.

'So, that would make it . . . ' Lou counted on her fingers. ' . . . five months.'

Recalling the evening in question, and how the two of them had fallen so deeply into conversation they'd become oblivious to the merriment going on all around them, Esme nodded. 'That's right. Our first proper date was on New Year's Eve. It turned out to be such fun that we went out again the next day as well . . . '

'So . . . '

'Then, shortly before Easter, he took me to the V&A for afternoon tea. On the way back through Thurloe Square Gardens, I was admiring the daffodils when he suggested we stop and sit on a bench. Next thing I know, he's down on one knee, ring in hand, saying 'Esme Colborne, will you marry me?''

'And you had no idea — that he was going to propose, I mean?'

'None whatsoever.'

'Golly. How romantic.'

In response to her cousin's remark, Esme smiled. 'It *was quite* romantic, yes.'

'And did you answer him straight away?'

'I did.'

'So, if you didn't hesitate *then*, why the doubts *now?* What's changed?'

'Well . . . '

'Because if the answer is *nothing*,' Lou observed, 'then I don't see what you have to worry about. In fact, rather than fret, you might want to count your blessings.'

Esme let out a sigh. Her cousin was right; she *was* fortunate. Richard was warm and caring. And terribly good company.

'Yes, of course,' she said. 'No doubt it's just a dose of last-minute collywobbles. By Saturday, I daresay I'll be fine.' With the sound of the dinner gong then echoing about the hallway, she again looked about for Richard. 'Anyway,' she said, failing to see him anywhere but giving her cousin's arm a quick squeeze, 'I asked Mummy to seat you next to Uncle Ned so that you'll have someone jolly to talk to. You'll find he has the most wicked sense of — ' Spotting Richard crossing the room towards her, Esme felt a surge of warmth. How daft to have got all het up; he really was lovely. 'Richard, there you are.'

'I believe that's our cue,' he said, offering a hand in her direction.

'And *my* cue to find Mum,' Lou said, before turning about and leaving them to it.

'Well, so far so good, don't you think?'

Taking his arm, Esme grinned. 'No one has challenged anyone to a duel yet. Is that what you mean?'

She loved how he threw back his head when he laughed. Unlike the rest of his family he was quick to see the funny side of things.

'Not that I'm aware of, no.'

'Still nerve-wracking, though, isn't it?' she said

5

as they started slowly towards the doors. 'Or is that just me?'

'Not just you, no. Navigating someone else's family is like picking one's way across a minefield. But, look at it like this, if our two clans can't get along, then once Saturday is over and done with, they need never see each other again. Whereas the two of us . . . '

When she turned to look at him, he was trying to keep a straight face.

'Will have no such choice?'

'None whatsoever. Stuck together for all eternity, I'm afraid.' Leading her out into the hallway he went on, 'And I can't think of anyone to whom I'd rather be stuck.'

Yes, how daft it felt now to have had doubts! She couldn't wait for Saturday.

Before then, though, they had this family dinner to get through, the sight awaiting them in the dining room causing her to withhold a groan. Staring expectantly in their direction from both sides of the long table were their two dozen relatives, while glinting under the light of the chandeliers had to be every piece of silverware the Colbornes owned, the place settings so elaborate they wouldn't have looked out of place in front of the King. Clearly, when it came to first impressions, Mummy and Grandmamma Pamela had decided to leave nothing to chance — wartime or not.

'Well then,' she murmured, angling her head towards him as she did so, 'let the tedium commence.'

'Now, now,' he whispered back as he escorted

6

her towards their seats. 'Don't be too hasty to write the thing off. This *could* turn out to be an evening we look back upon with great fondness . . . talk about for years to come . . . bore our grandchildren silly with . . .'

Lowering herself onto her chair, she sent him a despairing look. 'Then one can but pray it will be for the right reasons . . .'

★ ★ ★

Shifting her weight in her seat, Esme stifled a yawn. Surely her mother couldn't leave it *much* longer before signalling for the ladies to withdraw. They had finished eating ages ago and what she wanted more than anything right now was to kick off her shoes and fall into bed. Not helping was the fact that, with all the windows closed in order to secure the blackout blinds, the room was warm and airless.

Wondering how late it was, she pushed back the sleeve of her silk bolero and stared down at the face of her wristwatch, the tiny diamonds around the bezel sparkling under the lights. Ten past ten. No wonder she felt tired.

Stifling yet another yawn, she looked about the table: across from her, Daddy's forehead had begun to shine; further along, Mummy's cheeks had become flushed; Matilda Trevannion's nose had turned pink from overdoing the claret. Of course, it was wonderful that everyone had come together like this, especially given the fraught nature of travel these days but now, having sat through several hours during which the men seemed unable to talk of anything except the disaster unfolding on the beaches of northern France, she felt beyond exhausted. This close to the wedding she needed every hour of beauty sleep she could get.

Still, she mused, feeling her lips curling into a smile, at least she'd had Richard to talk to. Despite that earlier attack of nerves — surely only to be expected given the speed with which this had all come about — the prospect of becoming Mrs Richard Trevannion made her quite giddy with delight. At times, she still couldn't believe he'd been interested in her, let alone so quick to ask her to marry him.

'Everything all right, darling?' Drawn from her reflections, she turned to see him regarding her, his head angled, a light smile on his lips. 'You seemed miles away.'

She smiled back. 'Sorry. Just completely worn out.' Leaning forward to look beyond him along the table, she went on, 'And so must you be, too, having to converse for so long with Grand-mamma Pamela. I know what awfully hard work she can be.'

'If she hasn't been telling me about when she did the season, and about being presented,' he whispered back, 'she's been urging us not to leave it too long before starting a family. *The sooner the better*, she keeps saying.'

'Interfering old bat.' Careful to keep her voice lowered, she went on, 'Why is it that old people think they can say anything they like — that the usual rules of tact and discretion cease to apply once one reaches a certain age?'

'*Is* she that old? She seems remarkably quick-witted.'

'She's about to turn seventy. But she doesn't want anyone to know.'

Richard smiled. 'Would it be such a bad thing, though?'

'For most people, no. But Grandmamma likes to think she can pass for younger.'

Richard stifled laughter. 'No, silly, I meant about us starting a family. Might it not be a good idea to get on to it . . . so to speak . . . as soon as possible?'

For Esme, it was far too late in the evening to be discussing something as weighty as starting a family, not to mention entirely the wrong place. 'Well, no . . . '

'I was thinking four . . . '

She shook her head in dismay. 'Were you now?'

'Two of each — '

'As though one has any say in the matter.'

'I appreciate that. But it *would* make for a nice tidy little family.'

In truth, she'd always rather assumed that children simply came along, as and when, without the need to actually plan for them. She certainly had no preference for boys or girls, her only wish being that they arrived fit and healthy. Of course, it wouldn't harm if they were also beautiful and bright and grew up to become much admired and respected in decent society. They certainly wouldn't lack for pedigree: the Trevannions and the Colbornes — two old West Country families coming together. What better start could a child have? Respectability and privilege. The perfect combination. Granted, some years back there had been that whiff of scandal on the Colborne side but, as she'd only recently overheard Mummy reassuring Daddy, with both his parents now dead, and his brother long presumed so, there was no reason to fear *that unfortunate business* coming to light again now — even less so for the Trevannions to get to hear of it.

'Your father seems to be getting along famously with Mummy,' she said, noticing how, across the table, the two parents in question had their heads inclined towards one another as though in agreement about something. Although, even if they *weren't* getting along, their breeding was such that neither of them would show it.

'And Captain Colborne seems to be getting along nicely with mine,' Richard observed. 'But then, I think most people can usually find *something* they have in common.'

'Especially,' Esme said, 'if they have the good sense to steer clear of politics, religion and money.' *And from giving unsolicited advice about starting a family!*

'Indeed,' Richard replied. 'So, just two more nights under the family roof — '

'And then we'll be in our own home.'

'Our own little kingdom.'

'Actually,' she said, picturing the spacious mansion flat in St. John's Wood that he'd found through someone in Whitehall, 'I've been meaning to ask you about that.'

'Yes?'

'Once you'd found it,' she said, studying his face, 'why didn't you move in? Why keep living at home? *I'd* have been in there like a shot.'

He didn't hesitate. 'Because it was my wish that we embark upon our new life there *together*. I wanted it to feel like *our* home, rather than as though you were moving into mine. Besides, without *you*, I had no reason to be there in the first place.'

Esme stared into her lap; what a romantic thing for him to say. And how mercenary must he now think *her!* But then he was naturally so much nicer than she was anyway. She still didn't understand what he saw in her.

Struggling to fashion a suitably contrite reply, she glanced back up. Across the table, her mother was looking directly at her.

'Ladies,' Naomi Colborne chose that moment to announce, 'shall we adjourn?'

With the female guests murmuring their agreement, and the men making to get to their feet, Esme exhaled with relief. If only she didn't now have to go and make small talk over coffee in the drawing room. If only she could spend a few minutes with Richard — if for no other reason than to assuage her conscience, let him know how lucky she felt. Although, who said she *couldn't* spend a few minutes with him . . . ?

Reaching under the table, she put her hand on his thigh. Despite his leg twitching in surprise, all he did was raise an eyebrow.

'Five minutes,' she whispered, her head turned away from her mother's gaze. 'And then meet me in the morning room.'

'Bunk off?' he mouthed back at her, his amusement plain as he reached to the back of her chair and extended a hand to help her up.

Rising to her feet, she fought to keep a straight expression. 'Five minutes.'

'But aren't you expected in the drawing room? Coffee and petit fours? And what about Louise? Won't she . . . get in the way?'

'I'll speak to her. We'll slip out on the pretext of needing to powder our noses.' Leaning towards him, she whispered in his ear. 'So, what will it be, Mr Trevannion? Brandy and cigars with the old farts in the library . . . or five minutes somewhere quiet, just the two of us?'

She watched his eyes flick about the room.

'Five minutes. See you there.'

Out in the hallway, Esme caught up to her cousin, grabbed her arm and dragged her behind the aspidistra. Unsurprisingly, when she confided her intention, Lou was aghast.

'But won't your mother be suspicious? Mine will be.'

'Of course she will be. But she won't cause a fuss in front of her guests. Besides, we'll only be gone a couple of minutes. Then we'll reappear, innocent as you like.'

Clearly uneasy, Lou nevertheless followed her cousin's lead, and barely had they arrived in the morning room when Richard joined them.

'I feigned need of a comfort break,' he said, slipping in through the doors. 'Never been much of a one for brandy anyway and can't stomach cigars. Oh, hello, Louise.'

Lou shifted her weight. 'Hello again.'

With a brief frown, he went on, 'Captain Colborne did look at me askance when I declined his offer of a *Romeo y Julieta*. I suspect he thinks me soft.'

'No need to worry about Daddy,' Esme moved to assure him. '*He* was won over the moment he found out you're Admiralty. And as far as Mummy's concerned, you'd be hard pushed to put a foot wrong with her whatever you did.'

Richard's expression relaxed. 'Thank goodness for that at least.'

'Anyway . . . ' Hearing movement, Esme turned sharply over her shoulder; her cousin was closing the doors on her way out. Dear Lou, how tactful of her to withdraw.

'So, forty-eight hours,' Richard whispered, seizing upon Lou's departure to draw Esme close.

In his embrace, Esme sighed. 'Forty-eight hours. Ages and ages.' Two whole days to get through until they would stand together in St. George's and exchange their vows. To her mother's disappointment, and since there was indeed a war on, the wedding itself was to be small and their honeymoon brief, Richard's work at the Admiralty meaning he could only be spared for a couple of days. She didn't mind too greatly, though — certainly not nearly as much as her mother did.

With a swift glance towards the door, Richard drew her closer still. 'Forty-eight hours,' he whispered into the side of her neck. 'Best part of an eternity.'

The feel of his lips nuzzling her skin did something peculiar to her knees. 'Mm.'

'No last-minute doubts?'

She tensed. No point admitting now that she found the pressure to be perfect for him terrifying, that she feared not being able to live up to the expectations of his family; Grandmamma Pamela's standards were tough enough, but the Trevannions had elevated correctness into an artform. 'None . . . you?'

'Of course not. Never been more certain of anything in my life.'

'Even though it's only been five months?'

Lowering his arms, he took a step away from her, his expression quizzical. 'What's this, darling? Cold feet?'

She knew then that she shouldn't have said anything. Besides, being here with him like this made her earlier concerns seem quite ridiculous.

'No. No, of course not,' she hastened to reassure him. 'Just pre-wedding jitters, I expect.'

With a warm smile, he drew her back to him. 'Worried what I'll think once I find all those skeletons in your cupboards?'

'Skeletons are the *last* thing I'm worried about,' she said, truthfully. 'Seriously, I'm utterly dull.'

'Dull?'

'I'm afraid I am what you see before you. No hidden depths whatsoever.'

Burying his face in her shoulder, he groaned. 'Dear God, how I wish we could just slip away right this minute . . . skip the formalities and go straight to that suite at the Savoy.'

Yes, how daft it seemed now to have had doubts!

14

'There's always the broom cupboard.'

'The broom cupboard?'

She took his look of bewilderment to be an act but, just in case it wasn't, she decided to make light. 'It was a joke.'

'All right . . . '

Although, actually, he did look genuinely perplexed.

'Richard Vyvyan Edgcumbe Trevannion!' she hissed, certain he was having her on. 'All those weekend house parties your parents hosted . . . all those pretty young daughters of family friends who came to stay . . . and you never once sneaked any of them into a broom cupboard for a quick — '

'I most certainly did not!'

Was he serious? Was it possible he *hadn't* ever been in a broom cupboard with a girl? Given what went on at country house weekends — especially some of those she'd been to — it seemed hard to credit. For a young man, sneaking off to the broom cupboard at a house party was something of a rite of passage. And she knew for a fact he'd had a number of girlfriends over the years.

'Next you'll be telling me you never played postman's knock, either.'

'Postman's knock?'

Now she *knew* it was an act! 'Hm.'

'Hm.'

'Anyway,' she said, 'I lured you here for the chance to say a proper goodnight — you know, before you all depart together, and the best I can hope for is a chaste kiss on the cheek.'

15

'Your daring is to be applauded,' he said. 'And I'm more than happy to oblige.'

Eventually, letting go of her hands, he pulled away from her. 'Well, I suppose I'd better be getting back to the library. Can't risk your father catching me out in a lie. We could do without that sort of upset, certainly this close to the wedding.'

'All right,' she said, raising herself onto tiptoes to kiss him again, 'goodnight, Richard.'

'Goodnight, darling.'

'See you on Saturday at St. George's.'

'Three o'clock sharp. I'll be waiting.'

Once he had opened the door, made a quick check of the hallway and left the room with rather less purpose than when he'd come in, Lou came in the opposite direction.

'Thanks for making yourself scarce,' Esme said, flopping into one of the armchairs. 'I'll do the same for you one day.'

Lou shrugged. 'Should we be getting back to the drawing room? We have been gone rather a long time.'

Esme pulled a face. 'There's no rush. By the way, that Schiaparelli looks far better on you than it ever did on me.'

Coming more fully into the room, Lou stared down at the borrowed sheath-dress. 'Can't see how.'

'Stunning, in fact. I even caught Richard's brother giving you the once over. Mind you, that's not necessarily a compliment — given the plainness of his wife I should imagine he eyes rather a lot of women. Anyway, the designer of it,

Elsa Schiaparelli, claims to have invented that colour herself. Shocking-pink, she calls it.'

'I would think it must hang far better on you,' Lou said. 'You've considerably more bust to fill out this neckline. But thank you for lending it to me. My lemon satin would have looked right out of place, no matter how hard Mum tried to persuade me otherwise. Far too girly.'

'Then keep it,' Esme said, pulling herself more upright in the chair. Seeing the look of doubt that came across her cousin's face, she went on, 'Truly, Lou. Clothing shortages or no, I doubt I shall wear it again. That bias-cut satin never really did much for my hips.'

'Well . . . '

Poor Lou. This evening, in such formal surroundings, she'd looked like a fish out of water. Hardly surprising, really: in darkest North Devon a proper social life must be all but impossible. Perhaps, after the wedding, once things settled down, she should help her out in that regard — invite her up to town now and again. Actually, yes, she should do that; with the poor girl to herself for a weekend, she could take her to Bond Street and suggest she try a new hairstyle, show her a tip or two about using make-up. Like most country girls she had an enviably clear complexion, not to mention a perfect little rosebud mouth. Thank goodness she'd managed to persuade her to apply a touch of Guerlain's *Rouge Automatique;* her cousin's preference for lips *au nature!* had left the Schiaparelli looking horribly unfinished. If Louise Channer did but know it, with her willowy figure she had it in her to be a real beauty — a *stunner*, to resort to the vernacular.

Peering towards the door, Esme yawned. 'Golly, I'm exhausted. I wish they'd all hurry up and clear off. I'm desperate to go to bed.'

'Me too,' agreed Lou.

'Oh, and what I said to you earlier about haste. Forget it. It was just last-minute jitters.'

'Good,' Lou said. 'Because I don't think you realise how lucky you are.'

'No one special in *your* life at the moment?' Esme asked, changing the subject and fighting to stave off yet another yawn.

Lou shook her head. 'Fat chance of that.'

'What about that fellow you mentioned in your letter?'

'*Peter?* Hardly.' Getting up from where she had been perched on the arm of Esme's chair, Lou went to sit properly in the one across from it. 'Honestly, Essie,' she said, her expression one of despair, 'it's like having an orphaned puppy trailing around after me. Vic and Arthur even have a name for him — Lou's Pet Peter.'

Unable to help it, Esme burst out laughing but then, with a quick glance through the open door towards the hallway, quelled her giggles. 'That is unfortunate.'

'More unfortunate than *that*, is the way the name suits him down to the ground. It's as though the poor boy reached fifteen years of age and then got stuck there. But I can't be mean to him because he's harmless. And he thinks the world of me.'

'Not caring to disabuse him is still being mean,' Esme pointed out.

Lou gave a lengthy sigh. 'You might be right.'

'I am. Seriously, Lou, you should find someone — a proper man, I mean — and then let Peter see you with him. Borrow someone if necessary.'

'*Borrow* someone?'

'You know what I mean. There has to be *someone* you can parade about with now and again. You don't have to actually introduce him as your beau; just let Pet Peter work it out for himself. Better still, find someone you actually like and then it needn't be a charade. You can genuinely let it be known you're sweet on the chap.'

'There *is* Freddie . . .'

'The Freddie you went to school with?'

Lou nodded. 'We have *sort of* been walking out together . . .'

'There you go, then.'

'Hm.'

'Do you still have evacuees?' Esme asked, changing the subject yet again.

Lou shook her head. 'They went home. Couldn't get along with the quiet. Said they'd rather chance being bombed in their own beds than be bored out of their brains in the wilds of Devon. I'm not sorry they're gone. They were an ungrateful lot.'

Esme sighed. Woodicombe *was* rather remote — wouldn't do for her at all. It was bad enough having to spend the whole of August there every year while anyone of any consequence was in the

south of France. Although, there *was* Woodicombe Cove, its lovely little beach turning out to
be perfect for skinny dipping. What was the
name of that boy who'd dared her to do it?
Bernie? Barney? Barney something, yes. God,
she'd taken some risks that summer! Her mother
would have had a conniption: her sixteen-year-
old daughter, naked in the sea with the son of a
local farmer? Ye gods! The fall-out would have
been unimaginable. Worth the risk, though: in
anatomical terms alone, that particular August
had been instructional in a way nothing else
could have been for a girl with her upbringing.

But none of that was of any help to poor Lou,
who *was* rather cut off from real life. Perhaps,
when she invited her up for a weekend, she could
introduce her to some members of the opposite
sex. A girl as lovely as Lou deserved more than
some chap who came home every night covered
in mud or dung — both of those seemingly
unavoidable in North Devon.

'Yes,' she said, recalling Lou bemoaning the
remoteness of Woodicombe. 'I suppose it must
get terribly lonely. But it wasn't exactly a bed of
roses for me, even here in London, growing up
as an only child and having to bear the full
weight of my parents' expectations.'

'Trust me,' Lou retaliated, 'being the only
daughter amounts to much the same thing. I tell
you, if Pa had *his* way, I'd still be in liberty
bodices and ankle socks and wearing reins
whenever we went out!'

Esme smiled. In his own country way, dear
Uncle Luke was just as strict as Daddy. She

supposed Richard would also be like that one day with *their* daughters, too. Poor darlings. She would have to make sure they grew up in mixed company — got a good idea of what was what early on.

With a light shake of her head, she sighed. 'Well, if it's of any comfort, until I met Richard I hadn't the faintest clue what I was going to do with my life. I mean, obviously, I hoped to marry. But when the war started, well, I did begin to wonder . . . but then, meeting Richard, it was as though the missing pieces of my future all fell into place at once.' What hadn't harmed, she reminded herself, was that Richard was precisely the sort of outcome her mother had spent the previous five years trying so desperately hard to bring about: the son of an MP; family who were old money; respectable career in his own right. But there was no need to say that to Lou, whose own mother lacked not only Mummy's resources but her extensive address book as well. 'And then I just knew.'

'Easy for you to say — '

'Esme Colborne!' Caught off guard by her mother appearing in the doorway, Esme shot to her feet and hurried to straighten her dress. More slowly, Lou followed suit. 'What on earth can you be thinking, sprawled in that chair like a costermonger woman on a market stall?'

'Sorry, Mummy,' Esme said, careful not to look at Lou. 'But we're exhausted.'

'We're *all* exhausted, but you don't see any of the Trevannion women lounging in such unbecoming fashion, do you? Nor have you ever

21

seen me occupy a chair in such a disgraceful manner.'

'No, Mummy. I'm sorry.'

'Come and say goodnight to Richard's family,' — pausing briefly, Naomi Colborne cast her eyes to Lou — 'both of you. Then, Louise, once the Trevannions have departed, you may retire. You've had a long day.'

'Thank you, Aunt Naomi.'

'But, Esme, I need to speak to you.'

'Yes, Mummy.'

'Right, well then, come along, both of you.'

The Trevannions duly seen off, Esme and Lou exchanged weary glances.

'You go on up,' Esme whispered. 'Take first turn in the bathroom.'

Lou nodded. 'See you in a couple of minutes.'

'Hopefully, yes, with any luck this business with Mummy will turn out to be something of nothing.'

★ ★ ★

'Well, I think that went off all right,' Naomi Colborne said, closing the door to her sitting room and gesturing to Esme to sit down. 'I have to say, though, Hedley's wife isn't what I'd been expecting. Terribly vapid young woman. Doubtless chosen for her ox-like constitution and those child-bearing hips of hers rather than for her sparkling wit.'

Exhausted, and about to flop into one of her mother's armchairs, Esme lowered herself rather more carefully. 'That's a bit mean.'

'But true, I think you will come to find. You know how these old families are. You'll be quite the breath of fresh air to them.'

'Hm. I'm just relieved Richard and I don't have to actually live with them, as Hedley and Sophia do.'

'There, I would agree with you. Hardly the best way to start a marriage.'

When Naomi Colborne moved to the fireplace and stood peering into the mirror hanging above it, Esme noticed how drawn she looked. Tonight, with those pale shadows under her eyes, she looked every one of her forty-eight years. Not that she would ever say as much to her mother. Truth or not, it wouldn't go down well.

Perched on the edge of her chair, Esme stifled another yawn. What on earth could her mother possibly want to talk about at this time of night? Since she seemed in no hurry to get around to it, she was going to have to ask.

'Look, Mummy, I'm sorry to sound rude, but do you think you might cut to the chase? Only, I really am dead on my feet. As I'm sure you must be, too.'

The sigh her mother gave was an unusually weary one. 'Yes, of course. You're right. But it's . . . difficult. You see, there is something I've been meaning to tell you . . . '

Esme felt her shoulders sag. 'Something that can't wait?'

'Something that can't wait, no. Something I need to explain before Saturday.'

Before Saturday? Mortified by a thought, Esme withheld a groan. *Please don't let this be*

23

the talk about the birds and the bees . . . Steeling herself to that end, she cleared her throat. 'Do go on.'

'Very well. You see . . . Lawrence and I are not your real parents.'

Her mouth seeming reluctant to form words, Esme struggled to speak. '*What?*'

'You were orphaned. We adopted you as a newborn. You are not my daughter — nor Lawrence's — but my niece. Well, to be precise, my half-niece.'

As though winded by an almighty blow, Esme clutched the arm of the chair. Was this actually happening? Was this real? Beneath her palms she could feel the familiar cracks in the leather of the armchair, while, on the rug, her shoe was pinching her toe — both sensations she would ordinarily take to mean she wasn't dreaming. But were her senses to be trusted? She wouldn't put it past herself to have fallen asleep sitting up.

Unable to see her mother's face, she struggled to her feet. As she did so, her mother turned about, her hands clasped so tightly against the waistline of her frock that her knuckles looked as though they might burst through her skin.

'Mummy, please tell me you're joking . . . please tell me that either Richard or Uncle Ned has put you up to this. I've noticed those two becoming thick as thieves.'

'Darling, I assure you I am not joking. I only wish I were. Come, sit down.'

But when her mother reached towards her, Esme recoiled. 'Actually, no, I don't think I will sit down. Not until you tell me what's going on.'

'Look, darling, I realise this must be terribly hard for you to hear. I also realise that I should have told you a long time ago . . . but, now that you're getting married, well, clearly, it was something I couldn't keep from you any longer.'

The sight of her mother looking pained filled Esme with an urge to slap her. It was a difficult urge to fight down.

'So . . . this really *isn't* a joke?'

'I give you my word.'

Thoughts reeling, Esme glanced about the room: every piece of furniture, every swathe of fabric, every knickknack — all so well known to her. And yet, suddenly, their familiar shapes and forms held only menace.

Trying not to look at any of it, she spun back to her mother who now stood wringing her hands.

'And Daddy's not here with you to tell me this because . . . ?'

Naomi Colborne winced. 'Because I felt it *my* place to explain. You see, *I* was the one who took you in. When all of this came about, Lawrence was away, fighting with his regiment in France. I was alone, not long since having miscarried our baby — the first of several I was to lose. And not only had you been left with no one in the world, but you were related to me. *Are* related to me. So, you see, there was never any question. I *had* to take you in.'

Starting to shiver, Esme sank back down onto the chair. This *was* true, then? She really *was* adopted. Captain and Mrs Lawrence Colborne were *not* her real parents? No, it couldn't be true. For a start, she shared their same ebony-black hair. And she had her mother's nose, everyone said so. No, she wasn't having it. This *was* a joke. It had to be. There was no other explanation.

Her insides tightly coiled, she shot back to her feet. 'Prove it,' she said. 'If it *is* true, you must have papers.'

Without saying anything, Naomi reached to a buff-coloured folder on her desk. Placing it down on the occasional table, she opened the cover and drew out the uppermost document.

When she held it towards her, Esme noticed it tremble in her hand.

'This,' Naomi said, her voice suddenly small and uncertain, 'is your birth certificate. We *could* simply have registered you as our own child. There was no one to say otherwise, much less to object. But, to me at least, that would have felt as though we were stealing you. Besides, it was always my intention to one day tell you the truth.'

With her heart thudding in her chest and her head swimming with half-formed thoughts, Esme took the piece of paper. Across the top were printed the words *Certified Copy of an Entry of Birth*. With her eyes darting about the document, she picked out the column headed 'Name and Surname of Father'. In the box beneath it was written 'Ernest WARD'. In the box adjacent to that, under the heading 'Name and Surname of Mother' were the words 'Bertha WARD, formerly JONES'. Beneath 'Occupation of Father' it read 'Railway Platelayer/Soldier'.

26

She glanced again to the date of birth. In recognition that it was her own, she stiffened. Her real father had been a *railway platelayer?* What did that even mean? Wanting nothing to do with the piece of paper, she tossed it back onto the table.

'That . . . that means nothing,' she said, aware that she was only seconds from crying. But she would rather be angry and shout at the ludicrousness of this whole thing than let Naomi Colborne see her dissolve into tears. 'That could belong to anyone,' she said, her finger trembling as she pointed at the document on the table. 'How do I even know it's mine?'

'Because what reason would I have to lie to you about something like this?'

Esme felt the muscles in her stomach clench. Her legs weren't to be trusted. She felt sick. But the most overwhelming sensation was rage; deepening by the minute, it was stiffening her shoulders and tensing her jaw.

'How would *I* know why you might lie to me?' she spat. 'How would *I* know the myriad reasons you might have for doing this? I'm not even sure I know who you are any more. I mean, if *any* of what you say is true, why wait until *now* to tell me? Why wait until two days before my wedding? You must have known the shock it would be, how badly it would hurt me. So, why *now?*'

'Esme, darling, what you must remember — '

'*Esme?* Is that even my real name? I mean, is that the name chosen for me by these Ward people? Or did you change it?'

Naomi, although drained of all colour,

remained surprisingly calm. But then how many times in the last twenty-five years, Esme wondered, had she rehearsed for this very moment? Hundreds, probably. Thousands, even.

'Darling — '

'Talk about choosing your moment,' she said, a foul taste rising in her throat.

'I know,' Naomi replied quietly. 'And for that I am unreservedly sorry. But what you need to understand is that when you were small, the manner of your coming to us was unimportant. And then, when you were growing up, well, we only ever thought of you as our own. The more times I miscarried, the more precious you became, the circumstances of your birth ceasing to matter. We never . . . *I* never thought about it. I won't go so far as to say that we forgot about it but, to me, that you hadn't come from my own body was irrelevant.'

'Irrelevant for you, maybe!' Esme interjected. 'But did it never occur to you in all of those years to think about *my* feelings?'

Finally, Naomi's composure seemed to desert her. 'Of course we thought about your feelings! *Your* feelings were at the centre of every decision we ever made. For heaven's sake, Esme, we thought of nothing else. You only have to look around you to see that. The best tutors, the best school, getting you presented, finishing in Biarritz, it was *all* only ever about *you*. Always.' After a moment's pause to draw breath, Naomi's tone when she resumed was more placatory. 'Our primary concern, at all times, only ever centred upon how we could do the best for *you*.

We loved you. I simply can't stress enough how wanted you were.'

Utterly exhausted, Esme reached for the birth certificate and stared at the names written upon it. Seemingly, then, this absurd story was true; her parents were not Naomi and Lawrence Colborne, but this couple called Ernest and Bertha Ward. And she hadn't been born in Kensington but Whitechapel. *Whitechapel.* Hell's teeth. What a thing to discover.

With yet another slow and weary shake of her head, she let out an exasperated sigh. She supposed she was behaving rather badly. Granted, she had never expected to hear anything so bizarre and yes, she was in shock. But, if the Colbornes — and Mummy's family, the Russells — were guilty of anything, surely it was really only that they had waited so long to tell her. Apart from that, she had to admit their motives seemed admirable; taking in an orphaned child was no small undertaking. And one only had to look at Naomi Colborne's face to know that she was going through hell. They both were. But no amount of hell was going to change the fact that she wasn't Esme Colborne, nor that her world had just been turned upside down. Added to that, in her head were so many questions. For a start, how could this society woman, with her fastidious ways and privileged upbringing, be related to a railway worker from Whitechapel? How could she be her aunt? Well, that puzzle would have to wait. Of more pressing importance seemed to be to understand the circumstances of her birth, and to learn something of these people Ernest and Bertha Ward. Who were they? What were they like? Did she resemble either of them? Did she have real relatives somewhere? Christ — did she have brothers and sisters? Suddenly, her questions felt endless. But with so much to find out, what did she ask first?

Feeling a kind of reluctant resolve coming over her, she looked up to see Naomi staring towards the blacked-out window, her face taut and drawn, her expression empty.

'So,' she said, somehow overcoming her exhaustion to get to her feet, 'how about you ring for some tea? Then perhaps you would tell me what you know of these people — these people who to you are relatives . . . and to me are my real parents.'

★ ★ ★

Damn. Damn, damn, damn! She'd forgotten she was sharing her room with Lou tonight. Having made it all the way back upstairs without meeting anyone, she now had her cousin to face. Still, it could be worse; at least Lou wasn't the judgmental type. In fact, quite the opposite; if she was going to confide her true parentage to anyone, Lou would be as safe choice as any. Being one step removed from it all, she might even have some useful observations to share.

Arriving at the door to her bedroom, she reached for the handle. But then she stopped and withdrew her hand. Where on earth did she start with a tale so fantastical that she could hardly believe it herself? All she could do was tell it as it had been relayed to her. At least Lou wasn't the sort of person to get all histrionic.

Stopping long enough to draw a deep breath, she opened the door and went in. Across the room, dressed in a pink Viyella nightgown, Lou was brushing her hair. The sight of her caused a twinge of envy. How unfair that her cousin's life went on as normal.

At that moment, Lou turned towards her. 'Heavens, Essie,' she said, 'you look as though you've seen a ghost. Is everything all right? Oh, and I'm terribly sorry but I seem to have torn the hem of your dress. I expect I trod on it. I'm not used to high heels — they seem to give my feet a mind of their own. In the morning, I'll see if I can make an invisible mend. I'm sure I'll be able to. I'm quite good at mending — lots of practice. Mum despairs of what I do to my clothes.'

Unable to concentrate on what Lou was saying, Esme slumped onto the end of her bed. Here she was, her world fallen apart, and Lou was blabbering on about dresses and heels and ghosts. *Ghosts.* Sitting bolt upright she turned to look at her.

'Did you *know?*'

In the light from the single lamp on the table between the two beds, she saw her cousin frown.

'You've lost me. Did I know what?'

'Did you already know . . . that the people I have spent my entire life calling Mummy and Daddy . . . are not my real parents?'

Lou's frown deepened. '*What?*'

31

In a way, her cousin's puzzlement came as a relief since it suggested she'd had no idea. 'So, you didn't know either?'

'I'm not sure I even know *now*,' Lou replied, putting down her hairbrush and moving around the end of the bed towards her. 'Seriously, Esme, what on earth are you talking about?'

Wearily, Esme recounted a potted version of the story as relayed by her mother — *by her Aunt Naomi*. While she was doing so, she watched the colour slowly draining from her cousin's face.

'But . . . but if that's true, what happened to your real parents?' was the first thing Lou wanted to know.

Esme exhaled heavily; now she'd started the story, she couldn't really leave it half told. 'They died,' she said flatly. 'War started — the Great War, that is. Apparently, the moment the call went out for volunteers, my father, this Ernest Ward chap, joined the . . . oh, I don't know, the Essex Regiment or some such. I forget. Anyway, around the same time, he married my mother, who must have become pregnant pretty much straightaway, Then my father was killed — somewhere in France, I think. And not long afterwards, my mother, Bertha, who had supposedly been sickly throughout, didn't survive labour. Supposedly, she'd known for some time she was unlikely to make it because she'd made her best friend, some woman called Ada, swear that if she didn't survive, Ada would bring the baby — me — to Mrs Naomi Colborne because she was family.'

Now seated alongside her on the bed, Lou reached for her hand. 'Heavens, Esme. I don't know what to say.'

'Hardly surprising.'

'So, do you think that still means we're related?'

'Believe it or not, it does.' In all honesty, Esme didn't really care, but it would be unfair to vent her frustration on Lou. Poor Lou, who would never tell a lie even to save her own life — but whose own mother had clearly been in on the secret — had also been kept in the dark. 'If Hugh Russell is still my grandfather, then you and I are still cousins,' she said. 'But the woman you call Aunt Naomi, is now my Aunt Naomi, too.'

Beside her, Lou sat slowly shaking her head. 'Well, though I can only imagine the almighty shock this must have been for you, I don't suppose it really matters as much as it might once have done. I mean, you're grown up. You're getting married. If you choose to do so, you can leave it all behind. You can just leave and start your new life with Richard.'

Just leave and start a new life with Richard. To Lou, everything was always so cut and dried. Dear Lou, who only ever saw the — Christ almighty! Richard. She'd completely forgotten about him! Such had been her shock, and her anger about the deceit, that the greater ramifications hadn't hit home. Richard! Oh, dear God, she couldn't possibly marry him now — not now she was no longer Esme Colborne; not now she was nothing more than the daughter of a working-class East End couple. Dear God, no.

Feeling something in her stomach turning to lead, she doubled over. Thinking she was going to be sick, she slid from the bed, lurched across the room, flung back the door to the bathroom and stumbled towards the lavatory where she bent over and retched.

With no control over her body, she shuddered and retched again, feeling hot and cold at the same time.

Behind her, she could hear the sound of the tap running into the basin. Seconds later, Lou was bending down to her level with a toothglass filled with water. 'Here,' she said. 'Sit back a minute and sip this.'

With the contents of the room seeming to swirl about her, Esme somehow did as she was told, taking two small sips and then handing back the glass. 'Lou, I'm going to need your help.'

'Of course, Essie. Anything. You know that.'

Bearing down upon Lou's proffered arm, Esme struggled to her feet. Her throat felt dry and scratchy. Her head was pounding. And she was finding it hard to unclench her fists. But, despite all of that, her mind seemed in possession of a rare clarity.

'Empty my suitcase, would you?'

She could almost feel Lou staring back at her.

'Your suitcase? But I thought it was packed ready for your honeymoon?'

'Lou, what I need is your help, not the bloody Spanish Inquisition. So, are you going to help me or not?'

With that, and ignoring that her head was still swimming, Esme swivelled about and crossed the room. Dragging open the topmost drawer of the chest, she ran her eyes over the muddle inside, mostly undergarments deemed too worn and too sensible for Richard to see. Well, now they would do just fine. Grabbing the lot, she tossed them onto the bed. In the next drawer down she found her nightgowns and stockings. Those, too, she flung in the same general direction. Next, she went to the wardrobe, where she yanked open the doors and stood staring in. From the rail she clutched at hangers bearing skirts, jackets, day dresses, and dumped those too upon the eiderdown.

'Esme,' Lou began uncertainly, 'what on earth are you doing? Stop for a moment and talk to me, won't you?'

No matter how well-meant Lou's concern, Esme was determined to keep going. 'I'm leaving. I'm leaving this house and I'm not coming back.'

'Well, yes, you're getting married — '

'No, Lou, that's just it, I'm not. I can't. Don't you see? My life as Esme Colborne is over. Ruined.'

'Ruined? Of course it's not ruined. Look, Esme, please stop doing that and think for a moment. Nothing has really changed, has it? For certain you're feeling terrible hurt . . . and betrayed, too, I shouldn't wonder. But that's no reason to . . . to . . . '

Stopping what she was doing, Esme turned to stand, hands on hips, her expression rigid. 'No

35

reason to . . . what, Lou?' While she hated being mean, she had to make Lou understand. *Nothing has really changed* indeed!

'Well, to . . .'

'My mother . . . the woman I *called* my mother . . . knew all along that I was really the daughter of a man who earned his living laying railway tracks and a woman who was herself the illegitimate daughter of a liaison between our grandfather, Hugh Russell, and a dancer. A dancer, Lou! And I don't mean a ballerina, either. Ugh. It makes my flesh creep just thinking about it! And yet, despite knowing that — despite most of the adults in my *supposed family* knowing that, Grandmamma Pamela and Great Aunt Diana included — at no stage did anyone see fit to tell me. To tell *me*. Worse still, when Richard Trevannion, son of a member of parliament and descendent of one of the oldest families in the land, came to inform my father . . . *my adopted father* . . . that he was going to ask me to marry him, still none of them thought to take me aside and disabuse me. So obsessed were they by the dazzling match I was making that they chose to overlook the biggest single impediment to my accepting him — that I wasn't who he thought I was. Hell, that I wasn't even who *I* thought I was! And yet, and yet . . . you stand there and expect me to believe that where Richard is concerned, *nothing has changed?* Christ, Lou, you really do need to get out and see something of the world. This isn't North Devon, you know. No fairy godmother is waiting to come around the corner in a moment and tell me that Richard doesn't give a hoot who I really am — '

'But perhaps he really *wouldn't*,' Lou risked pointing out. 'Isn't that what true love is all about? Loving the other person for who they really are?'

Her frustration on the point of boiling over, Esme threw up her arms and let out a roar of despair. 'For God's sake, Lou. That sort of thing might happen in a fairy story but not in London society. Trust me. Matilda Trevannion already thinks her son is marrying beneath him because, although the Russells have wealth, they have no pedigree. In her eyes, my *only* saving grace was Daddy's lineage from the Colbornes of Avingham Park.'

'But that hasn't changed,' Lou said, apparently doing her best to understand Esme's despair. 'Captain Colborne is still descended from the Colbornes of wherever.'

'Louise Channer, are you deliberately being slow? *He* is, yes. But *I'm* not descended from *him. My* sole connection to this Godforsaken and unholy mess of a family is through Hugh Russell. Hugh Russell, Lou, son of an East End barrow boy-made-good, who, not content with marrying Grandmamma Pamela, went on to conduct an affair with a dancer, illegitimately producing my mother, Bertha Jones, in the process. For heaven's sake, just stop to take that all in for a moment and then think about Matilda Trevannion. *You've* met her. How do you think she'd react to learning of that sordid little saga? Especially with her precious Hedley about to be selected to stand as a member of parliament. She'd have a fit. Her heart would stop in her chest, that's what would happen.'

'But it doesn't have anything to do with her, does it?' Lou said flatly. 'It's Richard you're marrying. And since you're both over the age of twenty-one, nothing either of his parents say can stop you from going ahead and getting wed.'

'You underestimate the power of Matilda Trevannion,' Esme said sourly. 'She's . . . she's . . . well, she's one of those women who will go to all and any lengths to protect the family name. No, if she decrees that Richard can't marry the daughter of a Whitechapel railwayman — and trust me, she will — he won't go against her. Why would he want to anyway? Why invite the ridicule? Why make himself a laughing stock, a social outcast? Because you can be sure that's what the two of us would become. No, I can't do that to him. I *won't* do that to him. Not only will I not have that on my conscience, but he deserves better.'

'But wouldn't it at least be worth — '

'Besides which,' she rushed on, '*I* have no wish to be derided either. I don't have it in me to withstand the humiliation. No, for the sake of everyone in this mess, the best thing I can do is leave. And, when I'm gone, Naomi Colborne can explain to the Trevannions why there will no longer be a wedding.'

'Essie,' Lou pleaded, 'my dearest cousin and friend, please don't do this. Please, don't be so quick to decide. You're upset, obviously. But surely the thing to do is to talk to Richard, tell him what you've found out. Tell him about your real parents and how you came to be adopted and how, instead of being your mother, Naomi Colborne is actually your aunt. Think about it: it doesn't make *that* much difference. Hugh Russell was already your grandfather. So *that* bit of your past really *hasn't* changed.'

'Huh. That may well be. But at least before all of this my mother wasn't illegitimate. Nor was *her* mother a dancer.'

'Well . . . '

'No, Lou, I know you mean well. Truly, I do. But you don't see it — can't possibly.'

Yes, while what Lou had said about Grandpa Hugh might be true, Esme could see no alternative but to leave. Lou didn't understand how things worked for a family like the Trevannions. But there was no way she could marry Richard now. Going ahead with the wedding and simply cocking a snook at his family wasn't an option.

Reaching to unfasten the single button at the neck of her evening dress and cursing when it became entangled in its rouleau loop, she slipped the fabric off her shoulders and let the whole thing slide to the floor. In its place, she reached for a floral day dress, opened the first couple of buttons at the neckline, and then wrenched it over her head, hearing one of the seams ripping as she did so. Regardless, she refastened the buttons, poked the end of the belt through its buckle and tightened it about her waist. Then she kicked off her evening shoes, went to the wardrobe, ferreted about in the bottom and pulled out a pair of flat-heeled courts. They were old and needed a decent polishing, but they were comfy and sensible. And she had to be practical; who knew how far she might end up having to walk? Who knew where she was even going to go?

'Esme, please — '

'Sorry, Lou, no. If you're hoping to persuade me not to do this, you're wasting your breath. It's not your fault. You're from a different world, a world where things aren't so black and white and where people look for the good in one another, not the worst. No. I've made up my mind. Richard Trevannion is a good man. The best. And I will not have him humiliated. I'm not the woman he thinks I am. In fact, even were I to do as you said, and explain everything to him, he still won't know who I am. And do you know why he won't? Because *I* don't. So, no, I can't marry him, no matter how much I love him. In fact, *because* I love him. So, are you going to help me get away from here or not? Only, if you're not, that's fine. I value our friendship too much to drag you into this against your will.'

'I — '

With that, Esme had an idea. 'Of course,' she said carefully, wondering why the thought was only now occurring to her, 'you *could* always come with me. We could make a new start together somewhere — somewhere no one knows us. We could join the WRNS or the WAAF. I could be Esme Ward and you could be . . . well, you could be whoever you like. We could both choose completely new names. These

40

days, girls join up all the time. Or, if you don't want to join up, we could go to America. Or Canada. I've got money. Yes! We could go abroad and start afresh. Please, Lou, do say you'll come with me.'

When she saw Lou hang her head, she knew immediately that her cousin wasn't about to agree.

'I can't, Esme. You know that.'

'On the contrary, Lou Channer, I don't know it. As far as I can see, you can do anything you want.'

'That's not true. I don't have even an ounce of your strength and determination. No. I'm sorry, Esme. I can't.'

Honestly, Lou Channer could be so irritatingly timid! 'I don't see why not. I don't see one single reason for you to hang about at Woodicombe.'

'No,' Lou replied quietly. 'I don't imagine you do.'

'Unless you really are soft on Peter the Pet — or whatever your brothers call him.'

Now she was just being unkind. Now she was just trying to hurt Lou in the same way she had been hurt. And that was simply mean.

'I'm not soft on him. I'm not soft on anyone.'

'Fair enough,' Esme relented. There was no point in the two of them falling out. 'But, if you're not coming with me, please do me the courtesy of at least waiting until the morning before telling anyone that I've gone.'

From Lou's eyes, Esme read unease. Poor Lou. She shouldn't be putting her through this.

She was one of the few people who'd had nothing to do with this mess.

'Well . . .'

'Look,' she said. 'Tell you what, I'll make it easy for you. Get into bed.'

'But I haven't taken off this lipstick or brushed my teeth — '

'You can fuss with that when I'm gone. There's a pot of cold cream in the drawer of my dressing table. Have it. In fact, have anything you want. I shan't need any of it now.'

'But Esme, please — '

'Lou, dearest Lou, either get into bed or don't. Either way, I'm switching out the light so that tomorrow morning, when they question you about my disappearance, you can put your hand on your heart and swear that you didn't see me leave and it won't be a lie.'

Largely through seeming lost to know what else to do, Lou climbed into bed and pulled up the eiderdown.

Exhaling with relief, Esme bent to kiss her cousin's cheek and then reached beneath the lampshade to click off the light. Suitcase in hand, she then negotiated her way to the door, opened it and peered out. The dimly lit landing was empty. So was the rear stairwell when she reached it and, subsequently, the service hallway.

Making it unchallenged to the alleyway at the bottom of the garden, she paused to look up at the back of the house. She did wish Lou was coming with her — if for no other reason than for moral support; it was going to be scary on her own.

42

Well, scary or not, she had to go. Her parents — *her adopted parents* — had left her with no other choice.

2

Starting Over

It wasn't a bad area at all, really. Laburnum Avenue, Wimbledon, was a wide and tree-lined road, with solid-looking double-fronted villas set back behind low garden walls and neatly mown lawns. Granted, the name Wimbledon didn't carry the same cachet as Wimbledon Village, but it was quiet, the residents generally elderly, and the dwellings kept up nicely together. Convenient for the shops, Esme supposed it was the perfect example of life in the suburbs.

Arriving at the front gate to one particular house, she clicked open the latch. Nailed to one of the pillars on either side was a wooden plaque painted white on sky blue with the name 'Sandown' — chosen, she had been informed, after the location on the Isle of Wight where its elderly owner had met her late husband.

Stepping under the front porch, she poked her key into the lock and let herself in.

'Only me, Mrs Jeffreys,' she called along the hallway towards the kitchen. 'I have your medicine from the chemist, but I see that Mrs Smith has just done the floors and so I'll leave it here for you, on the hall table.'

Unsure whether Mrs Jeffreys had heard, Esme nevertheless deposited the paper bag, eased off her shoes, bent to pick them up and, in her stockinged feet, started up the carpeted stairs.

It was more than a week now since she had stood outside the newsagents on the concourse of Wimbledon railway station, peering through the grimy window at the handwritten advertisements in the hope of finding somewhere to lodge. The card that had eventually caught her eye had read: *Room to rent. Five minutes' walk from station. Single lady only.* It had gone on to state that references would be required but, when she had offered two weeks' rent in advance, and the householder, Mrs Jeffreys, had taken in the quality of her suitcase and smiled at her voice, such formalities had quickly been dispensed with.

'I shan't ask what it is you're running away from,' her new landlady had said, accepting the banknotes and pushing them into the sagging pocket of her arran-knit cardigan, her smile exaggerating the lattice of wrinkles around her eyes, 'as long as it doesn't follow you here.'

From that moment, an unlikely friendship had been struck up: Esme came and went as she pleased, offering to run errands whenever she was going along to The Broadway, while Mrs Jeffreys provided supper, and her daily, Mrs Smith, cleaned her room. Overnight, the privileged Esme Colborne had become Esme Ward, her supposed background that of governess to two young children in Kensington, who had lost her job when the family for whom she had been working decided to evacuate to relatives in Scotland, and she had declined to go with them.

'Can't say I blame you, love,' Mrs Jeffreys had said, catching sight of her reflection in the hall mirror and patting her newly set silver-rinsed hair, 'cold and wet old place by all accounts.'

Arriving now in her room on the first floor, with its deep window that gave out over the long garden to the rear, Esme set down her handbag and allowed herself a smile. In the end, leaving Clarence Square had proved easier than she might have imagined. After three nights spent in a small and anonymous hotel in Victoria, where she had done little more than lie in bed sobbing, she had awoken on the Sunday morning, determined to do as she had said to Lou and start afresh. To that end, she had repacked her belongings and walked around the corner to the railway station, where she had stood staring up at the departures board. Not wishing to make life too difficult for herself by travelling too far from town, she had spotted a train departing for the south coast, one that listed among its many stops, Wimbledon. Although somewhere she had never been, she thought it sounded respectable and so, on that basis alone, had bought a single ticket and hoped for the best.

Glancing now to the bedside table and seeing from her travel alarm clock that it wasn't even midday, she sat on the edge of the bed and sighed. The trouble was, whilst she might have removed herself from Clarence Square, and Richard and the Colbornes, she didn't feel as though she had left behind very much else. She was still the young woman with no idea of who she was, and with no thought as to what she was going to do next, much less how she was going to go about it. Staring out through the window of the train as it had pulled out of Victoria that morning, she had felt surprisingly calm, hopeful even. It had felt like a new beginning. But she was coming to realise now that for any new beginning to stand a chance of succeeding, prior loose ends ought to have been tied up — or, at the very least, have been laid to rest. Given the sudden manner of her departure, she had been able to do neither.

Be patient, she reminded herself each and every time she felt an onset of the wobbles; *it's barely even a week since your world was turned upside down*. But heeding her own advice wasn't easy. In quiet moments, her mind returned all too readily to consider the chaos her disappearance must have wrought. Her mother — for, despite everything, that was how she still thought of Naomi Colborne — and Grandmamma Pamela would be beside themselves, likely alternating between being worried sick one moment and bemoaning her selfishness the next. Then there was her father, who would almost certainly have alerted the police. Hopefully, the latter would have explained there was little they could do; not only was there no reason to suspect foul play but she was an adult, free to leave if she wished. Meanwhile, the Trevannions would most likely be trying to convince their son that, as it had turned out, the cancellation of the wedding was no bad thing: Esme Colborne, they were sure to have said, was clearly an unreliable young woman harbouring who-knew-what sort

47

of problems; sooner or later she would have been trouble, so better this had happened now, before the shameful matter of a divorce had reared its head. An ungrateful blot on both families — doubtless that was how she was being viewed.

Unsettled and restless, she heaved another sigh. How much would Richard have been told of the reason for her disappearance? Would the Colbornes have come clean with him, or would they, to save face, have pretended to have no idea why she had left? Some days she thought the former more likely. Other days, the latter.

And then there was Lou. Poor Lou. She did hope she hadn't borne the brunt of everyone's anger and exasperation. Anger. Hm, there was bound to have been a great deal of that. In recent days, she had tried telling herself she wasn't to blame for not going through with the wedding. But, in her heart, she felt differently. The Colbornes might have been responsible for withholding the fact that she was adopted but she *could* have waited until the morning to call off the wedding. She could at least have explained to Richard, in civilised fashion, why she had felt the need to do so. At the time, however, she hadn't wanted him to claim — as he surely would have — that it didn't matter who she was. She hadn't wanted to go ahead with the wedding only to one day find herself wondering whether he had done so purely from a sense of duty. Nor had she been prepared to risk that every time they went on to disagree about something, or Richard had raised his voice to her, she would be left wondering whether he regretted marrying her. To live surrounded by suspicion and doubt was no way to conduct a marriage, let alone to start one.

And so, here she was. But where, precisely, was that? Who was she now? Who was Esme Ward, and what did she want from life? In her rush to leave Esme Colborne behind, she hadn't thought that far ahead, the upshot being that she had begun to feel stuck. Rather than feeling liberated from her past, she seemed paralysed by the loss of it. Jettisoning the name Colborne hadn't changed who she was. Nor had leaving Clarence Square. Even absconding from her wedding, while most definitely changing the course of her future, had done nothing to fundamentally change who she was — at least, not in the way that discovering she was adopted had. No, as she was gradually coming to discover, not everything was easily discarded.

She glanced again to the clock. It was still only just coming up to midday. Who would have thought time could drag so when one had nothing to do and nowhere to be?

Running her hand distractedly over the candlewick bedspread, she felt the stirrings of idea. She would write letters; she would write and apologise to each of the people her disappearance would have upset. She would write and explain herself, let them know she was safe and well and trying to come to terms with what had happened. She would say sorry not for the things that weren't her fault, but for the manner of her departure. Then, hopefully, the guilt with which she was riddled might recede, releasing her to move forward. But first, since it was now after midday and she was ravenous, she would go and make herself an early luncheon.

Downstairs, eating a cheese and pickle sandwich — relieved to have recently discovered that cheese wasn't *on the ration* — the idea of writing to people grew on her. It felt like a way to wipe the slate in readiness for starting over.

Later, her lunch things cleared away and her jacket donned, she walked back up to The Broadway and went into Elys department store where she chose a Parker fountain pen, a bottle of Quink, and a square of blotting paper. At the display of writing paper, she reached for her usual Croxley but, upon enquiring the price for just fifty sheets, was forced to put it back on the shelf.

'There's always a run on writing paper in wartime,' the veteran soldier behind the counter remarked of the otherwise empty display, the only alternative to Croxley being a pad of Basildon Bond. In her straitened circumstances, it would have to do.

For the remainder of that afternoon, she sat at one end of Mrs Jeffreys' dining table where, for some time before putting pen to paper, she simply stared out of the window at the garden, trying to work out what on earth she was going to write. Eventually, her thoughts only marginally clearer, she started with the letter she considered to be the most straightforward — the one to Lou.

Quite by chance, I have found perfectly acceptable lodgings with a pleasant widow whose cooking, (I hadn't realised until now that meat was rationed on a shillings and pence basis!) is plain but wholesome. Please do not be offended that I have chosen not to furnish you with the address, but, for the present at least, I have no wish to be 'found'. I am sure you will understand.

Please apologise on my behalf to Aunt Kate for the wasted trip to London for you both. And please do not worry about me. I am perfectly fine and will write again should my circumstances change.

I trust that you are well and do not think too badly of me, with all my love, Esme.

Since she wasn't providing Lou with an address to which to reply, she felt it best to keep her letter brief and not give anyone at Woodicombe further cause for concern. It was an approach she went on to apply to her letter to the Colbornes.

I regret that it became necessary for me to leave in such a manner but would ask you to try to understand the confusion I felt upon learning of the circumstances of my birth. In that muddled state, I could not possibly have proceeded with the wedding and had no wish to be talked into doing so by anyone, no matter how well meaning.

Please be assured that I am safe and well and that there is no need for you to worry. I

have not yet decided what I shall do next
but, when I do, I will let you know.
Yours affectionately, Esme.

Unsurprisingly, the hardest letter to write was
the one to Richard. Indeed, she was to tear up
four sheets of her precious writing paper before
eventually settling upon words that, to her mind,
struck something close to a suitable tone. Upon
reaching the end, she read it back.

Dearest Richard,

Where to begin?
Well, firstly, although I am sure it will do
little to ease either your hurt or your
bewilderment and anger, I wish to apologise
to you for leaving as I did. I would hope
that by now you have learned of the news I
was given and can imagine the deep shock it
caused me. In all conscience, I could not
have gone through with our wedding whilst
in that state of upset and confusion. To do
so would have been unfair upon both of us.
That said, my decision to leave was not
taken lightly.
I do not know how, as a result of my
action, you now regard me. Nor do I know,
for my part, what I shall do next. I do know
that I need time to come to terms with the
shock of discovering that I am not Esme
Colborne.
If you can find it in your heart not to hate
me, I should feel relieved. However, if that

*is asking too much of you, then I shall
understand.*

Yours as ever, Esme.

After much dithering partway through, she
decided to make no mention of her own feelings
towards *him*. In all honesty, how could she? She
had no idea whether she would eventually feel
able to marry him — even were he to have her.
That being the case, she could hardly expect him
to wait around on the off chance that she might
one day decide to go back to him. On the other
hand, neither could she bring herself to tell him
not to wait; it felt too final. Where did that leave
poor Richard? Well, she hoped it left him free to
decide for himself — to wait for her or to move
on. Sadly, it was very much a case of what would
be, would be. The night she had run away and
left him, she had, as the saying went, made her
own bed. And now she was left with no choice
but to lie in it.

★ ★ ★

'Ah, there you are, dear.'
Waiting while Mrs Jeffreys made her way
slowly down the stairs the following morning,
Esme smoothed a hand down the front of her
dress. Of the several shirtwaist dresses she
owned, this turquoise one had always been her
favourite. With its white spots and large white
buttons, it never failed to put a spring in her
step.

53

'Yes, Mrs Jeffreys,' she said. 'What can I do for you?'

Clearly troubled today by the arthritis in her knees, and with her ribbed stockings wrinkled about her ankles, Mrs Jeffreys shuffled towards her. 'Don't suppose you're going up The Broadway this morning, are you?'

Esme smiled. 'I might walk up after breakfast, yes. Is there something you'd like me to fetch?'

'Couldn't nip into the post office for me, could you?' Fishing about in her purse for coins, she went on, 'Bit of a cheek, I know, seeing how long the queues are in there, but I've a niece who's just had her third, and I should like to drop her a line or two by way of congratulations.'

'Of course,' Esme said, accepting from her landlady a palmful of coins. 'How many stamps would you like?'

'Better fetch me three. Make it worth the queueing, love.'

'It looks very pleasant out there this morning,' Esme remarked as she followed Mrs Jeffreys and the smell of toast through to the kitchen. Through the crosshatch of pasted-linen tapes on the window — supposed to prevent glass from flying everywhere in the event of a bomb blast — the lawn looked emerald green. There were even a few early roses in bloom.

'Yes, and don't you look summery?'

Arriving behind her at the table, Mrs Smith set down a tray bearing the rack of toast. 'Pretty as a picture,' she agreed, nodding her approval of Esme's outfit. 'And though you wouldn't believe it to look at me now, I had hair just like yours

54

once. Long and dark and lustrous, it was. The talk of our street.'

'So, what have you got planned for today, then?' Mrs Jeffreys enquired once Mrs Smith had slopped back to the kitchen in her badly misshapen slippers.

Picking up her knife and scraping it as lightly as possible over the top of the block of National margarine, Esme shrugged her shoulders. It was a good question, and the same one to which she awoke every morning. 'I haven't decided yet.'

'Haven't decided or haven't the faintest?' Mrs Jeffreys asked, looking up from spreading a similarly meagre amount over her own toast. 'I swear this stuff gets greasier and less edible by the week. I doubt the army would even put it on their guns. Why we can't still have Stork, I'll never know.'

'Not very nice, is it?' Esme agreed. Though she didn't know how, at Clarence Square, they'd still had butter at breakfast. But only at breakfast.

'What you do or don't do is none of my business, dear,' Mrs Jeffreys picked up again. 'You pay your rent. We get along fine. But if you were one of mine, I'd being telling you to find something to do with yourself. Young woman like you, sat about twiddling her thumbs, it's never natural. I'm not suggesting you find a feller and settle down, but watching you coming and going, well, it strikes me you're lost. Why not put a card in the window of Cooper's, up by the station?'

Put a card in the newsagents? What, exactly, would Mrs Jeffreys have her advertise? 'I'm sorry?' she said, 'but I don't follow you.'

'Put in a card advertising your services as a governess . . . or a tutor or whatever it is that you were.'

Heavens, yes. She'd forgotten that was the story she'd spun.

'I suppose I *could* . . . '

'It mightn't be what you hope to do in the longer term, but in a place like Wimbledon, well, there's certainly no shortage of money to pay for such things. Around here, people get paid to do all sorts.'

'Yes, I suppose they do.'

'Or you could join a group of volunteers. The notice board in the church porch is chock-full of posters asking people to help out. Pick your cause, you can.'

'Actually, I have thought about it.' Oh dear. Now she was simply telling lies on top of lies. Although, as it happened, in this instance, the lie was only a partial one.

Barely half an hour earlier, when she had been trying to decide what to wear, the emptiness of the day ahead not helping in that regard, she had been comparing the differences between her feelings about the war before she had left Clarence Square — largely that it was a frightful inconvenience — to her rather more pragmatic view of it here, and had been struck by an urge to be of some use. But, as usual, she'd had no idea how to go about it; all she had ever been brought up to do was be a wife, run a household, and raise children. Oh, and, later, once the children were all safely away at boarding school, to bestow patronage upon a charitable venture of

56

some sort — preferably one spearheaded by a member of the royal family, or, if not, then for a cause that was at least fragrant and photogenic.

Talk about being of no earthly use. Even dear Lou had learned shorthand and typing, which at least made her employable. Mummy would never have countenanced such a thing, let alone permit her to go out to work. Not that it was fair to blame Naomi Colborne; she'd just been doing what women like her had done for centuries — raise sons to go out and conquer the world, and daughters to be supportive wives. It was still how things were for people of their class. Either way, it was hardly surprising that here she was, at the age of twenty-five, apparently fit for nothing but marriage.

She glanced up from her plate. It was tempting to come clean with Mrs Jeffreys — confide that her loss was even greater than it seemed on the surface — but at what cost? Mrs Jeffreys might not like to find out that she had been lied to. And, for the present, these lodgings suited her. So perhaps it was better not to give herself away.

'Why not have a look in the church porch while you're up there this morning,' Mrs Jeffreys suggested into the quiet. 'See if anything takes your fancy.'

'Yes,' Esme agreed, adopting a brighter tone. 'Perhaps I'll do that.'

In her heart, she knew she was unlikely to do any such thing. Volunteering was all well and good if one didn't need an income. No, what she needed was to start looking for something that paid, and the only way she could think to do that was either to visit the Employment Exchange — a prospect that made her shudder — or take the rather more discreet course of buying a newspaper and crossing her fingers that, among the Situations Vacant, there would be something to suit.

The newspaper. Actually, she didn't even need to go and buy one of those because, every evening, Mrs Jeffreys had one delivered. If she could get to yesterday's edition before Mrs Smith used it for one of her cleaning jobs, she could have a quick look — see whether there was any point in holding out hope.

Her breakfast finished, she went out to the scullery to discover that part of the paper had indeed already been put to use to wrap vegetable peelings. But, of the pages that remained, she could see one headed 'Situations Vacant'. Extracting it from between the rest, she took it upstairs and went to perch on her windowsill, the bright daylight helping with the small print.

Eagerly, she scanned the columns, the sheer number and variety of vacancies coming as a surprise: *driver for a bakery; grocer's delivery boy.* She ran her finger across the page: *cleaner for a factory; cleaner of railway carriages; attendant for ladies' conveniences.* Clearly, she was in the wrong column. *Coal Office Requires Accounts Clerk. Garage requires Bookkeeper (part-time hours).* Perfect for Lou but not much good otherwise. *Barmaid at the Crown & Sceptre. Waitress (afternoons only) Apply Copper Kettle Tea Rooms.* Oh, this was

58

hopeless. While she could probably make a reasonable hash of those last two, she wouldn't be seen dead doing either. *Bus conductress, Streatham Garage.* Hardly. Although, thinking about it, clippies, as they were known in popular parlance, did have natty uniforms. What else? *Piano teacher. Companion to elderly widow with three corgis. Research assistant to author — knowledge of military history preferred.* No, no and no. Heavens, this was a complete waste of time.

Disheartened, and feeling even more useless, she folded the remains of the newspaper and put it on top of the chest of drawers to take back downstairs later. What was she to do? She had to get fixed-up with something, but none of those jobs were in the least suitable. Those that sounded even vaguely respectable required talent or experience she didn't have. Talent? Huh, her only talent was for being of no use. Granted, if she was truly desperate, she could go to the Employment Exchange, be despatched straight away to 'war work' somewhere and, by Friday night, have a pay packet in her hand. Thankfully, it had yet to come to that. Nevertheless, alarmed by how quickly the balance in her account kept reducing, being frugal wasn't just a patriotic duty in her case but a necessity. And it wasn't as though she was being extravagant, either. Only yesterday, she had resisted the assistant on the cosmetics counter urging her to try the latest scarlet lipstick.

Yes, the unpalatable fact was that sooner or later her money was going to run out. Not

59

imminently, thank heavens; the funds invested by Great Aunt Diana twenty-five years ago had produced a surprisingly generous sum. But not a bottomless one. Even by practicing economies, she could already see that at some point in the coming months, her account was going to need topping up. In that regard, and despite her suggestion to Lou having been made partly in jest, her proposal that they join the WRNS or WAAF hadn't been without merit. Of course, just because Lou hadn't wanted to do it, didn't mean she couldn't go ahead and do it without her. But the idea of joining up on her own didn't hold nearly so much appeal. In fact, it smacked of desperation.

No nearer a decision about what to do, she glanced about the room, her eye unexpectedly caught by something on the floor beneath the dressing table. As it slowly dawned on her what it was, she slid from the bed, crossed the rug and bent down to retrieve it, only to hesitate at the last moment. If she was right, it was her favourite snapshot of Richard — the one she'd taken on his camera that afternoon in St. James's Park. He'd been leaning against a tree, smiling and waiting for her to press the shutter when a squirrel had darted down the trunk and come to a halt next to his shoulder. Bursting into laughter at the way the creature was peering at him, she'd accidentally pressed the button, recording for all time the goofiness of Richard's expression and the hilarity of the moment.

Weighed by sadness, she continued to stare down at the little white square of paper on the rug. Oh, but whatever was the matter with her? Yes, it was going to be painful to look at, but she could hardly leave it there. Eventually, shaking her head in despair, she reached out, picked it up and turned it over. At the sight of Richard staring back at her, she exhaled heavily, her shoulders sagging as she did so. He looked precisely as she remembered in that moment: having sprung away from the tree in surprise, he was teetering slightly off-balance, his eyes wide, his lips parted in laughter. By rights, such an accidental snap should have come out blurred, and been discarded as not worth keeping. But, to the astonishment of both photographer and subject, it had turned out brilliantly, conveying perfectly a moment of joyous abandon, the spontaneity of it beyond any formal pose to capture.

The longer she stared at the picture, the more clearly the details returned; a Sunday at the end of March, it had been unexpectedly warm. At her mother's invitation, Richard was coming to afternoon tea but, with both of them feeling a degree of trepidation about the likely grilling ahead of him, they had arranged to meet beforehand for a walk in St. James's Park. In a bid to calm their nerves — although, only with hindsight was that now apparent — they had carried on like a couple of tourists: stopping on the bridge over the lake for Richard to take pictures of her with Buckingham Palace in the background; watching a little girl feeding the mallard near Duck Island and fantasising about taking up residence in the little cottage there;

pausing by the bandstand to listen to a military ensemble playing patriotic marches. And then, suddenly realising how late they had left it, they had dashed back to Clarence Square, arriving flushed and happy, where her mother and grandmother had fallen for Richard with the same speed as she had done. The very next weekend, having in the intervening days obtained the approval of her father, he had proposed.

Heaving a long sigh, she hung her head, her eyes falling upon her hands and, in particular, her engagement ring. Why was she still wearing it? Through force of habit — simply slipping it onto her finger every morning without thinking about it? Because she adored it — the central and largest of the three stones being of remarkable clarity? Or was it because she had yet to accept that she was no longer getting married?

Swallowing hard, she continued to stare down, her view of the cluster of stones becoming blurred by tears. Swiping at them as they ran down her cheek, she reached into the pocket of her skirt for a handkerchief. Dear God, what had she done? What she had done, she reminded herself, was the right thing. She had spared Richard the need to call off the wedding himself on the grounds that her true parentage rendered her unworthy of joining his family. And yes, in this day and age, most people wouldn't have given a damn, but the Trevannions weren't most people, which was why she'd had no alternative. And, though the pain might still be unbearable, at least her conscience was clear. Her action had averted a scandal; the Trevannions' reputation was intact. Richard was free to marry someone more suitable.

Sadly, telling herself that leaving had been the right thing to do no longer brought consolation. It didn't even really feel true anymore. It certainly didn't make her feel any less alone. Nor was it going to help her find her way out of her current predicament.

Her eyes falling once again upon the ring, she slid it off her finger and went to the chest of drawers where she put it back into its plush little box and hid it beneath her underwear. The time had come to stop looking back and wishing, and to look forward instead. Mrs Jeffreys was right: the matter of money aside, she needed something to fill her days, to occupy her mind. Take now, for instance: what was she going to do with her afternoon? Trudge miserably around the park again? Save the money she might spend buying a book by going to borrow a dogeared one from the library? If those were her only two options, then perhaps she *should* go and volunteer. At least she would have to think about something other than her own heartbreak. The other thing she could do — and this was an idea only now occurring to her — was go along to Elys and apply to them for work. Even if they didn't have any vacancies on their counters right this moment, a store of that size must always be in need of new staff. She could ask them to keep her name and to let her know when something came up. A few hours a week somewhere like the perfume counter might be quite enjoyable. Or even on ladies' fashions. It was certainly worth a try.

So, yes, she would tidy her hair, reapply her lipstick, change into a pretty frock and go and see them. If nothing else, it would force her out of her state of inaction. Besides, as dear old Great Aunt Diana was so fond of saying, fortune did have a habit of favouring the bold. And if ever there was a time to stop wallowing and be bold, then surely it was now.

★ ★ ★

Well, it was a promising start. The woman in charge of staff at Ely's had been quite happy to take down her details and put them on file. Even so, Esme knew it would be unwise to trust her salvation to Elys alone; she would need to cast her net wider.

Waiting to cross the road on her way back to Laburnum Avenue, she found herself watching the people spilling from the station, among them two young children with a dark-haired woman, whose demeanour suggested she was exhausted, the cut of her clothes that she wasn't English. Fascinated by the possibility, Esme continued to watch, noticing how, every now and then, the woman let go of the little boy standing to her right and dabbed at her eyes with a handker-chief. Oh dear, she was crying. Or, perhaps more correctly, trying not to.

Once across the road, Esme paused to regard the little group further. The woman's dress was dusky pink with short sleeves, a square neckline,

and a wide band of pin tucks around the waist
— almost definitely haute couture. She was
slender, her complexion pale, her jaw-length hair
parted to the side and held back from her face
with a clasp. Unusually, she was wearing gloves
but no hat. The children were neatly dressed, her
little boy looking to be about three or four, her
daughter a couple of years older.

With a strong sense that something was
wrong, Esme found herself unable to look away.
Directing the children to stand by the wall and
depositing their luggage piece by piece next to
them, the woman stood, peering along the road.
Evidently not seeing the person for whom she
was clearly waiting, she again dabbed at her eyes.

It was no good; she had to go and check they
were all right.

Drawing close, she saw the little girl look up to
the woman's face. Then she heard her speak.

'Maman?'

Just as she'd thought — they weren't English
but French.

Only a day or two back, newspaper placards
everywhere had been plastered with headlines
such as *Paris Falls to the Germans. German
Troops Enter Paris. French Government aban-
dons city for Bordeaux.* In dismay at the news,
she had purchased a copy of the paper and read
about the fall of the French capital. The details
had sent a chill down her spine. Poor dear Paris!
How cruel that such a beautiful city was now in
the hands of the brutish Germans. And now,
here she was, hearing French voices. It couldn't
be a coincidence.

Unsure how her approach would be received, she went to stand a few feet away from the little group and affected to also be waiting for someone. The rag-tag nature of the family's luggage suggested that it had been hastily put together. She could only imagine they had left France with little notice, had maybe even fled Paris itself. What if the poor woman had been forced to leave without her husband? It would explain why she was upset.

She glanced to the children. They looked grey and restless.

'*Maman, j' ai faim*,' the little boy chose that moment to whine.

It was no good, she had to see whether she could help them. She couldn't ignore their plight.

'*Pardonnez-moi, madame, puis-je vous aider? Vous etes perdus?*'

The woman tightened her grip on her children's hands. '*Non, merci, mademoiselle. Nous attendons mon mari. Il vient nous rencontrer. Il est en retard.*'

Well, at least someone was coming to meet them. At least she had a husband, which must mean that they would soon be safe. '*Vous etes parti de Paris?*' she enquired.

'*Oui. Nous sommes partis quelques heures avant que l'armée allemande est arrivée.*'

Digesting the fact that this poor family had only just made it out of Paris before the Germans arrived, she was about to ask where they were headed when towards them came a man, dishevelled and breathless. In his late thirties, and wearing a crumpled grey suit, his face lit up. '*Cherie,*' he exclaimed before embracing each member of his family in turn.

With a relieved sigh, Esme watched the reconciliation. This little family was reunited, but how many others weren't? She knew from the newspapers, and from the nightly news reports on the radio that in France, terrible things were happening and yet here *she* was ruing that she'd had to deny herself a new lipstick.

She turned away.

'*Pardonnez-moi, mademoiselle. Vous parlez francais?*'

Expecting to see the man in the grey suit, she swung back. '*Un peu.*'

To her surprise, she instead carne face to face with a man in dark jacket and trousers, a pristine white shirt with a paisley tie, and a trilby hat.

'Forgive me for approaching you like this,' he said, his accent switching from that of a well-bred Frenchman to someone educated at a very expensive school in the English home counties, 'but I couldn't help overhearing that you are fluent in French.'

Puzzled, Esme frowned. 'I . . . speak it tolerably well, yes.'

'You have lived in France, perhaps?'

What was this? What did this well-groomed but otherwise ordinary stranger want with her? Since he didn't look threatening, there seemed only one way to find out.

'I spent a year finishing in Biarritz,' she answered matter-of-factly, 'during which *Madame* forbade us to speak English. Prior to that, I had accompanied my mother there for a couple of weeks each spring.'

When the man reached inside his jacket, Esme backed away. 'Then please,' he said, stepping towards her and pressing a business card into her hand. 'Take this. The government is looking for people just like you.'

She withdrew her hand from his grasp. What on earth did he mean?

'People just like me?'

'Please,' he said, his look earnest, 'telephone the number on the card. Ask for Miss Teal.'

'But I don't — '

'Miss Teal,' the man repeated. 'Remember that name. And please, do call. You could be just what we're looking for.'

She stared down at the card. *Marchant & Little. Consultants.* Printed beneath those few words was a telephone number: CRO 512. CRO? Wasn't that the exchange for Croydon? *Croydon?* The government didn't operate from Croydon. Surely, this had to be a prank. Although . . . hadn't Richard once told her that, given the risk of air raids, some of the more sensitive departments of government had relocated away from Whitehall? Richard. Was it possible he was behind this? No, he couldn't be. He oversaw a team who drew up plans for the admiralty, or so he'd said. Besides, he didn't know where she was.

Unsure what to make of the situation, she looked up. Not surprisingly, the man was nowhere to be seen, in his place just people going about their ordinary business. If it wasn't for the card in her hand, she might think she had imagined him.

Amused, she re-read the details. What did she do now? Did she telephone the number, ask for the mysterious Miss Teal and find out what this was about or not?

Undecided, she opened her handbag and slipped the card into the little pocket in the lining. Ultimately, whether or not she did as the stranger had urged would probably come down to whether she could summon the nerve to pick up the telephone and ask the operator for the number . . .

★ ★ ★

Miss Teal had been right. The building that was home to Marchant & Little was indeed an anonymous one.

'Take down these directions carefully,' her clipped tones had cautioned over the telephone, 'and when you leave the railway station, follow them precisely. We are rather hidden away and easy to miss.'

Despite the warning, Esme had pictured something very different to this — certainly something more swish and official looking. But here she was, standing before a black-painted door bearing the number 110A, the remainder of the modern and characterless building home to a parade of shops, among them a chemist's, a gentleman's outfitter's and an off licence.

On the train journey over — a trip of less than

half an hour including a change of trains at Streatham — she had tried to overcome a succession of uncomfortable feelings, fear of the unknown and a sense of unpreparedness foremost among them. After all, how did one prepare for an interview when one knew nothing of the job on offer? Worse still, now that she was here, rather than begin to feel more composed, her wariness had deepened to such an extent that the idea of hotfooting it back to South Croydon station seemed quite appealing. But no, she reminded herself, when presented with unfamiliar circumstances, fear was a perfectly natural state, there to prompt one to exercise caution and be alert to the possibility that something wasn't what it seemed.

Staring up at the brass numbers, she straightened her shoulders, drew a breath, reached for the brass handle and pushed open the door. Beyond it was a narrow flight of stairs. Stepping in from the street, she closed the door behind her and started up.

At the top of the first flight was a short landing with two identical doors. As directed by Miss Teal, she continued on up the second flight, and then the third. At the top of this last climb was just a single door, the sign on the obscure-glass panel of which read 'Marchant & Little'. Puffing lightly, she paused. *No, don't hesitate*, she told herself. *Pause now and you'll lose your nerve.* Heeding her own advice, she raised her hand and knocked.

The door was opened without delay by a slender woman in a plain grey suit and high-necked blouse. Oldfashioned, was Esme's initial assessment of the outfit. Frumpy, even. Her hairstyle did her no favours, either; mousy-brown, and pulled tightly back to the nape of her neck from a centre parting, it put Esme in mind of a schoolteacher.

'Good morning,' Esme greeted the young woman. It was hard to put an age to her: late twenties perhaps? 'Miss Ward to see Miss Teal.'

'Miss Ward, good morning. Do come in.'

'Thank you.'

The room into which she was shown was small, with a window that gave directly onto the brick wall of the neighbouring building. She glanced quickly about. Set out as a waiting room, the furniture comprised several upholstered chairs with wooden arms and a low table bearing an artificial pot plant. Against the far wall was a sideboard, on top of which sat an illuminated tank containing plastic coral and a dozen or so tropical fish.

'Thank you for coming, Miss Ward,' the woman said as she moved to close the door behind her. 'I am Miss Teal. How do you do.'

Ruing that her palms felt so clammy, Esme shook the woman's hand. 'How do you do.'

'Any bother finding us?'

'None, thank you. Your instructions were most precise.'

'Good. Take a seat and I'll tell them you've arrived.'

Them? She was to see both Marchant *and* Little? Fingers crossed she wasn't in for too much of a grilling then.

Perched on the edge of the nearest chair, Esme watched the woman cross the room to one of two doors, tap lightly upon it and go in. What on earth was this place? When she had called the number on the card and enquired about the nature of the business of Marchant & Little, all she had been told was that everything would be made clear when she attended for interview. Oh, and that the cost of her train fare would be reimbursed. Really? *That* was the most important piece of information to convey to a would-be employee?

Alarmingly quickly the door re-opened and Miss Teal came towards her. 'Miss Ward, please come through.'

The room in which Esme subsequently found herself was not unlike a living room in a modern house. Having been expecting something altogether more formal, she was momentarily thrown. *Curiouser and curiouser.*

By the window stood two men, both in grey suits, one older and portlier than the other. They turned to regard her.

'Ah, *Mademoiselle Ward. Je m'appelle Monsieur Le Grande*,' the larger of the two men said. As he crossed the room towards her, Esme gulped. She was to be interviewed in French? Who the devil were these people? And what *was* their business? Expecting to shake hands, she was further thrown to find herself being greeted, in the manner of the French, with a kiss on each cheek.

'*Enchantée*,' she felt drawn to reply.

The second man approached. '*Et je m'appelle Monsieur Ledoux.*'

'*Enchantée*,' she again responded.

Was it too late, she wondered, to offer an apology and leave — to say that she was terribly sorry to have wasted their time, but she had changed her mind?

'*Du café?*' the smaller of the two men enquired, gesturing to the table where there was a tray containing cups and saucers and a coffee pot.

She shook her head. '*Non, merci.*' In her state of apprehension, she felt it better not to trust herself with something she stood a very real chance of spilling.

The larger of the two men gestured to the sofa. Prickling with discomfort, she moved to sit down.

In flawless French, the two men proceeded to make general conversation, asking her how she had travelled there this morning and, learning that she had journeyed from Wimbledon, how long she had lived there and what she thought of it. From there, they asked what she knew of events at Dunkirk; surprised by the ease with which she was able to summon the vocabulary, and grateful to have lately taken a greater interest in the events unfolding in France, Esme answered them. Within moments, she no longer even found it odd to be speaking in French.

Then, without warning, the man who had introduced himself as Monsieur Le Grande leant forward in his chair and said, 'Well, Miss Ward, I suppose you're wondering why the devil you're sitting in an office in Croydon, speaking French with two men who, before this morning, you wouldn't have known from Adam.'

'Cigarette?' the second of the men asked, flicking open a silver case and offering it in her direction.

She shook her head. 'No, thank you. I don't.'

Withdrawing his arm, the man took a cigarette for himself, put the case down on the table and then reached into his jacket for a lighter. The smell, when he lit up, made her think of Benson & Hedges — the cigarettes smoked by Grandpa Hugh on account of them being favoured by the King.

'So, Miss Ward,' the first man picked up again, 'you have no idea what all this is about?'

She shook her head. 'Absolutely none. Which was why I was in two minds about coming at all.'

'But you came anyway.'

She nodded. 'It would seem so, yes.'

'Well, allow us to introduce ourselves properly. I am Mr Green — '

'And I,' the second man added, 'am Mr Brown.'

Esme held back a smile; clearly, these names were as false as their French ones. Green and Brown, she thought, looking between them. Large and green, small and brown: that was how she would remember which was which.

'Mr Brown and I belong to a department, set up by Winston Churchill himself, that has been charged with recruiting men and women to help the war effort,' Mr Green took it upon himself to explain.

Finally, they were getting somewhere. Now she might find out for what, precisely, she was

74

being interviewed. 'Help the war effort?' she said. 'Might I ask in what capacity?'

'I'm afraid not, Miss Ward. Until you have been thoroughly vetted, you will have to settle for knowing only that what we do, we do by . . . *operating outside of the usual channels*.'

Vetted? Her? Then she might not be able to see this through anyway; the last thing she needed right now was people poking about in her private business. That said, she *was* intrigued. 'When you say outside of the usual channels,' she said, 'would I be correct in thinking you mean as spies?' Unlikely though it felt, it was the only thing she could think of that would require such subterfuge.

Setting his cigarette on the edge of an onyx ashtray, Mr Brown looked across at her. 'We prefer to use the term *operative*.'

Operative. So, a spy by another name.

She glanced quickly about. Was this truly happening, or were these peculiar men about to start laughing and tell her that she'd been had? It seemed a more likely scenario than the alternative. After all, *her*, a *spy*? The possibility defied belief. Well, she would play along. But she would remain circumspect — and allow them to see as much. If nothing else, she didn't want them thinking she was easily duped.

'But I'm just an ordinary woman,' she said. 'And since I was approached in the street by a stranger who knew absolutely nothing about me, I fail to see what leads you to think me suitable for your purposes.'

It was Mr Green who replied. 'You are

convincingly fluent in French.'

She frowned. If being convincingly fluent in French was all that was required to help one's country, then schoolgirls everywhere would qualify. Surely there had to be more to it than that. 'Reasonably, I suppose,' she nevertheless agreed.

'Rather more than reasonably, I think,' said the smaller of the two men. 'By your own admission, you have spent time in Biarritz.'

'Well, yes,' she replied, remembering what she had told the man at the railway station. 'But only because I holidayed there a few times with my mother.'

'If I am not mistaken, you also finished there.'

She hesitated. Clearly, they knew what she had said, which did at least link them to the man who had handed her the business card. 'Well, yes . . . '

'You're not married?' For a moment, she wondered whether Mr Green's statement was designed to catch her out. Was it possible they had already investigated her? Did they know more than they were letting on?

'I am not, no,' she confined herself to replying. No need to do any more than answer the question as it had been asked.

'Any dependents? Elderly parents?' Mr Green enquired.

'None.'

'Then I do believe you could be just what we need,' Mr Brown concluded.

'But to do what, precisely?' she asked; infuriatingly, she still had no idea what it was they thought she could do.

'In the simplest of terms, we require ordinary people to be our eyes and ears, to fit into certain surroundings and report back to us upon what they see as they go about their daily business,' Mr Brown finally explained. 'Of course, there is rather more to it than that but, should you be interested in learning more about what we do, then we must first complete some enquiries. I'm sure you will appreciate that to be entirely sure of your suitability, there is much we must know about you. Assuming the answers to our enquiries prove satisfactory, you would be enrolled into a programme of training to give you the necessary skills to fulfil the role.'

'And where would this training be carried out?' she asked.

'Can't tell you that.'

'All right, then what sort of skills would I be learning?' After all of this dancing about, she did hope they weren't going to say shorthand and typing.

'For now, let us just say . . . skills to enable you to operate covertly.'

'I see.' She wasn't even sure what that meant, the description 'covertly' making the whole thing sound shady and dubious. But then spying was shady. Frantically, she tried to think what else she should ask. There had to be much. 'And by whom would I be employed?'

'Can't answer that precisely until after you've been vetted,' Mr Green replied. 'I'm sure you can appreciate why.'

'I suppose because you don't know that I won't go about blabbing.'

'Blabbing.' Her choice of word seemed to amuse him. 'In essence, yes.'

Digesting what she knew so far, she was struck by a thought. 'You wouldn't talk to my family, would you? Only — '

'We wouldn't *talk* to anyone, Miss Ward.'

'Only . . . well, let's just say that for the moment, I would prefer they didn't know where I am.'

She had expected that by hinting at some form of deceit on her part, she might put them off. In the event, they didn't even exchange glances.

'Rest assured, Miss Ward, nothing *we* do will give you away.'

Hm. They would say that, wouldn't they? 'But how do I know that I can trust what you say?'

To Esme, Mr Brown seemed to be trying not to smile.

'Because, Miss Ward, we are the government.'

Barely reason to trust them, she found herself thinking.

'And if I pass your . . . your *investigations* . . . this would be a proper job of employment?'

'It would. You would sign the Official Secrets Act and become a government employee.'

'I would receive a salary.'

'You would. And, whilst you were undergoing training, your board and lodgings, too.'

Suddenly this was becoming interesting! Training and a proper salary as well as the chance to help her country — precisely the thing about which, only the other day, she had been dreaming. Added to which, as a way of life, it had to beat lodging with Mrs Jeffreys, depleting her savings account at a rate of knots, and wondering how to fill her days. All told, it sounded like the perfect solution to her current predicament.

'Then where do we go from here?' she enquired of the two faces looking expectantly back at her.

★ ★ ★

Patience never had been one of her virtues. It was a shortcoming she attributed to having been raised without siblings — to always being able to command the full attention of the adults around her and to having her every whim indulged. Well, in this instance, no amount of wheedling and demanding was going to bring an envelope popping through the front door. Messrs Green and Brown had said they would write to her as soon as they could. It would take, they had said, as long as it takes. But *this* long? More than a week? Really?

So, when, later that morning, the flap on the letterbox gave its customary clunk, Esme didn't even bother to stir from the armchair in the living room where she was sitting reading the latest issue of *Vogue*.

'Post for you dearie,' Mrs Smith came through from the hallway moments later to announce.

Looking up from her magazine, Esme stiffened. On the lamp table just inside the door, Mrs Smith had placed a slender white envelope. Blinking across at it, she let her magazine slide to the floor, uncurled her legs and poked her feet back into her shoes. Could this be it? Had she really somehow summoned its arrival?

Breathing rapidly, she snatched up the envelope and ran her finger under the flap. Withdrawing the single sheet of paper from inside, she scanned the type-written words.

... wish to request that at your earliest convenience you telephone Miss Teal on the number previously provided to you.

Telephone Miss Teal? That boded well. Or did it? Rather than meaning their enquiries had thrown up nothing of concern, it might mean the reverse; it *might* mean they had uncovered her past and didn't like it. Either way, she wouldn't waste a moment. She would go straight to the telephone. If she wasn't going to be given the job, then she needed to be put out of her misery.

Her telephone call to Croydon, though, left her with no firm answer either way.

'I'll be frank, Miss Ward,' Miss Teal said once they had been connected. 'Mr Green and Mr Brown were very impressed with you.'

Esme grinned to herself. 'All right.'

'They would like to send you to the next stage of evaluation.'

Unsure what that meant, and with the crackling on the line not helping, Esme decided that Miss Teal appeared to be asking her to attend a further interview. 'When do you want to see me?' she asked.

'Can you make Saturday? But not here. They want you to go to our training centre in the

Weald. It will mean staying overnight. You'll be finished and on your way home Sunday afternoon.'

In the stuffiness of the telephone box, Esme could feel herself perspiring. A further interview wasn't what she had been expecting. Had it not been for the fact that she'd been the one to instigate this call, she might well have thought it a hoax.

'Saturday. Yes. All right,' she said.

'Since there's not much time, I'll arrange for your rail warrant to be waiting for you at the ticket office of Wimbledon railway station. Pack an overnight bag. Take the sort of things one might need if one was to go camping.'

Again, Esme thought she must have misheard. 'Did you say camping?' she raised her voice above the crackling on the line to ask.

'Good show. Thanks for calling so promptly. And good luck.'

With that, the line went dead.

Stepping out from the telephone box into the fresh air, Esme had no idea what to think. Seemingly, the day after tomorrow, she was going somewhere called the Weald in order for her would-be employers to get a second opinion on her abilities. And there might or might not be camping involved.

Turning back in the direction of Laburnum Avenue, she burst out laughing. Funny sorts, these spies. Sorry, *covert operatives*. But hey-ho, if it gave her a second chance at doing something useful for her country, then they could interview her wherever they liked!

3

The Interviews

'Miss Ward. Welcome to The Grange.'

Alighting from the staff car that had collected her from the railway station, Esme stood on the gravelled drive and looked up at the front of the building. Constructed of brown brick, and with generous bay windows, its original purpose as a country house seemed incidental now to the need for it to act as a support to a monstrous magnolia, clinging to which were still one or two waxy blooms.

After reaching into the motorcar for her overnight bag, she turned back to regard the man who had come striding out through the porch, and who was now stood, shoulders back, feet apart, arms behind his back. Even had he not been clad head to toe in khaki, it would have been clear from his posture alone that he was — or had been — an army man.

'Thank you,' she said. 'Good morning.'

He extended a hand. 'Major Lovat. I'm the one charged with putting you through your paces.'

'How do you do, Major Lovat.' Although trying to sound confident, at the mention of being put her through her paces, Esme felt her insides knot.

'Been to the Weald before?' he asked, gesturing

her ahead of him through the front door.

Beyond the porch, Esme found herself in a high-ceilinged hallway panelled with dark wood. Around the walls, lighter coloured oblongs suggested that longhanging paintings had recently been removed, presumably for safe-keeping.

'No,' she said, 'never.' The thing that struck her was the silence — not even the ticking of a clock nor the cheeping of a sparrow. 'It seems terribly remote.'

'Precisely why we commandeered the place,' Major Lovat said. 'With the nearest village over two miles away, no one knows we're here. It also has the advantage of being within the confines of a military training area and, thus, out of bounds to the general public.'

'Yes,' she said, recalling the concrete roadblocks and the barriers she'd seen at the various turnings along the route from the railway station. 'I noticed.'

Pleasantries over, Esme saw her chance to ask what was on her mind.

'Would you mind telling me why I'm here?'

The major raised an eyebrow. 'Nobody told you?'

'It all seems to have been a bit rushed. I was told only to pack a bag and get on the train. And so, I did.'

'Good for you,' the major said, seemingly amused. 'Well, in a moment, I'm going to ask you to sign a document. It's called the Official Secrets Act, and by signing it you are confirming that you will never, at any time, in any place, or under any circumstances, disclose or otherwise allude to anything that you see, hear or do whilst you are on these premises . . . or indeed, on any other government property.'

Esme nodded. Through Richard and his work at the Admiralty, she knew the significance of the Official Secrets Act. 'I understand.'

'After that, I will be taking you through some of the exercises we use with our operatives to see how well you fare. No need to panic,' he said, evidently reading the concern on her face. 'It's not a life and death sort of a test. I've simply been asked to gauge how well you might take to the work. It's not something we do ordinarily, but someone somewhere is clearly interested in you and trying to decide where you might be of greatest use.'

Oddly, his final remark made her feel a little less tense. Someone was interested in her: do well and she might have a job. In which case she would give it her all, peculiar set up or no.

'Thank you for explaining that,' she said.

'Right, then. Best foot forward. Time and tide wait for no man. Tomorrow, you are to be gone from here by eighteen-hundred hours — before the next intake of recruits arrives. And it's going to take all of the time between now and then to find out all about you.'

'Yes,' she said, 'of course.'

'So, up two floors to the dorms. Bunk wherever takes your fancy — you're the only one here. Facilities either end of the landing. Oh, and take this,' he said, going across to a table under the stairs and picking up a bundle of khaki, 'and put it on. We'll get you boots and a cap from the stores. Fifteen minutes do you?'

'Fine, thank you.'

Climbing the stairs and arriving at the first landing Esme glanced about, spotted behind her the next staircase, and went on up. At the second landing, it was obvious from the sloping ceilings that she was in the attic. Peering in through the first door she came to and seeing two beds, she went in. In the far wall, a tiny window was wide open and coming in on the breeze was the smell of woodland. Putting her bag down on one of the beds, she went across and closed the window, noticing as she peered out that there was nothing to see but trees and heathland. They really were in the middle of nowhere.

She glanced around the tiny room: two identical beds, each with a sheet and a grey woollen blanket, and between them, a small table. The only other furnishings were a wardrobe with a door whose hinge needed fixing, and a small mirror stuck to the wall. On the back of the door were two coat hooks. Thank goodness she was only there for the one night; spartan didn't begin to describe it.

Aware that she was expected back downstairs, she took off her jacket and picked up the garment handed to her by the major. Once unfolded, it turned out to be an all-in-one affair — overalls with long sleeves. Holding it by the shoulders and shaking it out, she fingered the material. It was stiff and heavy. And scratchy. Quickly, she unbuttoned her skirt and then took off her blouse. Realising that stockings were hardly appropriate, she removed those too and carefully folded them up. Precious things, these days, decent stockings.

Standing in her bare feet, she regretted that the socks she had gone out and bought for the occasion weren't thicker. *Far* too thin; she could see that now. Perhaps they could loan her some thicker ones — they were going to furnish her with boots, after all. Unbuttoning the front of the overalls, and holding them low to the floor, she put a foot into each leg. Then, realising that it might be wise to use the lavatory first, she hoisted the garment up over her thighs and grasped it about her waist. Peering out onto the landing, and seeing and hearing nothing, she scampered along to a door at the far end. As bathrooms went it was functional rather than comfortable — lavatory, washbasin with mirror above, bathtub. And on the floor was lino that felt surprisingly cold to her feet.

Back in the bedroom where she had deposited her things, she buttoned the overalls. Apart from where they strained across her chest, they were at least one size too large, possibly even two; with her arms straight, her hands didn't even reach beyond the ends of the sleeves. Sighing in dismay, she turned back the cuffs until her wrists appeared. Unable to see her feet at the bottom of the trousers, she bent down and turned up those several times too. Then, with no alternative, she slipped her feet back into her brogues. Thinking to grab a handkerchief from her handbag, she poked it behind her bra strap and then, somewhat pointlessly, hid her handbag under the pillow of the second bed.

Turning for the door, she wondered what Richard would say if he could see her looking like this. Would he burst out laughing, imagining her to be involved in some sort of prank? Would he admire her spunk and tell her to give it her best shot? Or would he be simply appalled and tell her she'd taken leave of her senses? What did it matter? Why, with everything else she had to worry about, was she concerned with Richard? If she was serious about getting a job with these people, then her appearance was the least of her concerns; she was here to undergo some sort of assessment — show them what she could do — not take part in a fashion parade.

When she arrived back down in the hallway, Major Lovat was waiting for her.

'Good show,' he said without so much as even looking her over. 'Let's get you something for your feet.' At the rear of the house, in what Esme could only think of as a gardener's shed, were wooden racks stacked with all manner of clothing, most of it in either black or lovat. *Lovat.* She gave a wry smile. The person responsible for allocating these false names clearly had a sense of humour.

'Size?' the major enquired, turning to look down at her shoes.

'Five,' she said.

'Nothing below a six, I'm afraid. You'd better take two pairs of socks.'

She hid her latest dismay with a smile. 'All right.'

Socks donned and boots laced, the major handed her a forage cap. 'If nothing else,' he said, 'it will keep your hair clean.' When she put it on, he adjusted the angle of it on her head. 'Might as well wear it properly.'

She smiled. 'Of course. My apologies.'

'Right, then, first stop PT.'

She frowned. 'PT?'

'Physical Training.'

Physical training — two words that conjured memories of being harangued by a humourless tyrant of a gym mistress at school. Perhaps, to save embarrassing herself, she should just point out that she wasn't terribly athletic — nip the humiliation in the bud and suggest they move on to another part of the assessment, saving time all round. Starting to open her mouth, but catching sight of the major's face, she shut it again. On the other hand, perhaps it would be best to keep quiet.

Departing the stores building, her stomach knotted with dread, she followed the major along a path that led away through a copse.

'When it comes to physical training,' he slowed his pace a little to say, 'the operatives we recruit must look to all the world as though they are ordinarily unfit people, while actually having rather more stamina and being rather more agile.'

Spotting that ahead of them in the trees was a clearing, Esme realised that this particular physical training was to be conducted out of doors. Feeling thoroughly wretched, she shook her head in dismay. If she'd known the weekend was going to entail this type of assessment she would never have come. Nevertheless, seeing the major looking at her, she nodded her understanding. 'I see, yes.'

'To that end, first thing each morning, rain or shine, our recruits come here to our commando battle course. By the end of their stay, they must be able to complete it without breaking into a sweat.'

Esme regarded the various timber constructions. 'It looks like an obstacle course,' she remarked dully. An obstacle course of nightmarish proportions.

'Correct,' the major replied, 'the start to which is at the far end.'

Studying the height of some of the wooden frames, Esme felt her stomach churn. She really and truly did not want to do this — job or no job at the end of it. 'Um . . . '

'HQ instructions, Miss Ward. You are to cover the same training course as the ordinary recruits, albeit in two days. Clearly, they think you're up to it. They didn't send you here solely to take up my time, or if they expected you to fail.'

Although it was too late now, she couldn't help thinking it would have been helpful had someone explained what she was coming here to do. Although, *had* she known, she probably wouldn't have come. Besides, *they clearly think you're up to it* suggested that someone, somewhere, saw something in her.

Resignation taking over, she sighed heavily. Finding oneself in a Sussex forest on a Saturday morning was peculiar enough. Having to tackle an army obstacle course — as the sole participant — only made it stranger still. But ever since she had accepted that business card from the man at the railway station, her whole life had taken a sharp turn towards the bizarre.

She stood looking ahead. *Ordinarily unfit*, Major Lovat had said. Well, she was *ordinarily unfit* personified. 'Then here goes,' she muttered.

Clambering up a ramp and running across a platform wasn't difficult; nor was jumping back down to the ground at the other side. The exertion didn't even leave her puffing.

'Move on,' Major Lovat instructed when she turned towards him.

The next obstacle, however, involved a pole of about ten feet in length supported at either end by wooden tripods, but, rather than being parallel to the ground, the pole sloped upwards, the tripod at the far end significantly higher than the first.

'I don't think I can walk that,' she said, concerned not only by the incline of it but by its height from the ground. Fall from six feet up — or more — and she was certain to break a limb.

'Few can at their first attempt,' Major Lovat replied. 'Some never do. And since I've instructions not to allow you to become injured, I suggest you do one of two things — sit astride it and move up leap-frog style or proceed on all fours like a chimpanzee.'

A chimpanzee indeed! 'Very well.'

'And I suggest you avoid looking down.'

In the event, the experience was less frightening than she had envisaged, the trickiest

90

part proving to be the dismount from the far end — in her case, an ungainly flop.

Relieved to feel grass beneath her hands, she exhaled heavily. 'Heavens.'

'Well done.'

'Thank you.'

And so it went on; wooden frames that resembled larger versions of the old trellis in Mrs Jeffreys garden to be clambered over; fallen tree trunks placed to bridge ditches; rope swings to traverse pits. And, whenever she appeared to flag, the major was there to urge her along.

'Come on, down with you, no time to hang about,' he said as she hesitated at the top of one particular obstacle. 'Imagine you're being chased by an SS officer with an Alsatian who hasn't been fed for several days.'

The thought was sufficient to both terrify and galvanise her. And when she finally reached the end of the course, the muscles in her arms and legs trembling from the effort, he was there with words of praise. 'After a few days, I guarantee you would be scrambling to the top of everything, hurling yourself over and dropping straight to the ground — all without drawing breath.'

'Dropping . . . straight . . . from the top?' Given her state of near exhaustion, it seemed unlikely.

'Alsatians, remember?'

'Alsatians,' she murmured, doubling over to nurse a stitch in her side.

'Overall, not bad for a first attempt,' Major Lovat told her. 'Those who fare best first time out are usually those who listen to my instructions and then do as I say.'

She laughed. 'In my case, it was do as you said or risk plunging to my death!'

'Miss Ward, I've not lost a recruit yet and I don't intend for you to be the first.'

'Thank goodness for that,' she said, wishing her heartbeat would stop pounding in her ears.

Having allowed her a moment to recover her breath, the major motioned to her to stand up. 'Next, we complete the hike.'

A *hike?* In these stiff old boots? With the way her feet felt at that precise moment she would rather stick pins in her eyes. But, which do you want, she asked herself: a job with the government doing valuable work, or one that involves cleaning public conveniences for a living? Because those two would seem to be your only choices.

Slowly, she nodded her head. 'All right . . . '

'And then, this afternoon,' he said, setting off into the trees, 'it's firearms training — '

'Firearms?' As in *guns*, did he mean? At no stage had anyone said anything to her about *guns*.

'Firearms. Ours and theirs.'

'Ours and theirs?' What the devil did *that* mean?

'Firearms of both British and foreign issue. No good being in enemy territory and wielding a British revolver.'

Enemy territory? No one had said anything about enemy territory either! Dear God, just what had she let herself in for?

But then she remembered the major's earlier advice: concern yourself only with your next challenge; to think any further ahead than that is to dilute your concentration on the task in hand. Well, she would try She wouldn't think about this afternoon — nor the guns. Although, now he'd mentioned them, they were going to be hard to ignore.

Nevertheless, to that end, she said, 'So, about this hike — '

'Ordinarily, pairs of recruits must cover twenty-five miles, completed solely with the aid of a map and compass, and carrying a backpack filled with sand to simulate the equipment they will one day have to carry. Oh, and they start out before dawn.'

'Tell me they at least have a torch,' she said, following him across the grass.

'They do if they've remembered what we tell them at the outset about keeping one on their person at all times. Otherwise, it's not something we remind them about in advance.'

Walking beside him between the trees, their way ahead unclear to her, she risked a look at his face. 'So, this hike we're going to do . . . ' She could only pray it wasn't going to be anywhere near twenty-five miles. Or that it involved darkness.

'A three-mile loop out over the heath. With the aid of map and compass, you'll be sticking mainly to marked rights of way.'

Three miles over a heath sounded bad enough. 'But I won't be going out alone . . . will I?'

'If I had my way, you would. But no, it was made plain to me that lose you and I'll be drummed out.'

Three miles with him accompanying her. Well, that was *something* of a relief.

To her surprise, the hike turned out to be relatively pleasant. For a while, the sun broke through and, eventually, her feet even seemed to grow used to the damnable boots. She also came to understand how to align the compass with the map to check their 'bearing' as she learned it was called, and to pick out distant features — such as the steeple of a church or the far hills — to keep them from wandering off course. All told, she found it surprisingly enjoyable.

When they arrived back at The Grange just after one o'clock, she realised that she was ravenous and, over a lunch of corned beef fritters with mashed potato and carrots, she learned more about what the rest of the day held in store.

And then, given fifteen minutes to herself, and in the privacy of her room, she peeled off three pairs of socks to examine her feet. To her surprise, her heels were only slightly red, and not blistered as she had feared. Nevertheless, she applied the plasters the major had fetched from a first aid kit.

When she reported back to the hallway, the major took her down to the basement where she was astonished to find herself in an armoury. There, from a couple of locked cabinets, the major selected four weapons, signed for them in a ledger, handed her two of them to carry, and then locked each of the doors behind them.

'We're going to the shooting range,' he said when they arrived back to the ground floor, 'where you will have the chance to practice using these.'

Ever since his first mention of the word firearm, Esme had found it hard to ignore a creeping sense of dread. Indeed, until he had just handed her what she guessed were a rifle and a revolver, she had never so much as seen a gun, let alone held one. To her surprise, though, the moment she was shown how to use them, her fear evaporated. And when, in the middle of the forest, the major stationed her inside a little timber building, telling her that her job was simply to come out and make it to the trees without being shot, she felt her heartbeat quicken and a surge of what could only be described as excitement.

Of course, she didn't react nearly quickly enough to his ambush, anticipating neither from where, nor when, the major — her gun-wielding enemy — would appear; within the first few seconds, she would have been shot dead a dozen times over. It was a realisation that took away her earlier excitement at pulling a trigger and hitting a target, and replaced it with the feeling that she was going to be sick.

'We always hope our people will never need to draw their weapon,' Major Lovat said, oblivious to her turmoil as he took back her revolver. 'Their purpose is not to get into combat but to blend in, to observe and report. We teach them to regard their weapon purely as a tool to protect themselves, not to take another life.'

Not to take another life. She couldn't believe she was even hearing those words. Nevertheless, as he stood examining her expression, she felt obliged to acknowledge his attempt to reassure her. 'No, of course not.'

'Now, on our way back, we'll go via the classroom where I will show you one or two other things and then we'll call it a day. Got that?'

Distractedly, she nodded. 'Yes, major.'

'So, in here,' he said when they reached the first floor of the house and the room he had referred to as the classroom, 'we provide recruits with critical information which they must be able to learn, retain and recall without reference to prompts or to written notes. Such as this,' he said, tugging the corner of a large cloth to reveal a board containing coloured drawings of uniforms and insignia for German military personnel. Alongside it was an organisation chart entitled *Geheime Staatspolizei*. 'This,' he said, seeing her staring at it, 'shows how the Gestapo is organised.'

'The German secret police,' she breathed. 'I've read about them in the newspaper.'

'If our people are to glean information that will be of any use, they must be able to identify German military personnel from their uniforms and understand how the organisation is set up. Misidentify someone and our chaps could end up in real trouble.'

'Goodness,' she remarked of the drawings. So many badges, so many titles, most of them as

incomprehensible as they were unpronounce-
able. How did anyone remember it all?

Still mulling the point, she followed the major
into an adjacent room.

'We also teach them how to evade capture,
along with skills such as how to get out of
handcuffs — '

'One can get out of handcuffs?' It was a feat
she wouldn't have thought possible. Besides, if
an operative was captured, it seemed to Esme
they would need to be able to do rather more
than just get out of handcuffs.

'One can and one must. But, to prepare them
for all eventualities, we also train them how to
resist interrogation.'

There was a picture she could do without. 'I
see.'

'Of course, if things go really badly, each of
our operatives is always in possession of a lethal
tablet.'

'A lethal tablet? I'm afraid I don't understand.'

'A suicide pill — although we try not to call
them that — for use as a last resort.'

A suicide pill? Such things really existed?
Feeling suddenly faint, she reached out and
grasped the doorframe. Could a situation really
become so desperate that someone would see no
option but to take their own life?

'But if they are just there to observe and
report back — '

'As I say, Miss Ward, it really would be the last
resort. A dozen or more things would need to
have gone completely awry for it to come to
that.'

On an adjacent bench she noticed radio equipment. To distract herself from what she'd just learned, she picked up one of the Bakelite headsets and examined it. Finding it heavier than she had been expecting, she put it back down. It was no good; the existence of a lethal tablet was all she could think about now, most of what the major went on to say after that insufficient to distract her: wireless operators; codes; messages transmitted within BBC News broadcasts. None of it seemed to stick. And then he was saying something about false identities and documents, and garments that were made to look more authentic by stitching into them the labels of French fashion houses. But still all she could think about was how desperate someone would have to be for a suicide pill to be their only option. Truly terrifying.

For the umpteenth time that day, she wished she could go home — return to a life where her most taxing consideration each morning was simply what to wear. It had already become clear that she wasn't cut out for this sort of work. No doubt many of the people who came here took to this espionage business like a duck to water. But, no matter how fervently she wished differently, and how deeply she regretted her unsuitability, it was evident that no amount of Major Lovat's training was going to make her one of them.

★ ★ ★

'Hot bath. That's all you need.'

When Esme followed the major back out into

the corridor, her legs were tired, her shoulders ached, and her neck was stiff. Coupled with that, she was finding it impossible to quell the constant feeling of being close to tears, and to banish the panicky sensation gnawing at her insides. Horrible, that was how she felt; frightened, cranky and horrible. And picturing the spartan little bathroom did nothing to engender any enthusiasm for the major's suggestion that she have a bath. More useful would be a couple of stiff gin and tonics.

'Dinner at nineteen-hundred,' he said as they arrived at the bottom of the stairs.

To Esme's surprise, though, a soak in the bath did at least ease the aching in her limbs. Unfortunately, it also served to harden the feeling she had been carrying around with her all day — the feeling that she had been got there under false pretences and that, had she known what she was letting herself in for, she would instantly have declined to have any part in it. The person who thought her suitable for this sort of work clearly needed their head examined.

Back in her room later still, after a supper of shepherd's pie and tinned peas — at which she could do little more than pick — she was even more convinced that she was wasting everyone's time. The only surprising thing was that she hadn't already said as much to the major. Not that it was *his* fault. As army types went, he seemed both fair and endlessly patient. It was just that the more she saw of what these recruits had to go through, the less she could picture herself among them.

Glancing to her travel alarm told her that it was approaching nine o'clock. With little else to do, she got between the covers on the bed. She wouldn't be able to sleep though; her body might be exhausted but her mind was racing. The wiser half of it was disappointed with the way she had let herself be duped. That same half was also ruing that she had allowed herself to get her hopes up. Having somehow made it through today, it couldn't be more evident that she was no more destined to become one of these government operatives than she was to becoming prime minister.

Trying to get comfortable on the lumpy mattress, she wriggled about. Changing her name from Colborne to Ward might have been partly about putting the past behind her, but it had also been to remind her that she was starting a new life, and that, relieved of the weight of her past, she was free to do anything she wanted. But the truth, in this particular instance, was that she was out of her depth. Completely unsuited. At the end of this torture there would be no offer of a job. And she had been foolish to even expect it. In fact, she should never have kept that business card; she should have laughed at the preposterousness of her being able to *help her country* and have confined herself instead to buying the newspaper and continuing to scour the vacancies for something more suited to her limited abilities. With the power of hindsight, that would have been far more sensible.

So, tomorrow morning, she would do what she

should have done today: admit defeat and ask to be allowed to go home.

★ ★ ★

'I'm sorry, Miss Ward, but no, you may not go home.'

'But, Major, I'm wasting your time.'

Arriving down to breakfast at seven o'clock the following morning, wearing the skirt and jacket in which she had travelled yesterday, Esme's intention had been to apologise for her shortcomings and request that she be taken back to the railway station. Coming clean and admitting to her failings seemed only fair. She couldn't imagine this was the first time there had been such an obvious mismatch of candidate to job, although it did make her wonder how she'd got this far, given her glaring unsuitability.

'Have some toast before it gets cold,' the major said. 'There's even a fresh boiled egg keeping warm for you over there.'

She glanced across to the sideboard. She was starving. And whether she stayed or not, she was still going to need some breakfast.

'Thank you,' she said, submitting to the major's suggestion.

'And then go and get into uniform because this morning we have a lot to cover.'

Seated opposite him at the table, the piece of toast growing cold on her plate, she withheld a sigh.

'But it's not going to work, is it?' she said. 'By

no stretch of the imagination am I cut out for this sort of thing.'

Across the table, the major's knife fell still. 'Miss Ward, *no one* is cut out for this sort of thing. That's why we pick the people we think have the capacity to be trained for it. The people we need don't arrive ready formed, they arrive raw and hapless but with open minds and a desire to help their country. We pick people not because they are outstanding but because they are ordinary.'

'Well, I'm certainly ordinary,' she said dully. 'More than ordinary, if such a thing is possible.'

Seeming to ignore her, Major Lovat continued. 'Added to which, you know very little about the role for which you are being considered.'

'If it involves firearms,' she said, using the major's term for the guns she'd handled yesterday, 'and the possibility of having to take a life, then I do know I want nothing to do with it.'

'Not all of our roles require firearms.'

Slowly, and unsure whether to believe him, she looked up. 'Hm.'

'Look, Miss Ward, someone at SOE sees something in you. In fact, from what I have gathered, they are split over which of two roles would suit you best. Either way, *my* job is to put you through this assessment, and *your* job is to complete it. That done, I shall submit my impression of you to HQ, with whom the decision ultimately rests.' Pausing for a moment, he looked straight at her. 'I've read your file. I know a good deal about you. In addition to which, I've turned far less-obviously suited candidates into top-notch operatives. Given a fortnight, I could do the same with you. And I'm not just saying that. It's my job to sort the wheat from the chaff. So please don't try to second guess me and consign yourself straight to the chaff bin.'

Although she tried really hard to raise a smile, it made no difference; despite the sincerity of his words, she knew that the life of an SOE operative would never be for her. She simply didn't have it in her to make a go of it. But, since the major wasn't about to let her go home, all she could do was see out the remainder of the day and then put the whole thing behind her: chalk it up to experience, get back on the train, and re-start her search for a less glamorous but ultimately more suitable form of employment.

★ ★ ★

' . . . while in Paris yesterday, Adolf Hitler is reported to have spent the day visiting sites including the Eiffel Tower, the Arc de Triomphe, and Napoleon's tomb at Les Invalides.'

Having arrived back at Laburnum Avenue late the previous evening, Esme had awoken this morning with a thudding headache, something not being helped by the monotone delivery of the newsreader on the BBC Home Service.

'Not hungry, dear?' Mrs Jeffreys enquired, looking across the table at her half-eaten piece of toast.

Esme didn't even attempt to smile. 'I thought I was . . . '

'Didn't go well?' her landlady went on. 'That interview you went for?'

The interview? Oh, yes, she'd told Mrs Jeffreys she was going to see a family in Sussex who required a private tutor, and that she would be staying the night with an old friend nearby. 'No,' she said. 'When I got there, it wasn't what I'd been led to believe.' Sticking to the essence of the truth, she went on, 'The duties weren't as my friend had been told. I didn't feel it was for me.'

'Listen to your heart, that's what I always say,' Mrs Jeffreys replied. 'Can't go far wrong like that.'

'No, I'm sure you're right.'

'So, what will you do now then? Keep looking, I suppose.'

'Yes,' she said, straightening her posture and affecting a brightness she didn't feel. 'I shall keep looking.'

'Best thing,' Mrs Jeffreys concurred. 'Only a matter of time, you see if I'm not wrong.'

To Esme, though, it didn't feel so cut and dried. Yes, she would need to keep looking for a job. And yes, the longer she looked, the more likely she was to find one. The trouble was, precious few prospects had excited her *before* she'd become muddled up with the department of government masquerading as Marchant & Little. In fact, having got up her hopes on their account, it was hard now to muster the enthusiasm to go and buy a newspaper, let alone go through the soul-destroying process of scanning the Situations Vacant. Indeed, edging its way into her mind was the notion of swallowing her pride and asking the Colbornes whether she could return to Clarence Square. So utterly dismal did her prospects seem that the idea of having to apologise for her thoughtlessness seemed by far the more palatable option.

The idea now firmly in her head, she spent most of the morning thinking of little else, reluctantly coming to decide that it was the only sensible course of action. Why waste time and money here in Wimbledon, she asked herself, when, if she went home, not only would the balance in her savings account be safe from further depletion but the need to consign herself to unsuitable employment would also be averted. There were downsides, of course. For a start, she would miss her new-found freedom. And the thought of having to eat humble pie made her shudder. But what other choice did she have? Principles were all very well but, if living as Esme Ward meant being directionless and, eventually, broke, then returning home seemed unavoidable. Sadly, and looking to the longer term, the only sane option was to swallow her pride, admit defeat, and retreat while the option was still open to her — assuming, of course, that it *was* still open to her! The thought that she might not be welcomed back at Clarence Square made her fingers curl into her palms and caused her heartbeat to quicken. Surely, she would be welcomed with open arms . . . wouldn't she?

With a quick check of her purse for coins, she slipped on her shoes, trotted down the stairs and let herself out though the front door. Then she headed briskly along the road to the telephone box. If there was any chance the Colbornes wouldn't want her back, she needed to know now. Equally, if she *was* going to go home, there was no sense delaying.

Stepping inside the telephone box and pulling the door closed behind her, she lifted the receiver and dialled the operator. 'Kensington 312, please.'

'Hold the line, caller.' Waiting to be connected, she stared absently through the filthy panes of glass. In keeping with every other telephone box she had ever used, the interior gave off an aroma of general despair. Was she being hasty — deciding to go home? No, rather than haste, what she felt was resignation: if this was what she had to do, there was no point putting it off. 'I'm sorry, caller, that line is engaged,' the operator returned to her to say.

Heaving a sigh of disappointment, she replaced the receiver and pushed open the door, the fresh air welcome. Bother. Not being able to get through to Clarence Square was a nuisance. But she wouldn't hang around here on the off chance of getting through in the next couple of minutes; instead, she would go back to Mrs Jeffreys, sort through her belongings in readiness to leave, and try telephoning again this evening. The delay would give her time to prepare what she was going to say to her mother so as to appear contrite without sounding a failure — no need to draw attention to the fact that she hadn't succeeded in making a go of things by herself.

Reassured by her plan, she arrived back at 'Sandown' and was just putting her key in the front door when, from behind her, she heard the creak of the gate hinges. Turning over her shoulder, she saw a young woman wearing the jacket of the telegram service. Assuming it to be an urgent message for Mrs Jeffreys, she turned the knob and opened the door.

'Good afternoon, ma'am. Telegram for Miss Esme Ward.'

With her hand still on the doorknob, Esme felt something in her stomach tense. 'Forgive me,' she said, 'but would you say that again?'

'I have a telegram for Miss Esme Ward of Sandown, Laburnum Avenue.'

A telegram for *her*? But how? No one knew where she lived . . .

'I . . . am she.'

'There you go, ma'am. Will there be a reply?'

Accepting the envelope and seeing her own name written upon it, Esme tried to think who might have died — and how anyone would have been able to track her down to tell her. 'One moment.'

She pulled out the message.

TELEPHONE MISS TEAL. URGENT.

Exasperated, but at the same time relieved not to be discovering that someone had died, she reached into her handbag, fished about in her purse for some coins and handed a couple to the delivery woman. 'No, no reply, thank you.'

She stared at the message. Was there to be no

escape from those dratted people? Since she wasn't going to be offered a position as one of their operatives, what could possibly be so urgent that it couldn't have been entrusted to a letter? What could be so critical as to require rattling her with a telegram?

With a dismayed shake of her head, she exhaled heavily. Well, she would go straight back to the telephone box and call them — bring to a close the whole sorry charade of Marchant & Little.

Checking she still had their business card in the pocket of her handbag, she stuffed the telegram in alongside it and closed the front door. With this final telephone call, she would draw a line under the matter. Then she would give her mind to the more important consideration of how to ask her mother if she could return to Clarence Square.

★　★　★

'Well, they weren't wrong, were they, Miss Black?'

This time, when Esme was shown into the room at Marchant & Little where she had previously been interviewed, she was not, as she had been expecting, met by Mr Green and Mr Brown but by a much younger man and a woman.

'No, Mr White, they were not in the least wrong,' the woman replied to her colleague's observation. 'She's perfect. Bags of 'it', as my mother would say.' Stepping forward, her hand

108

extended in greeting, the woman made to introduce herself. 'Welcome back, Miss Ward. My name is Miss Black and I'm delighted to meet you.'

Shaking the woman's hand, Esme stifled an urge to sigh in dismay. *Black*. Another false name; it had to be. 'Good morning,' she replied. 'How do you do?'

'And I am Mr White,' the second of her interviewers introduced himself. 'Please, won't you take a seat?'

Directed to the sofa, Esme sat down. That she was here at all was remarkable, her telephone call to Miss Teal yesterday having proceeded very differently to the way she had been expecting. Rather than the anticipated *on this particular occasion you are not what we are looking for speech*, Miss Teal had astonished her by requesting that she attend yet another interview — and as soon as possible. There were, she had said, two people who couldn't wait to meet her. Good job, then, that her mother's line *had* been engaged when she'd telephoned her! Even so, her instinct had been to decline the invitation. Sensing this, Miss Teal had proceeded to disclose that a new position had become available — one for which she was considered the perfect candidate. It was, Miss Teal's voice at the other end of the telephone line had gone on to add, an opportunity she really ought not decline.

And so, here she was, back in this peculiar little office, thoughts of Clarence Square momentarily on hold, but wary of what might be in store for her this time.

'We'll get straight to it,' the woman who had introduced herself as Miss Black said once Esme was settled.

'We have a proposition we'd like to put to you,' her colleague, Mr White, picked up.

'Mr Green and Mr Brown were very impressed by you — '

'In fact, they couldn't wait to tell us all about you — '

' — and how they thought that rather than recruit you into their department, you might better suit ours.'

'And now that the major has seen you, he agrees.'

Esme looked between the two faces staring eagerly back at her. Something about the way they interrupted one another suggested the two of them were, or had at some time been, more than merely work colleagues. But she mustn't let herself get distracted. Despite being desperate to find meaningful work, she had come here determined to establish, with all thoroughness, what, precisely, she was being offered. This time around, she would not be seduced into giddily accepting whatever they chose to tell her.

To that end, she smiled politely. 'And might I ask what department that would be?'

It was Mr White who responded. 'Miss Ward, before we go into the details, how much do you understand about the Official Secrets Act?'

'I know that in having signed it, I am bound not to disclose details of anything I see or am told about any government business.'

110

'Good. Just wanted to be certain you understood.'

'Someone I know — *knew* — works at the Admiralty,' she said, her intention being to show that this time around, she had her wits about her, even if it did mean referring to Richard. 'And so I was fully aware of the implications of that to which I was committing.'

Miss Black looked directly at her. 'Mr Richard Trevannion, one assumes your man in the Admiralty to be?'

Despite being unsettled by the mention of his name, Esme knew there was no point denying it; she *had* given his details on that form, after all — the one where they'd made her list the names of everyone she knew, from family members, friends, and acquaintances, all the way through to her doctor and dentist. 'That's right, Richard Trevannion.'

'Then perhaps this would be a good point to mention,' Miss Black went on, 'that if, once you see what we have in mind for you, you decide to join us, relationships such as the one you had with Mr Trevannion will become difficult . . . if not impossible.'

'I think what Miss Black wants you to understand, Miss Ward,' Mr White went on to clarify, 'is that all the while you work for us, the circumstances of your employment will not allow you to have a change of heart about your former fiance. Through the nature of your work, the one would preclude the other.'

If only they knew the irony of that warning! No, if she succeeded in getting this job, then

111

having already jettisoned the name Colborne, she would go forward and fully embrace life as Esme Ward — free from all constraints, free to do as she saw fit. Free from thoughts of marriage.

'I understand.'

With a single nod, Mr White continued. 'The operation Winston Churchill has been so keen to see established is called Special Operations Executive — SOE for short. While you won't previously have come across the name, I know you are aware of the purpose of its operatives and will know that its aim is to infiltrate German-occupied France to either observe and report back, or else to carry out specific missions within enemy controlled territory.'

Esme nodded. 'That much I gathered from Major Lovat, yes.'

'But, more recently,' Miss Black went on, 'it has been brought to our attention that our programme is missing a part — that is, a test of our operatives' ability not to leak, inadvertently or otherwise, details of their missions.'

'You know how fellows can be,' Mr White said, leaning towards her and grinning. 'There he is, in a strange place with a few days to kill, when he meets a young lady — if he's fortunate, maybe more than one. For some chaps, the desire to impress can rather loosen their tongues.'

'And it's not just the chaps, either,' Miss Black added. 'Although generally less gripped by the desire to impress, women operatives can fall into the same trap.'

112

Unexpectedly, the penny dropped. 'And those who might let slip secrets,' Esme said, 'must be weeded out.'

Miss Black smiled. 'Got it in one. Major Lovat said your questions showed a grasp of the situation.'

'You see, Miss Ward,' Mr White picked up, 'an operative who talks risks not only his own life, but the lives of others, too.'

Esme nodded. 'Yes, I see that.'

'So, we've come up with the idea of training what, for want of a better name, we're calling decoys.'

'And that, Miss Ward, is where you come in. With your looks — attractive but not so spectacular as to seem unattainable — '

'Thank you,' Esme said, raising her eyebrows and laughing. 'I *think* that's a compliment.'

' — and your lack of family ties, well, I'm sure you can see our thinking.'

'You want *me* to be one of these decoys.'

'Yes, Miss Ward, we do. Very much.'

'And you'll train me how to go about it,' Esme said. In her stomach, she could feel the stirrings of excitement. *Esme Ward can do anything she chooses.* 'Train me thoroughly, I mean.'

'Absolutely,' Mr White replied. 'We'll train you in all manner of techniques for putting male operatives to the test.'

'And we'll set you up in a flat or a hotel somewhere, along with a wardrobe of outfits and an out of pocket allowance.'

'The only thing is,' Mr White went on, 'no matter the excitement or the thrill attached to

113

your work, you will be unable to tell anyone what it is that you do. Ever. In fact, although we will provide you with a false identity, we strongly urge that you sever all but the most essential of ties with family and friends. That way, you will be presented with fewer opportunities to slip up.'

Sever ties with her family? She'd pretty much done that already. And somewhere to live as well as clothes and an allowance? Sounded perfect. Perhaps she should pinch herself to be sure this was real. And to think she'd been in two minds about coming here today!

With the business at The Grange still fresh in her mind though, she knew she had to maintain her detachment, try to appear non-plussed — at least until she was entirely sure that this *was* what it seemed.

'Well,' she said to that end, 'it does sound interesting.'

'Pleased to hear it,' Mr White replied. 'So, bearing in mind what we've told you thus far, what would you like to ask us?'

Esme thought for a moment. There were certainly matters she should check. 'I would become an employee of the government?'

'You would.'

'And, as well as the allowance, I would receive a salary.'

'You would.'

'And can you tell me where I would be carrying out this job?' Although not her most pressing concern, she would prefer it wasn't somewhere as remote as The Grange.

Her two interviewers exchanged glances.

'Still working on that,' Miss Black replied. 'But the obvious place would seem to be somewhere on the south coast.'

Unexpectedly, Esme felt a little rush of happiness. This really could happen! Unlike the previous role, this one sounded within her abilities to actually do. She still needed to exercise caution though, her experience at The Grange having taught her to be wary.

'Would it be safe to assume this job would have nothing to do with g — ' She paused. 'With firearms?'

Mr White looked taken aback. 'Good Lord, nothing whatsoever. If the chap fails, we don't expect you to shoot him.'

Miss Black, though, clearly understood her concern. 'Sorry to put you through that business at The Grange,' she said. 'But there was some disagreement as to where we could best use you. Mr Brown thought you had the makings of an operative. Mr Green thought you would make the perfect decoy. Having put you through your paces, Major Lovat thought you could do either, but that you were perfect for us.'

Reflecting upon Miss Black's explanation, Esme wished she had known all of that before being sent to Major Lovat; she wouldn't have felt nearly so terrified the whole time. Nor would she have come away with such a powerful sense of having failed.

'Now, I'm sure it won't surprise you to learn,' Mr White picked up again, 'that we're anxious to get this thing up and running soonest. In light of what's been happening in France, there's a bit of a flap on, and a need to get our operatives over there as quickly as possible.'

'Although not before we're sure they're ready,' Miss Black continued.

Esme nodded her understanding. 'So, you need a decision from me. Is that what you're saying?'

'I'm afraid so.'

'We appreciate you will want to think it over — ' 'But we really will need your answer by the end of the week.'

Think it over? Despite the caution with which she had vowed to approach this interview, what was there to think about? This sounded like something she could not only do but might also enjoy. Dressing up and attempting to get men to fall for her, all in the name of serving her country? Not only was this an opportunity she couldn't let slip through her fingers but the timing of it was perfect.

Careful to not to let her eagerness show on her face, Esme straightened up and looked at each of them in turn.

'I do have just one further question.'

Across the table from her, Mr White nodded. 'Which is . . . ?'

'Which is . . . when would you want me to start?'

4

Finishing School

Brighton! It was a stunning summer's morning and here she was in Brighton, with its salt-laden air and squawking seagulls dazzling white against the unbroken blue of the sky. So much had happened in such a short space of time that she could barely believe it.

Walking down the hill, she looked about. The street was an elegant one, lined by cream-painted Regency terraces with bow fronts and iron railings. Iron railings? In Wimbledon, all of the railings had been cut off at ground level and carted away, supposedly to make Spitfires and guns. *Do your patriotic duty*, householders were urged. *Help defeat Hitler* they were told as they surrendered pots and pans and garden gates.

With that, she saw a plaque on the house opposite: 'Les Marronniers'. The Chestnuts. And in the neighbouring public garden were the trees of the same name, their candles of blossom now crinkled and brown. Close by, a church clock chimed ten; by some miracle, she had made it on time.

Mounting the half-dozen steps to the front door of the house in question, she felt the muscles of her stomach tighten; just lately, trepidation was a feeling she had come to know well. Determining to ignore it, she reached for the brass knocker and rapped it against the door. When it opened, she found herself face to face with a smartly dressed young woman who simply looked at her and smiled. It was only then she recalled the instruction to introduce herself in French. Presumably, it was a sort of code by which she would be identified.

'Bonjour, mademoiselle,' she began. '*Je m'appelle Mademoiselle Ward. Madame Marron m'attende . . .*'

The young woman's smile broadened. '*Bonjour Mademoiselle Ward. Entrez.*'

When Esme stepped inside, she was surprised to find herself in the hallway of an ordinary home. But what had she been expecting — a secret bunker? Other than being told by Miss Teal that the language school was merely a 'front', she'd had no idea what to expect.

'Miss Ward, welcome.' From a doorway further along the hall appeared a woman in her late forties, her voice warm and deep but devoid of any discernible accent. With her chignon of auburn hair, her expensively cut navy-blue shift dress, and the single strand of pearls at her throat, she could easily be French. And yet, she almost certainly wasn't. Drawing closer, the woman extended a hand. 'I am Madame Marron, and this is my daughter, Violette.'

Shaking the woman's hand, Esme realised that while *les marronniers* did indeed translate as 'chestnut trees', the word *marron* was French for 'brown'. And the meaning of Violette was self-explanatory. Yet more colours posing as false names!

'How do you do, Madame Marron.'

'How was your journey? Not *too* fraught, I hope.'

As she had suspected, Madame Marron wasn't French at all.

'Not too bad, thank you. About halfway here we were held up for a good fifteen minutes while our identity cards were checked. I have no idea where we were because the names of the stations have all been taken away.'

'Such delays are common. Your identity card was checked because only residents and those on *bona fide* business are now permitted to be within twenty miles of the Channel coast. But you made it, and on time, too. So, welcome, Miss Ward, to Les Marronniers Private School of Languages. Come through, make yourself comfortable, and I'll tell you what it is we do here.'

Over a cup of coffee that tasted as though it had been brewed from actual coffee beans, Madame Marron set about explaining.

'As far as anyone passing on the street is concerned, Les Marronniers is still a language school. Before the war, my daughter and I gave private tuition — I taught French, Violette, German. Not long after war was declared, I was approached by someone from a board within the War Office, asking, in a manner that made plain it was less a request than an instruction, that in lieu of private pupils, we tutor civil servants and government officials. So, for a while, we did. More recently, they approached us about tutoring operatives from SOE.'

Following her story, Esme nodded. 'I see.'

119

'For the most part, the operatives are proficient but rusty, our task being to rehearse specific scenarios with them . . . scenarios that, well, let us confine ourselves to saying they feature official-dom — both French and German.' Recalling the display about the Gestapo in the classroom at The Grange, Esme nodded. 'More recently still, the same department approached me to do something different yet again, which was to work with you.'

'*Just* me?' Esme asked, it occurring to her only now that there might be others preparing for the same role.

'For the moment, just you. Our work coaching the operatives in French still continues but quite separately.'

'And you no longer take private students?'

'If anyone enquires about private tuition,' Violette joined the conversation to say, 'we tell them that for the present, we are not taking on new pupils.'

So far, it all seemed straightforward. But precisely how Madame Marron and her daughter fitted into her own role was still unclear. 'But *I* won't need to speak French, will I?'

'You won't, no. For you, the role of Les Marronniers will be to pass you details of each assignment and receive from you your report on the outcome. We will also help you with false identities, documents, the authorities, and so on.'

'This will be a place you can also come should you need help,' Violette added.

'My daughter and I occupy a separate apartment on the top floor, meaning that should the need arise, you will always know where to find us.'

'So . . . this isn't where I will be staying then?' Esme asked.

'That was the plan originally. But no, since there is now a night-time curfew, residing here would hamper your ability to come and go as you need. We also had concerns for your safety — '

'Given the increased likelihood of air raids . . . or even an invasion,' Violette interjected.

'So, instead, you'll be staying at The Aurelian.'

The Aurelian Hotel? She hadn't been expecting *that!*

'*The Aurelian?*'

Violette smiled. 'Is there another?'

'Right on the seafront?' she persisted, still thinking it had to be a mistake.

'That's correct,' Madame Marron replied, 'right on the seafront.'

'But that must be . . . well, it has to be the finest hotel in Brighton, if not on the whole of the south coast.'

'That would be the general consensus,' Madame Marron agreed. 'But do not flatter yourself too greatly. The choice is largely one of expediency. The management at The Aurelian have worked with the department previously and were amenable to doing so again. The manager and his deputy understand the clandestine nature of your work and will do everything to ensure that you are able to operate without hindrance.'

'Goodness.' She hadn't been expecting to be

put up at The Aurelian! Her mother would turn green with envy if she found out — not that she ever would.

'Rather exciting, isn't it?' Violette remarked, her tone conspiratorial.

But Esme was still struggling to digest the news. 'Very . . . '

'Something else within our remit is to facilitate contact between Esme Ward and her real life.'

Puzzled, Esme met Madame Marron's look. 'I'm sorry but I don't understand.'

'You have family who might need to contact you — '

'Well, actually, on that point — '

'Yes, I have been told that you are currently estranged from them. But situations change, especially in times of war. So, this afternoon, you will write to them, and to any close friends, telling them that you have taken up employment providing French tuition to minor government officials. It is plausible, is it not?'

Actually, it was more than plausible. 'Quite, yes.'

'Once your family know that you are safe and well, they should feel less tempted to try to track you down. You can write that owing to the nature of your work, you are not at liberty to divulge details but that, in an emergency, a message can be left with the agency who found you the position.'

'But if they know I'm in Brighton,' Esme ventured, 'what's to stop them turning up on your doorstep?'

Madame Marron smiled. 'The details you give

122

them will actually be for a government department in London whose role is to provide just this sort of support to operatives. They can also arrange for things such as fictitious postmarks for your letters.'

So much thought had gone into this and yet, for her own part, Esme felt utterly unprepared. 'Goodness' she said, hoping to conceal the fact.

'So, for you,' Madame Marron began again, 'these next few days will be all about settling in — settling into The Aurelian, into Brighton — '

'You will need to practice finding your way around until you know it almost as well as a local,' Violette pointed out.

' — rehearsing cover stories — '

'Don't look so worried,' Violette interjected. 'We will prepare you meticulously.'

'Leave nothing to chance,' Madame Marron echoed her daughter's remark. 'We will train you as thoroughly as we ourselves have been trained. Think of this week as a very particular type of finishing school — '

'A finishing school where you will have the chance to practice over and over.'

Unwittingly, Esme let out a long sigh. Finishing school. Hm. Back in Croydon, with Mr White and Miss Black, this whole business had sounded like a grand adventure. Now that she was discovering what it actually entailed, and just days from doing it for real, the prospect of going through with it was bringing her out in a cold sweat.

Well, it was too late now for second thoughts. Besides, at this precise moment, young men and women just like her were at The Grange, embarking upon their own course of instruction, except at the conclusion of *their* training, *they* faced real danger. *They* wouldn't be spending their time making small talk in the bar of a first-class hotel! No. So, if she ever felt her nerves starting to get the better of her, she would remind herself that, by comparison, what *she* was being asked to do was a doddle.

★ ★ ★

'A delight of a figure. Quite the hour-glass.'

It was after lunch that same day, and Esme was standing in her slip, on a low stool, having her measurements taken. At the same time, Madame Marron was relaying information from a file that lay open in front of her on the table.

'With each new target, you will assume a new name.'

Referring to the operatives as targets struck Esme as cold and impersonal. But then she supposed that's how she would have to be — detached and business-like. 'New name each time. Right.'

'But, for ease, the details of your background will remain much the same throughout. According to the chaps at SOE who came up with these instructions, it's best to keep people's new identities as close as possible to their real lives.'

Well, she could see the sense in that. 'Yes, I suppose so.'

Without looking down, Esme could see that by her feet, the tailoress was entering her measurements in a notebook.

'So, you will be an only child, orphaned in the last war and raised by a spinster aunt.' Recognising it as close to the truth, Esme stiffened. These people certainly didn't stint with their investigations, did they? But how did they find out such things? If, as they had told her, they didn't speak to family members, then how did they establish such personal details? Or was it just chance? Perhaps it was better not to know. 'Minor embellishments to that story,' Madame Marron picked up again, 'we leave to you. But my advice would be to keep it simple.'

'Simple. Yes.'

The taking of her measurements complete, the tailoress got to her feet.

'You will be able to supply everything on the list?' Madame Marron enquired of her.

The tailoress nodded. 'I will.'

'And when will you have some things for us to see?' Violette wanted to know.

'The first of the garments I should be able to bring to you tomorrow. The pieces I shall have to alter or run up from scratch . . . by Thursday or Friday.'

Accepting Violette's assistance down from the stool, Esme reached for her blouse and slipped it back on. So many clothes! Was it too much to hope that she would get to keep some of them afterwards?

'Excellent. Well, thank you for coming at such short notice. Violette will show you out.' Turning to Esme now buttoning her skirt, Madame Marron smiled. 'So, back to work. Every Sunday,

125

a file like this one will be delivered to your room at The Aurelian.'

Having finished dressing, Esme sat down next to Madame Marron. 'Sunday. Right.'

'You will then have twenty-four hours to familiarise yourself with the contents before your first meeting with the target detailed within, and so I recommend that you don't wait to start reading it.'

Esme nodded her understanding. 'I shan't.'

When Madame Marron slid the file towards her, Esme opened the cover. Fastened by a paper clip to several sheets of paper was a head-and-shoulders photograph of an unremarkable man in his thirties. She slipped it from under the clip and set it aside on the table.

'This is a dummy file, of course,' Violette explained, returning to sit next to her. 'For practice.'

Esme nodded. 'John Smith.' She giggled. 'Highly imaginative.'

'If you haven't already done so, this is when you must decide upon the name you will be using for yourself.'

'A different one each week,' Violette reminded her, 'to cover the possibility that although these men might not reveal anything to you directly, they might still suspect you of being a trap and pass on their suspicions to other operatives, something they are expressly forbidden to do.'

'So,' Esme said, deciding to check that she had correctly understood, 'even once they have left Brighton, they're still not allowed to disclose that they were here — or anything about the people they met during their stay.'

Madame Marron nodded. 'That is correct. Each man will understand that this is an opportunity for them to practice operating under an assumed identity and that their time here is to be regarded as though it was a genuine mission.'

Esme returned her attention to the file. *John Smith, thirty-five, unmarried, father deceased, one brother (younger). Born and raised in Suffolk. Occupation: Professor of History and University Archivist.* 'Golly,' she said in reaction to the last part, 'he sounds so terribly dull.'

'To you, perhaps,' Madame Marron remarked. 'Even so, were this real, it would be up to the target to live and breathe these details and convince everyone he meets that he is this man. He will have been told to think of this exercise as a steppingstone because, obviously, once in France, he will assume the identity of a Frenchman, whose details will be altogether more unfamiliar to him.'

'The targets — will they also be staying at The Aurelian?' she thought to ask.

Madame Marron shook her head. 'No, they will stay nearby.'

'In which case,' she asked, 'why will any of them choose to spend their evenings in the bar there, when, presumably, they could go any-where — sample any of the delights Brighton has to offer.'

'They will go to The Aurelian,' Violette interjected, 'because not only will it be just a short stroll from their lodgings — handy with the curfew and the difficulties with travel — but

127

because they will also be told that they may charge their drinks to a department account there.'

The more Esme found out, the more her mind brimmed with questions. 'All right. I see that. Even so, why will he get into conversation with *me?*'

'Heavens, Miss Ward!' Violette said, throwing up her hands in Gallic fashion. 'He will get into conversation with you because not only will you be the most stunning woman he has ever seen, but because you will be luring him into doing just that.'

Luring him. The picture that came to Esme's mind made her blush. Just how far were they expecting her to take this luring business? Just how much would she be expected to do to 'decoy' these men?

'Don't worry,' Madame Marron said, reaching to reassure her with a pat of her hand. 'There are many ways to draw a man into conversation without actually saying a word — ways to let him think he is making all of the running.'

'But if he doesn't want . . . if he doesn't want to converse . . . '

'He will,' Violette assured her. 'He will have been told to seek out interactions with people in order to practice his deceit.'

The cold truth, she thought as recognition dawned, was that she was there as bait. 'I see.'

'Oh, and the bartender is one of us.'

'One of us?'

Violette nodded. 'SOE helped the hotel to recruit a replacement for the young man who

128

tended bar previously . . . but who has recently received his call-up papers.'

Beginning to see how these things worked, Esme gave a wry smile. 'How fortunate — on both counts.'

'Indeed,' Madame Marron agreed. 'The new bartender is an older gentleman, a distinguished soldier from the last war.'

Reading between the lines, Esme studied the faces of the two women. 'A former spy, do you mean?'

'Let us just say that in the course of serving his country, he proved himself to be extraordinarily valuable. He has been briefed on your purpose at The Aurelian as well as that of your targets. In the manner of bartenders everywhere, you will find him personable and chatty. To the casual observer, it will be clear from his manner towards you that you are a long-time resident at the hotel.'

Beginning to appreciate the amount of planning that had gone into this operation, Esme couldn't decide whether to be alarmed or relieved. She also began to think she might have underestimated the scale of the responsibility about to settle upon on her shoulders. Until now, she had been guilty of viewing the operation as something of a jolly jape — an expression her Uncle Ned used to describe things he thought might turn out to be fun. But it was clear now just how much effort was going into ensuring its success — success that required her to fully commit to her own part in it. This wasn't just a final opportunity for these operatives to practise their craft of deceit, but the final chance for the department to be certain they were up to the task — up to maintaining their assumed identities while infiltrating German-occupied France. It was, she realised, a deadly serious affair, and one that was clearly going to require her to be deadly serious, too.

★ ★ ★

'A wedding cake. That's what it reminds me of.'

Staring up at the front of the hotel, Esme giggled. Already, she liked Violette and her sense of humour. 'Or a giant meringue,' she replied to the young woman's observation.

The architecture of The Aurelian was certainly of the over-the-top variety. Even heavily sand-bagged, and with every single one of its thousands of panes of glass criss-crossed with tape against bomb blasts, it still managed to appear regal and imposing.

'Go and wait over there,' Madame Marron instructed the two of them once they were inside, 'while I go and ask for Mr Bancroft.'

'Gosh,' Esme remarked as they took a seat in the vast foyer. 'There's not a soul about.'

'I was just thinking the same thing,' Violette agreed.

'If it's always like this I shall stand out like a sore thumb.'

Violette shrugged indifferently. 'I daresay it's busier than this in the evenings — with the restaurant and the bar.'

'Despite the curfew?'

'Despite the curfew.'

'I hope so.' Spotting a chance to satisfy her curiosity on an unrelated matter, she turned to Violette and, trying to couch her question without seeming nosy, said, 'Your mother . . . '

'Yes?'

'Forgive me for asking, but she's not actually French, is she?'

Violette smiled. 'Yes and no. Her father was English. As a young man travelling down the Atlantic coast of France one summer, he met a beautiful French girl, Marie-Laure, fell in love, married her and brought her back to England. So, although my mother was born *here*, she grew up speaking French and English in equal measure.'

That explained it. But she was curious about something else as well. 'But *you* speak German.'

This time, rather than smile, Violette grinned. 'Where I was at school, young ladies were expected not only to learn Latin but a modern language as well. However, as I was already more fluent in French than the mistress who taught it, the headmistress decided that she, herself, would teach me German instead. Until I started taking private students, though, I'd never found a use for it.'

With that, Madame Marron came back across the foyer. By her side was a sandy-haired man, fortyish, in a plain grey suit.

'Miss Ward, welcome to The Aurelian. It is a pleasure to meet you.'

Esme shook his hand. 'How do you do.'

'And Mademoiselle Violette, lovely to see you again.'

'And you, Mr Bancroft.'

Turning back to Esme, the manager went on, 'Miss Ward, my name is Raymond Bancroft, and it is into my care that you are being entrusted. Please, permit me to show you your room.' Once they were in the lift, and it was slowly climbing three floors, Mr Bancroft explained more about the hotel. 'As you might guess, the recent restriction upon travel to the area has effectively brought an end to private holiday bookings, leaving us with just our long-term residents and our regular businesspeople. That being the case, we have recently taken the decision to keep open just the rooms on the lower floors. We have also lost many of our staff to the war effort, including, as you will have noticed, our lift girl.' When the bell tinged and the doors opened, Mr Bancroft slid aside the scissorgate and gestured them ahead of him. Turning to the right, he picked up again, 'Given that you might be with us for a while, I have allocated you one of our nicest sea-view rooms.'

Turning a key in the lock of room 303, he opened back the door and, with a flourish, held out his arm.

Passing ahead of him into the room, Esme gasped. 'Goodness,' she said, crossing straight to the windows to take in the view out across the Channel.

'The ugliness of the army's defences is regrettable,' Mr Bancroft remarked, arriving

132

alongside her. 'The work to put them in place commenced about a week ago and I'm told there's still more to come.'

She could see what he meant. Directly across the road from the hotel, coils of barbed wire more than six feet high prevented access from the esplanade to the beach. In addition, concrete blocks at both ends of the flights of steps barred access between the two levels. On the shingle of the beach itself were gun emplacements. And then there were the pleasure piers, whole sections of which had been removed from their middles such that the traditional amusements at the far ends now stood like islets marooned at high tide. Even had the restrictions on visiting the place *not* come into force, she couldn't see why anyone would want to holiday here now anyway.

She looked back up. The view out to sea was still marvellous, though. And this room, complete with its very own little sitting area, was so elegant that she was finding it hard not to grin.

'It's lovely,' she said.

'It will suit you needs?' Mr Bancroft enquired.

How could it not! 'Perfectly, thank you.'

Across the room, she noticed Violette beckoning her into the bathroom. 'Come and see this. It's large enough to host a party.'

Violette wasn't wrong, over-sized mirrors on the walls giving the impression that the room was several times its already considerable size. 'Heavens,' she whispered, running her fingers along the marble top containing two washbasins with gold taps, the opulence of it all genuinely astonishing.

'I know it might be a bit dated,' Violette whispered back, 'but it's hard to beat *Les Arts Decoratifs* for a sense of style, don't you think? So terribly glamorous, is it not?'

'Shame about the 5″ mark,' Esme said, pointing to the line painted inside the claw-foot bath.

'Two things, my dear,' Violette replied, her eyes warm with mischief. 'Firstly, it has been painted onto the bath *in gold.*'

Bending lower to check, Esme noticed that it was indeed painted in gold leaf. 'And secondly?'

'And secondly, who's to know how deep you fill it, all the way up here in your ivory tower? Besides, you're on war work. *Vitally important* war work. And so I think you're entitled to flout the odd regulation.'

'Hm.'

'Seriously,' Violette went on, 'live a little. We might none of us be here tomorrow.'

It was a thought that made Esme shiver. While she understood the point Violette was trying to make, she was unable to shake from her mind the recruits who would, earlier today, have had their first sight of The Grange and who would, about now, be retiring to their spartan bedrooms and their draughty little communal bathroom. 'Tempting, I'll admit,' she said. 'But not terribly patriotic.'

Violette adopted a typically French moue. 'If the idea makes you feel guilty, fill it up anyway and I'll come and share it with you. Then we can both enjoy it with a clear conscience.'

Warming to Violette, Esme laughed, her laughter bringing Madame Marron to peer in. 'What are you two doing in here?'

Hidden behind the door, Violette sent Esme a wink. 'Just admiring the facilities, Maman.'

When the two Marron women had left with Mr Bancroft and her luggage had been brought up by a very young bell-boy, Esme returned to looking out the window. In a way, she wished she could tell the Colbornes where she was and what she was doing. She would like them to know how, through her own endeavours, she had secured employment. And not just any employment but employment with the government no less. But she couldn't tell them. Nor could she tell Richard, who, having seen how far she had come, would probably laugh and call her audacious. Dear Richard. Five weeks might have passed since that regrettable evening, but she still squirmed with discomfort to recall how badly she had treated him. True, in the last fortnight or so she hadn't thought of him *quite* so often, but she did miss being out on his arm and having him shower attention upon her.

Continuing to stare from the window, she sighed heavily. No sense looking back and wishing; thanks to the Colbornes and their deceit, her destiny was no longer to become Mrs Richard Trevannion. Instead, through a stroke of remarkably good luck, she found herself with a new purpose — the coming about of which couldn't have been more fortunate.

And anyway, she reflected, looking down at

the deserted esplanade, was Brighton not the place where the dreamers and the dispossessed came to lose themselves — to reinvent themselves and to start over? Because if it was, then Esme Ward — and her aliases — would fit in just fine.

The remainder of Esme's first week in Brighton passed in a blur. Madame Marron and Violette continued to explain how things were going to work and to provide Esme with even more information for her to commit to memory. They demonstrated how to casually ask the target questions about himself, tempting him into disclosing things he shouldn't. They even rehearsed little scenes to enable her to practise the techniques, which, as often as not, ended up with all three of them rocking with laughter.

'It's no good,' Esme said to Violette during one such exercise, tears streaming down her cheeks. 'If your idea of impersonating a man is to adopt *basso profundo*, I shan't be able to carry on!'

'Oh, very well,' Violette conceded, and from which point the exercise proceeded more smoothly.

'This afternoon, then,' Madame Marron said when the time came for them to break for lunch, 'we practise again how to converse with the targets.'

'*Again?*' Esme looked up to ask.

'Yes, Miss Ward, again. There is no substitute for preparation.'

'And tomorrow?' she asked, hoping that it wouldn't be something too heavy-going; although she wasn't

136

about to admit it, her head felt as though it might at any minute burst from being crammed with so much detail.

'Tomorrow morning, in so far as it is still possible to do so, Violette is going to show you around the town. Since you are supposed to have been resident here a while, it is important that you can at least converse about the main points of interest.'

At last, Esme found herself thinking — something that wouldn't require so much concentration.

'It will be fun,' Violette said with her usual enigmatic smile. But then, seeing her mother frowning, she hastened to add, 'But highly instructional, too.'

★   ★   ★

Everywhere looked so terribly sad. Exploring the town with Violette the following morning, it quickly became clear to Esme just how badly the restrictions on travel were affecting the place. Many of the amusements — such as the boating pool, now drained of water, its blue paint already peeling, and the putting green on the Esplanade — had simply been shut up. Even had there been holidaymakers to patronise them, there would have been no way for them to reach them through the barricades of barbed wire. The famous clock tower looked glum, too, sand-bagged at its base and draped, rather ignominiously, in banners exhorting passers-by to *Lend to Defend. Buy War Bonds. £5 & Upwards.* Other attractions, like the Aquarium, a fanciful and ornate building on Marine Parade, were no longer in operation by dint of having been requisitioned by the RAF

'It's rumoured,' Violette said to Esme as they alighted from the red and white Brighton Corporation trolleybus at the aquarium terminus, 'that they are using the buildings to instruct and test aircrew on Morse code and navigation.'

'Rather an odd place for that,' Esme said, taking in the white stonework of the facade and the little kiosks — now boarded up — at either end.

'I suppose to them they're just buildings. Just lately there are RAF chaps everywhere. You're bound to come across them. Some of the top brass are billeted at The Aurelian. Mr Bancroft said that as far as possible the hotel has resisted taking military personnel, meaning that most are being put up at The Grand or The Metropole. But he also said that if the war goes on for much longer, they might have to close altogether — give the whole place over to the Air Ministry and be done with it. Word is that's about to happen with The Grand.'

'Goodness,' Esme said. 'How tragic.'

Violette simply shrugged. 'There's a war on. What are you supposed to do if you own a hotel in a holiday resort with no holidaymakers?'

'Mm,' Esme agreed. 'I do see your point. But it doesn't make it any less sad.'

'Anyway,' Violette went on, swivelling about to face the sea, 'this is the terminus for Magnus Volk's electric railway. It runs along to the lido at Black Rock.'

'And is that far?' Esme asked, trying to show interest in a small ticket kiosk and a platform from which extended the railway track.

'Hardly. You can almost see the other end from here. Not even a mile, I shouldn't think. Anyway,' Violette continued, shrugging, 'it's academic — '

'Let me guess,' Esme said, noticing the padlock on the shutters and anticipating what Violette was about to say, 'it's closed.'

'Closed just recently, yes. The erection of all of these new defences saw to that.'

'Is there anything that *isn't* closed?'

'That, my dear,' Violette said, linking her arm through Esme's, 'is why we have come to this end of the town. Having shown you the railway and the aquarium, from here we can walk to the Royal Pavilion.'

'I've heard of that,' Esme replied as they set off. 'It's the building with all of those funny little domes, isn't it? Something to do with the Prince of Wales?'

Violette gave her arm a squeeze. 'A-ha! You did pay attention at school.'

Esme grinned. 'Occasionally.'

'Well, two things worth knowing about the Royal Pavilion today: one is that the wine cellar has been converted into an air raid shelter — '

'Handy.'

'And the other one is that the part of it known as the Dome now hosts dances and concerts. So, if you're desperate to meet a chap in uniform, the Dome is by far and away your best bet.'

Listening to Violette talking, Esme studied the

139

gaggle of exotic buildings that made up the Royal Pavilion. Though certainly eye-catching, it somehow managed to look just as forlorn as everything else, especially given that, this morning, in the adjacent gardens, exercise drills involving stretch bearers and volunteer casualties — the latter daubed with fake blood — were under way.

'Heartbreaking, isn't it?' she said.

'Hm?'

'What I mean,' she picked up again, 'is that it's diabolical how everything has had to stop, and how people's lives have been turned upside down, solely through the evil intentions of one little man in Germany.'

'It is sad, yes,' Violette agreed. 'But far worse, I think, if you live in France.'

Esme blushed. 'Yes. Of course. I didn't mean that the closure of a few attractions for holidaymakers is the end of the world. It's just that seeing everything as it is now makes it hard to picture how any of it will ever come back to life.'

'Then try not to think about it,' Violette suggested. 'Give your thoughts instead to your role in helping bring it all to an end. Take your sadness for all the gaiety that has been swept away from this once happy place and use it to be your very best at your job. Be alert for any sign, no matter how small, that one of our brave operatives will inadvertently spill details of his mission. Be our line of defence against betrayal — inadvertent or otherwise. We might all be ordinary people playing magnificent parts, but we are, each of us, only human. None of us is infallible.'

Golly, what an enigma Violette Marron was: one minute airy-headed and giggly, the next full of profound observations.

'Yes,' she said, spurred by her companion's words.

'Come on then, I'll just point out Hannington's to you — that's our best-loved department store, excellent for hats, hosiery, and everything in between — and then we'll get a trolleybus back.'

'Back to The Aurelian. To meet your mother for lunch.'

'That's right. And to toast the end of your training.'

'Mm,' Esme said. 'Though my training might be at an end, I don't feel anywhere *near* ready yet.'

'You will do, once you make a proper start,' Violette assured her. 'Besides, Les Marronniers isn't going anywhere. We will continue to be at your disposal. Whatever you need, we will come to your aid. In addition,' Violette continued, smiling broadly, 'this afternoon, the tailor is bringing the cocktail dresses she has run up from scratch. And ever since I caught a glimpse of her sketches, I can't wait to see them for real.'

'Come on, then,' Esme said, catching hold of Violette's arm as they crossed North Street, 'let's go and have some lunch. I really am rather ravenous.'

★　★　★

141

'Oh, my. Just look at you. Don't you look fabulous!'

It was much later that afternoon and Esme was once again standing on the stool with the tailoress this time fussing at the hemline of a figure-hugging pencil dress made from scarlet velvet.

'Does it look all right?' Esme asked Violette. Although in most respects it was quite demure, the overall effect was surprisingly racy.

'*All right?!* You look like a seductress from the silver screen.' When Violette approached to make a more detailed inspection, Esme stood stock-still. She wasn't sure she wanted to be a seductress; scarlet cocktail dress or not, that wasn't who she was. But Violette clearly found her appearance convincing. 'I adore this twist of fabric at your midriff, and the way the ruching fans out across your bust. It accentuates your assets beautifully.'

Unable to help it, Esme laughed. 'My assets?'

'But then, just as it gets interesting, these darling little cap sleeves rein in the effect just enough to prevent the whole thing from being over the top. *Very* clever.'

'There's a similar dress over there,' Esme said, nodding with her head towards the back of a chair. 'But in place of these little sleeves you're so taken with, it has shoulder straps.'

When Violette lifted the second dress from the chair, she nodded approvingly. 'Gorgeous. What would you call the colour?'

'Midnight blue,' the tailoress offered up.

'Can't wait to see you wearing it,' Violette went on.

'You should try it on.'

From behind Esme, the tailoress harrumphed disapproval at the suggestion.

'Don't worry,' Violette said, glancing in her direction, 'it's not my style.'

'But you're so lovely and slim,' Esme observed. And it wasn't a lie, either; today, in a white cotton blouse sprigged with geometric shapes and a pair of slender-cut navy slacks, Violette looked willowy. And very modern.

'I tell you, Miss Ward, in a clingy little bit of stuff like this I'd look like a ten-year-old wearing something she'd pinched from her mother's wardrobe.'

'You do think it's all right, though, don't you?' Esme whispered. 'It's not too . . . '

'It's absolutely not too *anything*,' Violette whispered back. 'Unless it's possible to be too stunning.'

'But that's what I mean,' Esme replied. 'Surely, I don't want to appear too conspicuous or too . . . unapproachable.'

'You worry too much,' Violette remarked. 'As we said to you the other day, you'll very quickly get an idea of your target's character — quickly determine whether he's desperate to impress and simply bursting to tell you what he's up to, whether there's no likelihood whatsoever of him letting slip a single word no matter your appearance, or whether, if you just try that little bit harder . . . Besides, who knows, in your very first conversation with each of them, they might all, to a man, confess everything.'

'I do hope not,' Esme said, 'because that

would make all of them hopeless traitors!'

In some respects, she was looking forward to what lay ahead; like any woman, she welcomed the occasion to don a fancy frock. But, despite her own extensive wardrobe of clothes in Clarence Square, she'd never worn anything quite so . . . well, quite as eye-catching as these cocktail dresses, had never been one to walk into a room and turn heads. In fact, in her former social circle, figure-hugging dresses like these would have been denounced as *fast* — especially by her mother. And that, she suspected, was the root of her unease. *If something doesn't feel right*, her mother was forever cautioning, *then one should take heed and steer well clear.*

Well, it was too late for second thoughts now. Her unease, founded or not, was something she would have to find a way to bury. This was her job — one that required her to assume a new identity and leave behind the concerns of Esme Ward. From now on, her personal likes and dislikes counted for nothing. So, when she stepped into these dresses, pinned up her hair and applied her lipstick, she would view it as putting on a uniform and going to work. In this time of war, plenty of women went every day to do jobs they didn't particularly like. And they went because it was their patriotic duty to do so.

Besides, she reminded herself, it wasn't as though she was here against her will. She had wanted to do something useful. She had wanted to help in the war against Hitler. And, since she had proved unqualified to do much else, working as a decoy was to be how she was going to do it.

144

5

The Decoy

'I don't think I can do this.'

'Here,' Violette said, holding out her hand, 'let me try. These tiny little clasps are rather fiddly.'

'I wasn't referring to these,' Esme said, unable to disguise her despair but dropping the earrings onto Violette's palm anyway so that she might secure them to her ears for her.

Leaning back against the marble washbasin, she sighed heavily. Any moment now she had to go downstairs to the bar and approach her first target — a stranger she would recognise solely from studying a photograph in a file. In readiness for the task, she had taken great pains with her hair, applied rather more make-up than usual, and struggled into the striking midnight-blue frock. Unfortunately, and despite all of that, she still felt underprepared, overexposed, and utterly terrified.

'There. Perfect. I knew they would set off this dress.'

'I meant,' Esme said, glancing only briefly in the mirror to see the effect of the marcasite earrings, 'that I don't think I can just flirt to command. It's not as though there's a switch I can just flick.'

'Actually,' Violette said, her tone relaxed, 'I think you'll find there is. And I think you'll also find that once you've done it the first time, you'll have no trouble flicking it again . . . and again and again.'

'Hm. I wish I shared your optimism.'

'Have you eaten?' Violette changed the subject to ask.

Eaten? Here she was, unable to stop trembling, and *that* was Violette's greatest concern?

'Hardly,' she said. 'With the way my stomach is tied in knots the last thing I need in it is food. So please don't try to make me eat something now. Not at this late stage.'

While she knew Violette meant well, she would have preferred that she hadn't come in the first place. This close to going downstairs to the bar she didn't need moral support as much as a few minutes alone to calm her mind, something that was impossible with Violette's constant enquiries and reassurances.

'Well, I do think you would have felt less nervy with some food in your stomach,' Violette went on, seemingly oblivious. 'Maybe bear that in mind for tomorrow. If nothing else, at least have a slice of toast. Have Mr Bancroft send some up just before you start getting ready. Yes, promise me you'll do that.'

Again, Esme sighed, but, since promising to ask for some toast was different from actually eating it, she had few qualms in agreeing. 'I promise.'

'Anyway,' Violette went on, reaching for Esme's hand and pulling her through to the bedroom, 'have I told you that you look

146

incredible? This dark blue really brings out the colour of your eyes. You're so terribly lucky. Blue eyes with dark brown hair is such a striking combination.'

Perhaps, Esme reflected, Violette was nervous too. Perhaps, for her and Madame Marron, a lot hinged on how tonight went — possibly not just tonight but every night. *Every night*. Dear God. The prospect of getting done up like this, four or five nights a week, to make scintillating conversation with an ever-changing parade of men, suddenly filled her with dread.

'Well, we can only hope that dark hair and blue eyes is a combination this Gregory Hatton chap goes for,' she said, staring at the photograph of a man who was actually quite nice-looking.

'You've memorised his details?' Violette asked.

She nodded. 'Of course.'

'And you'll remember to write up your initial thoughts before you go to bed?'

Again, Esme nodded. 'I know the drill.'

'At the very least, make some notes. Worst thing would be to get up in the morning and find it all a blur.'

Esme laughed. 'I doubt there's much chance of that. I have a feeling that no matter how it turns out, tonight is going to stick in my mind forever.'

Pushing back the sleeve of her blouse, Violette examined her wristwatch. 'Ten past seven.'

'Well then,' Esme said, still wishing her nerves would settle, 'I had better get on with it.'

'Just one more thing,' Violette said, swivelling

about and heading into the bathroom only to reappear seconds later brandishing a lipstick. 'A touch more colour. Open your mouth a little, please.' Esme parted her lips. 'That's it. Good. Yes, that's better.'

Deciding that she could always blot away some of it if it looked overdone, Esme reached for the evening bag that matched the dress and then gestured towards the door.

'You should go ahead, I suppose.'

'You're right. Best we're not seen together.' Halfway to the door, though, Violette turned back, retraced her steps and caught hold of Esme's hand. 'Repeat after me, I can do this.'

Reluctantly, Esme complied. 'I can do this.'

'I am ready.'

'I am ready.'

'Right. Then I'll see you tomorrow.'

'Yes,' Esme said as Violette opened the door and let herself out. 'See you tomorrow.'

★ ★ ★

'Good evening, Miss West. Your usual?'

Very slowly, trying to conceal just how badly she was trembling while at the same time appearing as though she had done this a hundred times before, Esme raised herself up onto one of the stools alongside the bar.

'Good evening, Anthony. Yes, that would be lovely, thank you.'

The stool immediately to her left was vacant but occupying the one next to that was her target — his likeness to the photograph in his file

148

reassuring. He was the first person she'd noticed as she had come through the doors — although he would have been hard to miss, the only other customers being a couple seated together in the corner, the woman in a simple summer's dress, the man in RAF uniform. *Always be aware of who is around you*, Major Lovat had told her. It was advice she intended to heed.

From the other side of the bar, Anthony placed a coaster in front of her and presented her with her drink.

'There you are, Miss West.'

She smiled, reached for it, and took the tiniest of sips. Then, summoning what little courage she could muster, she turned towards the stranger that she somehow had to draw into conversation. She knew the tactics well enough: catch his eye and smile, open the way for him to respond. It wasn't difficult. All she needed was for him to look in her direction. But when, with no warning, he did just that, her reaction was to hurriedly look away.

Silently, she cursed. What a gift of an opportunity wasted!

Forcing herself to breathe slowly, she looked back up again.

'Forgive me,' she was surprised to hear her target say, 'but I think perhaps we were both wondering the same thing.'

While she knew she should be grateful he had chosen to speak first, his taking of the initiative had thrown her, her carefully prepared greeting having deserted her, her mind suddenly empty of all useful thoughts. On top of that, she felt far

149

too hot. *At least he has presented you with an opening,* she told herself. *So, use it.*

'I suppose it is always possible,' she said, her voice sounding rather huskier than she would have liked — although at least it was working again. 'Tell me what it is you were wondering, and we'll find out.' Christ. Now she had overdone it. Now she sounded like a poor actress in a cheap film.

Her failed attempt at nonchalance seemed to go unnoticed.

'I was thinking we may have met somewhere. A while back perhaps.' Reaching across the vacant stool, he extended a hand. 'Gregory Hatton. And I know it's a cliche, but you do genuinely seem familiar. Although if we *have* met, it's terribly gauche of me to have forgotten your name.'

'Alexandra West,' she said, deciding that despite her best attempts to make a mess of this, fortune was clearly on her side. 'And yes, please accept my apologies for staring at you just now but I too feel we have met somewhere before. Might it have been on a previous occasion here, do you think?' To her relief, she felt some of the rigidness leaving her body.

In response to her question, her target shook his head. 'It can't have been here, no. This is my first visit.'

The ice broken, all she had to do now was keep her nerve. 'Your first visit to this particular hotel or to Brighton?'

'To both, actually.'

'Then welcome,' she said, turning more fully

150

towards him and pondering the wisdom of moving to the empty stool.

'Thank you. So, tell me,' he said casually, 'are there any places of interest around here? Any local sights that are still open to visitors? Only I gather from talking to the chap behind the bar just now that most places have been forced to close.'

'Well, Mr Hatton — '

'Please,' he said, 'do call me Greg.'

'Well, Greg,' she began again, 'when it comes to the fleshpots of Brighton, I'm afraid I'm not much of an authority.'

Just as she had hoped, Gregory Hatton burst out laughing. 'It's not the fleshpots I'm after,' he said. 'Just some ideas of how I might spend my free time. When I'm sent to a place I've never been before, I like to go out and try to get the flavour of it.'

'How admirable.'

Thank heavens he was chatty! Unless she bungled it completely from here, his natural warmth would make her task so much easier. With that in mind, she treated him to what she hoped was a friendly smile.

'So, Miss West, are there any sights that one can still visit?'

'Please, do call me Alex.'

'Alex.'

'Well, how long are you staying?' she asked, remembering only then that she was supposed to be the one directing their conversation.

'A week at most. And you?'

'I shall be here for quite a while, I'm afraid.'

'On business?'

'Sadly, no,' she said. 'My aunt died — '

'Oh, I am sorry to hear that. Please accept my condolences at this sad time.'

Feeling herself blushing, she lowered her head. It was a tip given to her by Violette for use when she needed a moment to think. 'Thank you.' she eventually replied and looked back up again. 'Mercifully, her passing was sudden. No prolonged illness or drawn-out suffering — just out like a light, how she would have wanted it, how anyone would want it, I suppose.' Giving her fictitious late aunt a quick and painless departure felt the least she could do for her. 'And she'd had a wonderful life. She would have been the first to admit that.'

'One imagines then,' he said, 'that you must be here to sort out her affairs?'

She nodded. 'I am, yes. Fortunately, the instructions she left were most precise. Unfortunately, in the course of her many exotic travels, she accumulated rather a lot of what I can only describe as *stuff.*'

'And it's the stuff that always causes the headaches.'

Goodness, he really was quite a delight: he listened; he showed sympathy. In any other circumstances she would be determining to get to know him better — quite a lot better. But that wasn't why she was here.

'Anyway, regarding your enquiry about places to visit,' she pressed on. 'As you are bound to have seen, anything connected to the seafront is out of bounds.'

'Plainly.'

'Even the aquarium has been taken over by the RAF — '

'What the devil are the RAF planning to do with an aquarium?' he asked, his bafflement seemingly genuine.

'Practise fishing?'

She laughed. 'I somehow doubt it. I expect they use it for something altogether more boring, don't you?'

'Almost certainly.'

To her surprise, she was beginning to enjoy this. If this was all she had to do every night, not only would it be straightforward but fun, too. 'There is always the Royal Pavilion, of course.'

'Yes, of course.'

'On Saturdays they use the part of it known as the Dome to hold dances. But I hear it's rather swamped with RAF.'

'Ah.'

'They seem to be everywhere. But anyway,' she said, deciding to move the conversation along, 'what is it that brings you to Brighton?'

'Well,' he said, 'that would be the RAF.'

Instantly, she felt her cheeks burning. 'Oh, dear God. I'm sorry. I didn't mean to be disparaging. I merely meant that they do seem to be rather . . . taking over . . . '

Seeing him grinning broadly, she realised she had fallen prey to a joke: of course he wasn't there for the RAF! She, better than anyone, knew *that*. And yet, so genuine was he that she'd been completely taken in — utterly hoodwinked. She must remember to note on his file that he was 'entirely convincing'.

'No, actually,' he said, 'I'm being rotten. I work for a bank and I'm here to carry out an investigation into . . . well, into some irregularities that have come to light. Deathly dull. Oh, and by the way, you can't tell anyone I've told you that. A successful inspection requires the element of surprise.'

'So that no one has time to destroy the records?'

'Or to cover their tracks, yes,' he said.

'Then my lips are sealed.'

What an odd start this had got off to — everything felt back to front and upside down. Not that she was complaining. As possible beginnings went, it was most satisfactory; she had engaged with her target and he was conversing freely with her — a dream of a start, Violette would say.

'But, since my task is unlikely to take the allotted five days, I'd rather thought to do some exploring.'

It wasn't lost on her that he had steered the conversation back to their previous topic. Clearly, he was throwing himself into this.

'I don't suppose you have a petrol allowance?' she said, content to see where it took them. 'Only, some of the countryside around here is very pretty.'

He shook his head. 'Sadly, no.'

'Then to be honest, I fear you are in for a bit of a disappointment. There really isn't anything still open that's worth doing.'

'Shame.'

Now it was her turn to take charge. She could certainly do with the practice. 'So, where do you reside when you're not being sent out investigating?'

'Twickenham in Middlesex,' he said. 'But my office is in the centre of London.'

'I see.'

That she was enjoying this was testament to how convincing he was, constantly needing to remind herself that nothing he said was true. Her biggest task seemed to be to maintain the momentum — ensure their conversation didn't peter out before she'd had a proper chance to test his loyalty.

Contrary to her fears, though, their conversation didn't wane. Indeed, an hour or so later, after they had at some point adjourned to a table away from the bar, she even found herself wishing that things were as they seemed. With his deep-brown eyes and neat hair, he was, in a slightly unorthodox way, good-looking. He was also just three years older than her. And charming. She could readily fall for him. But she only had to recall the *Sunday Times* yesterday and its chilling headline *LONDON SUBURB BOMBED Women Children & Firemen Machine Gunned*, to remember that no matter how appealing the idea of getting to know him better, nothing could ever come of it. He was about to be sent to France to do vital work spying on the operations of the nation responsible for those dreadful attacks on London — and for doing who-knew-what to the poor people of France.

'I say, I hope you won't think this forward,' he said, breaking into her reflections on the matter, 'but have you eaten?'

It *was* forward of him. But that wasn't the problem. The problem was that to play the game properly, she needed to remain alert — whereas already she was feeling utterly drained. And she couldn't afford, through weariness, to slip up.

'I have eaten, yes. Sorry.'

'Perhaps tomorrow, then?' he said. 'I don't know about you, but I dislike dining alone — especially in a strange town,'

'From what you have said, I imagine you are often in a strange town.' It was an observation she offered in order to give herself time to think. She did need to see him again but was it wise to do so over dinner? Might it not feel rather too much like an actual date?

'I'm away more often than I'd like to be, yes,' he replied. 'But I must go where the job takes me.'

Oh, for heaven's sake, she reasoned with herself, where was the harm in having dinner with him? He was only here for the rest of this week and then he would be gone, dropped into France, never to be seen again. Besides, on a purely selfish note, it felt as though it would be fun. And she hadn't seen anywhere in the rules where it said that she couldn't enjoy herself.

'All right,' she said, 'tomorrow. But here, in the restaurant. After that dreadful bombing just around the corner this morning — '

He straightened up. 'Just around the corner? Golly, what happened?'

'According to one of the staff coming down from fire-watching on the roof, a lone Dornier dropped nine bombs. Tragically, they landed on a row of houses, killing two residents and injuring several others.' What she stopped short of adding was that upstairs, in her sumptuous bedroom, she had been blissfully unaware of any of it, her sleep undisturbed — no siren even sounding. The subsequent discovery of what had happened, relayed to her by the room service waiter, had been enough to dampen her appetite for her tray of breakfast.

'Bastards,' he muttered. 'What's the betting the coward of a pilot was just dumping his bombs for the fun of it before turning for home.'

She sighed. 'That *would* seem to be the general consensus. Either way, I should prefer to remain close to a decent air raid shelter.'

She saw him smile.

'I've heard the shelter here is better appointed than most.'

'Better appointed is an understatement of the highest order,' she said, trying to shake the thought of bombs falling so close by. *Mind back on the job*, she remonstrated with her wandering thoughts. 'It's rather like a secret little club down there. All the comforts.'

'Very well, then,' he said. 'We'll dine here. What time would suit you?'

'Shall we say . . . seven?'

'Seven it is. And shall we meet here, for an aperitif?'

She nodded. 'That would be lovely.'

'Then if you will excuse me, this evening I

must go forth and forage a meal by myself.'

Once he had left, Esme glanced across to Anthony, but he was at the far end of the bar, talking to a couple of RAF officers, and didn't look up. Getting up from her seat, she decided it was probably just as well; with the way her cheeks felt to be burning, he would surely wonder at the nature of what had come to pass between the two of them. So far, she had been unable to ascertain precisely how much her guardian angel reported back — either to Madame Marron or to someone higher up in the department. With all the observing and the spying that went on, it was hard to believe there wasn't *someone* watching her as she went about her task.

Yes, she thought, heading across the lobby towards the lifts, if there was one thing she had learned tonight, it was that with the good-looking and charming targets in particular, she would have to be careful — and for reasons that none of her training or instructions had warned her about, either.

★ ★ ★

There had never been any question in her mind. For dinner the following evening her choice of outfit was obvious: the scarlet dress. It just felt appropriate, even if she did have to keep reminding herself that she wasn't going on a real date. The trouble was, it was long enough since she *had* been on a proper date, especially with anyone new, that this evening was taking on the air of one, even down to the fact that, rather than spending the afternoon growing steadily more apprehensive about the task ahead of her, she'd found that she couldn't wait. She also wanted everything about her appearance to be just right. And it quickly became apparent that she had succeeded, on that score at least, because when Greg Hatton saw her approaching the bar he leapt up from his seat and went towards her.

'Wow. You look a million dollars.'

'You're a fan of the cinema?' she asked, allowing him to lead her across to the table upon which she could see that there were already two drinks.

'Not especially,' he said, handing her into one of the seats. 'It was just the first expression that came into my mind. My apologies if it was *de trop*.'

Picking up on his use of a French expression, she wondered whether it was in some way a test. More likely, she decided, it was merely that her senses were on full alert.

'Well, thank you for the compliment,' she said. 'I almost didn't bring this dress with me from home. But I saw it in my wardrobe and — forgive me for how this is going to sound — I couldn't bear the thought that if a bomb were to fall upon the house, I would be devastated by the loss of such a beautiful garment.'

'Speaking personally, I couldn't be happier you felt that way. It's stunning.'

She blushed. She'd been missing the attentions of a man. 'Again, thank you.'

'I hope you don't mind but I asked the

barman what you usually drink and ordered you one. But if you fancy something different, I can take it back.'

She shook her head. Anthony would have known not to actually put any gin in her G&T. 'Thank you, this is just fine.'

Shortly after that, they went through to the restaurant, which turned out to be about half full, mainly of RAF officers and a few elderly people she recognised as longterm residents.

'Tell me,' he said, taking his place opposite her at their table, 'how is the food here?'

'Embarrassingly good, actually,' she said, browsing the choices. 'Considerably better than it is for people who must rely on rations alone. It was only when I came here that I found out private businesses aren't subject to rationing. I mean, I know restaurant meals are restricted to three courses, and the price to five shillings . . . but even so . . . '

'It doesn't feel right?'

She shook her head. 'Not when one stops to think about it.' For a moment after that, she watched him scan the menu. 'You didn't eat here last night?'

'No, I went somewhere less imposing around the corner. Steak and kidney pie, boiled potatoes and peas followed by fruit tart. Homely. And certainly not bad for under two shillings.'

'Are you ready to order, Madame?'

With a quick glance to their waiter, Esme nodded. 'The salmon in white wine with new potatoes and asparagus tips, please.'

'A starter for you, Madame?'

'Thank you, no.'

'And I'll have the same,' Greg Hatton said, handing back his menu.

'Will you be here at the weekend?' she asked when the waiter departed the table with their order.

Her dining companion shrugged his shoulders in a manner that suggested not. 'Unlikely but not impossible. Why do you ask?'

'Because believe it or not, on Fridays and Saturdays, the hotel almost returns to its former self. And yes, I know, looking around us at the moment that seems unlikely. But there are some wealthy people here in Brighton, and in neighbouring Hove, and every weekend they flock here to ignore the privations of war and make merry.'

'Truly?'

'Oh yes. On Fridays there's a supper dance with a band that plays until well after midnight. If there's an air raid, proceedings simply decamp to the basement. Of course, to stay beyond the curfew one must be a resident, so many of the partygoers take rooms for the night solely in order to stay to the bitter end. Saturday night is much the same, except that things come to a rather earlier close.'

'Reminds me of stories I've heard about Oddenino's — '

'In Regent Street?'

'You know it?' he asked, his surprise striking her as genuine.

'It was a favourite of my grandfather's, in his day.'

161

'Have you ever been?'

'Once,' she said, the occasion still clear to her. 'It was for my sixteenth birthday. I was served champagne and ate lobster. I remember it being terribly noisy'

He smiled. 'Are you truly not married?'

Feeling her cheeks colouring, she shook her head. 'Truly. Why do you ask?' It was a fatuous question. He was clearly as taken with her as she was with him. Despite her limited experience of men, she could tell.

His smile, when he replied, was rueful. 'No reason.'

'Hm. Then it was a most peculiar question.'

With that their food arrived, and she was spared having to relay the supposed story of how, during a blackout, her fiance had been killed in a motorcycle accident, and how she still wasn't in the mood to replace him.

Later still, when they were drinking their coffee and he proposed that they dine there again the next night, she didn't hesitate to accept. And when it seemed only natural that they do the same on the night after that, too, she was no less keen. It was then he explained to her that his work in Brighton was at an end.

'My findings are conclusive,' he told her. 'I have compiled my report — in fact I finished it yesterday — and must return to Head Office to present it to my superiors, after which I will be given details of my next assignment.'

For a moment, she wondered whether his fictitious report was not only real but actually about *her*. Was it fanciful to wonder whether his role in Brighton had been to evaluate her own performance whilst watching her evaluate his? She didn't *think* so. Given how they both inhabited a world of fake identities and subterfuge, it was hard to be certain. Just lately, she suspected the motives of almost everyone with whom she came into contact. *Comes with the territory*, she remembered Major Lovat warning her. *You will find yourself suspicious of even your nearest and dearest*, he'd said.

The news that her companion would be departing, and the prospect of him not being there next week, left her with a surprisingly profound ache in her chest. Apart from Richard, she thought, watching Greg Hatton tuck into a tiny crystal ramekin containing a fruit fool of gooseberries with Sauternes, she couldn't recall having ever been so instantly attracted to someone. This man with the captivating smile and the wicked sense of humour might very well, under different circumstances, have been *the one*. But the life she had chosen — the lives they had both chosen — meant that could never be; next week, when she was sitting in this same hotel with yet another man masquerading as someone he wasn't, the real man behind Gregory Hatton would have taken on yet another alias and would be somewhere in France, dodging the Germans to help the Resistance.

'Well,' she said, as he accompanied her across the lobby to the lifts, 'it's a shame you won't be here for one of the supper dances.'

For the first time, the smile he gave her

seemed genuinely regretful. 'It is.'

'I rather think we could have had fun.'

Lifting her hand from where she had been resting it upon his sleeve, he kissed it. 'For certain we would have,' he agreed, releasing her hand back to her side.

With little thought to what she was doing, she leant towards him. 'Do take care,' she whispered. When she pulled away, she noticed his puzzled expression. It made her flush hot and wonder whether she had tipped her hand. 'Only, I hear London is suffering more air raids now,' she added in an attempt to sound casual.

'Ah,' he said, 'yes. Air raids.'

'Well, goodnight then, Mr Hatton. I wish you well in your endeavours.'

'Goodnight, Miss West. I wish you well, too.'

When she pressed the button to call the lift, he remained where he was. And when the doors finally closed to leave him on the other side, she folded her arms across her ribs and the dull ache inside them. The report she had to write this evening would be straightforward and unequivocal: the real person behind Gregory Hatton was a fine man who, she was certain, could be relied upon not to betray his country. He had hinted at nothing of his true purpose; he could be sent undercover into France without a moment's doubt.

Having spent four enjoyable evenings in his company, though, of his true character she could say nothing more. She had no idea how much of what he'd chosen to display was genuine and how much of it was an act. And therein lay his skill, she thought, as the lift doors opened, and she stepped out into the thickly carpeted corridor of the third floor. For, if asked to describe the man behind the persona for whom she had undeniably fallen, she would have no idea what to say.

★ ★ ★

'Well done. This is just what they need.'

Pleased by Madame Marron's opinion of her report on Greg Hatton, Esme smiled; she had made it through her first assignment and now, at least for the next couple of days, she could relax.

'How do you feel?' Violette enquired, placing in front of her on the table a demitasse of dark coffee with a tiny almond biscuit in its saucer.

'Thank you,' she said of it, inhaling the aroma and thinking it was just what she needed. *Bless dear Violette for noticing.*

'Only, you look tired.'

'I feel it,' she admitted. 'I didn't sleep at all well last night.'

'A nap this afternoon, then,' Violette instructed. 'Because this evening, in celebration of the successful completion of your first assignment, you and I are going out.'

Wearily, Esme shook her head. So far this week she had been 'out' every night and had woken up this morning looking forward to an evening in. By browsing the copy of *The Radio Times* that was delivered to her room each week, she had noticed that after the nine o'clock news this evening there was to be half an hour of

Debussy, something she was looking forward to hearing.

'It rather looks as though Miss Ward would prefer to stay in,' Madame Marron observed.

Across the table from her, Esme sent her a grateful look.

'Then *I'll* come around to *you*,' Violette said, her enthusiasm no less.

As alternatives went, to Esme, it felt only marginally better. 'Bear in mind that curfew is ten past nine tonight,' she said, recalling the notice in the hotel lobby. Reading Violette's disappointment, and feeling mean at being the cause of it, she decided to offer up a compromise. 'How about we wait until tomorrow? This evening, I'll have an early night, and then tomorrow we could try the Supper Club.'

'Suppose.'

'And rather than let the curfew ruin it, you could stay over. I'm not exactly short on space.'

'Done! I'll be round at six.'

Esme leant back in her chair. 'Isn't six o'clock a bit — '

'Too early? No. Your nails need doing.' Esme glanced to her hands. Violette wasn't wrong. 'Once I've given you a manicure, we can get ready together — make more of a thing of it.'

Feeling the onset of a yawn, Esme tried — but failed — to stifle it, the earlier suggestion of an afternoon nap growing more appealing by the minute. 'All right. Six o'clock.'

'Needless to say,' Madame Marron looked up to remark, 'you must both be careful of what you say and do. And with whom. You might be

. . . off duty . . . both of you, but you never know who might be watching and listening. After making such a promising start, the department won't be pleased if the next thing you do is blow up the whole operation.'

'It's not *blow up* the operation, Maman,' Violette corrected her mother as Esme doubled over with laughter. 'It's *blow*. And no, you may rest assured we will be on guard at all times.'

Perhaps, Esme reflected, an evening out with Violette wouldn't be so bad after all — dancing, a nice meal, some young men in uniform: a palate cleanser before she moved on from Greg to her next target. Precisely what she needed, in fact.

★ ★ ★

'Well, what do you think?'

Turning absently in the direction of Violette's voice, Esme gasped. Gone was the sexless girl she was used to looking at, in her place someone who wouldn't have looked out of place on the silver screen. 'Wow,' she breathed, getting up and going towards her. 'You look . . . well, you look . . .'

'Seriously,' Violette said flatly, 'you don't have to try to think of something kind to say. I'm more than happy to settle for *nice*.'

Nice? Did Violette really have no idea of the impact she was going to make? She looked like a wispy young Hollywood actress; all she was missing was one of those long cigarette holders. 'Violette, you look stunning, gorgeous — '

' — only, I haven't worn anything formal since . . . well . . . since I don't *know* when. And I don't mind admitting to feeling gawky and ridiculous. In fact, I think I'll go and change into something else — '

'God, Violette,' Esme eventually managed, rushing to catch hold of her friend's arm. 'Don't do that. You look fabulous. I mean it. Surely you can tell from the fact that I'm lost for words.'

'Yeah, but there's lost for words in a delighted way and lost for words in disbelief.'

'The former,' Esme said. 'Definitely the former. You look incredible.' Gesturing a circle with her finger, she motioned to Violette to do a twirl.

With an exasperated little groan, Violette complied.

At first glance, her outfit appeared to be a plain black, slim-fitting floor length gown with a wrap over bodice, the satin lapels of which imitated a gentleman's dinner jacket. About her waist was a sash of the same contrasting fabric. But closer study revealed that the skirt was in fact slender trousers, cut just full enough to fool the eye. Ingenious. And so very, very Violette.

'I had it made up last year,' Violette seemed to feel it necessary to explain, 'since when, all it has done is languish in my wardrobe such that every time I clap eyes on it, I wonder what possessed me.'

'What possessed you,' Esme said, reaching to feel the fabric and finding it softer than she had imagined, 'was sheer brilliance.'

'Truly?'

'Truly. Was the design your own idea?'

Violette gave a little shrug. 'I can't lay claim to the whole thing, no. Some time back, one of our students from America left behind a magazine, and in it was a photograph of a model wearing something similar but summery and floral. It was described as a jumpsuit, and the one in the picture was clearly intended as daywear. But the more I looked at it, the more I thought that if I had one made for evenings, it would solve my perennial dilemma of what to wear when an invitation says *Black Tie*. Only, it can't have escaped your notice that I avoid dresses with the same vigour that I would avoid catching the plague.'

In that moment, Esme felt as though the penny had dropped. Of course! How had she never noticed that Violette always wore slacks? 'Your hair's perfect, too,' she said. 'Slicked back like that wouldn't suit many women. You're brave to wear it so short anyway . . . but you have the features to carry it off. And against this dark fabric, your complexion looks sort of . . . pearlescent. I've noticed before how it's often a trait of women with auburn hair. Anyway, you look terrific. Dressed like that, *you* should be the decoy, not me.'

'Huh, not enough up here for that,' Violette said, flapping the fabric across her chest. 'I'm too *straight up and down*. Men don't look twice at me. Thankfully.'

'Well, stood beside you in this, I feel positively frumpy.' With a laugh, Esme gestured to her own outfit — a sleeveless Grecian-style dress in a

169

shimmery lilac colour with a deep 'v' neckline and a trim of diamante at the shoulders. It was the first time she'd worn it and, feeling as matronly as she did in it now, she was minded to put it back in the wardrobe and forget about it. 'So, perhaps we had better go down before we both change our minds and take so long choosing something else to wear that we miss supper. And I, for one, am ravenous.'

Stepping out of the lift at the ground floor moments later, Esme's spirits lifted: she could tell from the crooning of a saxophone and the syncopated beat of the drums that the party was already well under way, the sheer exuberance of the music sending a shiver of anticipation down her spine. 'Hear that?' she said, grasping Violette's arm and drawing her on. 'That's Art Zilly and his Zillionaires.'

Something about Violette's expression suggested she was put out. 'I thought you said you hadn't been to Supper Club before?'

Sashaying across the lobby, her steps in time with the music, Esme shook her head. 'I haven't. Art Zilly used to play at the Empress.' Seeing Violette's nonplussed look, she added, 'It's a jazz club off Piccadilly. I went a couple of times with Richard. Terribly hard to get in, always packed. Great fun.'

As they approached the entrance to the ballroom, and the doors were opened ahead of them, a wall of noise stopped them in their tracks.

Raising herself on tiptoes, Esme scanned the room, eventually spotting Mr Bancroft making his way towards them.

'Miss Ward. Miss Marron,' he greeted them, his voice raised in order to make himself heard. 'So glad you could join us. Please, come with me. Your table is waiting.' The table Mr Bancroft had chosen for them was against the far wall, distant enough from the orchestra to be able to converse but close enough to the dance floor to be able to come and go with ease. 'I didn't think you would want to be somewhere too prominent,' he said. 'But if you don't like it, I can swap you with another reservation.'

'No, it's perfect,' Esme replied. 'Thank you.'

Once he had seen them settled, a barman arrived with a trolley containing an ice bucket from which was poking a bottle of champagne.

'Compliments of the house,' the young man said, proceeding to place in front of them a couple of champagne coupes. 'Would you like me to open it for you?'

Exchanging a look of delight with Violette, Esme nodded. 'Please do.'

Two glasses of champagne duly poured, Esme raised her glass. 'To what shall we drink?'

'To your success,' Violette suggested.

'And to you, dear Violette, without whom I would never have had the confidence in the first place.'

'Your menus for supper, mesdames.'

Accepting a menu from yet another waiter, Esme grinned. 'I'm so glad I thought of coming here.'

'Hm. Just as long as you don't expect me to dance.'

171

Not dance? Was Violette serious? With this music playing, *she* would be unable to keep still. She couldn't stop tapping her toes as it was. 'For all *I* know, no one will ask us.'

'Huh. They'll ask *you*,' Violette said. 'You can't possibly have missed the jaws dropping on that table of RAF officers as we came in. At this very moment they're probably drawing lots for the right to be first to come over and try their luck.'

'Then by turns, they will be disappointed,' Esme said, her eyes roving the list of dishes. 'Because first, I'm going to eat my way through every dish on this menu. Lobster. Duck. Beef Wellington. Crepes Suzette.'

As usual to such a remark, Violette's retort was a dry one. 'I wouldn't if I were you. Maman won't be pleased if she has to ask the seamstress to let out all of your gowns — especially not so soon after having them made.'

'You make a good point.'

'I usually do.'

When their waiter returned, Esme made her choice. 'The watercress soup and the veal, please.'

Violette, though, seemed overwhelmed. 'You choose for me,' she said, setting down her menu and shrugging.

'She'll have the same.' Once their waiter had departed, Esme leant towards her. 'Are you all right? Was I wrong to suggest coming here?'

Violette shook her head. 'No, of course not. I'm just not as hungry as I thought.'

With the bandleader urging the dance number to a riotous crescendo, and the audience applauding, the stage then fell to near darkness, a single spotlight casting a column of pale light upon a singer in a gold coloured dress. Her presence sent up a roar of approval and caused Esme to do a double take.

'It's Monica Scott!' she said, grasping Violette's arm. 'She has the most amazing voice. Just listen.'

But, as the pianist played the opening bars to an uptempo jazz number, a tall fellow with a pilot's brevet on his uniform approached their table. 'Please, forgive the intrusion, ladies.' He held a hand towards Esme. 'But might I have this dance?'

'Go on,' Violette said, her gesture seemingly one of resignation.

Getting to her feet, Esme allowed the young man to lead her to the very centre of the dance floor, where they quickly became absorbed into the throng.

'I'm Ralph,' he said, his smile all charm, his dance moves nifty.

Unable to help it, Esme laughed. 'Ralph from the RAF? That's unfortunate.'

'And don't I know it! And you are . . . ?'

Esme faltered. Did she use her real name or a false one? Which identity did SOE rules stipulate for such circumstances? She had no idea. 'Louise,' she said, it being the first name that popped into her head. *Sorry, Lou.*

'Louise. Suits you.'

'Thank you.'

'And do you have a boyfriend, Louise?'

She nodded. 'Uh-huh. Lieutenant in His

173

Majesty's Navy.' Not wanting to shut down completely the chance of further dance partners, she quickly went on, 'Though heaven only knows where he is. On the rare occasion when I do get to speak to him, it's all *Sorry, can't tell you, darling*. Careless talk, and all that, I suppose.'

When the song to which they had been dancing blended seamlessly into another, her partner seemed happy to continue dancing with her. But, when that song came to a close, and Esme made a point of thanking him, he escorted her back to her table.

'Good dancer?' Violette enquired as Esme sat down, lightly breathless.

'Well . . . he didn't steer us into anyone . . . nor did he step on my feet. So, I suppose . . . yes, quite acceptable.' For all his slick footwork, though, she hadn't thought him a patch on Richard.

'And will he be back later for another turn?'

'I doubt it,' she said, fanning at her face with her hand. 'I told him about my boyfriend in the navy. Ooh, look, here come our entrees.'

With the arrival of their food, Esme noticed Violette seeming to recover a little of her cheeriness. While they had been fussing to get ready — well, while *she* had been fussing to get ready — Violette had seemed bright and animated, livelier than she had felt herself, truth to tell. But, from the moment they had come into the ballroom, Violette's mood had changed. Granted, given the volume of the orchestra, conversation was proving difficult, but the change in her was noticeable. And odd. Equally odd was her claim that she didn't want to dance. Was it her way of protecting herself against the disappointment of not be asked, she wondered? Or could it be that she simply wasn't feeling at her best?

The ensuing break in the band's routine came at an opportune moment and allowed their conversation to proceed more naturally.

'I would never have thought to choose watercress soup,' Violette remarked.

'No?' Glancing across to her plate, Esme saw that she had scraped it clean.

'So I'm glad I left the choice to you. It was very nice.'

'I sometimes feel embarrassed at being able to eat so well,' Esme observed when their main courses arrived, and they had been served their vegetables. 'I mean, we've probably eaten more food already this evening than a family of four would see in a week.'

Violette didn't seem to agree. 'The situation with rationing isn't *that* bad. But this is definitely more food than a family would see in a day — and nicer, too. The thing Maman can't abide is the rationing of butter since it means that she can't make pastry. *What good is eight ounces of sugar a week and yet only two ounces of butter*, she is forever complaining. Whatever you do, don't make the mistake of mentioning margarine to her — she can't stand the stuff.'

'Even that's on the ration now, though, isn't it?' Esme asked. She was sure she had recently read something to that effect.

Violette nodded. 'And tea now, as well.

Thankfully, that doesn't bother *us*.'

Although Esme gave a sympathetic smile, she recognised how out of touch she had become. Having her every meal provided at the hotel meant never having to worry about food — a luxury she doubted even the Trevannions enjoyed.

Looking up, she noticed that over on the stage, the orchestra was returning after the interval. Accompanied by a new singer, they were soon playing a medley of well-known ballads.

Having both declined desserts, the two women sat listening to a song lamenting lost love. The wistfulness of the number once again brought Richard to mind. What would he be doing now? Did he ever think about her? Did he ever wonder if she was thinking about him? Why did it matter? It wasn't as though she would ever know.

Failing to notice the ripple of applause, and that the pianist was playing the opening bars to the next song, she glanced up to see two young men approaching their table. As they drew closer, a couple of words passed between them and then one turned back, the other continuing straight towards her. Mortified for Violette, Esme cringed — hardly gentlemanly behaviour.

'Would you grant me the pleasure of this dance, miss?'

When she looked to Violette, it was to see that she was staring at the debris of their meals. In two minds about accepting, she got to her feet; with that scowl on her face, Violette didn't exactly look as though she would welcome the chance to dance anyway.

The song turned out to be *A Nightingale Sang in Berkeley Square*, and one to which she had, on several occasions, danced with Richard. Richard, again. She *had* to stop thinking about him! She was no longer part of his life, and he was no longer part of hers. She led a different existence now, one filled with freedom and purpose. In no time at all, she had achieved things she could only have dreamt of during those days of worry and frustration in Wimbledon.

'Thank you,' her dance partner graciously said when the music came to an end.

She flushed. Poor man; she hadn't said a single word, let alone shown any interest in him. He might as well have been dancing with a floor mop.

'No, thank *you*,' she said with a light touch of his sleeve, deciding to stop short of apologising for being poor company.

Escorted back to their table, she sat down.

'And I suppose *he* was a good dancer as well.'

Straightening the front of her gown, Esme frowned. 'This was a mistake, wasn't it? You're not enjoying this in the least, are you?'

For a moment, Violette didn't respond but then, with a shrug, she said, 'Supper was nice. But no, you're right. Dancing's not my thing . . . at least, not with . . . oh, it doesn't matter. But *you* should keep dancing. You clearly enjoy it.'

Esme sighed. This was hopeless; Violette's gloom was taking the edge right off the evening. 'No,' she said, reaching decisively for her evening bag. 'If dancing means leaving you sitting here scowling, I don't want to. Let's go. Yes,' she said, warming to the idea, 'let's go upstairs and call down to room service for something decadent . . . something like . . . '

Now it was Violette's turn to frown. 'Like what? We've just eaten.'

'Like the sweet we didn't order . . . yes! And a glass of pudding wine to go with it!' When she got to her feet, Violette simply sat looking up at her. 'Come on. I'll ask Mr Bancroft to surprise us with something. I can see him over there at the bar.' When Violette still didn't move, Esme caught hold of her arm and tugged her to her feet. 'Come on. I can't bear to see you sitting there, suffering, as though every minute of this is torture.'

Reluctantly, Violette complied. 'All right. Just as long as you don't blame me for dragging you away from the attentions of all these men.'

Violette, it seemed, really was out of sorts. But, with Mr Bancroft consulted about the ordering of treats, Esme drew her towards the lobby. 'Who needs men?' she raised her voice over the receding music to ask.

In response to her question, Violette did at least grin. She also held out her arm, through which, with a smile, Esme linked her own.

'No sane woman, that's for sure,' Violette remarked, reaching to call the lift.

By the time they arrived on the third floor, Esme noticed Violette seemed to have already regained some of her sparkle.

'I don't know about you,' she said, heading

straight in through the door and leaving Violette to close it, 'but I could do with some fresh air. Put the light out, would you? Let's go out on the balcony.'

'Is that wise?' Violette called after her, extinguishing the light anyway.

'I can't think there's anything in the curfew directive that prevents standing on a balcony. It's not as though we'll be out on the street. If we're not showing a light, I don't see how anyone could object.' Grabbing her shawl from the chair on the way past, Esme raised the blackout blind and opened the door. The air outside was balmy and flat, the stars visible only where there were breaks in the cloud. With no need for it about her shoulders, Esme cast her shawl onto one of the steamer chairs.

'No moon,' Violette whispered, arriving to join her staring out over the railing.

'A dark night helps thwart the bombers,' she replied, remembering having read something to that effect in the *Telegraph*.

'Shame, though. Moonlight on a calm sea is lovely.'

'Mm. Romantic.' From beside her, Esme heard Violette sigh; on the railing, her hand had come to rest immediately adjacent to her own fingers, and she could feel the warmth of it. 'I'm sorry you didn't enjoy Supper Club,' she said.

'Rather too many cosy couples for me. But the music was good. You were right about Art Zilly — '

'*Cosy couples?*' Turning to regard Violette, Esme saw her shrug.

'Marvellous for a romantic date, not so comfortable if that's not what you're after.'

Lost to understand, Esme nevertheless felt moved to try. 'And that's *not* what you're after?'

'I should have thought it obvious — '

With that, there was a knock at the door.

'Dessert! I say, shall we eat it out here?' Expecting to be laughed at, Esme was surprised by Violette's response.

'Why not? There might not be a moon but it's still a lovely evening.'

In the blackness of the night air, the two women settled onto the steamer chairs and proceeded to tuck into tiny dishes of *mousse au chocolat* with which they sipped sweet *Beaumes de Venise* from narrow little wine glasses.

'This is delicious, isn't it?' Esme remarked of the combination. 'The dessert, the wine, the quiet . . . '

'Lovely,' Violette agreed softly.

'Happier now?'

'I am. But please don't spoil *this* by going on about *that*. I wasn't unhappy earlier. I was quite content to just be there with you.'

'Violette Marron, that simply isn't true. If you could have seen your face — '

'You were happy, so I was happy.'

Unable to help it, Esme scoffed. 'Well, if that was your *happy* face, remind me to give you a wide berth when you're grumpy.'

Beside her, Violette hung her head. 'You don't understand, do you?' She spoke so quietly that it took Esme a while to realise what she had said.

'I don't?'

'But, like I say, if you're happy, then I'm happy.'

Watching Violette lean forward to place her empty ramekin back on the tray, Esme frowned. Violette could be most strange at times. 'Well,' she said, 'that's a very considerate way to behave, but surely not very good for *you* . . . not in the longer term, I mean.'

'Probably not,' Violette whispered back. 'But that's just how it is. One can't always have what one wants.'

'And isn't *that* true! Here,' Esme said, tilting the bottle to top up Violette's glass before draining the dregs into her own. 'Let's finish the last of this gorgeous wine. Although it does seem quite strong . . . and seems to be making me squiffy.' With the freshening breeze raising goose bumps on her bare arms, she suggested they return indoors.

'Mind if I change out of this?' Violette asked, flapping at the fabric of her outfit. 'If we're done for the night, I shall feel more comfortable in my pyjamas.'

'Of course,' Esme said, seeing to the blackout and drawing the curtains. 'When you're finished in the bathroom, I'll do the same.'

And so, not long after that, the two of them, in their nightclothes, were sprawled on the bed, cushions and pillows positioned for comfort.

'Sorry if I spoilt your evening,' Violette said.

To Esme, her friend's remorse sounded genuine. 'You didn't. I did that by choosing entirely the wrong thing for us to do. Do you really not enjoy dancing?'

Violette stared into the distance. 'It's not the dancing, I don't like. It's having to pretend to like the men.'

Esme giggled. 'That's the *easy* part. You just smile and simper . . . and tell them what they want to hear.'

'Which is why *you're* the decoy and not me. I could never convince a man that I found him fascinating. But you're missing the point.'

'Well, next time we're looking for something to do,' Esme bowled on regardless, the wine making her feel light-headed, 'I shall leave it to you to choose.'

'So, if I suggested going to the theatre to see a play, you'd come?'

Violette's suggestion not appealing in the least, Esme tried to think how to say so without upsetting her. 'I doubt you would find a theatre still putting on shows.' *Nicely done*, she congratulated herself.

'There are still small ones managing to mount productions, if you know where to look. Or, if not the theatre, then how about . . . no, there's no point even suggesting that. You wouldn't want to.'

Rolling onto her side, Esme propped her head on her forearm and gave Violette a withering look. 'Wouldn't want to what? If you don't ask me, you'll never know. And I might love the idea.'

But Violette clearly thought otherwise, shrugging dismissively. 'No, you'd just laugh.'

'No, go on,' Esme said, pulling herself more upright. 'I promise I won't.'

Still, Violette prevaricated.

Why did she do that? Esme wondered. It certainly wasn't from a lack of confidence; ordinarily she was startlingly forthright.

'All right, well, it's just that one day . . . I should like to take you to a poetry reading.'

It was a suggestion that left Esme without a clue how to respond, her initial reaction being that not only was it a most peculiar thing to suggest, but that it sounded inordinately dull.

'Goodness . . .'

'See! I knew you wouldn't want to do it.'

Sitting up properly, Esme met Violette's look. 'Hold on. I haven't said anything yet.'

'But neither did you leap at the chance,' Violette pointed out, her tone sullen.

'Only because I'm stuck to picture what such a thing would be like. I mean . . . would it be someone ordinary reading something well-known — something I might know? Or is it a famous poet reading their latest work? Or is it people reading poems they've written themselves, a bit like a literary salon?'

Letting out a long sigh, Violette started to explain about a poetry group in Hove, and how she went there once a month to listen to readings and then discuss them afterwards with the group. Now and again they had guest poets, she said, not world-famous ones but people well known in poetry circles, nonetheless. 'Listening to poetry helps me to leave the world behind for a while,' she said, 'makes me stop, reflect, appreciate.'

Genuinely, Esme didn't know what to say.

'Goodness. I've never read a poem that I've understood. To me, they never seem to make any sense.'

'That's because you're reading them like you would a story, whereas to get the best from a poem, you need to understand how to listen differently. Perhaps I could read you something and show you what I mean?' Not waiting for Esme to reply, Violette slid from the bed to go and ferret about in her overnight bag. 'Something simple, where it's quite clear what the author is saying.'

'You brought poetry with you?' Esme was intrigued.

Climbing back onto the bed, Violette grinned. 'I never leave home without something to read. After all, these days it's not unusual to become stuck for hours in an air raid shelter, is it? Reading poetry transports me away from what would otherwise be a tedious waste of time.'

How had she never noticed this side to Violette? 'And you think I'll understand this poem you want to read?' she said. 'Only, at this precise moment, my head is a little on the fuggy side.'

'Get in to bed then.'

'What?'

Darting about the room, Violette extinguished all but one of the lamps. 'The more comfortable and relaxed you are, the more you will appreciate the imagery.'

It seeming churlish to make a fuss, Esme complied, pushing her pillow against the headboard, sliding between the covers, and then pulling them up under her chin. 'All right.'

'Comfortable?'

'Uh-huh.'

'Very well.'

Listening to Violette's voice, Esme closed her eyes, astonished to understand for the first time how words could be used to paint pictures. The poet was describing the craving she felt for someone she could only admire from afar, the language rich and warm and sensuous, the writer's passion undimmed even by the eventual recognition that the love burning inside her would never be returned.

'So tragic,' Esme whispered when Violette drew the poem to a close. 'And yet, at the same time, so very beautiful.'

'You'll come with me then?' Violette whispered back. 'You'll come to next month's meeting with me and try it?'

Feeling her eyelids closing, Esme sighed. 'Perhaps I will, yes.'

From the very edge of sleep, she felt a kiss on her forehead, heard the click of the lamp switch and then the sounds of Violette settling beside her.

'Goodnight then.'

To Esme, Violette sounded as though she was smiling.

'Goodnight, Violette. Sleep tight.'

Yes, where was the harm in going along to this thing with Violette? After all, the two of them had become friends. And showing an interest in each other's interests was what friends did . . . wasn't it?

6

The Traitor

'Good evening, Miss Woods. Your usual?'

It was Monday evening at the start of Esme's second week and, having the previous afternoon studied the file for her next target — adopted identity Roger Pryce — she had done her hair, made up her face, squeezed herself back into the midnight-blue pencil dress and, feeling a combination of anticipation and excitement, had arrived to take up her usual seat at the bar.

'Good evening, Anthony. Yes, thank you, that would be lovely.' She didn't need to look to know that the man occupying the next-but-one stool was her target. As usual at this hour, the bar was largely empty, besides which, even seen only in profile, he was a match for his photograph: thin face, pronounced nose, mouth set in a line not far short of disapproval. Oh, and a large forehead made to seem even higher by the combing back of his oiled hair. All in all, not a patch on Greg Hatton. Still, she didn't have to like the man; she just had to test his loyalty. But, for that to happen, she first needed him to look in her direction.

After several minutes of being presented with nothing but his profile, though, she decided that either he was so deep in his thoughts that he was oblivious to her presence or else, aware that she was looking at him, had simply determined not to respond.

Still failing to draw his attention, Esme sat watching the bubbles rising in the Indian tonic water masquerading as a G&T. Perhaps the real man behind Roger Pryce had a sweetheart somewhere and no interest in talking to a woman — no matter how glamorous. Perhaps he had no time for women full stop — some men didn't — and was planning on testing his cover by getting into conversation with another man instead. If that was the case, then she was never going to succeed. But wouldn't SOE have discovered that about him? Wouldn't they have known that, in those circumstances, a female decoy would never work? Their investigations had certainly been sufficiently thorough to miss nothing about her own situation.

So, what was she to do? Since she hadn't encountered this problem with Greg Hatton, she was at a loss. But then she realised that with Greg, it hadn't fallen to her to make the first move anyway; *he* had been the one to draw *her* into conversation.

With that, she had an idea. She would go out and come back in again. Easing herself from the stool, she gestured to Anthony. 'I shall be back in a moment.'

'Of course, Miss Woods.'

Leaving the bar, she went through the foyer to the ladies' powder room, relieved to find it empty.

Placing her clutch bag on the side, she stared at her reflection. Why wasn't it working? Why hadn't he even looked in her direction? Because, she realised then, she wasn't giving him any reason to. For all he knew, she was waiting for someone. Or, perhaps, hearing the bartender refer to her by name, he assumed that she was a regular and wouldn't wish to be troubled. There could be any number of reasons. If she was to overcome them, she had to do as she had been trained and take the lead. Her mistake had been to assume that all targets would be the same as the charming Mr Hatton.

Rinsing her hands under the tap, she reached for one of the monogrammed hand towels, dried her fingers on it and then dropped it into the little wicker basket. She would return to the bar and make more of an effort. With any luck, her return would cause him to at least look up and acknowledge her, thus giving her the opening she needed. If that failed, then tomorrow night she would have to try something different.

As she walked back into the bar, though, she was surprised to find it empty. The only person left was Anthony, polishing glasses. In her surprise, she laughed.

'Everything all right, Miss Woods?' he enquired.

'Was it something I said?' she asked. 'Only I seem to have emptied the place.'

Anthony gave a slow shake of his head. 'I highly doubt it, miss. The gentleman who was sitting here enquired about last orders for dinner for non-residents.'

'This war has a lot to answer for,' she said, affecting weary resignation. 'I for one never thought I'd find myself heading off, at this hour, to a good book rather than staying for another drink.' *Keep up the act until you are back in your room and have locked your door behind you,* Madame Marron had advised. *Even if you cannot see him, your target might still be watching you.*

'Calling it a night, miss?' Anthony enquired.

As though considering the matter, she inclined her head. 'Since there would seem to be little to stay up for, I do believe I am.'

'Good night then, miss.'

'Good night, Anthony. See you tomorrow.'

Back in her room, Esme kicked off her shoes and crossed to sit in one of the easy chairs. There, she unscrewed the earrings that had been biting into her lobes and dropped them into the cut-glass ashtray on the side table. Then, heaving a lengthy sigh, she got up again, crossed to the desk and pulled from the drawer the folder containing the details of her target. Although she had nothing to report, she knew that she still had to make an entry to that effect.

Unscrewing the lid from her fountain pen, she stared down at the blank page. Given that nothing had happened, all she could think to write was *Target did not engage.*

The lid back on her pen, she set it down on the file. Then, wandering into the bathroom, she pressed the plug into the bath and turned on the taps. Since she had failed in such spectacular fashion, she would have a soak and an early night. And then, in the morning, she would come up with a different approach.

Esme's heart sank. On her breakfast tray — along with her usual pot of coffee, plain omelette and rack of toast — was a letter addressed to her 'care of' the fictitious employment agency in London, the handwriting upon the envelope unmistakeably that of her mother. Were it to contain nothing more than idle gossip from London society and news of the family — as most letters from mothers would — she wouldn't have minded, but she just knew this was going to be a missive she would prefer not to read. Propping it up against the bud vase of dianthus, she poured herself a coffee. Well, it could wait until she had eaten her breakfast; no point letting Naomi Colborne's discontent spoil a perfectly made omelette.

Eventually, though, having finished eating, drained the coffee pot, cleaned her teeth and decided what to wear, she could avoid it no longer. Sliding the butter knife under the flap, she opened the envelope and pulled out what felt to be at least three sheets of her mother's headed paper. Oh, joy: a bumper edition. Preparing herself for a chastising, she took it out onto the balcony where she perched on the edge of one of the steamer chairs and began to read.

Dear Esme,

I shall begin by saying that although enormously relieved to receive your letter, I had been hoping to read that after a period of reflection you felt ready to return home and proceed with your wedding. Imagine then, my shock and dismay to learn instead that you have taken up a post of employment, giving no indication as to its likely duration. While it is thoughtless of you to be so vague, I choose to believe that you are not being deliberately hurtful, merely unable to think clearly.

Realising just how tightly she was gripping the sheet of paper, Esme loosened her grasp. Had Naomi Colborne really spent these last few weeks deluding herself that, after what had happened, she would just return home? If she had, then the woman was living in cloud cuckoo land.

Cross at allowing herself to have become so irritated before she had even reached the bottom of the first page, Esme straightened the sheets of paper, flexed her shoulders, and read on.

Prior to receiving your letter, I had been wondering whether a portion of the blame for the manner of your absconding might rest upon my own shoulders. With the benefit of hindsight, I realise that perhaps I should not have waited until the last minute to share the facts of your adoption. Had I ever, at any stage over the years, imagined that you would react as you did, then clearly, I would have handled the matter differently.

Shaking her head in dismay, Esme sat further

back on the chair. *With the benefit of hindsight?* Naomi Colborne had had twenty-five years to tell her the truth and yet here she was, only now wondering as to the wisdom of withholding it? Had she never even *tried* to picture how the news might prove devastating? Evidently not.

With a sigh of frustration, she turned back to the letter.

Those thoughts aside, I do believe that despite his distress and his humiliation, Richard would still be willing to marry you, something I feel speaks volumes to both his character and to the forbearance of the Trevannion family as a whole.

And so, I beg you, Esme, come home. Despite what you clearly think, you will not be able to remain in this precarious form of employment in the longer term, nor will you be mixing in the appropriate circles to meet and marry someone else. So, I implore you, put these nonsensical notions behind you and return to your family. Send word of your intentions to that effect and I will make a discreet approach to Richard in preparation for a reconciliation. Given time, I feel certain that all will be forgiven. In addition, as for as this household is concerned, I give you my word that once all of this is behind us, no further mention of it need ever be made.

In deepest concern,
Your loving mother, Naomi.

Her teeth gritted against her outrage, Esme tossed the letter onto the table. Then, seeing the breeze lifting the pages, she slammed the ashtray down on top of them. The venomous little letter contained not one word of apology, let alone a modicum of understanding. Its only concern was Naomi Colborne's desire to do right by the two families or, at the very least, to have her crawl back home, apologetic and contrite.

And yes, she hadn't forgotten she had recently contemplated doing just that — had considered admitting defeat and returning to Clarence Square. But that was when she'd thought she was useless and unemployable. But now look at her! She wouldn't deny it was a shame about Richard — she deeply, deeply regretted how humiliated he must have felt — and she did still miss him. But he wasn't the only desirable man on this earth as the rather fun Greg Hatton had demonstrated. But, now that she had tasted the freedom that came with earning her own living, she viewed the act of getting married quite differently, especially given that the family she would have been marrying into was the suffocating and traditional Trevannions. One only had to look at Richard's sister-in-law, Sophia, to see what marrying into that lot could do to a woman.

Heaving a long sigh of frustration, she gathered up the pages of the letter and went back inside. Since attempting to pen a reply would only distract her from the more pressing issue of how to get into conversation with Roger Pryce this evening, she would put it out of sight.

193

Naomi Colborne could stew in her own outrage. She would *not* allow her to spoil her enjoyment of her new life; it might not be perfect, but it was hers to live and do with as she chose.

★ ★ ★

'So, what are you going to do?'

'Do?'

'Hold still. Your hair is so silky that this last bit is going to need another couple of pins.'

It was later that same day and, while Esme had been getting ready to go down to the bar to try again with Roger Pryce, Violette had arrived, apparently for no other reason than to chat.

'Do about what?' Esme asked.

Taking a step back to check the finished hairstyle, Violette gave a satisfied little smile. 'Do about your letter from home.'

Esme held up her hand mirror. There could be no denying that her friend had a knack with hair. Odd, really, considering that her own barely reached to her jaw. Pleased with the finished effect, she set down the mirror and turned to face her. 'I'm not going to do anything. Why would I? I've already explained that I am now in employment. I see no reason to write further if all I'm going to do is refute the points she makes. It's not as though anything I say will change her views. By writing back, all I would be doing is prompting yet another letter from her, and then another and another, all in the same wearying vein. So, no,' she said, 'I really think things are best left as they are.'

194

Violette smiled. 'Good for you.'

'You think it's wrong of me not to respond?' Esme asked, wondering at Violette's tone.

Violette shook her head. 'She's not *my* family. It's not for me to have an opinion, is it? Anyway, I was just wondering whether you'd like to go out on Saturday?'

Selecting a crystal necklace from the tray on her dressing table, Esme held it to her throat and, studying her reflection, contemplated the effect; the plain black dress definitely needed something to finish the look. 'Mademoiselle Marron, you sound as though you're asking me out on a date!'

'Here, let me do it,' Violette responded, holding out her hand for the necklace. 'There, done. Turn around and let me see.'

'All right?' Esme enquired.

'Perfect. So, is that a yes or a no?'

'To a date?'

Violette raised her hands in a gesture of despair. 'Would it be so bad?'

There were two things in particular Esme liked about Violette. One was that she didn't have a malicious bone in her body; the second, her mischievous sense of humour. 'If the only alternative was Roger Pryce,' she said, pausing to grin, 'then as propositions go, it would be quite appealing.'

'But not if the alternative was young Mr Hatton?'

Esme made as though to think for a moment. 'Against Mr Hatton, I'm afraid you wouldn't stand a chance, no.'

'But this Roger Pryce bothers you.'

Esme shrugged her shoulders. 'Let's just say there's something about him. I can't put my finger on it but even were it not my job to get him to be disloyal, I have a feeling he's not a man one would trust anyway.'

'Then this evening might prove pleasingly straightforward,' Violette observed. 'And then you'll be able to have the rest of the week off.'

'Assuming I can get him to talk in the first place,' Esme pointed out.

'Then you'd better get to it.'

'Yes,' she said, 'I suppose I had.'

'And Saturday . . . ?'

Esme gave a rueful shake of her head. 'Possibly. Let's see what happens with Mr Pryce first.'

'Then go do your worst,' Violette said lightly, crossing to the door, opening it, and turning back to blow her a kiss. 'Toodle pip!'

Left on her own, Esme stood for a moment to compose her thoughts. As she often reminded herself, a degree of nervousness was no bad thing. Besides, until she got to know him, who was to say that Roger Pryce wouldn't yet turn out to be not only easy-going but utterly charming as well? It was worth hoping for, she reflected as she let herself out of her room, turned the key in the lock and headed downstairs to find out.

★ ★ ★

'Good evening, Miss Woods. Your usual?'

Just as she had done the night before, but with

slightly more apprehension this time, Esme raised herself up onto the stool.

'Good evening, Anthony,' she replied to the bartender's greeting. 'Yes, my usual would be lovely, thank you.'

'And might I enquire how you fared today, miss? Any further interesting finds in your late aunt's abode?'

For a moment, she simply stared back at him. And then she realised that having witnessed her failure last night, he was stepping in to help out, his remark a reference to the fact that she was supposedly in Brighton to attend to the affairs of her recently deceased aunt.

'There were certainly plenty more finds, yes,' she replied to his enquiry, her smile one of gratitude.

'There you go, Miss Woods.'

'Thank you,' she said as he placed her drink in front of her. 'Is it dreadful of me to admit to having been looking forward to this all afternoon? Sorting through someone's affairs after they're gone is such a terribly sad business. Possessions that probably meant a great deal to my aunt, to me seem little more than junk.'

Very carefully, she was working towards what she felt certain would leave her target unable to resist joining their conversation.

His head lowered slightly, Anthony sent her a look of encouragement. 'I can only imagine it must be, miss, yes.'

'She has what I do believe — sorry, I mean she *had* what I do believe are a couple of rather fine pieces of furniture. Late eighteenth century, possibly. Not my taste, of course, but nice enough nonetheless.'

Rather more quickly than she had been hoping, her target offered an observation. 'If you suspect them to be of any worth, then for heaven's sake, do have them properly valued.' Adopting an expression she hoped conveyed a mixture of curiosity and surprise, she turned to regard him. 'Forgive the intrusion,' he said, meeting her look, 'but I couldn't help overhearing what you were discussing.'

Last night, when he had failed to even look in her direction, she had been horrified to find that almost every detail she had read about him had deserted her — including the fact that he was supposed to be an antiques dealer. Thanks to Anthony's intervention, and to the time she had spent re-reading his file this morning, this evening was already off to a better start.

Stay in character, she reminded herself. *And don't stop talking.*

'But I could so easily be wrong about them,' she said, ignoring his apology, 'and they might be of no value whatsoever. I should so hate to waste someone's time.'

Holding his look, she felt a degree of smugness; it felt good to be aware of how he would be appraising her — to understand what would be going through his mind. It was a situation that put her one step ahead in the game. With Greg she'd felt his equal, with this man it was different.

'Better to waste the time of a professional than let something of real value go for a song to some rogue who clears houses for a living . . . and who will be adamant that by taking it off your hands he's doing you a favour, only to then make a pretty penny on it for himself.'

With that piece of advice, he had just gifted her an opening. But she knew not to get too confident; this was just the beginning. Carefully, she got down from her stool and moved to the empty one between them. From behind the bar, Anthony repositioned her drink.

'And which of those two are you?' she asked, hoping this time that her smile made her appear enigmatic. 'The professional or the charlatan?'

Throwing back his head, he laughed out loud, the relaxation of his expression lifting years from his appearance. 'Ha!'

'Only, you clearly have some experience in one or other of those fields.'

'Roger Pryce,' he said, extending a hand that she accepted and shook. 'Pryce with a 'y'.'

'Well, how do you do, Roger Pryce with a 'y'. Beatrice Woods, with not a 'y' in sight.'

'It is a pleasure to meet you, Miss Woods.'

'Please,' she said, her smile owing as much to relief as to her ability as an actress, 'call me Bea. Everyone does.'

He leant slightly closer. 'Bea.'

On Sunday afternoon, and in accordance with the instructions for choosing her name for the week, she had tried desperately to think of an appealing name beginning with the letter B. The only ones she had been able to summon — Barbara, Bertha, Brenda and Beryl — had sounded neither attractive nor interesting. Bea, which she was pronouncing *Bee-a*, was something of her own invention and infinitely preferable to anything else she had come up with.

Risking a glance to her target, she recalled her initial impression of him as quite an oily little man — not to be trusted. And rather full of himself. But she couldn't afford to let that put her off; she had a mission to accomplish and, according to Major Lovat, there was no place on a mission for sentiment of the personal variety.

'I notice you haven't answered my question,' she said, fixing his stare.

He responded with a slippery smile. 'Which was . . . ?'

'Which was whether, in the field of antiques, you are a professional or a charlatan.'

'I should hope general opinion,' he replied, 'would be that I am closer to the former than the latter.'

When she affected to laugh, her intention had been to sound gay. She feared afterwards that she might have sounded drunken. Hopefully, he wouldn't have noticed.

'Well,' she said, 'that's good to know. Although . . . isn't that precisely what a charlatan would seek to have me believe?'

'Since you ask,' he said, shifting his weight on his stool and turning to face her more fully, 'my father dealt in antiques. All that I know of the subject I learned from him.'

'Locally?' she asked, struggling to ignore the urge to short circuit the small talk and advance her cause. *Slow down,* she cautioned herself. *Be patient.*

Roger Pryce shook his head. 'Not locally, no. In any event, I'm out of that game now.'

She affected disappointment. 'That's a shame. Based on your recommendation to employ a professional, I was rather hoping you might know of someone trustworthy nearby.'

'Sorry, I don't. But I'm sure you will find the hotel manager only too happy to recommend the services of someone reliable.'

'Yes, of course,' she said. 'How clever of you to think of that. I shall make a point of asking him.' Since he was now leaning towards her, she slowly edged further back on her stool. 'So, what brought about your departure from the world of antiques?' she asked. Finally, he backed away. 'Silly question,' she said, bringing her fingers to her lips in a gesture of foolishness, 'since it can really only be the war.'

When he took a sip of his whisky and then toyed with the tumbler, she had to remind herself to breathe. If he was ever to be tempted to divulge anything he shouldn't, it was now.

'In a manner of speaking, it was as you suppose, yes.'

'*In a manner of speaking?* Sounds intriguing.' Inside, she was squirming; she detested having to act airheaded. On this occasion, though, she recognised it as necessary.

For a while, Roger Pryce didn't respond, instead simply swirling the remains of his whisky. Lifting her own drink, she took a sip, repositioned her glass on its coaster and then waited. *If they're reluctant to talk, don't press. They've been trained to sense traps.* It was surprising how much of her own training was coming back to her now that she needed it — especially since *last* week she hadn't needed to draw upon it all.

Draining his glass, he cast a quick glance to her still full one and motioned to Anthony for a refill of his own.

'Actually,' he finally said, 'it's all rather hush-hush.'

When he tapped the side of his nose, she had to steel herself against a shudder. Golly, he was odious. 'I knew it!' she said, nonetheless.

The look he gave her was one of genuine puzzlement. 'You knew what?'

In exaggerated fashion she looked about the room before leaning towards him, lowering her voice, and whispering, 'That you are here on secret business.'

His grin told her that he was flattered.

'Secret business? Whatever gave you that idea?'

She sat back again. 'Oh, I don't know.' With her right hand she gestured airily. 'Perhaps it was something about the intensity of your frown.'

'Frowning is solely the prerogative of spies?'

She gasped. 'You see! I was right! I knew it.' Leaning towards him, she whispered, 'You *are* a spy!' When he joined in her laughter, she realised her mistake: she had given him the perfect opportunity to deny it. Desperate that he shouldn't back track now, she brushed his sleeve with her fingers. She would reverse her approach. 'I'm teasing you. Of course you're not a spy. But I did notice that you were frowning rather deeply. I trust everything is all right.'

For a moment he didn't respond. Neither did he move.

Fighting an urge to press on, she forced herself to sit perfectly still and wait.

'Actually,' he eventually picked up again, 'you were right on several counts.'

She feigned surprise. 'I was? Golly. Perhaps I'm a better judge of people than I always think!' Lifting her drink, she waved it about before taking a mouthful, gulping it down and rushing on, 'My friends are forever telling me I'm hopeless. Especially when it comes to the opposite sex.'

'Hm.'

'Oh dear, I'm sorry. Is that why you were frowning? Do you have lady-friend troubles?'

He shook his head. 'No. You were right earlier when you mentioned the war.'

'Ah. You are about to join up.'

'Already have.'

'Air Force?' she asked, careful to keep her tone casual. 'There's an awful lot of them in town.'

Again, he shook his head. 'Not the RAF, no. The service I've joined is . . . well, let's just say that its operations are covert.'

Deep within her chest she could feel a powerful thudding. She mustn't blow it now. 'Covert,' she repeated uncertainly. 'You mean you *are* a spy?'

'*That* I can neither confirm nor deny, and by which, I mean that I am genuinely and legally prevented from saying.'

Rather helpfully, her excitement had caused her breathing to become rapid and shallow. She hoped it gave her the appearance of being impressed. 'Golly.'

When he went on, his voice was so quiet as to be barely audible. 'So, I suppose if I *was* frowning, it was because the task ahead of me carries a heavy burden.'

'Of course,' she said. 'Your work must lead you into terrible danger.'

He nodded. 'It will do, yes.'

Glancing about, she, too, lowered her voice further. 'Are you going . . . ' Again, she glanced about. ' . . . to Germany?' He shook his head. 'France then,' she said. 'It must be France.'

Very slowly, he nodded. 'Uh-huh.'

Now her heart was pounding even harder. 'But . . . they surrendered, didn't they? The French, I mean.'

'Their government did, yes. But there are those among the ordinary population who would work against the Germans.'

She deliberately widened her eyes. 'And you're going to help them?' Again, he nodded. 'But how? How do you even get there? You can hardly take the boat train to Dover and just cross the Channel as though going on a holiday, can you?'

'A colleague and I — a junior colleague, you understand — will be dropped by parachute into an area where it is expected we will be able to make contact with an organisation called the Resistance.'

'And they're on our side?' she asked. In a way, she wanted to stop; she didn't want him to disclose anything further. She felt guilty just to be hearing such secrets even though it was nothing she didn't already know. She also wanted to get herself away from him, the mere act of sitting alongside him making her feel tainted by his disloyalty — because that's what he was being: disloyal not only to the organisation who had trained him but to his fellow operatives, indeed to the whole of his country.

'They are on our side, yes. But they're going to need our help.'

'Which is where you come in.'

'That's right.'

'Are there lots of you doing this? Only, although I find it heartening to learn this is all going on, I should think it's going to take rather more than just one or two of you . . . brave souls.' She was so nearly there. All she needed from him now was one or two specific details to relay back to SOE. Then there could be no doubt. 'I bet you have code names . . . and everything.'

He nodded. 'We do.'

'Tell me,' she said, her voice so quiet that it had become husky, 'what's yours?'

'Actually, I don't know it yet. For the moment I'm in what's called 'holding' but, any day now, I will be given my instructions. And then . . . ' With his hand he mimed the action of an aircraft taking off. ' . . . it will be up and away.'

'To France.'

'To be parachuted into enemy territory, disguised as a Frenchie, and to wreak as much havoc as possible.'

For a moment, she thought she might be sick.

'Golly, how brave,' she said, swallowing down a vile taste. 'That really is quite something.'

'All in a day's work for an undercover operative.'

Reaching for her glass, she took a sip of her drink. How, though, now that she'd heard enough, did she get away from him? Having fulfilled her purpose, she didn't want to spend a moment more than necessary in his company. If Madame Marron had advised her what to do in such circumstances, she seemed to have forgotten.

Carefully — given how badly her hand was shaking — she replaced her glass on the bar. Perhaps, in future, she should set up some sort of signal with Anthony. But, for now, all she could think to do was fall back on something simple.

'I'm afraid I'm going to have to ask you to excuse me, Roger,' she said, easing herself from her stool, 'because I've just noticed the time and I have to telephone my aunt — my other aunt, that is. She lives alone, and if I don't telephone on time, she gets upset. You know how the elderly can be.' Unsure what would happen once her report reached SOE, she glanced to Anthony. Presumably, it would be unwise to close down the possibility they might want her to keep going with this, even though her target had already failed the test. Thinking on her feet, she said, 'Another drink for Mr Pryce, please, Anthony. Put it on my account.'

'Of course, Miss Woods. Will we see you tomorrow?'

There. That was his lead, and to which she gave a casual shrug. 'All being well.'

Once in the lobby, she walked straight to the lifts. Glancing over her shoulder, her heart beating a tattoo in her chest, she pressed the call button. Surely, she must have gleaned enough to convince SOE that this man presented a danger to the programme? Surely, he had betrayed it beyond a shadow of a doubt. Surely, she would never have to see Roger Pryce — or whoever he really was — ever again.

★ ★ ★

'This is good work, Miss Ward.'

'Excellent, in fact.'

'Well done.'

It was late the following morning and almost no time at all after Esme had gone to Les Marronniers to report what had happened, two officials from SOE arrived to interview her.

'You have spoken to no one of this?' the older of the two men checked.

She shook her head. 'No one other than Madame Marron — and only then just in order to ask what I should do.'

'Good. You did the right thing. Rather fortunate we were already at The Grange, observing training, since it meant we could get here without delay. You're our first decoy, and with this,' he tapped the file with his pen, 'just your second assignment, you have already proved not only your own worth but the value of the programme as a whole.'

'In some regards rather worryingly,' the second of the men observed. 'For the sake of the integrity of the programme, we must hope this proves to be an isolated incident. If you get the same results with your next man, we're in trouble.'

Watching as he closed the file containing her report, Esme nodded. She hadn't considered the longer-term aspect of what she was doing; she had been concerned only with Roger Pryce. 'What will happen now?' she asked.

'Now,' the man with the file said as he got up from the table, 'we will report back to our superiors, who will almost certainly authorise us to pick up Mr Pryce and take him to HQ.'

'And then?' she asked. Failure or not, she didn't like the idea that on her say so, something terrible was going to happen to him — something *final*.

'Other than recommending that he be pulled from the programme, that won't be for us to determine. But, given the extent of his training, we can't just return him to civilian life. He will need to be placed somewhere . . . somewhere he can be closely monitored at all times.'

She wondered, but didn't like to ask, whether that would mean him going to jail.

With the two men from SOE then departing, Madame Marron and Violette came into the room.

'You are all right?' Madame Marron wanted to know.

Esme nodded. 'Yes, I'm fine, thank you. Exhausted, but fine.'

'I know what we'll do,' Violette said, slipping

her arm through Esme's and smiling warmly. 'We'll go out to lunch. And then, afterwards, you can go back to the hotel and catch up on some sleep. You do look a little grey under the eyes, and we can't have that.'

Although Violette's offer was well meant, inwardly Esme groaned. She didn't feel like going out to lunch but neither did she feel like going to sleep. What she wanted to do was to talk to someone and sort out her feelings — feelings that veered from satisfaction and pride one moment to guilt and shame the next. Worse still, she knew that although this particular assignment had come to a close, in a couple of days' time, she would have to reprise the charade with another target. And then do so again. And again.

She looked between the faces of the two women. 'Am I allowed to discuss with you what happened?'

Violette released her arm. 'Yes, of course. The three of us operate at the same level.'

'Then rather than go out, might I just talk to you?'

Madame Marron nodded. 'I'll go and make some coffee.'

'And we'll all go upstairs to the drawing room,' Violette added. 'And you can talk for as long as you need.'

★ ★ ★

'I really and truthfully don't want to do this.'

'I know. And I'm really sorry that we have to ask you — '

'But, understandably, HQ are concerned,' Madame Marron finished her daughter's sentence. 'This is the first time they have been confronted by a traitor in their midst and it is of paramount importance they ensure the situation is as it seems.'

It was much later that same day — almost seven o'clock — when, to Esme's surprise, Violette and Madame Marron had arrived at The Aurelian. In inviting them in, she'd had no inkling of what lay in store, which was that, while SOE felt she had done extraordinarily well, when it came to Roger Pryce and his disloyalty, they needed more. They needed him, as Madame Marron had just explained, to *thoroughly and properly hang himself*. A specific name or location, they had apparently said, was all she needed him to divulge and they would be content.

'Apparently, since this is Winston Churchill's own initiative,' Violette picked up again, 'they can't afford to be wrong. If nothing else, it would bring scrutiny to bear upon the wider operation — possibly even shut it down altogether.'

Collapsing heavily onto the end of the bed, Esme sat shaking her head in dismay. She'd thought she would never again have to be anywhere near the unctuous little man masquerading as Roger Pryce. Now she had to spend a further evening in his company.

Moving to sit beside her, Violette reached for her hand and squeezed it tightly. 'Come on, let's get you dressed and made up. The sooner you go down and see him, the sooner it will be over.'

Wearily, Esme sighed. 'I suppose.'

'Look at it this way,' Violette went on. 'If he's as keen to talk as he was last night, half an hour and you'll be back up here having a well-earned soak in the bath. I'll even stay here and wait for you if you like.'

'No,' Esme said, getting reluctantly to her feet. 'There's no need for all three of us to have our evening ruined. I wouldn't say no to some help getting ready but then you should go home.'

To Esme's mind, Violette looked put out. But she couldn't help that; when she was done, all she would want to do was go to sleep.

With Madame Marron leaving them to it, it took less than half an hour for Esme to wash and dress, and for Violette do her hair and make-up.

'You might need to do away with the frown,' Violette cautioned when Esme was searching about for her evening bag. 'And are you *sure* you wouldn't like me to wait?'

Esme nodded. 'Certain. I'll see you tomorrow morning with my report anyway.'

'You do know, don't you,' Violette said, evidently detecting the reluctance in Esme's tone, 'that if there had been any way to persuade them that this wasn't necessary, we would have done so.'

'Of course. I fully understand what they need and why. So, you just have to let me go and get on with it — get it over and done with. Truly. Comes with the territory, as you so often say.'

'I do say that, yes.'

'Well, out you go then,' Esme said. 'I'll wait

until I've heard the lift arrive and then I'll follow.'

The only good thing, Esme decided as she made her way across the lobby towards the bar a few minutes later, was that tonight she knew what to expect. Unlike last night, when she hadn't even been sure that he would talk to her, she now knew that he enjoyed the chance to boast. She would just have to hope that overnight he hadn't been wracked by such guilt that tonight, he wouldn't utter a word.

Entering the bar moments later, she saw that he had chosen to occupy the same stool as previously. That he was a creature of habit bolstered her confidence.

'Well, good evening,' she said, slowing her approach in order to give him time to turn in her direction and see her sashay the last few steps. 'Mr Pryce, how are you today?'

'Drink for Miss Woods,' Roger Pryce instructed, clicking his fingers to attract Anthony's attention.

Mortified by the man's lack of grace, Esme made sure to send Anthony a warm smile. 'Good evening,' she said.

'Good evening, Miss Woods.'

'Did you speak to the manager about an antiques dealer?' Roger Pryce asked as she made herself comfortable on the stool adjacent to his.

'I didn't have the chance today,' she said. 'I spent much of it with my aunt's solicitor. Since I don't have the faintest understanding of death duties, I had no choice but to sit and listen to them explaining how it all works. Dreadfully dreary.' When he didn't seem about to reply, she said, 'What about you? I trust you found an interesting way to fill your day?'

It didn't escape her notice that this evening he seemed less chatty. Was it possible that he regretted being so free with the information last night? Either way, she couldn't push him. If she was to get what she wanted, she was going to have to be patient.

'I did a little exploring,' he finally volunteered. 'Found somewhere pleasant for a spot of luncheon. Usual things.'

'Tell me, do you get on edge?' she asked, her voice lowered. 'Having to wait around for your instructions, I mean? *I'd* be terrible. I'm utterly hopeless at waiting for anything.' Her nerves in danger of making her prattle, she reached for her drink, raised her glass in his direction and took a sip.

'It can be hard not knowing what's going to happen next, yes,' he said. 'Or when.'

'So, still no word then,' she leant closer to remark. 'Not even a code name?'

'Nothing yet.'

Her instinct being to sigh with frustration, she caught herself just in time. 'You sound like a man in need of another drink,' she commented, waiting to catch Anthony's eye and then motioning to the dregs in Roger Pryce's glass.

'Coming up, Miss Woods.'

'Tell me,' she said when the drink arrived, her voice lowered even further, 'how *does* one get a job as a spy? I was thinking last night about what you'd said and couldn't imagine it being advertised among the Situations Vacant.'

From Roger Pryce came a sort of scoffing noise. 'One is approached.'

'I thought as much,' she said, affecting pleasure at finding her supposition to be correct. 'Someone spotted that you're a natural.'

'They did, yes.'

Was he thawing a little? Was playing to his ego beginning to work? 'Ooh, I say, do you have . . . ' She glanced over her shoulder. ' . . . a gun?' Continuing to stare ahead, he responded with just a single nod. Heavens, this was hard work tonight! At this rate she would probably have to come back again tomorrow. And her nerves wouldn't stand that. She leant closer. 'Have you ever . . . fired it?'

Again, he nodded. 'Of course. We do firearms training.'

Finally, she felt as though she was getting somewhere. 'How incredibly exciting. Although, please tell me that you don't shoot at bunny rabbits.'

She saw his lips curl at the corners, his expression bearing an uncanny resemblance to the snarl of a fox.

'No, we practice with targets.'

She drew her hand to her chest. 'That's a relief.' The trouble was, with so little coming from him tonight, their conversation kept getting stuck. 'Tell me,' she went on, 'are there women spies as well? Or is that just in films?'

'No,' he said, 'there were a couple of women on our course of instruction.'

'And do they have guns as well?'

'Of course.'

214

'Golly,' she said. 'How glamorous. And how brave you all must be. I mean to say, they can train you how to fire a gun, but I don't suppose they can train you how to be brave. Or can they?'

'No,' he said, 'they can't. Some people are just naturally more brave than others.'

'Like you.'

He shrugged. 'I suppose so, yes.'

'You do look like someone who would be brave. You've got one of those lofty foreheads that heroes have.'

He turned to regard her. 'I do?'

'Definitely. I bet you finished top of your class — or whatever.'

'Actually,' he said, 'The Grange isn't about competing with one's peers, it's about learning to do all sort of top-secret things whilst otherwise carrying on quite normally — you know, without drawing attention.'

The Grange. He had just given away the name of SOE's training centre! She had him. But just in case . . .

'The Grange,' she said, struggling to hide her relief. 'What's that?'

Vaguely aware of him explaining about an army training camp not far from East Grinstead, Esme knew that what she had to do now was catch Anthony's eye. But he was busy delivering a tray of drinks to a party of RAF officers and their young ladies at a table in the corner.

When Anthony returned to the bar, he briefly met her look. 'Any more drinks for you?'

This was her chance. 'Actually, do you think I might have a glass of water,' she said, as ordinarily as she had been taught earlier that evening. 'I have a fearful headache.' *Ask Anthony for a glass of water, Madame Marron had said, and Anthony will understand that the target has failed the test. After that, just go along with whatever happens next.*

'Of course, Miss Woods. One glass of water coming up.'

Moments later, and before she knew what was happening, mumbling arose from the other customers present, as a police sergeant, a constable, and two men in grey suits came into the bar. And then Mr Bancroft was addressing the room.

'Ladies and gendemen, I apologise for the intrusion upon your evening, but please would you have ready for inspection your identity cards. Just a routine check. No cause for alarm.'

Unsure whether this was something she had triggered or merely coincidence, she looked about the room.

'Don't worry, Miss Woods,' Anthony leant across to say, as he put in front of her the glass of water. 'It's just the usual check. Same as we get every week.'

'Yes, yes of course,' she said, poking about inside her clutch bag.

All around them people were holding out their papers while, in the general hush, the officers could be heard asking questions and confirming identities. And then the two of them seemed to be surrounded. Breathing rapidly, she tried not to panic. No reason to feel guilty, just doing your job, she told herself.

'Miss Woods,' Mr Bancroft said, placing his hand on her elbow, 'could I prevail upon you to step over here a moment?'

Mr Bancroft's grip upon her arm was firm, giving her no option but to go and wait with him by the door. Desperate to know what was going on, she reminded herself not to drop her cover until she was back in her room. No matter the confusion or the pandemonium, she was to maintain her identity. Those were the rules.

At the end of the bar, all attention was now on the target.

'Your name, please, sir?' one of the men in plain clothes asked.

'Roger Pryce,' Esme heard him reply. Was this her doing? Or was this just a routine check? It could so easily be either.

'Mr Pryce, I must ask you to come with us.'

'Come with you? Might I ask why? Is there a problem with my papers?'

'Just come with us, please.'

And then, with the customers in the bar looking on in fascination, Roger Pryce was led from the room.

By Esme's side, Mr Bancroft released her arm. 'Thank you, ladies and gentlemen, for your patience,' he said, addressing the room. 'Please, enjoy the rest of your evening.'

Perspiring heavily, and feeling horribly light-headed, Esme allowed Mr Bancroft to walk her to the lifts.

'Is that it?' she asked when the doors closed on the hubbub of the lobby, her voice little more than a scratchy whisper.

'That's it, yes. It's over.'

'And did . . . did *I* do that? Did those men arrive because of me?'

'Yes, Miss Ward, they did. Congratulations on uncovering your first traitor.'

Traitor. It had such a nasty ring — left such a nasty taste. 'So . . . what will happen now? What I mean is, what will they do with him?'

'I couldn't say.'

'Only, although he failed, I shouldn't like to think something awful is going to happen to him.'

When they reached her room, Mr Bancroft took the key from her hand and opened the door. 'Is there anything I can get for you?'

'Actually, yes,' she said, stepping inside. 'I should quite like a bottle of that nice spring water you serve in the restaurant — '

'The Harrogate? I'll have some sent up.'

' — because all of a sudden I find that I actually do have a truly terrible headache.'

7

Wallace

'Madame Marron, that was delicious. It's a long time since I've had authentic French onion soup.'

'I'm glad you enjoyed it,' Madame Marron replied to Esme's observation. 'The recipe was my grandmother's. Fortunately, in these days of rationing, a perfectly acceptable beef bouillon can still be made even from the cheapest cuts of meat. And at least onions seem readily available.'

Seated next to Esme at the table, Violette grinned. 'Does it take you back to your days in Biarritz?'

Ah, Biarritz, Esme reflected. Simpler times, when one's future as the mistress of an overly large home felt all but assured. For why else would one have been learning how to interview a prospective servant? 'Actually,' she replied, still never entirely sure when Violette was teasing her, 'it does remind me, yes. It reminds me of travelling back there, after a Christmas spent at Clarence Square, to find the town blanketed in snow, and a steaming bowl of soupe a l'oignon gratinée waiting for us at supper. Simple but perfect.'

Despite talk of onion soup and Christmas, it was in fact the height of August and, after the commotion surrounding what was now referred to within the confines of Les Marronniers as *The*

Roger Pryce Affair, life for Esme had settled into a predictable routine. By Thursday of each week, she had usually gained sufficient understanding of her target to report upon his reliability and trustworthiness. That being the case, on Friday mornings, she would walk around the corner to return the file to Les Marronniers and, as often as not, stay for lunch, usually a rustic dish of ratatouille, or cassoulet, or a salad niçoise, all as authentically French as these days of rationing would allow. In addition, there was often a bottle of wine, which, from what Esme had been able to deduce, seemed to find its way there from the cellar at The Aurelian.

Their meal finished, Violette would banish her mother from the tiny kitchen while she and Esme did the clearing up.

'So,' Violette remarked on this particular occasion as she stood scrubbing at the base of a saute pan, 'that's another of your operatives safely on his way.'

Waiting with the tea towel, Esme nodded. 'Uh-huh.'

'Makes me think Roger Pryce was a one-off'

Esme hoped so. 'To be perfectly honest,' she said, 'these last few targets have been so dull that I really don't think any of them had it in them to blatantly disobey the rules.'

'Mm,' Violette agreed, 'I must admit they did all look rather bland.'

'And while I know that's precisely the point,' Esme went on, 'they were *so* bland that I can no longer recall a single detail about any of them. They've all blurred into a single grey mass.'

'I remember your first one after dear Roger,' Violette said, finally handing her the pan to dry. 'You were terrified he was going to do the same thing and blab.'

'Maurice Smith,' she said, vaguely recalling his pudgy face. 'For him, I had decided to use the name Cassandra Wells. I rather liked the idea of having a man calling me Cassie. What a waste of a perfectly nice name that turned out to be!'

Beside her, Violette laughed. 'That does explain why the next name you chose was quite hideous.'

Now it was Esme's turn to laugh. 'Dorothea Wykeham was not hideous. Had the target turned out to be attractive, I was going to suggest that he call me Thea.'

'But he didn't? Turn out to be attractive, I mean?'

Trying to picture his face, Esme frowned. 'Graham . . . Thomas. That was him. And no, he was utterly tedious. And after him came Alfred Cox, who was no better. You know, sometimes, when they are droning on, I play little games in my head. I try to guess their real names . . . or come up with even more dull ones for their aliases.'

'Helps to pass the time?'

'Something like that.'

'But you're still glad you're doing it — this job, I mean?'

Reaching to hang the dried saucepan on the rack, Esme nodded. 'I am. If all I wanted was to earn a living, there would be far easier ways to do it. But I wanted what I do to matter. *I* wanted to matter — '

'You certainly do that,' Violette said, taking the tea towel from Esme's hand and hanging it on its hook. 'You matter to SOE. And, although none of them know it, you matter to the operatives you're putting to the test, too.'

'Hm, they *don't* know it, do they?' Unlike Major Lovat at The Grange, whose words would forever stick in the operatives' minds, the moment the targets left Brighton they would never give *her* a second thought. They would never even realise their loyalty had been tested, nor that they had emerged not only more practised for it but stronger, too — which was just how it was supposed to be.

'Any thoughts as to what you will do once the war is over?'

Absently, Esme watched Violette reach to the cupboard for the coffee service. 'Hm?'

'When your work here comes to an end, what will you do?'

It was a good question. 'I haven't thought about it,' she said.

And nor did she particularly want to, either. Never far from her mind just recently was something her Aunt Kate had once said, which was that when the last war had ended, no one wanted women in the workplace anymore. Even when the numbers of men returning home fit enough to work were insufficient to keep things running, pressure was still brought to bear upon employers to send their female workers 'back where they belonged', which meant to the kitchen sink, no regard given to the fact that, for the previous four or five years, households had got along just fine without anyone at home all day. She supposed it would be the same this time around, too. Her own job was different, of course; it would come to a natural end, her role only existing while there remained the necessity to send operatives into occupied France. Beyond that, the need for her to do what she did ceased to exist. At least once the war did eventually end, Violette could return to teaching languages — even if that language wasn't German.

Wishing Violette had never put the thought in her mind, she sighed heavily.

'Coffee?' Violette chose that moment to ask, gesturing with one of the cups.

She nodded. 'Thank you, yes. I suppose what I do after this will depend upon how long the war lasts, and how soon afterwards things get back to normal.' *Back to normal.* For her, the word 'normal' would once have meant marriage and a family. But now, with her bridges in that regard well and truly burnt, and eligible young men doubtless hard to find, who knew whether that would even still be possible.

'I suppose it will, yes,' Violette agreed.

'I like having a salary. I like the independence of it. Until you've actually earned your own money and tasted the freedom it brings, you have no grasp of how it can make you feel — or how you've been missing out.'

'You can still earn a salary,' Violette remarked, placing the coffee pot on the tray with the cups and saucers.

'Not if I get married.'

'With your ability to speak French,' Violette

continued, 'you could teach. You could take on private clients like we do. Like we *did*. You could even stay on here with us, you know, for a refresher . . . or even as a tutor . . . '

'My dear Violette,' Esme said, reaching to open the door to the drawing room, 'that does rather assume that not only are we destined to defeat Mr Hitler — such that the people of France don't end up speaking German — but that this war doesn't make people less likely to want to travel to France and thus learn French to start with.'

Passing ahead of her through the door, the tray in her hands, Violette scoffed. 'Or . . . perhaps defeating Hitler will make them want to learn it even more.'

Sometimes, Esme reflected as she crossed the room to the sofa, Violette was hard to fathom. She seemed to exist in a very small circle from which it wouldn't harm her to occasionally get out: broaden her social circle; find herself a boyfriend. Curiously, for someone with so many opinions, the subject of men was something she rarely mentioned. She certainly never spoke of suitors — past *or* present. But what did that matter? The Marron women were nice. She liked being invited into their home; they had become almost like family. And, in the same way that she never enquired as to the whereabouts of Monsieur Marron, she wasn't going to jeopardise her relationship with them by prying into Violette's affairs, affairs that really were none of her business.

★ ★ ★

It was a shame all of the beaches were closed. With the weather as it was today — warm and clear with just the lightest of winds — a dip in the sea would have been just the thing. As it was, all Esme could do was look longingly at the expanse of summery blue and take pleasure from the fact that at least she had a balcony from which to do so.

Regrettably, those same clear skies had recently been affording German bombers — with the help of their fighter escorts of ME-109s — unrestricted views of their targets in southern England. Wave after wave of them, black specks against the blue, were all too often seen swarming across the Channel. And, although those same clear skies had been enabling the boys of the RAF to pick out these formations, Esme knew from the newspapers that the resulting skirmishes were causing heavy losses on both sides.

When a tap at the door broke into her thoughts, she rose from her wicker chair, slipped her feet into her shoes and went to answer it. In the middle of a Sunday afternoon there was only one person it could be: Mr Bancroft arriving with details of her next assignment. Accepting it from him, she closed the door and wandered back into the room, peeling back the flap of the envelope and pulling from it the contents. Letting the envelope drop onto the desk, she flopped onto the sofa and opened the cover. *12th August 1940. Target No. 107: Wallace Teague.*

Staring at the photograph of yet another earnest-looking man in his late twenties or early thirties, she sighed. His cover identity was that of a cartographer visiting Brighton to help the RAF with a specialist project. Involuntarily, she yawned. Why couldn't any of these men ever be something interesting? Because, she reminded herself, their assumed identities and reasons for being in Brighton needed to be realistic. As much as she might relish the variety, she was never going to open a file to find that her next target was a tightrope walker in a circus, an explorer in the jungles of the Amazon, or a bank robber on the run from the police. Even so, her targets over the last month, certainly since the departure of the charming Greg Hatton, had been dull, dull, dull. And now, this week, she was faced with pursuing someone who drew maps for a living. Dear God, what a prospect. Pretending to find *that* fascinating was going to require every ounce of her acting skills.

Kicking off her shoes, she stretched her legs along the sofa. What name should she adopt for Mr . . . she glanced back to his profile . . . Mr Wallace Teague of Southampton in Hampshire? Florence? No, too nursey. Frances? No, that carried the risk of being shortened to Fanny Flora? She shook her head; that was the sort of name Grandmamma Pamela would have picked for one of her parlour maids. Freda? Faith? Filomena? No, wait, Fenella. Fenella Wentworth. That's who she would be this week. And she would do her best to stop looking upon these poor men as dull. Not only was her job important to the war effort, but she was fortunate. Since that fateful night when she had left Clarence Square with no idea of what she was going to do, she'd come a long way. Of late, she hadn't even thought about Richard — which had to mean she was getting over him. Moreover, none of the other people she had been so desperate to leave behind knew where she was. And that was without, as she had said to Violette only the other day, reckoning upon the salary and the freedom this job afforded her.

As it happened, when she went into the bar the following evening, Wallace Teague wasn't there. As it also happened, she didn't mind; to relieve the monotony of waiting, and to minimise the risk of being approached by one of the several RAF officers already drinking there, she took a seat in the lobby, from where she watched the comings and goings, inventing identities and stories for her fellow guests. Then, just when she thought he wasn't going to show, and she was about to call it a night, Wallace Teague walked straight past her into the bar. Allowing him a moment to order a drink and settle, she waited. Then she followed him in.

As luck would have it, the first three stools at the bar were taken by the RAF officers, her target occupying the middle of the remaining three. Excellent — now she had no choice but to sit next to him, something that made her task considerably easier.

Arriving at the bar, she gestured to the end stool. 'Pardon me . . . but is this seat taken?'

'Be my guest.' Then, as though registering from

her voice that she was female, he turned sharply. 'Forgive me, no, please, do take it. Here,' he said, getting to his feet. 'Allow me to assist you.'

Accepting his hand, she raised herself onto the stool. 'Thank you.'

From behind the bar, Anthony acknowledged her presence. 'Be with you in a moment, Miss Wentworth.'

From further along, three immaculately groomed heads turned to regard her. From one of them came a faint whistle of appreciation. Using it as an excuse to turn away from them, she swivelled upon her stool, accidentally kicking her target's shin as she did so. The fortuitousness of this mishap not lost on her, she brushed his sleeve with her fingers and apologised. 'I'm so terribly sorry. Perhaps I should find somewhere else to sit.' As though about to do so, she looked over her shoulder.

'What, and make life easier for whichever of those Brylcreem Boys fancies his chances? I wouldn't, not unless one of them is your type.'

Containing an urge to roar with laughter, she instead smiled broadly; a target with a sense of humour — and a dry one, at that. This might not be so bad after all.

'Good point,' she said, her tone confidential. 'Then if you don't mind, I'll stay put. But I promise to try not to kick you again.'

Her first impression of him was that his photograph did him few favours, the frown he bore in it giving him an air of standoffishness.

'Wallace Teague,' he said, offering his hand in her direction.

She shook it. It felt warm and surprisingly soft. 'Fenella Wentworth.'

'Pleased to make your acquaintance, Miss Wentworth.'

'Likewise, Mr Teague.'

From among the RAF officers came guffaws of laughter. Deciding them to be at the expense of either her or her target, she chose to ignore them. In any event, her drink arrived.

'There you are, Miss Wentworth.'

'Thank you, Anthony.' Making a point of peering at the glass in front of her companion, she added, 'And another for Mr Teague, please.'

'Actually — '

'Please,' she said. 'Having kicked your shin, I feel it's the least I can do.'

'What I had been going to say was that if you're going to buy me a drink, you might also want to call me Wallace.'

This time she didn't bother restraining her laughter — nor did she attempt to hide the colour that flooded her cheeks. In fact, she couldn't have planned it better.

'In which case, Wallace, may I buy you a drink?'

'You may. Solely to relieve the pain, you understand.'

'Of course. So, are you residing here?' she asked when Anthony left them to attend to her request.

'In Brighton, yes,' he said. 'But at The Aurelian, no. You?'

'I've been staying here a while now, yes.'

'Ah.'

'Your work brings you here?' she asked, anxious now not to squander such a promising start.

On the other side of the bar, Anthony reappeared. 'Your drink, sir.'

'To your good health,' he said, raising his glass.

She tilted her own in his direction. 'Chin-chin.'

'When it comes to my reason for being here, you assume correctly,' he said. 'I hold an official document permitting me to remain, and I quote, *for up to, but no more than, seven days.*'

'Golly,' she said. 'Things *have* become officious, haven't they?'

'With good reason, I suppose,' he agreed. 'And you? What brings you here?'

'Oh,' she said, 'well, I've been here since before the coming about of these latest restrictions. Largely for want of something better to do, I was staying with my elderly aunt until one day, out of the blue *fft.*' In emphasis of her point, she clicked her fingers. 'She died.'

'Goodness. My condolences for your loss.'

From his increasingly relaxed demeanour, Esme knew the hard work was done. They had turned a corner. She would have little trouble now steering things where she wanted them to go.

'Tell you what,' she said, raising her voice above the laughter from further along the bar, 'shall we go and sit over there. It's rather noisy here.'

'Good idea,' he said. Motioning to her glass he went on, 'Allow me.'

From the moment they moved away from the bar, things progressed more agreeably than she could have hoped. The man purporting to be Wallace Teague had a calm and gentle way about him, listening as much as he talked, and considering the opinions she offered without belittling her. Genial, that was the word for him. And how much easier was her task when her interest didn't have to be feigned?

When she enquired more about his work, he answered in some detail, leading her to decide that he had genuinely once worked with maps. With features that were soft and kind but otherwise unremarkable, and with a manner that leant towards bookish and academic, she suspected that he was often overlooked — not only by employers but by women, too. In that regard it was a shame but, from the point of view of the operation he was about to undertake, such natural inconspicuousness could only improve his chances of success.

'Excuse me, sir, Miss Wentworth.' Absorbed by their conversation, neither of them had noticed Anthony arriving at their table. 'I am obliged to point out that the curfew starts in five minutes.'

In disbelief, Esme raised her wrist, only to realise that she wasn't wearing her watch. 'Truly?' she said. 'It's that time already?' How quickly the evening had flown!

'Thank you,' Wallace said, acknowledging Anthony and getting to his feet. 'I don't suppose,' he said, folding his jacket over his arm in preparation to leave, 'there's any chance you will be here again tomorrow evening?'

To at least give the appearance of propriety, Esme hesitated. 'Well, yes. I do believe there might be.'

'Then perhaps we might resume our conversation tomorrow? I should welcome the company.'

As she got to her feet, her smile came naturally. 'Shall we say around seven?'

His smile hinted at relief. 'Seven it is. Goodnight, Miss Wentworth.'

'Goodnight, Mr Teague. Do hurry home. The DVF around here are red-hot.'

'Thank you. I will.'

Moments later, as the lift carried her up to her room on the third floor, she realised that at some stage during the evening, the despondency that had been hanging over her for a while now had evaporated. She felt less jaded, more enthusiastic. Able to attribute it solely to the amenable nature of this latest target, she shrugged her shoulders. What did it matter why she felt brighter? Surely the main thing was that, for the first time in a while, she did.

⋆　⋆　⋆

Deciding against the scarlet cocktail dress had been a wise move. By opting instead to wear the dark blue one, Wallace Teague couldn't be led into believing — or even fearing — that she was out to impress him. Indeed, by appearing much as she had previously, their rendezvous the following evening picked up precisely where it had left off — no fuss, no manoeuvring. No anxiety. The only thing Esme had to keep reminding herself was that she wasn't there to build a friendship; she was there to test his loyalty to his country.

'So, how is your work with the RAF going?' she asked to that end. They had chosen to sit on a buttoned sofa adjacent to a low table, well away from the bar and the same trio of officers in airforce blue.

'Pleasingly well,' he said. 'They are clear on what they want, which always makes the task easier.'

'And will you have to come back again after this week?' Waiting for him to answer, she raised her glass and sipped her drink.

He shook his head. 'No. By Friday morning my work here will be complete. What happens after that will be down to someone else.'

'You will be heading back along the coast.'

Rather than reply, he frowned. 'I don't remember telling you where I live.'

The sip of drink she had just taken seemed to lodge in her throat while, in her chest, her heart felt as though it missed a beat. Had she, for the first time, mis-stepped?

Trying not to panic, she made a little coughing noise. 'I do beg your pardon,' she said, coughing for a second time. 'I don't think you did tell me. I suppose I merely assumed that you would live somewhere close to your work.'

He grinned. 'Not an unreasonable deduction, I suppose. And, as it happens, correct. Yes, I'm hoping to get a train in the direction of Southampton as soon as I finish on Friday.'

That she felt disappointment was no surprise;

this man was good company. But those same feelings of regret should also serve as a caution: did she really want a repeat of how she had felt with Greg Hatton? No. But enjoying the company of a charming man needn't compromise her operation; it was already apparent that the alter ego of Wallace Teague wasn't going to let anything slip. Besides, after the last three or four dreary targets she'd been sent, she deserved not only an easier time of it but also some fun. So, yes, she would follow her instinct on this.

'That's a shame,' she said, 'since I was rather hoping to talk you into accompanying me to Supper Club on Friday. I went once with a friend but would welcome the chance to go again.'

She watched him give a little smile. 'I suppose I could stay one more night. My lodgings are paid for . . . and my travel warrant seems to be valid for a while longer yet . . . '

'Excellent,' she said, determined that he shouldn't change his mind. 'Curfew still applies for non-residents, I'm sorry to say, but we can book for the earlier dinner and still catch some of the dancing.'

'Now hold on,' he said, his expression deadpan. 'This is the first you've said of any dancing!'

She treated him to one of her enigmatic smiles. 'I think you'll find it was implied.'

'Implied, was it? Well, then I feel duty bound to warn you that I have two left feet. Some might say three.'

She pulled an amused face. 'I'll take my

chances. Besides, since I have already kicked your shin, it seems only fair that I give you a chance to even the score . . . '

★ ★ ★

She hoped he would be there. Forgetting to make a definite arrangement last night — or even a casual one — to meet him this evening had been remiss of her and showed all too clearly what happened when one forgot one's purpose.

She needn't have worried, though; as she walked into the bar, he was seated on the sofa, clearly watching for her arrival.

'Miss Wentworth.' Getting to his feet, he gestured to her to sit down.

'Goodness,' she said, his greeting striking her as oddly formal. 'How very proper you are tonight, Mr Teague.'

'Forgive me,' he said, sitting down beside her. 'Good evening, *Fenella*. But you see . . . I've been sitting here, wrestling with a dilemma.'

Oh dear. This didn't sound good; had she said or done something to make him suspicious? 'Which is?'

'Which is . . . whether or not, by proposing something to you, you might think me overly forward . . . '

Still with no idea what was going through his mind, she felt her heart gathering speed. 'Well,' she said, 'I suppose there's really only one way to find out.'

'Very well. Then would you have lunch with me tomorrow?' *That was his dilemma?* 'You see, tomorrow, the chaps I'm working with have some grand pow-wow to attend, meaning that from eleven o'clock onwards, my day will be my own. I've asked around and it seems that if we take a tram, and if you don't mind a short walk afterwards, on the outskirts of the town there's an excellent restaurant run by an actual Frenchman.'

Well, this was a surprise. Not only was he charming, he had initiative, too. 'French food?' she said, lacing her tone with amusement in the hope of burying the irony she felt. 'Now that *would* make a change. What time did you have in mind?'

'Well, what if I were to call for you at twelve-thirty?'

'Yes,' she said, wondering at what point, precisely, she had lost control of the situation — and whether or not she should care rather more than she seemed to. 'I shall be ready.'

'Excellent. And bring your best appetite. By all accounts, although the cooking is homely, the portions are generous.'

'I'll do my best.'

'But now, of more immediate importance is to catch Anthony's eye and order us some drinks.'

★   ★   ★

Violette looked bewildered. 'For lunch? The target has asked you to *go out for lunch* with him? Today?'

'That's right.'

'Well, *that's* not allowed.'

236

When, the following morning, Esme had decided to take a detour on the way back from browsing in the bookshop to call in at Les Marronniers and share her news with Violette, this wasn't the reaction she had been anticipating. What did Violette mean it wasn't allowed? As far as she knew, there was no rule governing when or where — or even how — she could meet a target. Why would there be?

'It's only lunch,' she said, trying to play down the significance of her earlier announcement, and grateful that she hadn't gone as far as mentioning that the restaurant in question was French. She could do without *that* ridicule. 'I hardly think I'll be taken to task for swapping the bar at The Aurelian for a modest restaurant somewhere. Especially not since *he* will be paying. Truly, I don't see what there is for anyone to get het up about.'

'Well, *I* think it's asking for trouble.'

Unsettled by Violette's inexplicably bristly manner, Esme opted for caution. Whatever had Violette rattled, she didn't want to make it worse. 'Well,' she said, 'the rules are there for a reason. I do appreciate that. And I wouldn't dream of flouting them. But I have seen nothing to indicate restrictions upon meeting the targets. Besides, Wal — Mr Teague is just beginning to trust me. And, if I can build upon that, who knows what he might go on to say or do?'

He wouldn't spill information, she knew that for certain. But Violette didn't.

'Hm. From where I'm standing,' Violette said, 'I think there's more to this than meets the eye.

237

You like him, don't you? I can tell.'

Esme decided not to lie. 'I do like him, yes, but not in the way — '

'You do realise that you're not dating these men, don't you?'

'Violette, really. Of course I do.'

'That you're not supposed to fall for them — '

'Violette,' she said softly, anxious to defuse a situation that showed all the signs of turning into an argument, 'It couldn't be clearer. You know that.' But, as soon as she'd said it, she wondered whether it was strictly true. Was she, as Violette was implying, falling for Wallace Teague? No, how ridiculous. Wallace Teague wasn't even a real person. Yes, she found him fun and enjoyed his company. But that was all she was doing — making the most of the chance to have a nice time.

'Look,' Violette said, her tone close to exasperation. 'I'm not cross with you. I could never be cross with you. I'm just concerned, that's all. I still remember how . . . how melancholy you were when that Gregory Hatton fellow left. And so, all I'm trying to do is remind you that none of these men are real . . . and that no matter how much you like them, it's always, always, going to end the same way. Every Friday, in accordance with their instructions, they will leave. They have no choice but to. They're going to war.'

'I know that.'

'What's more, no matter what they might draw you into believing, none of them is going to come back and marry you. Use you, yes. Marry you, no.'

'Look,' Esme said, Violette's statement causing her to squirm. 'I appreciate your concern, really, I do. But I must say I think you're being ridiculous. Only the other day, you and I had a long discussion about what we will do once this war is over. Among other things, I pointed out how getting married would mean not only having to give up earning my own living but also having to forgo the freedom that goes with it, and how I wasn't sure I was ready to make that sacrifice just yet. So, contrary to what you suddenly think, I do not harbour a secret hope that one of the targets will want to marry me. The very notion is absurd. And, frankly, insulting.'

With that, Violette seemed remorseful, reaching for Esme's arm as though trying to placate her. Uncertain of her motives, Esme pulled away.

'Can't you see?' Violette said. 'I'm only looking out for you. I only want you to be safe, not taken in, only to later be cast aside and hurt.'

To Esme, none of that felt true; rather, it felt more as though Violette wanted to exercise some sort of hold over her. The only other motive she could think of was jealousy — not jealousy in the usual sense of Violette wanting these men and their attentions for herself, but rather more as though Violette was jealous of *the men*. In fact, yes, their contretemps bore all the hallmarks of a lovers' tiff.

Heaving a sigh of dismay, she glanced to her wrist-watch. It was already eleven fifteen. 'Look,' she said, 'I'm grateful for your concern.'

'Huh. *Are* you?'

Now she'd had enough. Now she felt as though she was being called a liar.

'Violette,' she said, precariously close to snapping at her, 'I don't appreciate having my professionalism called into question. So, before one of us says something that can't be taken back, I think I should leave. I shall see you tomorrow morning when I file my report. But I don't think I shall stay for lunch. Please pass my regrets to your mother.'

Making her way back to The Aurelian, Esme walked rapidly, her hands clenched into fists. Becoming aware of this, she deliberately slowed her pace, rolling her shoulders to ease the tension in her neck as she did so. Violette's remarks had left her feeling uneasy. And she knew why. There *was* truth in Violette's observations — in *some* of her observations, anyway. If she was brutally honest, she did like Wallace. She liked that he was charming, thoughtful, and easy to talk to. Last night, when he'd asked her out to lunch, she'd been thrilled. And, yes, it did feel like a date. And yes, that did make her feel warm in a way that she hadn't in ages. But, despite those feelings, she was under no illusion that anything could come of it; there would be no happily ever after. Violette, though, clearly didn't believe her — or didn't want to.

Waiting at the kerb for a couple of military motorcyclists to pass, she sighed. With hindsight, she should never have told Violette about Wallace's invitation; it was a confidence too far and one she should have kept to herself. And, in the future, she would do just that. In the meantime, she would look upon this unpleasant episode as a lesson learnt: going forward, she would discuss with the Marrons only those matters relating directly to her assessment of the target.

Her other mistake, she was beginning to realise as she turned the corner and The Aurelian came into view, had been in allowing her relationship with Violette to develop beyond the merely professional. By doing so, both of them had allowed the distinction between friendship and work to become so blurred that, as had just become abundantly clear, neither of them could separate the two.

Arriving back at the hotel, she went up the front steps. To either side of the entrance, men in overalls were stacking extra sandbags on top of those already there.

'Mornin', miss,' one of them said as she passed.

She raised a smile. 'Good morning.'

Crossing the lobby and pressing the button to call the lift, she was clear about what she had to do. From now on, where Violette was concerned, she would keep her counsel. Unfortunately, where Wallace was concerned, the appropriate remedy was rather less palatable, because, as Violette had been quite correct to surmise, she was already quite smitten.

★   ★   ★

'Hullo? Hullo? Lou, is that you?'
'Yes? Hello? Who is this please?'

Oh, for heaven's sake, this was ridiculous, Esme thought, pressing the telephone receiver closer to her ear.

It was now Friday, the day after her lunch with Wallace and, with time on her hands before she needed to get ready to meet him for Supper Club, Esme had thought it an opportune moment to telephone Cousin Lou, have a quick chat, and find out how she was. Had she known how difficult it would prove, she would have waited until she'd had an entire evening free. As it was, she could be forgiven for thinking she was trying to speak to Lou on the moon rather than barely two hundred miles along the coast.

'Lou, it's Esme.' Having announced herself yet again to the voice on the other end of the line, she waited, dismayed to hear nothing but crackling. 'Lou, is that you? Are you there?'

'Esme! Good Lord, it *is* you! I wasn't sure. How on earth did you know to ring me *here*?'

Finally!

'I rang Woodicombe first,' she said. 'Your father answered. Told me you'd got fixed up with something in Plymouth. Something about the dockyard?'

With that, the static on their line seemed to settle and their connection became a little clearer.

'That's right,' Lou replied. 'I have a job as a clerk at the Royal Canadian Navy depot in Devonport Dockyard. I share a room in a house just up the road. Quite a few of us from there lodge here.'

Little Lou Channer had left home and gone

out to work? Well, there was a surprise. 'And are you enjoying it?' she asked.

'I am. I really like it. What about you? Where are you now? Mum mentioned being able to write to you care of somewhere in London.'

'That's right. I'm working for the government, but I can't talk about what I do or where I do it. Not that I'd want to. It's quite boring.'

She heard Lou giggle.

'Top secret. Goodness. Do you like it?'

'I do,' she replied. 'Has there been much bombing where you are?'

'Very little. You?'

'A lot of activity nearby but only the odd incident here. So far, at least.'

'That's good.'

'Anyway, how are you?' Esme enquired. 'Are you all right? I feel mean about being quiet for so long but, well, with this job . . . you know how it is.'

'I'm fine,' Lou replied. And to Esme she sounded it, too — bright and bubbly like the Lou of her childhood. She also sounded as though there was a lot of activity going on around her. 'More than fine, to be honest. I was seeing this chap — my roommate's step-brother, actually — but that's ended now and . . . well, let's just say I've got my eye on someone else, someone . . . older and nicer.'

'Lou Channer. You little minx! You'd better not let your father find out.'

'Don't worry. I don't tell Mum and Dad the half of what we get up to down here. It would send them grey. Anyway, what about you? Are you seeing anyone?'

Through Esme's mind flashed a picture of Richard. 'No time for it,' she said, coiling the telephone cable absently around her fingers. What she wanted to do was tell Lou about Wallace. Having had such a lovely lunch with him yesterday — but with relaying the details to Violette now out of the question — she was just bursting to talk about the delightful little restaurant and their delicious meal and what attentive company he had been. Instead, remembering just how much was at stake from loose lips, she said, 'With everything being so secretive all of the time, I couldn't see anyone on a regular basis anyway, even if I wanted to.'

'No. Suppose not. Look, Esme, I'm sorry to be rude, but I'm getting dirty looks from the girls queueing to use the telephone — '

'It's all right,' she said, 'I have somewhere to be, too.'

' — but it's real lovely of you to call. And I'm so pleased you're all right. Truly I am.'

'And I'm pleased you've escaped from Woodicombe,' Esme replied. 'It sounds as though you're having fun.'

'I am. Well, thanks again, Esme. Bye!'

'Bye, Lou. Do take care.'

Who would have thought it, Esme reflected as she replaced the receiver on its cradle? Cousin Lou had left home and got a job. And not only had she been seeing someone, she'd apparently just thrown him over for someone else. Talk about *a turn up for the books*, as Aunt Kate would say. She did hope Lou wasn't getting too carried away, though — that she was exercising some degree of caution. After all, finding her way about in the world was new to her. And they did say it was the quiet ones who were always the first to get into trouble.

With a little sigh and a quick check of the time, she got up from the desk and went towards the wardrobe to choose her outfit for the evening ahead. How life had changed for the pair of them, she thought as she pulled from the rail a floor length dress of black satin with a lace overlay. Seven or eight weeks on from that fateful night in Clarence Square and who would recognise either of them now? They had both broken free from the shackles of family and domesticity. And, although they might be doing very different things, they were both enjoying life. Yes, she reflected, laying the dress on the bed, things had worked out all right for both of them.

★ ★ ★

She should have guessed he hadn't been truthful with her! She should have guessed that Wallace's protestations about being a poor dancer would turn out to be untrue — after all, everything else about him was!

It was later that evening, and Esme and Wallace were at The Aurelian's Supper Club, where, the instant the band leader had announced that the next tune was to be *Begin the Beguine*, Wallace had got smartly to his feet and held out his hand. 'It was, I believe, your wish to dance.'

To a contemporary rendition of the classic piece, he then proceeded to lead her in a foxtrot with footwork so light it took her breath away. She'd always thought that Richard was a competent dancer, but Wallace put his efforts firmly in the shade.

'Thank you,' she said, when the music came to an end. 'You are extremely nimble.'

'Not quite up to the standard of Fred Astaire,' he quipped, returning her to their table and handing her back to her seat.

'You've seen *Broadway Melody of 1940?* Already?' Having only recently read about Astaire's spectacular routine with Eleanor Powell to the same song the band had just played, she was both surprised and impressed.

'My mother knew someone who knew someone who . . . well, I'm sure you get the picture. Anyway, I ended up taking her to see it.'

If just one of the things he had told her this week was true, for certain this was it. Something about the softness of his features as he spoke of his mother gave him away — just the briefest letting down of his guard, but there to see, nonetheless.

Her own response was also truthful. 'I don't mind admitting to being envious. You can probably tell from the shade of green I'm turning. All *I've* managed to do is read about it in a magazine.'

As the band struck up a swing number, he caught the attention of a waiter and ordered drinks.

'Do go and see it if you get the chance,' he

said, raising his voice to be heard. 'That particular number is a triumph in the truest sense of the word.'

Discovering this snippet about him had her intrigued. 'Do you go to the cinema often?' The moment she asked, she wished she hadn't; picturing him taking a young woman to see a film made something inside of her curl up.

He shrugged indifferently. 'From time to time. But not often, no. I'm not the world's greatest fan.'

'You prefer to go dancing perhaps?' Oh, for heaven's sake, why was she torturing herself like this! A chap like him was bound to have a girlfriend. And what did it even matter if he had? He was about to be sent undercover into occupied France; as she kept reminding herself, there was no future for them.

'Haven't been dancing in years,' he said. 'And before you ask, yes, I did have lessons — my mother's doing. I realised later it was her way of ensuring I was in demand — you know, when competent dance partners were in short supply.'

She smiled. 'Astute of her.'

'Hm. Perhaps. Ah, here come our drinks.'

With the arrival of the waiter, she changed the subject. 'I keep thinking about our lovely lunch.'

'From the Kir at the start all the way through to the Armagnac at the end, it was quite superb, wasn't it?'

'And rather more sophisticated than the homely fare you sold it to me as.'

'I only sold it as homely because that was how it was sold to me — which must say rather a lot about that particular chap's idea of home.'

'Well, anyway,' she said, 'thank you again. It is a meal I shall remember for a long time to come.'

'As shall I.'

After that, they danced again, a couple of waltzes to slower numbers, her floor-length dress adding to the feel of romance as he led her around the floor. At the same time, she felt a creeping sadness such that, when the dance came to an end, she excused herself and went to the powder room. Unsurprisingly, she found it packed with glistening women repairing their make-up and was forced to wait for one of the basins to become free. When it did, she rinsed her hands under the tap, dried them, and stood staring at her reflection. Dinner and dancing — the epitome of romance. First Greg, and now Wallace — both of them men with whom she was tempted not to leave it at just that. It would be so easy not to: upstairs she had a magnificent room, and nothing and no one to stop her . . . and as everyone was always so quick to point out, by tomorrow they could all be dead.

Opening the clasp of her clutch bag, she pulled out her powder compact and dabbed at her nose. No. For all her odd little ways, Violette was right; the evenings she spent with these men were *not* dates, which was definitely how, with Wallace in particular, she was guilty of starting to view them. Violette was also right to say that she was in danger of blurring the lines between her work and her feelings. It didn't need a genius to spot that falling for her targets would make it difficult for her to remain objective — and that was without the toll it would wreak upon her own welfare. Yes, unpalatable though it was to accept, perhaps she should be grateful that Wallace was leaving tomorrow. Painful though it was going to be, she should look upon his departure as a reminder of why it was unwise to become so involved.

'Excuse me, but are you finished at the mirror?'

Realising where she was, Esme snapped her attention back to her reflection to see behind her a woman with blonde hair and smudged red lips.

'Forgive me, yes,' Esme said, dropping her lipstick back into her clutch and stepping aside. 'Go ahead.'

Not quite ready yet to return to the revelries, she pushed open the door and stood for a moment in the corridor. The band were bringing to a close their rendition of Glenn Miller's *Moonlight Serenade* — a dreamy tune that she utterly adored — and Wallace would be wondering where she was. Perhaps tomorrow, once he had left, she would go to Les Marronniers and patch things up with Violette — apologise for leaving in such a huff the other day. Handing in her report and talking through her findings with the Marrons would help to reinforce in her mind why she was here in the first place, help her to see this business with Wallace for what it was, and get herself back onto an even keel before taking on the next target.

Making her way back through the throng to

their table, she heard the band leader making the announcement that always brought groans from the dance floor. 'Ladies and gentlemen, for those of you not resident at The Aurelian, this evening's curfew is just this one last dance away'

'I'm afraid,' Wallace said, moving to stand with his hands behind his back, 'that has to be — '

'Your carriage. Yes.'

'Walk with me to the door?'

She nodded. 'Of course.'

When he proffered his arm, she took it. And, as they headed out of the ballroom towards the lobby, she tried more than once to rid herself of the horrible and familiar tightening in her throat.

'Thank you, Miss Fenella Wentworth,' he said, raising her fingers to his lips, 'for turning what could have been an unbearably dull week into an utterly enchanting one.'

'No,' she said, 'thank *you*.'

'It was just what I needed.'

She tried to make her smile appear natural but knew immediately that she hadn't succeeded. 'In a different time . . . '

He smiled back. 'In a different time.'

'Do take care when . . . well, wherever you go next.'

'I will. I promise.'

With that, he turned away and headed to where the doorman was assisting people out through the blackout curtain.

Concerned that she might be about to cry, she turned sharply in the direction of the lifts. Despite the rules, she wouldn't write up her report tonight; she would wait until the morning.

It wasn't as though a few hours were going to change her conclusion that *the target acquitted himself without incident, above suspicion, and proved himself to be entirely trustworthy.* That he was also the perfect gentleman and wonderful company, and that she had fallen for him completely, need be of no concern to anyone else — certainly not to Violette Marron, whose words the other day might just possibly have saved her from ruining her reputation as a first-class decoy.

8

Casualties

Knock-knock-knock. Knock-knock-knock. 'Miss Ward?'

Awoken from a vivid dream by someone at her door, Esme struggled to sit up, the wailing of an air raid siren immediately sending her spirits plummeting. Not again. Not more night-time bombing. It really was becoming too much to bear.

Hauling herself out of bed, she stumbled towards the door. 'Yes, all right,' she called back without opening it. 'I'll just get some things.'

'As quickly as you can please, Miss Ward.'

Retracing her steps to the bed, she switched on the lamp. Squinting against the brightness, she lifted her nightdress over her head, slipped on her camisole and then stepped into the siren suit she had taken to leaving ready on the ottoman at the foot of the bed. Picking up the overnight bag, left there for the same purpose, she pushed her feet into her shoes and went to the door.

Out in the corridor she found Mr Bancroft escorting two of the hotel's elderly residents to the lift. 'I'll take the stairs,' she said, catching sight of two other couples already waiting.

He nodded. Still in his dinner jacket, he didn't look as though he had even gone off duty yet.

'My staff will be waiting for you in the basement.'

Descending three flights of stairs, she arrived at the bottom to the sound of a Count Basie 78 being played at full volume and the sight of the night porter coming towards her. 'Would you like a bunk, miss?' he raised his voice above the music to ask.

The main shelter, set up like a cross between an underground club — complete with small stage — and a hotel lounge bar, was sizeable but, by virtue of its low ceiling, felt cramped and claustrophobic. Leading off it were two smaller rooms set up as dormitories, and a third containing lavatories, both apparently installed during the last war to accommodate staff in the event of an emergency that never came.

'What time is it?' she asked the porter.

'A little after midnight, miss.'

Hence the music, she thought, glancing about at the two dozen couples carrying on as though Supper Club was still in full swing. Pound to a penny none of them were married. Well, not to one another.

'A bunk? Yes, please. If there's one spare.'

'Mr Bancroft had me keep the one in the far corner for you.'

Going ahead of her, the porter opened a door. Beyond it, a dim nightlight picked out the forms of female guests settling into bunks. Although little more than timber frames bearing mattresses, they were kept made up with the hotel's best pillows and finest linens, each bunk having two clothes hooks on the wall and a small shelf for personal belongings.

'Thank you,' she said to the porter as he made to close the door behind her. 'Goodnight.'

With the help of the little torch she kept in her overnight bag, Esme squeezed her way between a couple of women organising their belongings. Reaching the farthest bunk, she climbed the ladder, put her bag on the shelf and slipped between the bedcovers. In the main room, someone quietened the gramophone. Pity they couldn't do the same with the laughter, she thought, listening to the unrestrained bellowing of several male guests. Not that she would be able to sleep even if they fell silent; having been awoken from a deep slumber, she was now fully alert.

Turning onto her side and wriggling herself comfortable, she found her thoughts wandering to Wallace. Hopefully he would have gone to whatever shelter arrangements were in place at his lodgings. Until the last fortnight or so, night-time air raid warnings had been routinely viewed as false alarms and often ignored altogether, the German bombers responsible for raising the warnings never troubling the coastal towns this far west. Over time, the seemingly false sirens had engendered in householders a reluctance to leave their comfy beds for the rudimentary provisions of their Anderson shelter. This last week, though, with bombs falling much closer by, few people now chanced remaining in their homes, no matter the hour or the inconvenience. In all likelihood, she reflected, Wallace would have heeded the siren and headed to safety. Safety. Huh. There was irony; by protecting himself from an air raid, he would simply be saving himself for even greater danger in France. Despite knowing that his role within SOE was critical to the overall success of operations, she still thought it criminal to risk the life of such a good man, the knowledge that he would be in possession of a suicide pill — sorry, *lethal tablet* — only making it worse.

In the confines of her bunk, she wriggled onto her back. Somewhere nearby, someone was snoring softly. Lucky them. Having now unsettled herself with thoughts of Wallace heading for France, she would never get to sleep.

In a bid to distract herself, she tried thinking about Lou instead. She really should have made the effort to telephone her sooner. At least she felt better for knowing she was all right, and was glad she had sounded so joyful. With the way things appeared to have worked out for her, failing to convince her to come 'on the run' wasn't the shame it might have been. During those first few weeks in Wimbledon — while she'd had no idea what she was going to do to support herself — Lou's presence would have been a liability. Furthermore, since her dear cousin didn't have a single dishonest bone in her body, she would never have been cut out for this life of subterfuge. It had been risky enough, that night she'd left Clarence Square, trusting her not to blab about her disappearance to the Colbornes.

Wishing the confined little room didn't feel so stuffy, Esme returned to lying on her side. She still couldn't believe she'd found the courage to leave that night — most definitely couldn't believe the manner in which she'd done so! Unfortunately, it was the nature of her departure she regretted most; pretty much straightaway, she had regretted not stopping long enough to explain to Richard why she felt unable to go through with the wedding. Not that he would have understood. None of them would have.

How was Richard now, she wondered? Did he pine for her or did he despise her? Despite her mother writing that he might be willing to take her back, he clearly hadn't felt sufficiently moved to pen a letter himself, leaving her only able to assume that Naomi had been wrong, and that he wanted nothing more to do with her. She sighed heavily. He would have made a good husband — he was kind, handsome, nicely set up in a respectable job — but, as she often reminded herself, it was better this way. Besides, she was devoting herself to war valuable work. She couldn't have it all.

Finally beginning to feel drowsy, she plumped her pillow and tried to make herself comfortable. With her mind on relationships gone by the wayside — and her part in putting them there — her thoughts turned to Violette. Now *there* was a friendship she *could* repair. *Should* repair. After all, Violette only ever looked out for her. So perhaps, tomorrow, she would go and make amends, apologise for having lost her temper, and patch things up. Furthermore, while she was putting things to rights, she would also banish from her thoughts, once and for all, her girlish infatuation with Wallace. In fact, now would be a good time to bury *all* of her recent mistakes: to learn from them and to move on; see to it she treated her next target —

Wheeeee. Thud-thud.

She stiffened. Bombs exploding. Somewhere close by. And they never came in just ones and twos. She held her breath.

Wheeeee. Thud-thud.

Thud.

The force of the last explosion shook her bed. Two further thuds rattled the door in its frame. Plaster rained down from the ceiling. The night light went out. Belatedly there came a response from the big guns: pom, pom, pom. Pom, pom, pom.

'Close tonight,' a woman observed from within the darkness.

With that, the door opened and a yellowy beam of light from a torch roved the floor, the walls, the ceiling.

'No cause for alarm, ladies.' The voice belonged to Mr Bancroft. As usual, he sounded unruffled. With her heart still pounding, Esme wondered whether he was still in evening dress. Nerves, she told herself, recognising the absurdity of her concern. 'My apologies, but we appear to have lost the electricity. I've sent someone to see to the generator. Shouldn't be too long.'

After that, with everything beyond their little haven returning to silence, some of the women settled back down and went to sleep — she could tell from the pattern of their breathing.

But, knowing she wouldn't be so fortunate, Esme lay rigidly, able only to hope that dawn wasn't too far off.

After another half an hour or so, during which the electricity didn't return, Mr Bancroft once again opened the door to announce in a whisper that the All Clear had sounded and that anyone who wished to do so could return to their room. Having failed to sleep a wink since the explosions, Esme gathered her belongings and climbed down from her bunk. Guided up the stairs and back to her room by a bell boy with a torch, she wasted no time in stripping off her siren suit and climbing back into her own bed.

Three thirty, the luminous hands on her alarm clock said. Ages yet till dawn. But maybe, she thought as she tried to get comfortable, having had some fun, the Luftwaffe would now return home and allow them all to get some much-needed sleep.

★ ★ ★

Knock-knock-knock. Knock-knock-knock. 'Miss Ward?'

Please don't let this be another air raid warning, Esme thought, forcing her eyes open and casting about in the darkness for the switch to the lamp.

Knock-knock-knock.

'Yes, yes. I'm coming,' she called, pushing back the covers and noticing that she must have forgotten to wind her alarm clock because it had stopped at eight thirty. Eight thirty? She glanced over her shoulder to the windows but, so efficient were the blackout curtains that she had no way of telling whether it was daylight.

Stopping just short of the door, she tied her wrap and then reached to turn the key in the lock. Waiting to greet her was Mr Bancroft with one of the young waiters from the restaurant. And she could smell coffee.

'Good morning, Miss Ward. I apologise for disturbing you, but may I come in?'

Too bleary to even enquire why, she stood aside and watched, puzzled, as the waiter crossed the room and proceeded to set out the contents of his tray. When Mr Bancroft then closed the door behind the waiter's departing back, Esme studied his face. It looked greyer than usual — as though he hadn't managed even a moment's sleep.

'Mr Bancroft, is everything all right?' Something about his expression made her steel herself against the possibility that it wasn't.

His response was to turn to the windows. 'May I draw the curtains?'

She shrugged. 'Of course.'

Squinting against the ensuing brightness, she realised that her clock hadn't stopped at all; the day was well under way.

Turning back and glancing about the room, Raymond Bancroft went to switch off the lamp and then gestured to the sofa.

Dutifully, she sat down.

'Miss Ward,' he said, lowering himself alongside her and proceeding to pour the coffee, 'I'm afraid I bring bad news. One of last night's bombs fell on Les Marronniers.'

Watching him put one of the cups of coffee in front of her on the table, she fought to understand what he had just said. 'Les Marronniers? Golly. Was anyone hurt?'

His expression didn't alter. 'I'm afraid it was a direct hit. The entire terrace was destroyed.'

She felt her throat tighten. 'But Madame Marron . . . and Violette . . . they *are* all right?'

He looked straight at her. 'I'm afraid not. Volunteers searching the rubble have recovered the bodies of two women.'

Reaching to the arm of the sofa, she gripped it hard. 'But are they . . . '

'I'm afraid they are those of Madame and Violette Marron.'

No. No, that couldn't be! It just couldn't. She had been going there this morning to see them, to apologise to Violette. 'Has anyone checked their shelter?'

Mr Bancroft gave an almost indiscernible nod. 'Their shelter was empty. The position of their bodies among the rubble suggests they had been on the top floor of the building, which would have been close to where the bomb landed. Occupants from the other three properties in the terrace were found unharmed in their shelters.'

The only feeling Esme could make sense of was disbelief. 'But it *could* still be that they are alive . . . '

'I'm sorry, Miss Ward, but no. The moment word reached me I went straight there, my intention being to collect them and bring them to stay here. Regrettably, the only thing I could do for them was confirm their identities to the authorities.'

Feeling as though she had been punched in the midriff, Esme doubled over and let out a low moan. 'So . . . where are they now?'

'Their bodies have been removed to a relief centre set up in St. Margaret's. As soon as I have seen to a few things here, I shall be going back there to complete the formalities.'

'Then if you can wait while I dress, I'll come with you — '

'Miss Ward, while I fully understand why you would want to, I'm afraid I cannot let you do that. I have instructions that you are to remain here.'

'Instructions? Whose instructions?'

Ignoring her challenge, Mr Bancroft contin- ued. 'Ordinarily in these circumstances, I would offer to call a family member to come and be with you, but, in your case, I appreciate that isn't possible. With that in mind, I have spoken to SOE. They are sending a Miss Black. I'm told you've met her.'

Esme nodded. 'Miss Black. Yes.'

'Until then, if you would prefer not to be alone, I can have one of our ladies come and sit with you. Or I could ask someone from the WVS if you would rather.'

Esme shook her head. She didn't want a stranger sitting with her. She didn't want Miss Black either, truth be told. 'Why is Miss Black coming? What can she do that I can't?'

'As I understand it, she is coming to take charge of the necessary arrangements. She will

261

know, better than I, for what the rules do and do not allow.'

The rules. Yes. Of course. Even in death there were rules. 'Then if I can't come with you, forgive me but I think I should like to be alone.'

'Yes, of course,' Mr Bancroft said. 'But should you want anything, anything at all, just ring down to reception and someone will come straight up.'

With Mr Bancroft letting himself out, Esme climbed back into bed. But only when she had heard him turn the key in the lock did she let out an anguished howl and start to cry. The bloody unfairness of it! Dear, kindly Violette. Dead. Killed by a German bomb. And the last words she had said to her, and which there could now be no taking back, had been designed to hurt.

★　★　★

If only she could run faster. If only she wasn't so out of breath. If only the building didn't keep getting further away! The enemy bombers were close now, the thrum of their engines making her ribs vibrate, the constant wailing of the air raid siren jarring her head. But there! There was Violette — waving from that little window on the top floor. She would shout up to her that the German bombers were coming, warn her to go to the shelter. But the harder she tried to shout, the more her lips fastened themselves shut. Unable to make a sound, she waved her arms above her head. Go to the shelter! But Violette was simply smiling and waving back . . . and the bombers were really close now, droning low above her head . . .

Shooting up from her pillow, Esme gasped for breath. She looked frantically about. Her room: thank God, she was in her room. It had been a nightmare, that was all.

Finding her camisole stuck to her skin and her hair damp about her face, she threw back the covers, lowered her legs over the side of the bed and reached for her wrap. But then, spotting the tray of coffee things on the table, she froze, her throat constricting at the sight of it, a dull ache of recognition returning to her chest. Violette was dead. Les Marronniers had been hit by a German bomb. Those few seconds of relief upon discovering she'd been dreaming had been a false dawn. In those few moments, the truth had escaped her. But now it was as though Violette had died all over again. And the pain was tearing her in two.

Slumping onto the side of the bed, she hung her head. Yes, Violette was dead, which meant that either she could dwell upon her loss and wrestle with the *if onlys*, or else she could get up and get on with it. Even befogged by grief, she knew it had to be the latter. Dwelling would do no one any good. It certainly wouldn't bring back Violette or Madame Marron. Nothing would. So, she would get dressed, see Miss Black when she arrived, and explain that it was her wish to carry on as usual.

To do any of that, though, she needed to look presentable. She turned towards the clock: eleven fifteen. Time to get moving.

263

Trudging to the bathroom, her head pounding, she pressed the plug into the bath and turned on both taps. Leaving the water running, she went to the chest of drawers and pulled out clean underwear. Then she went back to the bathroom, filled the toothglass with water, forced herself to drink the contents and then brushed her teeth. With no idea what would happen without the Marrons, she must expect things to be different. Their absence would mean changes, but she would take them in her stride. She would rise to the challenge. She owed it to them.

As soon as there was a couple of inches of water in the bath, she got in and sank low. Then, as the water level around her rose gradually higher, she dunked her head, the feel of the warm water on her scalp bringing momentary relief from the hammering going on inside. Even so, she still couldn't think beyond one action at a time: soap her body; shampoo her hair; rinse it with clean water from the hose attachment. Pull the plug. Get dry. Whether the result of fatigue or shock she didn't know, but everything seemed to need phenomenal effort.

With her head swathed in a towel, she stood in front of the mirror. Now what did she do? At the very least her hair needed rolling up and drying. Crossing to the desk, she picked up the telephone receiver.

'Switchboard? This is Miss Ward in room 303. Please put me through me to your hair salon.' Arrangements made for someone to come and see to her hair, she once again dialled the switchboard. 'Housekeeping, this is Miss Ward in room 303. I'm afraid your chambermaid was unable to gain access to clean my room earlier. Could you please send someone up in say . . . one hour? Yes, twelve thirty would be fine. And would you have such a thing as a black armband? For mourning, yes. Thank you. You have been most helpful.'

Later, once her hair had been styled and her room was shipshape, the telephone rang.

'Sorry to disturb you, Miss Ward. This is Billy at the concierge desk. I have someone here asking to see you. She says her name is Miss Black. Should I show her up or would you prefer to come down?' Agreeing that she would go down to the lobby, Esme pulled on her jacket and made a cursory check of her appearance. It was good job she'd brought her navy-blue suit. In the absence of a black outfit that was neither cocktail nor evening wear, it was just about sombre enough to pass for mourning. Her hair looked better, too, she decided, turning to examine it from several angles — a bit matronly but at least it was clean and tidy.

As soon as the doors of the lift opened at the ground floor, she spotted Miss Black and headed towards her.

'Miss Ward. Thank you for coming down to see me. The news was so deeply shocking that I came straightaway in case . . . well, in case you needed anything.'

As usual, Miss Black was wearing a plain grey skirt and jacket over a white blouse. On her sleeve was a black crepe band.

'Thank you.'

'Tell me, how are you holding up?'

Esme gave a slow shake of her head. 'It hasn't sunk in yet.'

'Don't suppose it has. Look, have you eaten anything?'

She tried to remember. 'I don't think so. It was a badly disturbed night and I seem to have slept through most of the morning.'

'Well, look, how about we get something to eat and have a chat. Not a full-blown three-course meal — '

'We could go to the Orangerie,' Esme said. 'At this time of day, they'll be serving light lunches.'

'Sounds perfect. Lead on.'

Seated at a table in the Orangerie, two dishes ordered from the menu, Esme felt better for having some company. In the last hour or so, sitting with her head under a dryer, she'd realised just how little she'd known about Violette and Madame Marron. With both of them now gone — *oh, dear God, they were gone!* — it seemed only respectful to discover something of their backgrounds.

'Did the Marrons have family?' she asked once the waiter had left their table. Only then did it occur to her that their name probably wasn't even Marron.

'Not according to the details they gave when they signed up, no.'

'So . . . Violette's father . . . '

'We don't know. The box on her form for his details was left blank. And Madame Marron gave her marital status as 'single'.'

'Oh.' Well, that raised more questions than it

answered! Now it felt as though she had been given a puzzle with several pieces missing, the result being that, despite being tantalisingly close, she would never fully appreciate the complete picture.

'So . . .' But the question in her mind was one she could barely bring herself to ask. 'So, what will happen about . . . the arrangements?'

'With Mr Bancroft's help at this end, SOE will take care of the funerals. We haven't discussed it yet but, in the absence of the Marrons seeming to have a connection to anywhere else, I should imagine they will be buried here, in Brighton.'

What a sad state of affairs, Esme reflected: no family to know you had died; no one to speak as to your wishes. Awful.

'What was her real name — Violette, I mean?'

Miss Black looked torn. 'You know I can't tell you that.'

'But it wasn't Violette, was it?'

Miss Black gave the slightest shake of her head. And then, leaning across the table, she whispered, 'The name in her file is Valerie. But you didn't learn that from me.'

Valerie. Yes, she could see Violette answering to that. Valerie. Pretty.

When their food arrived — a grilled fillet of Dover sole with new potatoes and peas for Miss Black, and a plain omelette served with mushrooms and asparagus tips for herself — they ate for a while before Esme asked, 'So what will happen now — with the operation, I mean?'

Finishing her mouthful, Miss Black brought her knife and fork to rest on her plate. 'The target who was due here on Monday has been told not to travel — has been told the situation in Brighton isn't safe at the moment and that we can't risk losing a fully trained operative. Since he didn't know he was coming here to be assessed, it's all he needs know. Either way, we think you should take this week as leave. You're welcome to stay here at The Aurelian, but just take some time to grieve while we work out what to do going forward.'

It wasn't what Esme wanted to hear. 'I'd rather work,' she said. 'I'd feel better carrying on, using the skills the Marrons taught me — honouring their memory, so to speak.'

Miss Black smiled. 'I'm sure you would. And I'm not saying that I don't understand, but it's not that simple.'

'Actually,' Esme said, surprised by how determined she suddenly felt, 'It's perfectly simple. You forward the file for my assignment to Mr Bancroft and then, at the end of the week, I give it back to him. It's not as though I don't know what I'm doing now. If an unexpected situation does arise, I can always telephone you or Mr White.' Granted, it would be peculiar operating without the Marrons, but she wasn't going to let their demise bring the operation to a close, certainly not without a fight. Violette would have expected no less.

'Actually, Miss Ward, when I said it wasn't that simple, I wasn't speaking from an SOE standpoint. I was talking about giving you some time to come to terms with what has happened, to grieve.'

Esme tensed. Grieve? Her? 'Oh, no . . . I'm not the sort of person to lie about, weeping and grief-stricken. I'm more the sort to work on, to — '

'I don't doubt you feel that way now — feel you can simply continue, possibly even believe yourself more determined than ever. But I can tell you from experience, Miss Ward, grief is a peculiar beast. It doesn't play by the rules or work to a timetable. It is not easily blunted. At this moment, you are still in shock. But, once the news sinks in — properly, I mean — and the shocks fades, you will find yourself in a state of denial . . . and after that, most likely anger. All of which are entirely natural but not conducive to carrying on as normal, especially in your line of work, where you cannot even be yourself, let alone confide in anyone. So, take this week and do with it as you please. If there is somewhere you would like to travel, let me know and I will arrange for a rail warrant. As for the decoy operation, I'm inclined to agree with you. Going forward, you should be able to operate with only minimal support. That being the case, I will relay your wishes to HQ and get back to you at the end of the week.'

'You'll send me details of a new target next weekend,' Esme pressed.

'It's certainly possible. In the meantime, do as I've said. And if you find yourself in need of someone to talk to, or you need help of any variety, call me. That's an order.'

When Miss Black had settled the bill and taken her leave, Esme went back up to her room and, for want of something better to do, went out onto her balcony. There, she drew deep breaths of the briny air. Grief. Hm. Violette and Madame Marron deserved to be mourned, but that was different from grieving. Mourning someone's passing was about showing your respect, which she could surely do best by continuing to operate as they had trained her to. Grief, on the other hand, was about indulging personal feelings — not a habit she viewed as particularly helpful, even less so in a time of war.

Staring out across the gently undulating waters of the Channel, and picturing the sky above it filled with the dark specks of German bomber formations, she came to a decision. Since she had been given no choice, she would treat this week as time to rest. If nothing else, she would catch up on some sleep. But she would *not* spend the time in tears or lamenting her loss. Not only would the Marrons have been dismayed by such carrying on from her, it simply wasn't who she was.

★ ★ ★

She didn't know what had drawn her there. All she knew was that she had felt the need to go to Les Marronniers and see for herself what had happened. Guessing that anyone she told of her intention would try to stop her, she mentioned to no one where she was going, simply walking out through the hotel entrance as though going for a stroll. Since it would take less than five

270

minutes to get there, she would be back in no time.

Nothing, though, had prepared her for what she would see, such that, when she turned the final corner, she stumbled to a halt and gasped. The entire regency terrace, the farthest end of which had been occupied by Les Marronniers, was completely gone. The only section even recognisable as having once been a dwelling was the end closest to her, where the gable wall was still standing to the level of the first floor. The rest was nothing more than a mound of rubble: bricks, roof tiles, window frames. A washbasin attached to a small section of tiled wall. A bedstead. Scraps of fabric that could have been curtains or, just as easily, bedclothes. Picking his way across it all, prodding with a long metal rod, was a workman wearing blue overalls and the steel helmet of an air raid warden. The sight of him stabbing away made her want to yell at him to stop. It might be the way rescuers checked for people still trapped, but it was also disrespectful; those were people's belongings he was clambering over. Somewhere among the lumps of masonry and fractured lengths of timber would be Madame Marron's jewellery — the ornate brooches she favoured: the oval one with the garnet surrounded by sprays of diamante; the jade-coloured enamel one in the shape of a fan that had a pair of matching earrings. And somewhere in the devastation would be Violette's poetry books, one or two of them first editions. And there he was, that warden, prodding away as though it was all nothing more than rubbish. At least they had recovered their bodies, she found herself thinking, the idea of them being sniffed out by stray dogs or, worse still, found by rats . . . well . . .

Her vision blurred by tears, she reached out and, clutching at a railing, fought down the urge to be sick. Ridiculous though it seemed, she hadn't been expecting the destruction to be so complete; Les Marronniers had been completely obliterated. Its two occupants wouldn't have stood a chance.

Keeping to the pavement, she edged a dozen or so paces closer. On this side of the street, council workmen were boarding up windows damaged by the blast while a woman in a flowery housecoat stood sweeping glass into a shovel that she periodically emptied into a dustbin.

When the woman saw her approaching, Esme raised a weak smile. 'Did everyone on this side of the road escape unharmed?' she asked. Having caught the woman's eye, it seemed only polite to enquire.

The woman nodded. 'Silly fool next door was blown off his feet and cut by flying glass, but no worse than he deserved. Daft beggar won't ever go down the shelter.'

'But everyone else is all right?'

'No thanks to the damn Luftwaffe. The ARPs reckon the bombs were intended for the railway station. Me, I think it more likely some ruddy pilot couldn't be bothered going all the way to his proper target and thought he'd dump his load and scarper while he could, before the ack-acks got him. Bloody cowards, the lot of 'em.'

In a way, Esme hoped the woman was wrong. It was unfair enough that the Marrons had been killed, but to think of them having died simply because the pilot couldn't be bothered to find his proper target made it even worse.

'I knew the people in the house at the end,' she said. She hadn't meant to; the admission just sort of slipped out.

'Those two teacher ladies?'

Esme nodded. 'They were mother and daughter.'

Leaning her broom against the railing, the woman came down the steps to the pavement. 'Oh, love, I'm sorry to hear that. Friends of yours, were they?'

Feeling more tears welling, Esme bowed her head. 'Yes.'

'Look, dearie, I might not have any glass in my windows, but I've a kettle and some tea. And you look like you could do with a cup. So, come on, in you come.'

To her own surprise, Esme went along with the stranger's suggestion, allowing the woman to lead her up the steps, along the passage and through to her kitchen. Beyond the blown-out window, in a back yard that was little more than twenty feet in either direction, her attention was caught by the mound of earth covering the Anderson shelter. From it was growing a clump of dandelions, a single bloom blazing the most vivid of yellows in the sunlight.

'Do you always go down to your shelter?' she

asked. 'Every time the siren goes?'

Looking at the woman in profile as she stood filling her kettle from the tap, Esme tried to guess her age. With her hair tucked out of sight under a navy-blue turban, and her lips painted an orangey scarlet that did little to flatter her complexion, it was hard to tell. If pushed, she would say she was in her late forties.

'Without fail, love,' the woman replied. 'Blowed if I'm going to let the Germans take *me* out. I lost my father and all three of my brothers to them in that last business. So, when this latest quarrel started up, I made a vow. Winnie, I said to myself, they've taken enough of us Carters. Don't let them get you, too.'

Esme managed a smile. At least she now knew her benefactor's name. 'Good for you,' she said. 'But I'm sorry you lost so many of your family. My father, my uncle, and my aunt's husband all fought, too. All of them were injured . . . one way or another . . . but at least they all made it back home.'

'Sit down, love,' Winnie directed, pulling out one of two chairs tucked under the kitchen table. 'Tea's just brewing. No, first moment I hear that siren, I'm down the garden quicker than you can say Hermann Goering.'

And that's why she was still here, Esme thought — living proof of the wisdom of heeding the warnings. So, why, oh why, hadn't Violette done the same? Why, when it came to air raids, had she always been so gung-ho? *They won't be aiming for us*, she was forever saying. *Even if it is a real raid, and not yet another false alarm, we'll be fine.*

She wished now she had remonstrated more strongly with her — had pointed out that firstly, no one could possibly know for whom the Germans were aiming and, secondly, as casualty figures attested, even the most committed of bombers sometimes missed their targets. And that was without taking into account those who simply didn't care if innocent civilians died — probably even rejoiced when they did. So, yes, why couldn't Violette, just this once, have got out of her bed and gone to the shelter? It wasn't as though they'd had the bother of trudging along the street to a public one. Nor was it the middle of winter and freezing cold. It hadn't even been raining. The inconvenience would have cost her nothing but a few minutes of her time. Instead, it had cost both of them their lives.

'Thank you,' she said when Winnie put a thick pottery cup and saucer on the table in front of her. The contents of it were the colour of Heinz Baked Beans.

'No sugar but there's a hefty dollop of condensed in there. Good for the shock.'

Used to drinking Earl Grey with a slice of lemon in the mornings, and Darjeeling in the afternoons, Esme stared at her cup. No matter how it tasted, somehow, she was going to have to drink every last drop of it. Tea, she had recently discovered from Violette, was the latest thing to have *gone on the ration*, and amounted to just two ounces per person per week. And yet here was a woman she didn't know, not thinking twice about offering to brew her a cup.

'Sweet tea, yes,' she said. 'Good for shock.'

Somehow, by taking rather large mouthfuls, she managed to drink it and, after what she felt was a decent amount of small talk, prepared to take her leave.

'Feeling a little less wobbly?' Winnie enquired as the pair of them got to their feet.

'Yes,' she said. 'And thank you so much for the tea. It was incredibly kind of you.'

'Think nothing of it, love.'

'Please, do keep heeding the sirens.'

'Have no fear on that score, love. Not after this close shave.'

Picking her way through the remaining shards of glass on the front step, Esme glanced again at the pile of rubble where Les Marronniers should have been.

Bubbling away inside her was a cauldron of emotions, shock swirling around with sadness, hatred bubbling around denial. Recognising that any one of those had the power to reduce her to tears, she bit hard on her tongue, ducked her head, and walked quickly back to the corner of the street. From there, she kept walking, not fully looking up again until she was back in the lobby of The Aurelian, where, since there was already a young couple already waiting for the lift, she trotted up the three flights of stairs and let herself into her room without having had to converse with anyone.

Dragging the curtains across the window, she undressed, pulled back the eiderdown from the bed and got in. Finally, she was alone. Finally, she could cry. Finally, she could weep for

Madame Marron, and for Violette, whose refusal to see sense had cost *them* their lives and her, Esme, two of her dearest friends.

★ ★ ★

Why was she in darkness? Moments ago, when she had got into bed, chinks of daylight had been showing through the gap between the curtains. But now the room was completely dark. Uncertainly, she lifted her head and turned towards her clock. Quarter past ten? She had been asleep six hours? *Six hours?*

Carefully she pulled herself upright. Her throat was parched and her head pounding. Fumbling about, she found the lamp and switched it on. Blinking several times and spotting that her curtains weren't fully drawn across the windows, she hastily clicked it off again; the last thing she needed was a reprimand for not observing the blackout. Crossing to the window, she risked parting the curtains; everywhere outside was pitch black. Without much thought, she opened the door and stepped out onto the balcony. Left and right along the coast, searchlights were performing their night-time ballet, while, straight ahead, out over the open sea, she could see stars twinkling against the velvety blackness. It was the strange thing about war, she decided, folding her arms about her waist, that while the activities of humankind grew ghastlier and more threatening by the day, nature went on as though nothing had changed. The sun rose and set. The tides turned. People came into the world and people departed.

Shivering in the light breeze, and realising that she was wearing only her slip, she let herself back in through the door, secured the blackout blinds and drew the curtains. Then she felt her way across to the bed and switched on the lamp. Finding its light dim and depressing, she went about the room, switching on all the remaining lights. Yes, it was a criminal waste to have so many light bulbs burning, but nowhere near as great a waste as the loss of Violette.

Feeling her stomach grumbling and realising that she hadn't eaten since her lunch with Miss Black, she picked up the telephone and asked whether it was possible to have a rack of toast and a pot of tea. The kitchen was just closing, she was told, but for her, yes, of course it was possible.

For company while she munched on her toast, she turned on the radio. The programme being aired was a play and, since it was already more than halfway through, she turned it off again. Instead, she picked up the morning's newspaper, as yet still unopened. *Terrific Air Battles Over London*, a headline on the first page read. Reports further down were just as grim. *Scores of Bombs Dropped by German Raiders. Seventy-one Shot Down.* And then, more worryingly still, *German plan to disable military targets fails. South London suburbs bear the brunt. Shops, homes, railway stations hit.* Was this, the newspaper wanted to know, the pre-cursor to a German invasion?

Briefly, she skimmed the remaining pages

until, desperate to hear something that put matters in a less terrifying light, she switched on the radio again, this time for the midnight news broadcast. At that moment, the station was replaying part of an earlier speech by Alfred Duff-Cooper, Winston Churchill's Minister of Information. But he, too, was talking about a German invasion, appearing almost to mock Hitler, goad him even, saying that the nation was ready for him, and that all would be disappointed if he didn't turn up. Finding the man's rhetoric not in the least comforting, with a flick of the knob she silenced him. And then she lay on the bed, staring at the ceiling: so many worries crowding her mind and no one with whom to discuss them. Ordinarily, Madame Marron would have had a soothing observation to offer, while Violette would instantly have dismissed the very notion of Hitler invading as nonsense, pooh-poohing it and suggesting that to take their minds from the possibility, they go to a matinee and then for an ice — if one was to be had. *The searching is half the fun*, she would have said. Equally, if it was reassurance in the form of calm facts she was after, then Wallace — or even Greg — would have provided her with a rational assessment of the situation. It was always something she had liked about Richard, too — the way that he could take her fears and, through presentation of the facts, dissolve them away. Despite the way things had turned out, she did hope he was safe; Whitehall would surely be one of the Luftwaffe's primary targets.

Not in the least tired, she continued flicking

the pages of the newspaper back and forth, pausing to read things as they caught her eye. Seeing on the theatre pages that *A Midsummer's Night Dream* was playing at the Open Air Theatre in Regent's Park, she suddenly felt wistful, recalling how, last year, she had seen an open-air production of Romeo & Juliet. Higher up the same page, she noted that Daphne du Maurier's *Rebecca* was still playing at the Queen's. It starred Celia Johnson, Margaret Rutherford and Owen Nares. Just after Easter, when it had been due to open, Richard had suggested getting tickets for them to go and see it. Somehow, arrangements for the wedding had got in the way and they never had made it. By all accounts, it was enjoying great success.

Eventually, with her eyes growing heavy from peering at the newsprint, she tidied the bed, applied cold cream to her face and wiped it away, brushed her teeth, extinguished the lights, and lay down to sleep.

With the arrival of the following day, though, she still felt entirely without purpose. The weather was glorious, turning out to be everything an English summer's day should be, which, for a Sunday at the height of the holiday season, only made the deserted promenade and the empty beaches seem even more unreal. For something to do, she took a late breakfast in the Orangerie, where the irony of having run out of orange juice wasn't lost on her good-humoured waiter, and where Mr Bancroft asked whether she might like to join him for lunch. Looking down at the food on her plate and seeing from her wristwatch that it was already after eleven o'clock, she thanked him for the kind offer but declined. Instead, she went for a walk. Not wishing to stray too far from the hotel in case of an air raid, she went to sit in a nearby park, where, for a while, she watched two young girls taking it in turns with a skipping rope, and kept a watchful eye on two similarly-aged boys sitting high up in the branches of one of the plane trees. But none of it distracted her for long; within moments she found herself thinking it was all very well Miss Black telling her to treat the week as leave while she came to terms with the loss of Madame Marron and Violette, but it wasn't that straightforward. With nothing to do, her mind was going to keep dwelling. And it wasn't only about the Marrons, either. Having read about the bombing raids on London, and the aerial battles that had cost one hundred German aircraft, and one hundred and thirty-six British ones, she wasn't surprised to find Richard once again in her thoughts. It could just be grief playing with her mind, she told herself — a natural reaction to losing someone close. Either way, she needed to be busy. She couldn't drift without purpose for much longer.

After two further days spent lurching from frustration to pity, and from certainty to doubt, she turned on the radio one evening to hear the address Winston Churchill had given to parliament earlier that afternoon. With the whole country now fully expecting the Germans to invade, and with the RAF fighting what was being referred to as the Battle of Britain, he was clearly aiming to engender in the public renewed confidence about the war effort. When he went on to say, 'Never in the field of human conflict was so much owed by so many to so few', she knew she had to stop flailing about. Grief and grieving be damned! She had to get back to work. Her part in the war effort might be miniscule, but a part it was, all the same.

Lifting the receiver to the telephone, she spoke to the switchboard operator.

'Croydon 512, please. Yes, I'll hold.'

Unsurprisingly, it was Miss Teal who answered. 'I'll put you through to Miss Black now,' she said.

'Miss Ward, is everything all right?'

'In the sense that you probably mean, then yes,' Esme said to her. 'But in the sense of me needing a reason to get up each morning then no, it's not. So, I'm calling to ask that you resume sending targets for evaluation.'

'Right-ho. Understood. If you're certain that's what you want.'

'I am. And it is.'

'Expect a file on Sunday.'

'Thank you.'

Replacing the receiver, Esme raised her eyebrows in disbelief. If she'd known it was going to be *that* simple, she would have asked sooner. Now she could stop wallowing in indecision and regret and get back to work. Now she could resume doing her bit. She might not be able to help the Battle of Britain by flying a Hurricane, or one of those new Spitfires, but she *could* make sure SOE's covert operatives were fit to play their parts in France. Madame Marron and Violette would have expected nothing less.

9

The Proposal

Esme glanced at her wristwatch. Already it was seven o'clock; less than an hour and it would be getting dark. And, if the last couple of days were anything to go by, then less than an hour after *that*, the first of the night's air raid sirens would force her to seek shelter in the basement again. It was vital, therefore, that she rein in her thoughts and finish her report on this week's target.

It was now two weeks since the bombing of Les Marronniers and the loss of Violette and Madame Marron, and ten days since she had attended their funerals. In a small Victorian chapel within the cemetery, together with Miss Black and Mr Bancroft, she had sat through the brief service and then witnessed the interments into adjacent plots on the hillside. A couple of miles from the town centre, the only thing Esme thought the Marrons would have liked about the location was the speck of sea just visible on the far horizon. Apart from that, she found the cemetery characterless and utilitarian — the sort of place no one aspired to end up but where you grudgingly conceded you would have to be buried because you had to be *laid to rest* somewhere. For two people who had so recently been serving their country, it didn't seem in the least bit fitting.

The burials complete, the little party of mourners had returned to The Aurelian for a memorial luncheon, held in the hotel's Golden Palm restaurant. It had been a sombre affair, just the three of them, each seemingly preoccupied, the atmosphere not in the least noisy and celebratory as she thought Violette would have preferred. *Sing. Laugh. Imbibe.* Those were the instructions she could hear a despairing Violette yelling at them.

Reining back her thoughts yet again, she looked down at the file in front of her. This last week her mind had been all over the place, such that she was struggling to recall any details with which to support her recommendation. And SOE did like to read specifics. Lance Edwards, aged thirty-three, a history teacher from Bromley with a classical education — five languages to his name including Latin and Greek — and with a passion for all things military. Unsurprisingly, he had turned out to be just as dull as she had been expecting. *Initially reluctant to engage,* she wrote in the box on the form entitled 'Observations Pertaining to Manner and Appearance'. Further down the page she added, *Suitably unassuming. Intense. Unforthcoming. No desire to impress. Lived up to his profile without even trying.* But had that been, she wondered as she finished that last sentence, all part of the act? Had the real man behind the profile done as instructed and thrown himself fully into the role of academic? What did it matter, she thought, reaching the box headed 'Recommendation' and crossing through the various pre-printed statements so that it read *Unlikely to betray purpose*. Finally, having written the word *Recommended*, she signed her name and closed the file.

In a moment she would go downstairs and find Mr Bancroft — consign the real person behind the false identity of Lance Edwards to his fate in France. And then, on Monday, she would start all over again with yet another new target.

With no visits to the Marrons to brighten her days, Esme had begun to feel isolated and alone, her time filled with nothing but the seriousness — and, increasingly, the dullness — of assessing targets. Life seemed to have become nothing more than a repeating round of sleep, idle, worry, work. Sleep, idle, worry, work. But it was no one else's fault; *she* had been the one to say she could do this on her own.

'Would you like to join me at Supper Club?' Mr Bancroft enquired when she went to deliver the folder containing her report. Already, chatty young women in silks and diamonds were being escorted on the arm of their partners to the ballroom. 'Just for supper if you like. I would see to it that you weren't troubled.'

By that, she knew he meant he would ensure she wasn't harassed by requests to dance from unaccompanied RAF officers.

'Thank you for the kind invitation,' she replied without even needing to think about it, 'but I'm afraid I'm not in the mood for merriment. It feels . . . '

'Too soon?'

She nodded. 'I knew you would understand.'

'Then choose something to eat from the menu

and I'll have it sent up. Come,' he said, seeing her reluctance, 'even amid the fog of grief one still has to eat.'

In the end, upstairs on her balcony, she sat in the fading light with a bowl of bouillabaisse that had arrived with a basket containing thin slices of French baguette and a tiny ramekin of olive oil into which to dip them. Fragrant with the scents of the Mediterranean — of fennel, citrus, Pernod and saffron — the broth was rich with perfectly cooked chunks of red mullet, monkfish, gurnard and what she suspected to be John Dory. Savouring every mouthful of it, she was glad to have gone with Mr Bancroft's recommendation.

Away to her right, she watched the sunset slowly deepening through shades of apricot and lemon to crimson and indigo while, to her left, there rose a bomber's moon. The latter would mean another noisy night in the basement — such a criminal waste of an evening that might, ordinarily, for other people at least, have been heady with the promise of romance.

Looking down and spotting the first of the DVF wardens setting out on his patrols, she got reluctantly to her feet, opened the door, picked up her tray, and went inside. There, she pulled down the blackout blinds and drew the curtains. Ahead of her stretched another long night with only her thoughts for company.

For the sound of another human voice, she clicked on the radio. On the Home Service was 'Follow the Flag', a programme billed as *a collection of patriotic songs*. Finding the deliberately rousing nature of the music jarring, she turned the dial to locate the Forces Programme, where she came across the news being broadcast in French. At least it was a voice rather than falsely jolly music. And at least the fact that it was in French made her concentrate, which was ironic, really, she found herself thinking as she listened to reports of the number of sorties being flown by the RAF, since it was her fluency in French that had brought her here in the first place.

As it happened — and against all expectations — the night that followed was a quiet one, and the next morning she awoke feeling purposeful and refreshed. Drawing back the curtains and raising the blinds, she was also pleased to find the weather bright and dry. She would do some shopping. She would go to Hannington's to see what lipsticks were to be had and perhaps browse for a pair of shoes that would take her through the autumn and into winter. And, perhaps, now that it was clear she was going to be here for a while, she should purchase a raincoat; it was the last day of August, after all. If rumours were to be believed, clothes would soon be going on the ration, and so it made sense not to leave it too late to take care of her needs in that regard. A warm sweater might not go amiss, either, she thought, watching the hotel's flag fluttering from its pole; the wind off the sea would probably be quite bracing in the colder months.

Arriving in Hannington's, she was disappointed to find many of the cosmetics' displays largely empty.

'No,' the assistant said when it was Esme's turn to be served, 'I'm afraid Elizabeth Arden's *Victory Red* is out of stock. We do have Tangee.'

She had to force herself not to groan; not for her the ubiquitous and cloggy Tangee. 'Helena Rubenstein?' she asked without much hope.

The assistant reached under the counter. 'You're in luck,' she whispered. 'I have two I was keeping back for a friend, but she's just told me she's going up the munitions factory, and up there they get *given* lipsticks. *Given* them. Apparently, it's to keep up morale. Can you believe it?'

Esme couldn't. But of greater concern was to secure what appeared to be the last two decent lipsticks in the store.

From cosmetics, she went to ladies' footwear and came away with a pair of dainty black-leather lace-ups with a stylish three-inch heel, and a pair of burgundy suede court shoes with small suede bows. She also bought a navy-blue trench coat of gaberdine with a wide belt and gilt buckle. An expensive morning? Yes, but not an extravagant one; her purchases were essentials. Or so she thought until, taking a short cut along one of the side streets that led to the seafront, she was forced to step down into the gutter in order to pass a thicket of people. Only as she drew close did she realise that the shop outside of which they were gathered was a butcher's, and that the predominantly female customers were queuing for their ration of meat.

'At this rate,' one of the women moaned, 'there won't be nothing left but bloomin' tripe.

And you won't get none of mine eating *that* again. You should have heard them last time. Our Bert's better fed on that destroyer of his than we are here on dry land.'

Deftly, Esme dropped her stiff little paper bag with its Rubenstein logo inside one of her others and then, leaving only the box containing her gas mask over her left shoulder, shifted all of her packages to her right hand in order that they might be less conspicuous. With all of her meals provided by The Aurelian, she gave so little thought to rationing. *Rationing.* Heavens, her ration book had been at Les Marronniers; Madame Marron had put it with her file for safe keeping. She must remember to enquire of Mr Bancroft about getting a replacement.

Back in her room at the hotel, her new raincoat on a hanger, her shoes unpacked from their boxes and her lipsticks on the dressing table, she was saddened to realise that her earlier delight at their acquisition had already worn off. Instead, into her mind kept returning the pinched expression on the face of the woman in the queue for the butcher's. Her complexion had been grey, her expression one of weary resignation. It made her think of the meals Mrs Jeffreys had prepared: edible if you were hungry enough but otherwise stodgy and lacking in flavour. By comparison, the way she lived at The Aurelian made her wriggle with discomfort, even though it could be argued that she had sacrificed — and was still sacrificing — a normal life to be there.

Surprised from her thoughts by the sound of

the telephone ringing, she went to answer it.

'Hullo?'

'Sorry to trouble you . . . but would that be Miss . . . um . . . Miss Wentworth?'

Wentworth? Wasn't that the name she had used for Wallace?

She supposed she had better play along; for all she knew, it could be some sort of test by SOE. 'I am she.'

'Then there's a gentleman in the lobby asking to see you.'

She drew a sharp breath. 'And does this gentleman have a name?'

'The name on his card says Wallace Teague, ma'am. I mean *miss*.'

Wallace. Heavens. It *was* him. But how? And why?

'I'll come down,' she said quickly. 'Tell him, please, that I will be down in two minutes.'

Thrusting the telephone receiver back onto its cradle and grabbing one of the lipsticks, she hurtled through to the bathroom to examine her appearance. Thanks to a good night's sleep and some fresh air she looked better than she had for a while, certainly better than she had been expecting. Even so, running her fingers under the tap, she moistened a few wayward strands of hair. Then she applied a coat of Regimental Red over the remains of her earlier lip colour. Startled by the effect, she blotted some of it away. What the devil was Wallace doing back in Brighton? Shouldn't he be in France? Even given that he wasn't, what was he doing *here?* There was only one way to find out.

When the doors to the lift opened at the ground floor and she stepped out, unable to see him anywhere she approached the concierge.

'The gentleman is waiting outside,' he informed her, understandably confused to discover that she went by the name Wentworth as well as Ward.

Peering out through the entrance and seeing him halfway down the steps, staring across the road to the promenade, she felt her heart speed up. It really was him. He wasn't in France at all. Now what did she do? *Remain vigilant,* she cautioned. *Remember, Fenella Wentworth wouldn't have known that Wallace Teague was supposed to be in France.* The trouble was, Fenella Wentworth had faded so far from her mind that she wasn't even sure what the two of them had talked about — how much she had told him about her deceased aunt, or whether she had mentioned to him any other family members. In fact, coming down to see him now felt like a huge mistake. She should have said she was indisposed. So, why hadn't she? Was it too late to ask the concierge to apologise for a sudden change of heart on her part?

It was now, for, without warning, Wallace Teague turned and saw her standing just inside the plate glass door. His face lighting up, he mounted the half dozen stairs two at a time and reached to open it for her.

Breathing far too rapidly, she stepped outside.

'Wallace!' Sounding surprised took no effort whatsoever. 'What are *you* doing here?' Whether her memory had chosen that moment to let her down she wasn't sure, but he looked quite different; for a start, his hair seemed wavier than she remembered. A quick once-over of his clothing revealed that he was wearing summery grey-check trousers, the matching jacket to which was over his arm, and a white shirt with patterned tie beneath a sleeveless V-neck pullover of blue stripes. In his hand was a dark grey trilby. He also looked as though he had spent several of the last few days out in the sunshine, the effect being that he appeared considerably younger.

'Forgive me for surprising you like this,' he said. 'The office didn't have anywhere for me to be — still don't next week — and so I decided to take a few days' leave.'

Presumably, his mission in France had been scrubbed.

'And you came back to Brighton?'

He gave a casual shrug. 'I did.' When she stepped aside to allow people to pass, he went on, 'Come for a coffee with me somewhere? Lunch, if you'd prefer. Nothing flash.'

She glanced over her shoulder. This felt wrong. And yet, how could it be? As long as neither of them dropped their cover, or let slip anything they shouldn't, where was the danger?

'Can you wait while I go and fetch my handbag and a jacket?'

'Of course.' He gestured down the flight of steps. 'I'll wait for you over there.'

'And I'll try not to be too long,' she said, turning about.

Well, here was a surprise: the lovely Wallace

Teague had come back to see her. And, although she was struggling to remember what they had told each other about themselves, it didn't require any effort at all to remember that she had liked him a lot. She also knew from just those few moments spent talking to him that she still did. So, what on earth did she do now? Wait and see why he was here, she supposed. And avoid doing or saying anything she might later have cause to regret.

★ ★ ★

She had been to this little cafe once before, with Violette. Back then, there had still been tables and chairs on the pavement out the front, where they'd sat drinking tea and eating slices of a surprisingly respectable bread pudding. Since then, the tables had been cleared away, not, apparently, on account of the onset of autumn but on the advice of the ARP, who had said that, in the event of a blast, they could be sent flying through the air and cause fatal injuries. So, this afternoon, the two of them were seated inside — at Esme's instigating, far from the bay window.

'Well,' she said, once the young waitress had taken their order for a pot of tea for two and the only cake available — an eggless carrot cake. 'This *is* a surprise.'

'Yes,' Wallace agreed, 'that's becoming apparent to me, too.'

'But not an unpleasant one,' she rushed to add.

He gave a little laugh. 'Thank goodness for that at least.'

'You look well.'

'So do you,' he was quick to respond. 'That's a very pretty frock.'

Inwardly, she groaned. While it was nice to see him, the small talk was already rattling her nerves. 'Wallace, may I be direct?'

'Please, do.'

Waiting while the waitress placed their order on the table, she went on, 'What, exactly, are you doing back here?'

He grinned. 'Yes, sorry, I shouldn't have just turned up, should I?'

With her fork, she sliced off the corner of her piece of cake. 'Well, that's hard to say when I don't even know what *this* is.'

His grin changed to something more sheepish. 'Genuinely, Fenella, I found myself with time on my hands, the assignment I was to undertake after *I* left here being shelved for the moment.'

'And so, you took some leave. Yes, you said. But why come back to Brighton? It's not as though there's anything to do here.'

'I enjoyed your company. And I rather thought you enjoyed mine.'

Now they were getting somewhere. 'I see.' This was dangerous — and for more than just the obvious reason.

'Have dinner with me. And yes, I realise it will have to be an early one so that we can both go our separate ways before the curfew. Not that I have a clue what time that will be tonight.'

Closing her eyes, she tried to picture the sign

in the hotel lobby. 'A quarter to eight.'

'Goodness! Then it *will* have to be early. Is there anywhere around here we can eat at about six? Other than The Aurelian, I mean.'

At least he appreciated the need to be discreet. 'Well . . .'

But before she could finish, there came the winding up of an air raid siren.

He gave a hapless grin. 'Seems we'll have to finish our discussion in a shelter somewhere.'

'Too far to make it back to The Aurelian,' she said, following his lead and getting to her feet.

In the doorway, the patron of the tea rooms was directing people down the alleyway between the buildings. Taking no notice, Wallace grabbed Esme's hand.

'I remember seeing a sign,' he said, pulling her in the opposite direction. 'Quick, this way.'

She scampered to keep up. 'You remember seeing a sign? When?'

'Last time I was here,' he said, lengthening his stride, 'I made a point of finding out where the public shelters were.'

Having to trot to keep up with him, she tried to digest this rather peculiar revelation. 'You did? Odd way . . . to spend your time . . . I must say.'

With that, he unhooked a gate in a rickety length of chestnut fencing and drew her through it. 'The school,' he announced. 'Come on, look, the shelter is over there, built into the bank on the far side of the playground.'

'Why here?' she asked, making a quick glance to the sky as she trailed after him.

'For the school children, obviously.'

She shook her head. 'No, I mean why did you want to come here rather than the shelter behind the tearoom?'

He looked at her as though it should be obvious. 'It's Saturday. No school. It should be almost empty.'

He wasn't wrong. When they opened the door to the concrete shelter and started down the steps, there was just an elderly man, trying to get a light to work and clearly surprised to see them.

'Come on in, children,' he said, beckoning them on down the steps. 'Bit of dodgy wiring, that's all. It just needs a bit of a . . . there you go. *And God said, Let there be light: and there was light.*' Esme frowned. Now they would be stuck here with this peculiar little man. 'You won't come to no harm in here,' he continued. 'Safe as houses, this place. Just make sure to stay put until you hear the All Clear.' With that, he went up the steps, out through the door, and closed it behind him.

Alone with Wallace, and feeling too unsettled to sit down, Esme looked around. The shelter was surprisingly large, with a string of three lights running the length of the ceiling, only the central one of which was working. Around the walls — of concrete panels painted cream — were wooden benches, and down the centre of the floor were moveable wooden forms that looked as though they had come from the school hall. The pervading smell was of damp earth, rubber-soled plimsolls, and Jeyes fluid.

'Hey, sit down,' Wallace said, perching on the bench and extending a hand towards her. With little option but to comply, she chose to leave a gap of at least three feet between them. 'I doubt the warning will last long. It's daylight. It'll pretty quickly be evident whether the threat is real.'

She wished she believed him. She wished she didn't feel as though she was in a tomb. She also wished they'd gone where there were other people in case there really was a raid — people who knew helpful things like first aid. Of course! That's why she was so fidgety; she had spent every other air raid in the basement of The Aurelian, where it felt substantial and safe, and where there were always people on hand . . . and facilities. Being somewhere like this — somewhere more exposed — was making her think about what had happened to Les Marronniers.

'Two weeks ago,' she said without meaning to, 'I lost a friend — two friends, in fact — in a night-time raid. A stick of bombs fell just around the corner from the hotel.' When she paused to study his reaction, he remained quiet. 'They weren't meant for Brighton. But they dropped them there anyway. One of them landed on my friends' house. They hadn't gone to their shelter. It killed them instantly.'

He slid along the bench, closing the distance between them. 'I am so very sorry. No wonder you're jittery. Here,' he said, 'hold my hand.'

Again, she complied. 'I went to their funeral. It was awful. They had no family and so it was all . . . horribly impersonal and rather without meaning. If funerals are meant to bring comfort to those left behind, that one failed dismally.'

298

He gave her hand a gentle squeeze. 'I'm sorry to hear that. Coming so soon on top of your other loss, it must have been doubly hard.'

She raised her head and looked at him. 'Other loss?'

'Your Aunt Mabel.'

She exhaled heavily. Close shave! 'That was a while ago now. And she was old. And it was — '

'Peaceful.'

Golly, he remembered. She was going to need to be even more careful than she had first thought.

She nodded. 'Altogether different.'

'Will you have to remain in Brighton for much longer?' he asked.

She noticed that he hadn't let go of her hand. She didn't mind. Physical contact was something she missed: Violette had been forever hugging her; Madame Marron often touched her arm or hand in reassurance; Richard . . . well, when no one else was there to see, Richard used to wrap her in the warmest and loveliest of hugs.

Bringing her thoughts back to Wallace's question about Brighton, she shook her head. 'I doubt I'll be here too much longer. My aunt's property has finally been sold. And the solicitor is in the throes of working out the duties, so I suppose that shortly now it will all be done with.'

'You will be free to go back to your normal life.'

The little scoffing noise she made was instinctive. 'Normal life? Does anyone still have one of those? Every day I listen to the news and read the reports in the papers and I can't see how life will ever be normal again. Some people say the threat of a German invasion hasn't completely gone away. Hardly surprising with that man Duff-Cooper giving that speech practically inviting Hitler in . . . '

'Fenella,' Wallace said gently.

Failing to recognise it as her name, it took her a moment to respond. 'I'm sorry I'm so gloomy. You came here to spend your free time — presumably in agreeable fashion — and yet here you are, stuck in an Anderson shelter in a school playground with the gloomiest woman on earth — '

'And I don't mind at all,' he said, stroking the back of her hand. 'But, given what you've been through recently, I do wish we weren't stuck down here, yes.'

With that, and to their surprise, they heard the All Clear start up.

'Thank God,' she said, feeling her shoulders sinking several inches lower. 'Now we can get out of here.'

When she got up from the bench, he made no move to follow, his expression that of someone about to say something profound. In the event, all he said was, 'Only when you tell me where you have decided upon for our unsociably early dinner.'

★ ★ ★

The restaurant at the Colonnade Hotel proved a good choice. Only about half of the tables were occupied, mainly by older couples who, Esme

300

assumed, also had an eye to the curfew. The other thing that proved to have been a good choice was her outfit. Arriving back at The Aurelian after the All Clear, she had dashed up to her room, stripped off for a quick freshen up, thrust some rollers into the front of her hair and touched up her make up. Then she had stood for a while in front of the wardrobe agonising over what to wear. Her cocktail and evening dresses all felt too formal for such an early meal, her ordinary frocks not dressy enough. In the end, she plumped for an old favourite, one she had brought with her from Clarence Square, but which she'd so far had no occasion to wear. In a rich claret colour, the soft fabric hung beautifully without clinging, the wrap-over front giving a deep neckline over which to wear a simple necklace. With a lightweight shawl in lieu of a jacket, she felt she had somehow stumbled upon just the right look.

'Lovely,' Wallace had remarked, offering her his arm when she met him outside of the hotel.

Now that they were seated, their starter of celery soup turning out to be light and flavoursome, she was glad she had come. Sitting in a hotel bar for as many as five evenings a week had somewhat spoiled her enthusiasm for getting dressed up on a Saturday night and going out. And yet, perversely, it was also something she had missed.

'This is delicious,' she said when her main course of sole bonne femme had arrived and she had taken her first mouthful.

'So is this,' Wallace replied. 'Perfectly sea-soned.'

His choice of jugged hare had surprised her, it being a dish one didn't often see on menus. But, if she remembered correctly, August was the month when hare came into season.

Throughout their meal, their conversation remained light and broad ranging, steered by her onto and around topics she hoped would prevent him from straying into traitorous territory. Her efforts seemed to pay off.

'Have you always lived in Hampshire?' she asked at one point.

'My entire life. My father was an accounts clerk for a shipping company and worked from an office in Southampton docks. We always lived within a couple of miles of the sea.'

'Brothers and sisters?' she enquired, piercing a piece of boiled potato with her fork.

'Sister, older, married.'

She tried to remember whether she had read any of this in his file. The fact that none of it rang any bells suggested he was answering her questions as himself — whoever that was — rather than as Wallace Teague. From her perspective as a decoy, she wasn't concerned. The information was innocuous enough.

'What about you? Any siblings?'

In her own case, it didn't matter too greatly how she answered, her false identity based so closely upon real life. 'No. My mother died when I was tiny, and I was adopted by my aunt. Sadly, she was never able to have children of her own.'

'That is sad.'

'As a result, I was rather doted upon.'

He raised an eyebrow. 'Why am I not surprised?'

She gave him a dismayed shake of her head. 'I had no idea I was adopted until . . . well, until I was grown up. Since I had never suspected, the news came as a profound shock. I had lived with this family all of my life and yet no one had ever given the least hint. As you might imagine, it took me a while to come to terms with it.' As she was speaking, she realised that this was the first time she had told anyone the whole story — well, anyone other than Lou. She wondered why, of all the people she could have told, it had turned out to be him? Because she knew they wouldn't meet again? She had thought that once before! Because he was good at listening? Or was it because she had finally accepted the facts of her birth and her upbringing for what they were: facts that had no bearing upon who she became or what she did with her life; facts with which she had now come to terms? The slow dawning of the possibility came as a pleasant surprise, a relief, even. She might have been born to the working-class Mr and Mrs Ward of Whitechapel, and raised by the middle-class Colbornes of Kensington, but none of that mattered. Her surname was irrelevant; as had become evident with her targets these last few weeks, names were meaningless — merely labels chosen and stuck on you by someone else. Goodness, what an unexpected and liberating thing to realise! What a weight to have lifted from her. And how strange that it should happen here, with Wallace.

'Do we have time for a dessert?' she asked when they had finished their main courses.

He pushed back his cuff to look at his watch. 'Just about. I'll ask for a menu.'

There being no ice cream, Esme chose blackcurrant sorbet. Seeming suddenly preoccupied, Wallace signalled to the waiter for the same.

'Is everything all right?' she enquired. 'If you're not keen on dessert I can do without.'

Instantly, his expression lightened. 'You'll do no such thing. We shall enjoy our sorbets and then I shall walk you back to The Aurelian.'

'Where are you staying?' she thought to ask.

'Same place as previously. It's clean and homely. Comfortable enough for a few nights and just a couple of roads back from the sea front.'

'Sounds just the ticket.'

Their desserts finished and coffees declined, Wallace settled the bill and then escorted her out. 'I know it's not terribly scenic,' he said, glancing both ways along the deserted road, 'but shall we cross over and walk back along the upper promenade?'

'Yes, let's do that,' she said. 'The defences might all be hideous eyesores, but the sea still looks wonderful.'

'Come on, then. Take my arm.'

They walked slowly, careful to maintain their distance behind the couple in front and nodding politely to other couples walking in the opposite direction.

'Hard to believe summer's over,' she said as he led her to a halt at the railings and they stood looking out. Below them, beyond the lower promenade, the waves were curling so gently onto the pebbles that they barely made a sound. And the breeze was so light that it wasn't even troubling the loose strands of her hair. It was almost a perfect evening.

'September on the south coast can be quite nice,' he eventually replied, reaching for her hand and taking hold of it.

'In any ordinary year, yes,' she agreed.

'Yes.'

'Well,' she said, noticing a change in his mood — a change towards the sombre, 'it's almost sunset. And I suppose that if you are to be back indoors before the curfew, we should probably go on.'

'Probably. But before we do,' he said, his expression straightening, 'I have a confession.'

In the moment while his hold on her hand slackened, she carefully withdrew it. Now what was he going to tell her? So far, she had kept him away from saying anything he shouldn't. 'Look, Wallace — '

'Fenella, that's part of what I want to confess. My name isn't Wallace. It's Marcus. Marcus Latham.'

With her breath seeming to catch in her chest, she gave an involuntary gasp. Marcus Latham. It suited him so much better than Wallace. The problem was, they really were now in dangerous territory: the decoy in her knew to let him talk; the woman in her wished he would stop. His final assessment for SOE might have been completed several weeks back, but targets were sworn to secrecy for all time — not just while they were on an operation. It was something made clear to them at the outset.

'Why are you telling me this?' It was the only thing she could think to ask that didn't lead him more in one direction than the other — left him in charge of his own destiny.

'Because certain things I have led you to believe about me aren't true — '

'So why tell me now?' It was as much as she could do not to shout at him to stop.

'Because it's important that you don't think me deceitful. I do live in Southampton. I *am* a cartographer. I joined the Ordnance Survey straight from school and they trained me to draw maps. It wasn't something I planned as a career, but I turned out to be good at it. *Am* good at it. But, this last year, I was recruited into a department of the Government. No one was more surprised than me as to the manner of its coming about, though more than that I'm not at liberty to say.'

'Then don't,' she whispered. 'Stop now, this minute. And leave before you say something you shouldn't.'

'I can't,' he said, searching her eyes as she looked back at him. 'At least, not just yet. You see, I've come back to Brighton for a very specific reason, to do something before the opportunity is lost to me.'

All she could think was that, so far, he still hadn't given anything away. But he was getting perilously close. At the same time, *she* had to be careful not to fall into the trap of confessing to her own secrets, one confidence begetting another. In her role as a decoy she knew the obvious thing to do would be to lead him, to ask him about *the very specific reason* for his return. But she couldn't do it. Although practised in the art, she couldn't do it *to him*. She could, though, act confused, lead him in a different direction altogether — well away from danger. 'Look, Wallace . . . Marcus . . . I really think we should be going . . . '

Preoccupied with thoughts of how to prevent him from transgressing any further, she failed to spot him once again reaching for her hand.

'I've come back, Fenella, not to tell you anything I shouldn't, but to prove my sincerity when I ask . . . will you marry me?'

'On Friday, London was once again subjected to heavy bombing, as were RAF bases all across the south east. Fighter command flew more than one thousand sorties, their highest number yet in one day. The first German aircraft were spotted across Kent and Sussex at around ten thirty in the morning, with successive raids lasting well into the afternoon. Severe damage was inflicted upon hangars at Biggin Hill airfield, further extensive damage occurring at the Vauxhall factory at Luton and the Handley Page Halifax bomber production line at Radlett. Eyewitnesses in Kent are reported as saying that wherever one chose to look, the skies were filled with bombers and fighter planes. Elsewhere on Friday — '

Esme clicked off the radio. If she had thought it would serve as a distraction, she'd been wrong. Even news of such dreadful losses wasn't going to take her mind from the dilemma that had just been thrust upon her. Wallace — *Marcus* — had asked her to marry him. And she had teetered on the verge of saying yes. Fortunately, she hadn't. Fortunately, common sense had intervened. But now, having told him that there were just too many reasons why she couldn't accept him, she was wondering whether it *was* so fortunate.

Sitting on her bed in the darkness, propped up against the pillows, she let out a long sigh. Wallace — *Marcus!* — had explained that his proposal wasn't made with a view to them getting married in haste, but solely so that she might understand the desire he had to build a life with her once the war was over and things returned to normal. But what did *he* mean by normal? For him, it seemed to suggest returning from operations in France to marry Fenella Wentworth, a young woman apparently without family and clearly of some independent means. Whereas for her, normal meant slipping back into the identity of Esme Ward, and wondering what on earth she was going to do with herself, the bridges back to her old life now well and truly burned. For her, normality would most likely mean facing a world in which Wallace Teague had gone to do his duty in France, where he would probably have been unmasked by the Nazis and sent to perish in a prison camp or, if fortune was on his side, had been swiftly executed by a bullet to the head. Nowhere within either definition of normal did their two separate definitions seem even similar, let alone to meet. And that had to be down to their completely different start points; *he* couldn't tell *her* the real truth about who he was, and *she* couldn't tell *him* about the deception she kept up — a state of affairs he had no reason to even suspect. To make matters worse, her dilemma was further deepened by the matter of whether or not by telling her what he had, he had committed the degree of treachery that warranted her reporting him to SOE.

And then there was the fact that, given the chance, she could truly fall for him. He was intelligent, personable, sensitive. Nice looking. Articulate. Confident. She could go on. And, if further proof was needed, when he had asked her to marry him her heart had skipped at least two beats and her instinct had been to say yes, despite knowing next to nothing about the real Marcus Latham.

There was also something else she was doing her best to ignore — and that was Richard. In the last week or so, she had found herself thinking about him more and more, even though, given the months that had elapsed with no contact between them, a reconciliation was clearly out of the question.

Poor Marcus. Thank goodness he didn't know just how much was stacked against him — none of it of his own making. *I don't think I can*, she had answered his proposal. *Under different circumstances*, she had said. *In a different time*, he had replied, echoing the sentiments they had expressed the first time they had parted. And the irony and the cruelty of it was that it was true. If she hadn't had to face explaining to him that, just as he wasn't Wallace Teague, she wasn't Fenella Wentworth, let alone that she had yet to finally decide whether to go forward in life as Esme Ward or Esme Colborne, then there might have been a real chance for them. Even so, would she have wanted to accept him, plan her future around him, knowing that in all likelihood he would never return home? She didn't think so. And yet, there was something about him, something that made her think — as apparently did he — that they were right to dream of a future together.

In her frustration, she let out a long sigh. Well, on the back of his card he had written the address of his lodgings in Jasper Street. And he had said he would remain there until he was called back to take up his next assignment. *His next assignment*. With those few words she had been reassured that he hadn't broken the rules; apart from telling her his real name, the pretence was intact.

She wouldn't go to him though. She wouldn't change her mind. What she *would* do, was take this as a sign to stop and take stock of her life. This business with Marcus had shone a light upon feelings and situations she had clearly been ignoring and so, perhaps the time had come to act. Perhaps the time had come to heed her confusion and to make some decisions once and for all. But, to do that, she was going to need the help of someone who would ensure that she thought things through and did nothing in haste.

★ ★ ★

'Lou? It's Esme.'

For a moment, Esme's greeting met only with silence. But, just as she was about to repeat herself, she heard Lou reply.

'Oh, hello, Esme. How are you?'

Alone at her end of the line, Esme frowned. Lou sounded unusually glum.

'A bit up and down of late. I lost a couple of friends when a German bomb fell on their home and I don't seem able to quite get over it but otherwise, well, much the same. You know how it is. What about you?'

'Woeful, truth to tell,' Lou replied, her voice leaden. 'There's been a . . . well, a bit of a to-do at work. I can't tell you over the telephone. And then there's been some bad news from home. But I don't want to talk about *that* because if I do, I'll start crying. And I'd really rather not. Cry, that is.'

Not used to Lou being anything other than bright and cheery, Esme didn't know what to say. It certainly didn't seem appropriate now to ask her for a favour. 'I'm sorry to hear that, Lou. But you have friends there, don't you? People you can talk to?'

From the other end of the line came the sound of sniffing.

'I *did* have. But since this business at work, everything's all turned upside down and . . . well . . . '

Unable to bear the idea of Lou being not only upset but friendless, too, Esme knew she was going to have to re-think her earlier plan. She had been going to suggest travelling down to Plymouth for a visit, but it appeared now that of greater help would be to get Lou away from there for a while.

'Lou,' she said, thinking on her feet, 'can you get leave from work for a few days? Can we meet?' From the other end of the line there now came only soft crying. 'Lou?'

'Perhaps . . . '

'Then how about I book us a hotel somewhere? Could you get to Exeter for a couple of days? That wouldn't be too far for you to get a train, would it?'

'C-Can't,' Lou sobbed. 'N-No m-money.'

Esme sighed. For Lou to sound so distressed, things had to be quite bad.

'Right. Well, then I have another idea. I'm due some leave. And I also know someone who can organise things. So, how about we go to Aunt Diana's in Windsor? We can meet in town and travel out from there together. It might take me a couple of days to arrange, but how about next weekend? How about I get a rail warrant for you for Friday? And maybe one back for the Sunday evening? How does that sound?'

'N-Nice,' Lou replied. 'That sounds n-nice.'

'All right. And don't worry about money'

'You're s-so kind, Esme.'

'Hm. Look, tell me your address and leave it all to me.'

When Esme hung up, she wondered what on earth could be so awful to have reduced Lou to such misery. By the seem of it, there had been bad news at home as well as trouble at work. She did hope the Channers were all safe and well; without knowing what had happened, it seemed risky to just ring them out of the blue and ask. She also had to hope that Lou hadn't done anything stupid — young girl in a big city and all that. She *had* talked rather excitedly about two men last time they'd spoken.

Well, on Monday, she would telephone Croydon and ask Miss Black for some time off and for a couple of favours. She would say that a cousin had suffered a tragedy — a suitably vague sounding cover all — and that she needed to offer support. In the crudest of terms, it would be killing two birds with one stone: not only could she find out what was going on with Lou, but the very act of being back in London might help to bring clarity to her own situation — which was, after all, why she had telephoned Lou in the first place.

Yes, she thought, beginning to warm to her plan, and if Lou wasn't up to it, there was always Great Aunt Diana; when it came to impartial advice, she was always completely reliable and thoroughly discreet. And if she was going to be truthful about what had been going through her mind earlier this evening, then truth and discretion were going to be of paramount importance.

10

The Unravelling

'Darlings. How wonderful!'

The sight of Diana Lloyd sweeping down her grand staircase made Esme smile. Her great aunt might be closer to eighty years old than seventy, but she had lost none of her sprightliness, nor her style.

'Aunt Diana,' she said, hurrying towards her. 'It's so lovely to see you. Thank you for allowing us to descend upon you like this.'

'Nonsense, my dear. Always a joy to have you. And Louise, how grown up you look now.'

'Hello, Mrs Lloyd,' Lou replied as she submitted to an embrace.

'For goodness' sake, dear, do call me Diana — Aunt Diana if you prefer. Now, come on, the pair of you, come through to the conservatory and we'll take some tea. Which would you prefer — Assam or Ceylon? We don't have any Darjeeling — our usual man has shut up shop and gone *orf* to fight. Dreadful inconvenience. Tell me, are you finding this war as tedious as I am? Hopeless, isn't it? Did we not learn anything from that last debacle?'

Following Diana Lloyd through the drawing room, Esme nudged Lou's arm. 'It would seem that we learnt nothing at all from it, Aunt, no.'

She might only have been there two minutes

but, already, she could feel the tension draining from her limbs. She was even smiling — not something she'd been doing much of lately.

In the conservatory, over slabs of spiced raisin cake and cups of tea, the girls politely answered Aunt Diana's enquiries or, rather, they nodded or shook their heads as the tone of her remarks seemed to require. Yes, they were both keeping well — patently untrue, Esme reflected. Yes, they were horrified by the terrible losses on both sides of the so-called Battle of Britain — but tried not to think about it — and, yes, they too hoped those nasty little men Hitler and Goering got beaten back and taught a lesson.

Everyone seeming to agree upon everything, Aunt Diana rang for their tea things to be cleared. 'I'm down to three now,' she said.

'Three, aunt?' Esme sought to clarify.

'Three staff. Wootton in the kitchen — been with me years. Has some surprisingly inventive approaches to rationing. That said, much of what one can get is, of course, down to who one knows. And with your Uncle Ned's business, well, let's just say he clearly inherited his father's creativity and that we fare better than most. Then I still have Dolly, although with the way her knees are when it's damp, I don't suppose I shall have her for much longer. And dear old Bennett, who, since I have no petrol allowance and thus no call for a chauffeur, I now refer to as my general factotum. Everyone else went to do their bit. Not that there were many left to start with. Still, as Bennett pointed out, at least we haven't been lumbered with evacuees. Too close to town for that.'

Glancing to Lou, and sensing she was finding it hard to maintain her dutiful smile, Esme risked interrupting her great aunt's ramblings. 'All right with you if we go and freshen up, Aunt? Only, poor Lou spent the whole morning crammed into a railway carriage.'

'Dear me, child, yes, of course. Where are my manners? I asked Dolly to put you in the ladies' twin. You remember where that is, don't you?'

Getting to her feet, Esme nodded. 'Near enough.'

'Drinks at six then,' Diana said. 'I'm afraid I dine rather early nowadays.'

'Six it is.'

After more than two months residing in one of the plushest rooms at The Aurelian, Esme thought Great Aunt Diana's ladies' twin felt old-fashioned and dark, the furnishings the same incongruous mix of last century run-of-the-mill and genuine antiques she remembered from her childhood. The view from the window was also just as she remembered: the castle hidden from view by trees; the racecourse visible away to the left; Eton College to the right; between them, the water meadows.

'Which bed do you want?' Lou asked as she stood looking about.

Replacing the chintz curtains neatly at the window, Esme turned back into the room. 'You choose. I have no preference.'

Watching as her cousin picked the bed closest to the door, unfastened her bag and started pulling out her belongings, she wondered how long she should leave it before asking her what was wrong. From a selfish standpoint, she would prefer to leave it as long as possible. But why invite the poor girl all the way up here if not to lend a supportive ear?

'Can you tell me where the bathroom is?' Lou chose that moment to look up and ask.

'Down the landing, last door on the left.'

'Then I'll just take my things along and splash my face.'

While Lou was in the bathroom, Esme had an idea. 'Let's go for a walk,' she said when Lou returned. 'If we go around past the church, we can pick up the footpath along the river. We *could* go down through the orchard, but the churchyard is usually less muddy.' With a glance to Lou's slacks, she went on, 'Come on, grab a sweater and we'll snatch an hour while it's sunny. You can tell me what's upsetting you.'

Lou's smile was a weak one. 'Yes. All right.'

And so, as they walked, entirely oblivious to their surroundings, Esme listened to Lou giving a rather muddled and meandering account of the events that had led to the predicament in which she now found herself. By the sound of it, what had happened to her cousin had been ghastly, but it did appear as though — apart from the dreadful events with her brother — she was now over the worst of it, able to put her bad luck behind her and make a choice between two clear alternatives. Not that, to Esme's mind, there was any decision to be made. To her, it was quite plain not only what Lou *should* do, but also what she *wanted* to do. To her, it seemed as though all

Lou had needed was someone's permission to follow her heart and take the leap.

By contrast, she thought her own situation rather more complicated, there seeming to be no one clear choice but rather a minefield of smaller ones, just one single misstep in the negotiating of which would have ramifications for the direction of the rest of her life. But it wasn't to be until after dinner that the chance arose for her to even begin explaining as much to her cousin.

Their meal finished, and Aunt Diana having forbidden them to clear the table in order to assist poor Dolly — *She'd be mortified, dears, absolutely mortified* — Esme and Lou carried their coffees through to the drawing room.

'You go and have a good old chat,' Diana said, smiling fondly. 'Put the world to rights. You know, you two remind me so much of your mothers. I remember them clearly at your age, determined and independent, making the best of being without their menfolk, indignant and hot under the collar about some or other injustice one moment, giggling like schoolgirls the next.'

Esme smiled. Aunt Kate she could picture at Lou's age; Naomi Colborne not so much. 'You must tell us all about them one day,' she said, largely from politeness. 'One day when we're not both so weighed down with affairs of our own.'

'I should, shouldn't I?' Aunt Diana agreed. 'Well, I'm going to head up for an early night with a cognac and Steinbeck's *The Grapes of Wrath*. Dying to get stuck. By all accounts it's rather good. Oh, and by the way, when the siren goes, which it undoubtedly will, it's down to the wine cellar with you. Don't worry if I don't join you. I rarely hear the warning. Besides, at my age, I'm prepared to chance the odds for the comfort of staying in my own bed.'

Aunt Diana's words made Esme's shiver; Violette had been of the same opinion and look where it had got *her*. Six feet under. But it wasn't her place to remonstrate with the formidable Diana Lloyd.

'All right, Aunt. We'll see you in the morning, then.'

Having removed themselves to the drawing room, Esme and Lou settled into the wingback chairs either side of the fireplace — the latter, home today to a dusty display of dried flowers.

'Are you feeling a little better now?' Esme enquired of Lou as, in identical fashion, they kicked off their shoes and curled up their feet beneath them.

Lou nodded. 'I am, thank you, yes. I can see what I have to go back and do. So, now it's your turn to tell me what's on *your* mind.'

Inexplicably, now that she had the chance, Esme found she had no idea where to start; there was so much that Lou didn't — and couldn't ever — know about her life in Brighton that made the situation tricky to explain. Even adapting the real-life details to suit her supposed role as a tutor of French would be mired with traps.

'What's on *my* mind?' she said, gesturing airily. 'Men.' Surprised to have spotted the nub of the matter, she burst into laughter.

'Whenever isn't it?' Lou replied, setting her

cup and saucer on the side table and grinning.
'But as for where to start . . .'

Lou merely shrugged. 'Just do as you would tell me to — start with the man causing you the greatest amount of anguish and we'll take it from there.'

* * *

Hearing Lou breathing softly, Esme reached to feel about on the bedside table for her wristwatch. Finding it, but unable to make out the time, she put it back again. It felt as though she had been tossing and turning for hours. Hardly any wonder: over and over in her mind kept going fragments of her conversation with Lou.

'To my mind,' her cousin had said after sitting through what Esme considered to be the abridged version of her woes, 'you're guilty of doing just what you accused me of — muddling up lots of different things, some of which really aren't things at all.'

And therein lay the value of an impartial bystander, Esme realised; they weren't usually trying to see the situation through a fog of despair. 'Precisely how do you mean?' she had nevertheless been forced to ask.

Lou's answer had cut to the chase. 'Have you found yourself thinking about Richard and London because you truly long to be back there, or because other things are making you unhappy and he seems the only other alternative? You say you don't trust your own judgement anymore, and that it all started when you found out the truth about your parents, but I think that's a red herring. I think that's because you're looking for something to blame, when, in fact, to sort out every single problem you reeled off to me, there's only one question in need of answering.'

Taken by surprise at that point, Esme had hauled herself more upright in her chair. 'And that is?'

'Do you still regret not marrying Richard? And if so, given the chance, would you still like to? Once you're true to yourself about that, then it's simple. Everything else decides itself.'

Esme's response to such a straightforward assessment of her situation had been to prevaricate, to remark that it *wasn't* that simple, and to which Lou had once again shrugged. *I thought you wanted me to be honest*, she had retorted.

Reflecting upon it now, she could see Lou's point; the key to resolving her dilemma was to be truthful about her feelings for Richard. If she did regret what she had done and did still want to marry him — assuming there was any chance whatsoever he would have her — then her work in Brighton would, of necessity, have to come to an end. On the other hand, if she cherished her independence above all else, then she had to accept not only the repetitive nature of the work but also the necessity of her solitary existence — and make the most of it for as long as it lasted. Having stepped away from her life in Brighton, she could see now it wasn't so much the work she was reluctant to give up but the perks and the freedom that went with it. Moreover, the very chance to escape Clarence Square — to start over, to do something useful and have fun in the process — had ultimately brought little more than exhaustion and isolation. Even had Violette, her one friend and ally in all of it, not died, she could never have been a substitute for family, not in the longer term. And this honest assessment of her situation told her that now, more than anything, what she really craved was a return to normal.

Normal. Huh. After all the turmoil she'd been through, and all the luxury and the glamour she'd had at her disposal, who would have thought it?

Plumping her pillow, she tried to settle. If she did give up her life in Brighton, the 'normal' that took its place couldn't be just any old normal, though; it would have to be a new and different sort of a normal. And to stand any chance of bringing *that* about was going to mean eating a horribly large portion of humble pie . . .

★   ★   ★

Esme sighed wearily. Having seen Lou safely onto the 10.20 to Penzance, a service that — unfortunately for Lou — was scheduled to stop at almost every station between Waterloo and Plymouth, she was still standing around, waiting for it to depart fifteen minutes later. *Please don't bother to wait,* Lou had urged, *go on and do what you have to do, and then write and let me know how you get on.* Esme, though, thought it mean not to stay to wave her cousin off; it was a brave thing she was going back to Plymouth to do, and a few more minutes spent waiting for her to leave cost nothing but the mounting of her own apprehension.

Eventually, a full twenty minutes behind schedule, and with a clank of couplings, the train pulled out and, her duty done, Esme made her way towards the tube station. There, in the dank and fetid air of the platform, she stood close to the wall, curling and uncurling her fingers. She hadn't expected to feel so nervous about doing this, or so beset by doubts: should she have telephoned beforehand; what if they weren't in when she got there? Of greater concern should perhaps be what if they were there but didn't want to see her? Where would that leave her then?

Arriving at South Kensington underground station, she set off to walk the short distance to Clarence Square. Yes, this was going to be difficult, she told herself. But she had to do it anyway. Lou was right; this was just one of several uncomfortable steps she had to take if she was to have the life she wanted. If her mother declined to see her, then she would have no choice but to accept the situation and move on to the next stage of her plan without her. The main thing, Lou had said, was that she at least *attempt* a reconciliation.

Absorbed in her thoughts, she rounded the corner onto Thruxton Street, only to find her way blocked by a barrier. Looking up, she saw that beyond it workmen were clearing rubble from where, further along, the middle of one of the elegant terraces had been reduced to little more than a shell. *Les Marronniers*. It was just like the scene at Les Marronniers. Reaching to the barrier to steady herself, she averted her eyes from the devastation. More lives taken. More families grieving. Why bomb a row of houses? What good did killing innocent people do?

'All right there, miss?'

She looked up. A workman in dusty overalls and flat cap was leaning on his shovel. She gave him a single nod. 'I was going to walk along here to get to Clarence Square. I didn't know it had been bombed.'

'Happened a couple of days back,' the man said.

'But Clarence Square . . . is all right?' It hadn't occurred to her until now that the house could have been bombed, everyone within it wiped out.

'Clarence Square missed it, love.'

She exhaled heavily. 'Thank goodness.'

'But to get there you'll need to go up through Hanson Place.'

'Thank you,' she said, her heart still racing. 'I'll do that.'

'Mind how you go, miss.'

Eventually reaching the corner of Clarence Square, Esme paused. Her dress and jacket were smart enough, but she wished now that she'd worn a hat; it *was* Sunday after all. And, while many churches might have softened their stance on the necessity of a hat for attending services, her mother's rules were rather less flexible.

Suddenly uncertain about coming here, she tutted. What the hell did it matter about Naomi Colborne's rules? There was a war on. The neighbouring street had been bombed. People were dying in their beds. She'd come, hadn't she? Wasn't that what mattered most?

Walking up the steps to the porch, she noticed how, even in this, one of the smartest areas in London, things had taken on an air of shabbiness: paper blew along the streets; grass grew from between the kerb stones; even the door knocker lacked its usual gleam. What was it Great Aunt Diana had said? War always strikes first at the foundations of respectability?

Nevertheless, when she rang the bell, the door was opened promptly by Smedley, who, if he was surprised to see her, didn't let it show. One of the last of the old school, she thought, offering him a smile: the only remaining member of staff from Grandmamma Pamela's days.

'Smedley. Good morning. Would my mother be available to receive me?'

As though she were unknown to him, the ageing butler signalled towards the hall chairs. 'Please take a seat, Miss Esme. I shall go and enquire.'

When he started up the stairs, what she wanted to do most was turn around and let herself back out. Unfolding her hands from where they had once again become curled into fists, she straightened her fingers and laced them loosely in front of her. Then she adjusted the strap of her handbag on her shoulder. *Then* she realised that in her haste to ensure Lou caught her train, she had forgotten to bring her gas mask, a recognition that only added to her panic, even though, as she reminded herself, it was probably the least of her worries.

'Darling, oh, darling! It *is* you.' At the sound of her mother's voice, she turned sharply. 'I hardly dared believe it.'

Coming quickly down the stairs, dressed in a plain navy skirt and pale blue jumper with a single strand of pearls at her throat, her mother looked precisely as she always had.

Heartened by the warmth of her reaction, Esme got to her feet. 'Mummy.'

'Darling, you're safe.'

Once wrapped in what was, for her mother, an unusually lengthy embrace, Esme allowed herself to relax a little, even laughing from relief. 'Of course I'm safe.'

'And you're all right? You're not . . . in any trouble?'

'No, Mummy. I'm not in any trouble.'

Releasing her daughter from their hug, Naomi Colborne looked about the hallway. 'No . . . luggage? You're not staying?'

Aware that her reception could have been very different, Esme reminded herself to tread carefully. 'Not today, no. I'm afraid I must return to Bri — be back at work in a couple of days. I came in the hope that we might talk.'

Naomi Colborne's smile didn't falter. 'Of course, darling. We'll go up to my sitting room. We can talk to our heart's content up there.'

Accepting her mother's hand, Esme allowed herself to be led up the stairs.

326

Who would have believed, she thought, following her mother into the first-floor sitting room, that such a short absence could bring back distant memories with such vividness — not only memories of being young and moving here from Hartland Street for her mother to take over the running of the house from her own parents, but back farther still, to the days when Grandmamma Pamela would hold court in this same little sitting room and she, Esme, would sit and play on the landing, listening to the chatter of the women within. The only real change, she decided, was the scent of the place, her mother preferring the less heady Chanel No. 5 over the sultry vanilla fragrance of Guerlain's Shalimar as favoured by Grand-mamma.

'So, Mummy, how are you?' she asked once they were both settled upon the small velvet sofa. And then, to circumvent any heading in the wrong direction, she quickly went on, 'You look well.'

'All I shall say is that I feel so very much better for seeing you.'

'Mm.'

'And you? I must say you have quite the healthy glow about you. Outdoorsy.'

About to reply that it was down to the sea-air, Esme stopped herself. Even a throwaway comment like that could give her away.

'I'm well, yes. And Daddy?'

'Will be so cross to have missed you, but this Battle of Britain business has him in Whitehall seven days a week at the moment. Other than that, he's well. Exhausted, but well.'

'I see a bomb fell in Thruxton Street,' she said.

'Yes, dreadful. The whole house shook so badly I thought it was us that had been hit.'

The scene of devastation around the corner so fresh in her mind, Esme said, 'I'm surprised you haven't thought about evacuating to Woodicombe.'

'What and leave your father? And Ned? I don't think so. But, if it gets much worse, I think Mamma might be persuaded to go to Aunt Diana's.'

After a moment spent reflecting in silence, they both spoke together.

'Look, Mummy — '

'Esme, I just want — '

'Please, do go on,' Esme said. Hearing what her mother had to say first would serve to guide her own remarks.

'I want to say that I'm sorry. You can't know how deeply I regret the way things unfolded that evening. Not knowing where you were these last months has caused me to go over and over in my mind how I could have handled things differently. And while it doesn't help you to know any of this now, I do wish to offer something by way of explanation. You see, it wasn't until I had to find the certificate of registration for your birth that I realised . . . well, that it occurred to me how we had never explained to you that you were adopted. And then . . . well, even once I realised *that*, I kept putting off telling you. So *many* times I tried to . . . but by then you were so in love and so happy to be getting married . . . and Richard was so . . . perfect . . . that I didn't want to be the one with news that might break the spell.'

'No,' Esme said softly. 'I suppose I can understand that.'

'And then, once you were gone, I was so deeply, deeply, upset. My daughter, my only child, gone without a word. As anyone will tell you, I was beside myself. And then when you wrote saying that we could only contact you through that strange address, well, I'm afraid I rather let my response be coloured by my fear. I wasn't thinking clearly. I just wanted you to come home.'

Esme contained a sigh. Perhaps this was going to be all right after all. If she adopted the same tone of reconciliation as her mother, then perhaps the rift between them could be repaired, the mending of their relationship could begin. She could consign all her buried anger to history.

'Well, thank you, Mummy, for explaining. In return, I should like to apologise for the manner of my disappearing. With the benefit of hindsight, I, too, could have done things differently. I still believe I would have wanted to postpone the wedding . . . but running away like that was disrespectful and hurtful to so many people. It was just that I was . . . well . . . that I was — '

'Deeply shocked.'

She nodded. 'Deeply. All I could think was how could I expect Richard to make a commitment to me, till death do us part, when even *I* didn't know who I was? You and Daddy

329

. . . and even Richard . . . would no doubt have done your best to reassure me, I know that. But I had to work it out for myself — find out who I was and see where that left me.' At this point, she looked up to gauge her mother's reaction. 'Can you understand that?'

'I have come to, yes. At the time all I could think was that you were being petulant and selfish, cutting off your nose to spite your face . . . or making some sort of gesture solely with a view to hurting us — '

Very slowly, Esme shook her head. 'I did want to hurt you, that's true. But it wasn't why I left as I did. I left so that no one could talk me into going ahead with the wedding. I left because you had turned my world upside down and I couldn't bear the thought of staying here with you and Daddy and simply carrying on as though nothing had happened. If nothing else, it didn't seem fair on Richard.'

'But now? Now that you have had time to yourself?'

She knew what her mother was asking. She was asking whether she was now ready to return home — a question she had determined with Lou not to answer in haste.

'My position,' she ventured, 'is that I am thinking very carefully about what I should like to do next — about how much of my old life still feels appropriate to who I am now.'

Whether that was what her mother had been expecting to hear, she couldn't tell.

'And does any part of that life include Richard?'

Esme felt her face colouring. 'If I say to you it is something I am considering, please do not start reorganising the wedding. I know it's only been three months but, in that time, I've changed. My thoughts and feelings about what I'd like from a marriage are no longer the same. *I'm* no longer the same. And even if Richard hasn't . . . changed . . . and was still prepared to have me back, I would need to be sure he understood who I have become . . . and was prepared to take the plunge on that basis.'

'One assumes you haven't spoken to him then.'

'I haven't, no.' Unsettled by her mother's frown, but trying to sound light and inconsequential, she said, 'Are you still in touch with the Trevannions?'

Naomi shook her head. 'Not the family, no. But, back at the beginning, when you were first gone, Richard did leave me a telephone number, asking that I call if you came back.' Getting to her feet, Naomi went to her desk, pulled open a drawer and lifted out her leather-bound address book. 'Would you like me to write it down for you?'

What she really wanted was for her mother to offer to call Richard for her. But that would set the wrong tone. Besides, for all her own undesirable traits, cowardice wasn't one of them. She could fight her own battles. 'Yes, please. If you think he wouldn't mind me having it.'

The number copied onto the back of one of her cards, Naomi handed it to her. 'I believe it is the number of his home.'

Esme stared at her mother's handwriting. JUN? Juniper? Wasn't that the exchange for St. John's Wood? The recognition caused something inside of her to lurch; he had gone ahead and moved into the mansion flat that was to have been their home together? Surprised by how indignant she felt, she had to press her lips together against laughter: it wasn't *their* flat; the moment she jilted him she had forgone all rights to think of it in those terms. It was nothing short of ludicrous to feel affronted by the idea of Richard moving into his own flat! But she couldn't help how she felt — nor what that told her about her feelings for him.

'I shall call,' she said, her tone neutral. 'Perhaps later this afternoon. But please, promise me *you* won't leap to conclusions. Even if he is prepared to see me, there's no telling that either of us will feel like taking things any further.'

Returning to sit on the sofa, Naomi angled her head. 'You haven't been working as a French tutor, have you?'

Thrown by her mother's change of tack, Esme blushed. 'What makes you say that?'

'Because you're different. You said just now that you've changed, and I can see it for myself. You always were spirited, even as a young girl, but now you have a . . . well, let's call it worldliness, shall we?'

'And that's a good thing?'

Her mother smiled. 'As the Americans are so fond of saying, the jury is still out. But yes, I think it probably is.'

Slowly, Esme got to her feet. Her return to

Clarence Square had gone well — not necessarily as she had expected, but well, nonetheless. Her mother had been respectful of her feelings and neither of them had raised their voice. They had both learned a lesson, which would surely serve them well going forward. But reconciling with Naomi had never been the greatest cause of her anxiety anyway. No, that nagging fear stemmed rather more from what she had to do next.

⋆ ⋆ ⋆

Closing the wrought iron gate behind her, Esme glanced about at her surroundings. Yesterday evening, when she had finally plucked up the courage to telephone Richard and ask to meet him, he had suggested for their rendezvous this little walled garden off Whitehall. To her relief, now, he was already there.

'What a charming little place,' she said when he got up from where he had been sitting and came towards her.

'Something of a Whitehall secret,' he replied. 'Those who know of its existence tend to keep it to themselves.'

When he directed her back to the bench, she nodded. 'And I can see why. It's a perfect little oasis of peace and quiet.'

'I thought it a good choice for our purpose,' he said as they sat down. 'Public and yet, at the same time, private.'

Despite the knotting of her insides, Esme allowed herself a light laugh. 'Good thinking.'

Glancing about at the well-tended flower borders, it occurred to her that this would be the perfect place for a meeting of covert operatives.

'You look well,' he said.

She forced a smile. 'Thank you. *You* look tired.' While it was true that he looked in need of a good night's sleep, her first sight of him had still caught her breath. When he had then turned and met her look, she had felt the same old sensations — the lurch inside her chest that always accompanied a quickening of her pulse and a heightening of her senses. At that precise moment, her doubts about coming to see him had evaporated into thin air.

'I've been working some long days just lately, we all have. And quite a few nights, too.'

'Yes, I suppose so,' she said.

Oh, but how ridiculous to be making small talk! There was so much she wanted to say — probably much he wanted to say too, and yet, here they were, both of them wary of being the first to show their colours.

'Well — '

'The thing is — '

'Forgive me,' Richard said when they both started to speak at the same moment, 'you were the one who asked that we meet, and so it is only right that you go first.'

She forced herself to swallow. She'd forgotten just how little Richard had to do to make her lose her train of thought. *For goodness' sake*, she chided herself, *pull yourself together*.

'All right. Well, firstly,' she said, 'I asked to see you because I wanted to apologise. To leave you,

334

so close to the wedding, without a single word of explanation, was unforgiveable. To then stay away with little more than a few scribbled lines was even worse. So, for my appalling behaviour, I am deeply sorry. Rather late to apologise now, I appreciate that, especially considering the scale of my transgression. For what it's worth, I have been in an agony of anxiety over it. Whenever I recall what I did, I squirm with embarrassment.'

All the time she had been talking, Richard had been sitting, his elbows resting on his knees, his head angled towards the ground. When she fell silent, he looked up.

'Thank you. As you say, rather late in the day, but apology accepted.'

She unclenched her hands. His response was a tiny step in the right direction.

'With hindsight, I should have come straight to you and explained. But I was devastated . . . and confused . . . and more than a little angry.' At the mention of anger, she noticed him raise an eyebrow. 'And the last thing I wanted was everybody smoothing over it all and saying that it didn't matter.'

He nodded. 'I can understand that. But I still wish you'd come to me. We could have postponed the wedding, waited until you felt ready.'

'I see that now. But, at the time, all I could think was that if *I* didn't know who I was, how could I expect you to? How could I expect you to commit to marrying someone who wasn't who you'd always supposed? And then there was your family. Out of the blue, I had turned out to be the daughter of a labourer from Whitechapel. Not only did I fear being despised . . . ridiculed . . . gossiped about, I feared how it would affect all of you. I know it's nineteen-forty, but I mean, the son of Vyvyan Thurston Trevannion MP marrying a railway worker's daughter? I think not. The respect I had for you and your family was too great to allow all of you to be derided and mocked on account of *my* situation. Indeed, it was, in large part, thinking about the Trevannion reputation — certainly as much as my own — that drove me to flee. My conscience simply wouldn't allow my real identity to result in you being ostracised from polite society. Going ahead with our wedding was simply out of the question.'

Having heard her out, Richard sat up straight. 'When your father telephoned me that morning, it was to ask if I'd seen you — to ask whether you were with me. Not knowing what had happened, I told him of course not. When he then went on to tell me you had disappeared, without leaving word where you were going, my first thought was that you'd got cold feet. But when he explained about the news they'd broken to you, do you know what I wanted to do more than anything?' Meeting his look, Esme shook her head. 'My first thought was to find you, hold you in my arms and reassure you. Knowing how shocked *I* was, I could only imagine the state *you* were in, and I knew instantly that I had to be by your side. After that, Captain Colborne and I looked everywhere for you. And your Uncle Ned spent the whole morning on the telephone, speaking to all of the local constabularies and hospitals, giving them your description, each of us terrified of him discovering the unthinkable.'

Esme stared at the ground. She hadn't thought about anyone trying to find her, only about how cross they would be at the inconvenience and the embarrassment. 'I'm sorry,' she said quietly. 'Truly, I am.'

With that, from between the buildings came the sound of an air raid siren winding its way up to full pitch.

'Bloody Luftwaffe,' Richard muttered, getting to his feet. 'Come on, there's a public shelter beneath one of the buildings on Whitehall.'

Together, they walked quickly back out onto the main thoroughfare and the short distance to where an air raid warden was directing people in through a doorway. Inside, a further warden was ushering everyone down a flight of stairs.

To Esme, the shelter looked as though it had once been a storeroom. Lined up in rows across it now were two hundred or more folding chairs. They didn't look very comfortable.

Going ahead of her, Richard beckoned her to the far wall.

'Sorry to ruin your lunch hour,' she said as she took a seat at the end of a long wooden form.

Unbuttoning his jacket, he sat down next to her. 'As it happens, it will probably be longer than an hour now.'

'Will you be in trouble?'

The effect of his grin was to bring an ache to her chest. What the hell had she thrown away? Feeling as though she was about to cry, she bit hard on the side of her tongue. Momentarily at least, it staved off her tears.

'Getting caught in an air raid is one of the few acceptable reasons for not being back at my desk on time.'

She sighed. 'Well, thank goodness for that, at least. On top of everything else, I could do without having you being reprimanded on my conscience.'

'Hm.'

When they both fell silent, she sat staring ahead. The shelter was still filling up, the chairs now almost completely taken. Most of the occupants were what she thought of as *Whitehall types* — dark suits, umbrella over one arm, *The Times* under the other. There were a few women, too. A couple of them had taken knitting from their bags. One or two were reading novels; others were browsing women's magazines. For all of them, this seemed a well-worn routine.

She glanced to Richard. He was staring straight ahead. How, now that they could be stuck here for some time, could she say what was on her mind?

Evidently feeling her looking at him, he turned to regard her. With no clue what he was thinking, she gave him a short smile.

'Richard — '

'Rotten luck, this.'

She nodded. She mustn't allow herself to be deflected. She had to go on. 'Richard,' she whispered again, 'Do you hate me?'

The few seconds it took him to answer seemed to stretch for an eternity, an eternity in which she would have given anything to be able to wind back time.

'No,' he said with a slow shake of his head. 'I've certainly experienced some extreme feelings. It would be lying to say otherwise. But the worst of those were aimed at the circumstances, the timing of the revelation, for example, than at the girl I adored . . . even if, by denying me the chance to tell her that I loved her anyway, no matter the circumstances of her birth, I felt utterly exasperated with her.'

Unable to help it, Esme started to cry. She could bite on her tongue all she liked; it would do nothing now to stem her tears.

Beside her, Richard reached into his pocket and handed her a starched handkerchief. 'Here. And please, keep it.'

Listening to him speaking only filled her with even more regret. Worse still, nothing he had said so far suggested he was entertaining taking her back. On the other hand, if it wasn't *her* he had hated as much as what had happened to her, then perhaps there was still hope. And, in which case, she owed it to herself to keep going. 'Do you think you might forgive me?' she whispered.

He didn't hesitate. 'I already have.'

It wasn't what she had been expecting; she had been expecting him to prevaricate and say something along the lines of 'maybe' or 'perhaps, in time'. *I already have* was better than she had dared hope for.

'Then would it be too presumptuous of me to ask whether we could meet again, whether you might be willing to grant me the chance to show you how I have changed? Among other things, the work I have been doing has helped me to take less for granted, appreciate what's important . . . and I truly think . . . '

When he turned fully towards her and met her look, she felt a surge of relief. He was going to give her a second chance.

Feeling her body softening, she smiled warmly. 'I can't.'

In her shock she recoiled. 'You . . . can't?'

'I'm sorry. I can't meet you again because I am seeing someone else.'

Seeing someone else? Bringing her hands slowly to her sides, she curled her fingers around the front of the bench, the only sound in her head that of her blood pounding. How could that be? Barely three months ago he had been on the verge of marrying *her* and yet, in the blink of an eye, he had taken up with someone else? How could he do that? More to the point, how could it never have occurred to her that he might? The one thing she had never stopped to consider in all of this was that he might have moved on, and that the outcome of this attempt at a reconciliation might not be down to her at all.

On the other hand, what right did she have to feel affronted? Had she not entertained a future with Wallace/Marcus? And before that with Greg? Perhaps, before getting in a huff, she should remember the saying about people in glass houses being ill-advised to throw stones. But *really? Seeing* someone? Of all the possible responses from him, she hadn't banked on *that*.

'Well, no,' she said briskly, 'then of course you

can't meet me again — '

'In fact, I should probably tell you that yesterday morning, on the way back from church, I proposed to her . . . and she accepted.'

Had it not been for the near silence all around them, Esme would have thought she'd misheard. 'You . . . proposed? But isn't that — '

'Sudden? I can see why you might think so, yes,' he said. 'But I've actually known her a long time. Our two families have always been close, our names linked by both sets of parents for more than a decade . . . and so it isn't as though I've proposed to a stranger.' To Esme, even seen through a blur of complete disbelief, he looked suddenly uncomfortable. 'You see, what you must remember, is that your one and only letter to me made no mention of you returning — either in the short term . . . or at any stage in the future.'

'But that . . . ' she said, lost in her disbelief but determined to defend herself, 'was because I didn't for one moment think you would be in such a hurry to push a ring onto someone else's finger.'

'I wouldn't say I was in a hurry, exactly. Not given the time we've known each other . . . or that there's a war on.'

Unable to comprehend any of this, Esme sat shaking her head in disbelief. This wasn't the Richard she knew. The Richard she knew was cautious. Conventional. A romantic. Marrying someone he'd known since childhood simply because there was a war on was completely out of character.

And then it came to her: this was his mother's doing. Yes, of course it was! Over dinner that fateful evening in May, she'd heard her say, more than once, how Hedley, Richard's elder brother, had been selected to stand at the next election. Mentioning the *increased scrutiny* this had brought upon the Trevannions as a whole, the malicious old trout had even glanced across the table at that point to meet her look. *Two members of parliament in the family*, she had said, her implication hard to miss.

Feeling herself growing crosser by the moment, Esme couldn't help herself. 'Your mother's behind this, isn't she?' she said, less concerned now with keeping her voice down.

At least he had the grace to look embarrassed by the accusation.

'My mother? No, of course she isn't.'

'Really? One whiff of scandal about me and the minute I'm out of the way you're marrying the daughter of friends of hers? It has Matilda Trevannion written all over it.'

'I'll have you know', Richard said, his voice rather quieter than her own, 'that she had nothing to do with it. Admiral and Mrs Povey came up to stay one weekend and Caroline just happened to come with them. Finding ourselves seated next to one another at dinner, we started reminiscing — '

'She *just happened to come with them?*' Well aware that people around them were turning to look at her, she didn't care. 'You *found yourselves seated next to one another at dinner?* Have you heard yourself, Richard? The whole thing was set up. In your state of shock, you were easy prey, ripe for being manipulated by two snooty mothers acting in concert.'

'Now, hold on a minute. That's hardly fair — '

With the sound of the All Clear came a collective sigh of relief, people around them gathering their belongings, getting to their feet and stretching.

'Well,' she said, shooting up from the bench, 'fair or not, for your own sake, I hope you love her. I hope you look at her and can't wait to make her your wife . . . because, for your mother, a divorce in the family would be one scandal too far. So, rush into this if you want but, when you end up hoping that the next air raid *is* your last, don't say I didn't warn you!'

In too much pain to remain there for a moment longer, she pushed her way through the throng of people heading towards the daylight that had come streaming down from the street and stumbled blindly up the stairs. Reaching the top, she lurched out onto the pavement, stood for a moment looking about, and then began to run in what she hoped was the direction of Charing Cross tube station.

★ ★ ★

'Really, dear, you must *try* to eat.'

'I'm sorry, Aunt . . . I don't mean to be ungrateful . . . but I *can't*.'

It was later that same day, and not only could Esme not remember finding her way back to Windsor, she also had no idea how long she had been crying. All she knew was that her head was throbbing, her throat was dry, and Aunt Diana kept trying to persuade her to drink some pungent-smelling broth.

'And you're sure you don't want me to call your mother.'

'No-o,' Esme wailed, clutching the bed covers to her chin. Beneath her cheek, her pillow felt sodden.

'All right, well, then I am going to find your nightdress, draw you a bath, bring you up a jug of water and a nightcap, and say goodnight. Then, in the morning, you can decide what you are going to do. As I see it, you have a number of choices. You can go to Clarence Square and stay with your mother, you can remain here — for as long as you want to, you know that — or we can find out the train times and you can go and throw yourself back into your work. But what I *will not* let you do, is lie here, bawling your eyes out and making yourself ill. You might be heartbroken, and I don't belittle the pain that brings, but I will not let you wallow in pity, when, from what I can tell, for more than three months you have been going along without Richard just fine.'

'But Aunt . . . he's marrying . . . someone . . . else.'

'So you say, dear. And my heart breaks to see you in such pain. But ask yourself this: are you crying because you genuinely want him back but can't have him, or because, without reference to you, he has decided to move on with his life?'

'No. Yes. Oh, I don't know!'

'No need to raise your voice, dear. As you well know, a lady doesn't do that.'

'But that's the problem, isn't it! I'm not a lady, am I? If I was, that witch Matilda Trevannion wouldn't have been in such a rush to marry Richard off to someone more suitable, would she, the evil, conniving — '

'Esme, I'm telling you now, if you're going to keep this up, you will lose what little sympathy I have left. So, get up out of this bed, remove your underthings, and come and get into the bath I am going to run for you. While you're getting cleaned up, I shall go and ask Dolly to bring you another pillow and remake this bed.'

Catching sight of the expression on her great aunt's face, Esme knew she had no choice but to comply. What did it matter anyway? Richard was getting married. She had lost him for good. And it was nobody's fault but her own.

11

The Reckoning

'Is everything all right, Miss Ward? Only, if you don't mind my saying, you seem . . . dispirited.'

Wearily, Esme raised a smile. 'Everything is fine, thank you, Mr Bancroft. It was just a rather tedious journey back.'

'Yes, I'm sure. Well, SOE asked me to convey to you that while three days isn't long to complete a full assessment, they would nevertheless be grateful for any opinion you can bring to bear on this next one. *Do your best in the time available* was the instruction they asked me to convey.'

Accepting the envelope from Mr Bancroft, Esme nodded. 'I'll do what I can.'

'Then I'll leave you to it.'

Unpacking her bags upon her return from Great Aunt Diana's, Esme had overlooked that Mr Bancroft would have a file waiting for her. The prospect of a new target so soon filled her with dismay, the thought of having just three days to assess this one only adding to her general gloom. With her thoughts still in turmoil over what had happened in London, she could do without the nightly charade of dressing up and pandering to the baser instincts of male operatives. If she was to reach a decision about the direction of her life from here on, she really needed a clear head — not one filled with SOE business. But, as everyone was forever pointing out, there was a war on. And this was her job. And anyway, with going back to Richard no longer an option, what was there to decide?

Crossing to one of the easy chairs, she sat down and flicked open the file. Staring back from the photograph inside was a surprisingly angular face with a strong nose, heavy brows and deep-set eyes; the first man with features that were memorable rather than bland, he put her in mind of a villain in an adventure film. That being the case, she wondered how well he would be able to blend in. If he stood out to *her*, wouldn't he stand out to other people? She scanned his details: Charles Sutton, aged thirty-five, of private means, widowed. *Widowed?* That was a first, as was the description *of private means*. An odd choice all round, she reflected, surprised by the extent of her fascination with the man. With someone like this, she would need to appear captivating and yet enigmatic. So, who should she be? Helena? Honoria? Hermione? Yes! She would be Hermione Wallis, her choice of surname a subtle nod to what she was toying with doing now that she was definitely no longer destined to become Mrs Richard Trevannion . . .

★ ★ ★

Perhaps she should have given this more thought. While it was one thing to be decisive, it was quite another to be reckless. And, this

morning, walking along this street of unremarkable houses, she felt woefully underprepared for
what she had come here to do. Even so, she had
to see it through; sitting around wondering
would do nothing to relieve her turmoil. Besides,
time wasn't on her side. Taking too long to work
out what she wanted last time had cost her
Richard; she couldn't — and wouldn't — let the
same thing happen again.

Spotting the name on the gate post ahead of
her, she came to a halt. This was it: 'Tamarisk',
number seventeen, Jasper Street — the private
boarding house run by Mrs Jones. Clicking open
the latch, she pushed back the gate and then
closed it behind her.

The distance from there to the front porch was
no more than a couple of yards but even that
afforded sufficient time for doubt to take hold,
and for her to flirt with the idea of turning back.
Stay calm, she reminded herself. *You've only
come to say you've been doing some thinking.
That's all.*

With that in mind, she pressed the button for
the bell. Beyond the front door its shrill ring
echoed about a hallway and, after a short delay,
looking her up and down was a short woman in
a floral housecoat.

'Mrs Jones?'

'That's right.'

'I'm terribly sorry to bother you but I'm given
to believe you have a resident by the name of Mr
Wallace Teague.'

'Did have, love. He left.'

There it was again, that terrifying sense of

having been punched in the stomach — the same winded feeling she'd experienced in that air raid shelter in Whitehall.

'*He left?*'

'This weekend past, duck. Telegram came. Let me see, Friday afternoon, was it? That's right, because he came straight through and told me he'd received his marching orders and needed to be on the first train the following morning. I made sure to be about early so as to make him a decent breakfast. Nice chap, he was. Lovely manners. Left his suitcase and just took an overnight bag.'

He'd gone. She'd missed him. Damn her prevaricating!

'Did he . . . did he say where he was going?' Her question was pointless, she knew that, but it did at least keep up the pretence.

'He didn't say, and I didn't ask, love. Between you and me — ' With that, Mrs Jones leant beyond Esme to peer down the path. 'I'm minded he was going overseas. Just the impression I got. See, the entire time he was here he was fidgety. To begin with, I thought to myself *that chap's expecting a visitor.* Poor feller — turns out it wasn't a visitor he was expecting but his embarkation orders.'

No, no, he had definitely been expecting a visitor. He had been expecting — or at least, hoping, Esme knew — that she would arrive to tell him she'd had a change of heart. *Change of heart.* Huh. She was expert at those; it was the dilatoriness with which she had them that stank.

'And what is to happen to his suitcase?'

349

She had no idea why she was asking; if SOE had a mission for him then, by now, he would be in the final stages of preparation for being dropped into France. He was as good as gone. Wallace Teague and Marcus Latham had already become someone different yet again.

'Chap came Monday morning to collect it, just like Mr Teague said he would.'

Standing on Mrs Jones' doorstep, Esme felt her bottom lip beginning to tremble. How could she possibly be too late yet again? 'Well, thank you,' she said, tears welling. 'It seems I've missed him.'

''Fraid you have, love. And by no more than a couple of days at that.'

Turning away, Esme heard the door close behind her. A couple of days or a couple of weeks, what did it matter? She had missed him. She had missed her chance. And she had no one but herself to blame.

★ ★ ★

Checking her appearance in the full-length mirror, Esme tried to recall the last time she'd worn this dress. *The outfit of last resort*, Violette had called this scarlet number. Well, tonight, it was being promoted; tonight, it was being worn to create a memorable first impression.

Swivelling about and craning over her shoulder, she examined what she could see of her rear. The seams of her stockings looked straight, her hair tidy. She was almost ready — one last glance at the file for this Sutton fellow and then she would head downstairs.

It was in turning away from the mirror that she noticed an envelope slipped under her door. Spotting that it was addressed to *Miss E Ward, Room 303*, she bent to pick it up. Inside was a telephone message card, at the top of which had been written *7.13 pm*. She squinted across to the clock: barely ten minutes since. When it came to relaying messages, that department in London didn't hang about; no sooner had they taken the message than they must have rung it through to The Aurelian. Scanning the wording on the card, she groaned. *Please telephone your mother as soon as possible*. Clearly, Naomi was after the ins and outs of her meeting with Richard. Well, reconciled with her mother or not, she wasn't in the mood this evening to sit and listen to her begging her to go home — nor would she be tomorrow. Nor, for that matter, the day after. Besides, this was no time to let herself become distracted. If she was going to devote herself to this job, she had to be all in.

Ramming the card back into its envelope, she went to the wastepaper basket and dropped it in. Message dealt with.

Buoyed by her resolve, she went into the bathroom and reached for the little tube of Regimental Red. Slicking it across her lips, she stood back to examine the result. Well, no one was going to overlook that mouth! Nor the rest of her for that matter. Tonight, given that she had to attract and hold the attention of a widower — something of an unknown quantity to her — the look she was aiming for was dazzling. To that end, she had taken a bolder approach with the eyeliner, had applied more than her usual amount of mascara, and had scraped her hair rather higher, leaving just a few strands loose to frame her face.

Satisfied with the overall effect, and congratulating herself on having left nothing to chance, she picked up her clutch and extinguished the light. Off to work. She had a job to do for her country. And she was going to give it her all.

⋆ ⋆ ⋆

'Nice to see you back, Miss Wallis.'

'Thank you, Anthony. It's jolly nice to *be* back.'

Arriving in the hotel bar, Esme was surprised to find it deserted; apart from her target, the place was empty, devoid of the customary air force officers ordinarily responsible for making the place feel noisy and alive. Well, she reflected, hoisting herself up onto one of the stools, at least in this church-like solemnity, it would be impossible for her target to miss her.

'Your usual, Miss Wallis?'

'Yes please.'

Presenting her with her drink, Anthony kept their conversation going. 'I trust your friend appreciated you going all that way to visit her. And that she's recovering well.'

Esme gestured airily. 'She's on the mend, thank you for asking. Unfortunately, while it was lovely to see her, I spent as much time trying to get there and then get back again as I actually

352

spent with *her*. But, with the state of the trains, some would say I was fortunate to be able to get there at all. By the way,' she said, casting about the room, 'what's happened to all the fly-boys?'

'The RAF officers? They haven't been in since before the weekend.'

'One imagines them to be tied up defending us from the Luftwaffe.' Coming from her target, this unsolicited observation took Esme by surprise.

Raising an eyebrow, she turned towards him. 'Yes, I suppose so, poor things. This war has become truly ghastly, hasn't it?'

Her target's steady appraisal of her face moved to her chest. Probably not even aware he was doing it, she surmised, wishing now that when she had been in the lift, she hadn't tugged the neckline of her dress lower for good measure.

'Charles Sutton,' he said, moving smoothly to occupy the vacant stool between them. With him came the smell of lavender, vanilla, sandalwood and moss: an oddly feminine combination; Caron, if she wasn't mistaken.

Well, at least there was to be no wasting time, she reflected. And thank goodness for that — with any luck she would be back upstairs and in bed by nine.

'Hermione Wallis, how do you do.'

'Pleasure to meet you, Hermione Wallis.'

'So, Mr Sutton,' she said, 'what brings you to Brighton in these days of restrictions and curfews?'

'What brings me here? A fancy for some fresh air.'

The dryness of his retort made her laugh. 'And for that you chose Brighton, of all places?' 'A haunt from my childhood.'

'I'm amazed you were given permission by the authorities. Indulging a whim wouldn't ordinarily constitute reason for entering our little exclusion zone, let alone permit one to remain here for any length of time.'

Charles Sutton didn't flinch. 'Let's just say . . . I know people.'

'Helps, doesn't it?' Suggesting that she, too, *knew people* could only enhance her mystery.

'By that same token, then, what brings *you* here?'

'What brought me here originally was family business. As to what keeps me here . . . lethargy, I suppose. Residing at The Aurelian permits me to indulge a predilection for comfort without the effort of having to maintain my own staff. Do you have any idea how tedious it is to run a decent household these days?'

When he angled his head to regard her, she found herself studying him in greater detail: his five o'clock shadow and thick moustache lent him a swarthiness, his olive complexion a hint of the eastern Mediterranean. When he parted his lips, elongated canine teeth gave him an air of wolfishness.

'It might surprise you to know that I understand the issue very well. In the end, difficulties with my own household became so tedious, to borrow your own words, that I took the decision to close it up altogether. Rather than have the army commandeer it, I then loaned it to

354

a church orphanage desperate to evacuate from Lewisham.'

A church orphanage? Did he think displaying charity and compassion would make her swoon?

'How very public spirited of you.'

He shrugged. 'The place was far too large for me on my own.'

Hm. Hinting at considerable wealth was the play of a man with designs on one thing. Well, she would make that work to her advantage.

'And where is it, this vast home of yours?' Reminding herself not to press him *too* hard, she picked up her glass and took a sip of her drink.

'Surrey. Not far from Guildford.'

'Ooh,' she said, deliberately returning her tumbler rather heavily to its coaster, 'then you must know the Veaseys. Terribly old family with roots all the way back to the manor of . . . heavens, what's the name of that rambling pile of theirs? It seems to escape me. Anyway, it's just outside of Guildford. I went there once — finished in the south of France with their daughter. Arabella. Very horsey girl.'

Appearing to think for a moment, he shook his head. 'I'm afraid the name doesn't ring a bell. To be honest, I had very little time for the place. The country life was very much my late wife's thing. I rarely went there.'

If this was an act, it was a remarkably convincing one, his words barely concealing his loathing. If it *wasn't* an act, then why had someone like him, with genuine wealth, signed up to train as a covert operative for SOE? For the excitement? For the danger? It was hardly for the glamour or the recognition. Perhaps, if he genuinely was widowed, it was for the escape it appeared to offer.

'Too quiet for you,' she surmised.

'Absolutely too quiet.'

'Do you have children?'

'None.'

'Me neither,' she said. 'I'm not saying I shouldn't *ever* want them. Merely that I shouldn't want them for a while yet.'

'So, there's no *Mr* Wallis?' he came back with.

She shook her head. 'The last man who came anywhere close dumped me at the last minute for an old flame.' Wincing at the similarity of the story to real life, she took a mouthful of her drink. 'Can you believe it?'

He appeared to be trying not to grin. 'The man was clearly a fool.'

'That's what *I* said!' Bizarrely, she was starting to enjoy herself. Acting the part of some well-to-do but empty-headed socialite was liberating. She could say anything she liked — let off a little steam.

Pleased with the start she had made, she drained her glass.

'Another couple of drinks here, please, barman,' he beat her to it to say.

'Why, thank you,' she replied, making a point of fixing his eyes. 'But I really must make this my last. All that travelling has left me in need of an early night.'

'Is that so?'

The nature of his smile, and the way he seemed to be slowly and surreptitiously closing what remained of the gap between them, put her on alert. Something about him didn't add up. For a start, how had a man with no occupation and no family not previously seen fit to enlist? Moreover, how had he got himself recruited into SOE?

'Do you know,' she began, determining to try to find out, 'before you introduced yourself, I could have sworn you were military. *This chap has the air of a major*, I said to myself.'

'Disappointed to learn I'm not?'

She gestured vaguely. 'Disappointment doesn't really enter into it. But I'm rarely wrong. So, if not army, then something in the government . . . ooh, yes, an official in a secret department somewhere. You did mention *knowing people*.'

He pressed his lips together as though amused and shook his head. As denials went, it was convincing. 'No,' he said, his voice lowered to a whisper, 'I serve only myself. But something tells *me*,' he went on, leaning so close that she could smell the whisky on his breath, 'how, in that regard, you and I are probably rather alike — live by your own credo, rely upon nothing but your own wits to get what you want.'

With that, one of his hands settled upon on her knee, his fingers coming to rest upon the hem of her dress. She felt a stab of arousal. Somewhat contrarily, she also felt her palm itching to slap his face. It was an urge she fought back; allow his fingers to remain there and who knew what he might say, especially if he thought there was a chance of getting what he so clearly wanted. In reluctant admiration for his audacity, and remembering how Violette had made her rehearse for the possibility that one of her targets would become amorous — or, as the dear girl had so succinctly put it, *fresh* — she pressed her own hand on top of his.

'You're right,' she whispered back, 'I do find it best not to rely on others.'

'You know,' he said, his voice now little more than a murmur, 'striking looks and a streak of determination in a woman make for a heady mix, and I don't mind admitting to finding you most . . . alluring.' The tips of his fingers slid beneath her dress. 'Tantalising . . . ' They edged beyond the top of her stocking. 'Tempting . . . '

With his fingers meeting her skin, she contained a gasp, her insides giving an involuntary lurch. Just how far would he go? Why not find out? If all they were both after was a little diversion, where was the harm? All she need do was pull her room key from her bag and let him see the number stamped upon it. He certainly didn't strike her as the sort to look a gift horse in the mouth. She was in the mood for a little distraction herself; an intriguing stranger she would never have to see again — what better way to let off some steam, deaden the pain of recent disappointments?

Reaching for her bag, she opened the clasp. But, as she reached inside and her fingers folded around her key, a glint of light drew her attention to where Anthony was loading a tray with glasses. Dear God, what was she thinking! This *intriguing stranger* she was minded to take up to

358

her room was an SOE operative whose weakness she was here to test not to indulge. Mortified by the recognition, she withdrew her hand from her bag and snapped it shut. Now, by getting carried away, she had compromised her impartiality, the operation beyond salvaging. So, what to do? Make an excuse and get away? Yes, safest to cut her losses. And quickly. She could stew over what to tell Miss Black in the morning.

Her heart pounding, she knew to make her departure appear casual. Sickened to even be touching him, she lifted his hand from her thigh. 'Well, Mr Sutton,' she said, hoping he wouldn't detect that she was shaking, 'as I mentioned earlier, I've had a dreadfully long day and fear I must now wish you goodnight.'

Careful to keep her movements slow and relaxed, she then lifted her clutch bag from the bar, got down from her stool and, as she always did, signalled to Anthony that she was calling it a night.

Across the bar, where he seemed to be on the point of making a telephone call, Anthony acknowledged her with a smile. 'Good night, Miss Wallis. See you tomorrow.'

Once out in the lobby, she went straight to the lift, pressed the button, and then stood, fanning her face with her hand. How narrowly had she avoided that disaster? It was all very well telling herself now that she had only been tempted for a split second — that all she had done was momentarily entertain a fantasy — but deep down she knew otherwise. Not only had she been on the point of acting upon an urge, she had been about to jeopardise the whole operation.

Stabbing again at the button to call the lift, she stood shaking her head in disbelief. Perhaps she had yet to recover from the shock of what had happened with Richard — and then Wallace — to the extent that the fallout was clouding her judgement. Perhaps she was even suffering in part from delayed grief over the loss of Violette. Perhaps, courting danger was a reaction to all that she'd been through. Charles Sutton, on the other hand, was unlikely to have any such excuse, and was almost certainly just a bad lot through and through.

Regrettably, she reflected, glancing up to see from the indicator that the lift was finally on its way, being obnoxious and overly forward didn't render him unsuitable for undercover operations. Although, did it? His task in France would be to blend in and observe, not draw attention to himself or cause trouble.

With the arrival of the lift, she stepped inside and pressed the button for her floor. While her unease about his character warranted reporting to SOE, of greater urgency was to reflect upon this evening and learn from what could so easily have been a disaster. True, she had brought a stop to his advances, but she should never have let things get that far to start with. It was this dress, she thought, tugging the fabric higher up her chest. It gave men ideas and made her feel . . . well, no matter how invincible it made her feel, she wouldn't wear it again. No matter how close she thought a target was to telling her everything, she wouldn't put herself in a position where he might think she was there for the taking.

Making her way along the corridor, thankful to have come to her senses when she did, she felt about in her handbag and pulled out her door key. Perhaps the best way out of this unfortunate situation would be to telephone Miss Black and ask to be relieved of this particular target — say she didn't feel safe with him and that she wasn't convinced he could be relied upon to follow the rules of engagement once overseas. It would certainly remove the need for her to see him again.

Pleased to feel herself breathing more freely, she imagined for a moment that she could smell his cologne. Funny, wasn't it, the furtive methods used by a guilty conscience to remind one of one's transgressions!

'So, that nightcap you offered me.'

Her hand extended towards the door, she froze. She hadn't imagined the smell of his cologne: he was there, beside her. But how? How the devil had he known where to find her? More importantly, what did she do now?

'Forgive me,' she began, seeing no alternative but to turn and acknowledge him. Despite the renewed thudding of her heart, she hoped she sounded casual. 'But I don't recall offering you a nightcap.'

His response was to smirk. 'No?'

Sensing it unwise to provoke him, she edged back against the doorframe. 'I'm afraid not . . . no.'

As he reached out a hand to lean against the wall, his fingers brushed the top of her arm. With rather more purpose, his other hand arrived in the small of her back.

'The offer,' he said, and with which she found herself being pulled towards him, 'was implied.'

Now what? To stand any chance of getting away from him she would have to catch him by surprise. And she wasn't sure she was thinking clearly enough to do that.

'Well, I'm sorry that you misunderstood — ' The hand that had been on the wall moved to her thigh. She forced herself not to react. ' — but I clearly recall telling you that I was in need of an early night.'

'And you can still *have* your early night.' Grasping a handful of her dress, he forced it up her leg, 'all we'll be doing is helping it along with a little nip of something first. Come on,' he said, gesturing with his head towards the door, '*tonight could be our last* and all that?'

The firmness of his hold meant she wouldn't be able to get away from him now anyway; the power was all his. The only ploy left to her was to try to reason with him. 'Thank you,' she said, her voice quivering, 'but I don't think so.'

'You know . . . ' His face was now so close to hers that she could no longer make out his features, his cologne so powerful she felt queasy. ' . . . I like a bit of a dance about as much as the next man. But at your invitation I came up here for a nightcap. So, a nightcap we're going to have.'

It was the feel of the door key pressing into her

palm that finally gave her an idea.

'Perhaps you're right,' she said, softening her limbs so as to appear to be surrendering to him, 'where's the harm in a nightcap?'

Just as she had been hoping, his grasp on her slackened. 'That's more like it.'

Her plan wasn't without risk, she knew that, but with anger now overtaking her fear, simply getting away from him was no longer enough: now she wanted him held to account, made to pay.

Tightening her hold upon her key, she drew a breath and poked it into the lock.

'Pour us . . . some drinks?' she suggested, opening the door, flicking on the light and going ahead of him into the room. 'I'll just . . . ' Stepping aside to let him pass, she gestured to the bathroom. But the moment she saw him reach the cocktail cabinet, she darted back out into the corridor, pulled the door shut behind her, thrust the key back into the lock and turned it sharply, the clunk of the mechanism barely a second ahead of the pounding of his fists on the other side.

With his cursing in her ears, she tore along the corridor and flew around the corner to the staircase. There, smacking into someone coming the other way, she let out a shriek, the sound of her terror echoing around the stairwell.

'Miss Ward?' Aware only that a pair of hands had hold of her arms, she fought to shake them off. 'Miss Ward, it's me, Raymond Bancroft.'

Jerking her head in the direction of the voice, she saw that it was indeed Mr Bancroft, along with Billy from the concierge desk. Gasping for breath, she gestured over her shoulder. 'It's . . . he's . . . Sutton, I locked him in.'

Above the sound of her panting, she heard Mr Bancroft address Billy. 'Go to the house phone. Have switchboard summon the police.'

'Yes, sir.'

The flooding of relief through her limbs made her feel faint. And with her knees then buckling beneath her, it was Raymond Bancroft's hand under her elbow that slowed her descent to the floor. There, slumped into a heap, she started to cry. Relief, she told herself, sobbing noisily. It was just the relief.

'Miss Ward,' Mr Bancroft said, bending down beside her, 'are you hurt?'

'No . . . no . . . '

'Then please, remain here for a moment while I go and fetch assistance.' Hunched on the floor and crying, she nodded. When he returned moments later, with him was a woman Esme didn't know. 'Miss Ward, this is Mrs Coates, my duty housekeeper. She will take you along to one of our vacant rooms and sit with you until the police arrive.'

Too tired and teary to protest, Esme allowed herself to be helped to her feet, events after that becoming a blur. She remembered the woman called Mrs Coates being kind, bringing her fresh handkerchiefs, a blanket to warm her up and a glass of water to sip. She also recalled that, not too much later, Mr Bancroft arrived with a police sergeant, whose reaction upon entering the room was to look her up and down, shake his head and tut. With little urgency and even less enthusiasm, he suggested she recount what had happened, it being plain from his demeanour that he considered the whole thing to be a waste of his time, no crime having been perpetrated, no laws broken. He didn't even trouble himself to open the cover of his notebook.

For Esme, the experience of being questioned by the police was sobering. Sutton's behaviour might have terrified her, but the sergeant's unspoken opinion couldn't have plainer: what, exactly, had she been expecting to happen, sitting alone in the bar of a hotel, dressed like that? And he had a point.

After that, having declined an offer to move her belongings to a different suite, Mr Bancroft escorted her back to room 303, where he went to the drinks cabinet and poured a finger of whisky.

When he held the glass towards her, she accepted it and took the merest of sips, the effect of it making her shudder.

'Has he been arrested?' she asked. 'Only — '

'At my request,' Mr Bancroft replied, 'he has been removed to the police station to await the arrival of SOE, into whose custody he will shortly be passed.'

She nodded her understanding. Then, despite the effect of her first sip of the whisky, she took another, surprised to find herself relishing the feel of it burning her throat on the way down. Already, the strength of it seemed to be steadying her nerves and helping her to think. 'And then what will happen to him?'

'Even were I to ask, I doubt SOE would tell me.'

'In the bar,' she said, feeling she owed it to Mr Bancroft to explain, 'when he put his hand on my thigh, I brought our conversation to a polite close, bade him goodnight, and took my leave. I have no idea how he knew my room number — I certainly didn't give it to him — nor do I know how he got up here so quickly.'

'No. Thankfully, Anthony had been watching and telephoned to alert me.'

'He knew Sutton was going to follow me?'

'He suspected as much.'

Dear Anthony. She must make a point of thanking him; without his quick thinking, things might have turned out very differently.

'You know,' she said, exhaling heavily, 'the first time I read Sutton's file, I had a feeling about him. And then, when I met him in person, I was even more certain things weren't as they seemed. You see, all the targets so far have been much of a muchness, similar in character, temperament, even in appearance. But Sutton . . . well, he was nothing like any of those before him.'

'Then you must include those observations in your report to Miss Black.'

'I shall.'

'And I will of course submit my own thoughts. As you are aware, my business is The Aurelian, not the operations of SOE, but I do know that while no one expects these men and women to be saints, they do not expect them to draw attention to their presence, worse still, to cause trouble.'

'No.'

'Feeling better now?' he asked after a while longer.

With a weary sigh, she nodded. 'Thank you, yes. Rather badly shaken but otherwise fine.'

'Then if you have no need of anything further, I shall bid you goodnight. Try to get some rest, Miss Ward. Easy to say, I know, but try to put the incident out of your mind. Don't let this one bad apple spoil the whole barrel for you.'

Accompanying Mr Bancroft to the door, Esme wished him goodnight, glanced in both directions along the corridor and then immediately turned the key in the lock.

Crossing to the drinks' cabinet, she picked up the whisky tumbler and downed the remaining contents, the peatiness of the liquid unexpectedly pleasing as it hit the back of her throat. Setting down the glass, she picked up the decanter and poured another measure, larger, this time, than the one she had just finished. Then she unfastened her shoes, pulled the pins from her hair, switched on one of the lamps and went to extinguish the ceiling light. Returning to collect the tumbler, she started towards the bed, only to pause part way there and return for the decanter.

Sinking onto the mattress, she sighed with exhaustion. What the hell was she doing — not just what was she doing putting herself in such a situation tonight, but what was she doing in this job? As exciting as it had once seemed, tonight's little episode had left her feeling shabby, and made her life in this hotel, surrounded by privilege and luxury, seem false and shallow. And that was without stopping to consider her life more generally. For goodness' sake, here she was, still reeling from her disastrous meeting with Richard and yet the moment she had arrived back, where had she gone? Straight after Marcus Latham, that's where. That act of desperation alone surely raised questions about her state of mind.

'Seriously,' she said out loud, swilling the amber liquid around in the tumbler, 'you jilted your fiance. You upset and abandoned the people who raised you. You allowed yourself to be swept along by the idea of becoming a covert operator. I mean, really, *you*, a *spy*. Absurd. Then . . . the moment it was apparent you wouldn't be any good at that, you leapt at the chance to get all dolled up every night in order to try and lure men into betraying their country. You've fallen for *at least* two of them. Worse than that, in a belated attack of remorse for jilting your fiance, you go and ask him to take you back, only to be . . . to be astounded by the discovery that he has moved on with his life. And now, tonight, the icing on the cake, you go into the bar of a hotel, wearing a tight dress and far too much make up, to sit like a sixpenny harlot . . . only to be left wondering how the target of your attentions could possibly have got the wrong idea.' Pausing for a moment to stare at the contents of her glass, she raised it to her lips and then downed the lot in one go. Shuddering from the aftereffects, she let out a growl and reached to the decanter for more. 'You're lost,' she mumbled, gloom descending more heavily with each mouthful. 'That's what you are. Lost. It's one thing . . . it's one thing to . . . damn. Now you can't even . . . think straight. Well, you're not going to sleep until you've listened to me.' To that end, she held herself rigidly. 'It's one thing to want to work out who you are . . . ' God, she felt strange. 'But quite another to . . . to . . . ' It was no good, she was going to have to lie down. Just for a moment. Just until she didn't feel so hot and . . . woozy. Just while she . . . ah, thank goodness for that, a nice soft pillow . . .

★ ★ ★

Something to four? How could the clock be saying it was something to four? And anyway, was that four in the morning or in the afternoon?

Raising her head from the pillow, Esme screwed up her eyes. Why was the bedside lamp on? And what was that smell, that damp earthy, manly aroma?

Unable to work out why everything seemed wrong, Esme slowly pushed herself up from the bed. Before her eyes, the room spun like a carousel. Oh, dear God. Of course. The whisky.

Carefully, she inched towards the edge of the bed. What a state — still fully dressed and with no idea whether it was morning or afternoon. Padding to the window, she eased apart the curtains and tweaked the edge of the blackout blind. Darkness. Beyond the window was utter darkness. Four in the morning then.

Taking care to replace the blind, she turned

back into the room. Water. The first thing she had to do was ease this cracked feeling in her throat. To that end, she went to the bathroom, switched on the light, narrowed her eyes against the brightness and turned on the tap. Having filled a glass, she sipped the contents, her throat initially too dry to swallow it without discomfort. Flexing her shoulders, she held up her head, the sight staring back from the mirror making her gasp: her hair was flat on one side; the skin beneath her eyes was stained with the black of her mascara; the smudging of her lipstick making it look as though she had been drinking blood. Ghoulish, that's how she looked. Throbbing headache or not, she had to get cleaned up. Then she had to go back to sleep. Then, in the morning, she had to sort herself out. She couldn't go on like this. There might be a war on, and she might want to do her bit, but carrying on like this would be the death of her — although not, as had been the case with poor Violette, through anything the Germans did. So, she would get some more sleep, pray that when she awoke it was with a clearer head, and then decide how to get herself out of this terrible mess.

★ ★ ★

There was someone at the door. Glancing to her travel alarm and seeing that it was nine o'clock, Esme heaved herself up. At least the room had stopped spinning.

Grateful for the wherewithal to have got

herself cleaned up and into her nightdress, she pushed back the covers, reached for her wrap, pulled it on, and went to see who it was.

It turned out to be a waiter with a room service trolley.

'Good morning, Miss Ward. Forgive me for disturbing you but Mr Bancroft thought you might like breakfast.'

Coffee, she thought, catching the aroma of it as the waiter wheeled his trolley into the room. 'Thank you,' she said, watching him remove the covers from various dishes and trays.

'Would you like me to open the curtains?'

She nodded, immediately regretting the dizzying effect upon her head. 'Please do. And open one of the doors if you would. I should like some fresh air.'

'Yes, Miss Ward.'

'And please ask housekeeping to leave servicing my room until later. I have some work to do.'

'Of course. Oh, and Mr Bancroft asked me to tell you that SOE have him.'

Esme frowned. 'SOE have him?'

'That's what he said, miss. 'SOE have him.' He said you'd know what that meant.'

Ah, SOE had Sutton. Well thank goodness. Hopefully, they would cart him off to one of those top-secret Scottish island bunkers they were rumoured to have and put him to some sort of hard labour there — at least until the war was over.

Unexpectedly ravenous, she went to the table and surveyed the breakfast tray. A rack of toast, a basket of tiny pastries and, under the cloche, a plate of salmon, saute potatoes, spinach, and poached eggs. Along with the packet of Alka Seltzer and the carafe of water, it constituted the perfect remedy for a hangover. Dear Mr Bancroft: when it came to anticipating the needs of his guests, he didn't miss a trick.

Sometime later, having devoured almost every morsel of food on the tray and drained the coffee pot, Esme got up and went to sit at the desk, where she directed her thoughts to the matter of what to report to SOE — even if it did no longer matter. Unsure where to start, she found a loose sheet of paper and scribbled a list of her observations about the man masquerading as Charles Sutton. Then she set about completing the form, ending by crossing through the word at the bottom that said 'Recommended' and writing instead, *Grave concerns as to suitability of temperament.*

Signing her name at the foot of the document, she tore up her list and reached for the bin, the sight of something in the bottom of it causing her to bend and lift it out. Ah. Yes. The telephone message from her mother.

Turning it over in her hand, she pondered what to do: to telephone as requested or to ignore it? Really, she should call; after all, something awful might have happened. And how would she feel to find out that, say, Grandpa Hugh was at death's door and all the family had gathered to say their goodbyes except her? Hoping to discover nothing of the sort, she went back to the desk, lifted the telephone receiver, and dialled 'o' for the switchboard.

'Good morning. I should like to place a person to person call to Mrs Lawrence Colborne, Kensington 312. Yes, thank you, I'll hold.'

Waiting to be connected, she tried to think what — other than an illness or accident — might be so urgent as to prompt her mother to telephone in the first place.

'Caller, I have Mrs Colborne.'

'Mummy? It's Esme.' From the other end of the line there was only crackling. 'Mummy? Are you there?'

'Darling, thank goodness.'

Detecting the relief in her mother's voice, Esme tensed. 'Mummy, is everything all right?'

'Yes, darling, all fine. I left that message for you because Richard telephoned.'

Esme tightened her grip on the receiver. 'Did you say Richard? Golly, this is a terrible line.'

'Richard, yes,' Naomi Colborne repeated. 'He enquired whether I knew how to contact you. And when I said that I could get a message to you, he asked if I would do so.'

She tightened her grasp further still. Where was this this going?

'All right. And what is his message?'

'I'm sorry, darling, you're terribly faint.'

'*I said* what was his message?'

'Oh! Oh, well, he asked me to say that he'd like to talk to you — '

He wanted to *talk* to her? 'Did he say why?'

' — which struck me as odd because only yesterday I saw it in *The Telegraph*.'

'Saw what in *The Telegraph*?'

373

'In Hatch, Match and Despatch. His engagement to the Povey girl.'

Oh. Yes. That.

'Of course. So, he gave no hint as to why he wants to talk to me?'

'None, darling. No.'

'All right, well, I'll think about it.'

'Do you still have his telephone number.'

She hesitated. 'Somewhere, I think.'

'Juniper 2579. Write it down.'

'Juniper 2579.'

'If you do decide to telephone, might I suggest not leaving it too long?'

'If I do decide to, I'll try this evening.'

'All right, darling. Goodbye then.'

'Goodbye, Mummy. And thank you.'

Replacing the receiver on its cradle, Esme wondered what possible reason Richard could have for wanting to speak to her. He had made his situation perfectly clear. Even had he wanted to do something as insensitive as invite her to the wedding, he would have no need to speak to her; he could just send the invitation to Clarence Square. Besides, he wouldn't invite her anyway, would he? No, of course he wouldn't.

Remembering what he'd said about working long days, she knew there was no point trying to telephone until well into the evening, which would mean spending the remainder of the morning, followed by an entire afternoon and then several hours after that, burdened by curiosity. At least she had no decoy duties tonight; at least the evening was her own. Thank goodness.

Going to stand at the window, she looked down upon the deserted promenade and sighed. Whatever Richard wanted to talk to her about, she must remain circumspect. She'd had enough upsets recently, without courting more, and her mind was already bursting with matters requiring decisions — her work and the very course of her future among them. What she didn't need now, was a mind cluttered with Richard Trevannion — someone she should be doing her utmost to forget.

★ ★ ★

Watching the progress of the second hand around the dial of the clock, Esme pressed the telephone receiver closer to her ear. How could it possibly be taking the operator so long to connect her?

She glanced again to the time. Eight-thirty. Surely, he would be home by now?

'Juniper 2579.'

Thank goodness!

'Hullo? Richard, it's me, Esme.' Concerned more with sounding business-like than with giving him the chance to respond, she hurried straight on. 'I had a message from Mummy to say you wanted me to telephone.' Pleased with her matter of fact tone — something she had spent a good part of the day perfecting — she paused long enough to allow him to respond.

'Esme. Yes. Thank you for telephoning. Did you try earlier?'

'No, I recalled you saying you often have to

work late.' *Well done. Still nice and impersonal. Keep it up.*

'Yes, that's right. Good. Anyway, look . . . Christ, this is difficult. Definitely not the sort of conversation to be having over the telephone.'

'Richard, whatever it is, just say it. I promise I won't hang up without warning.'

'I've broken it off with Caroline.'

Reaching to the edge of the desk, she gripped it tightly. 'What?'

'Caroline. I've broken off our engagement.'

'Sorry, yes, it's not that I didn't hear you, it's more that I'm wondering why you would do such a thing when you've only just asked her to marry you. Mummy said it's only just been in *The Telegraph*.'

'I know, which is why having this conversation over the telephone is so . . . Anyway, the truth of the matter is that I thought about what you said and I — '

'Thought about what *I* said?' Ignoring her decision to let him do the talking, she went on, 'Look, Richard, if you're going to blame this catastrophic turn of events on me, then I'm telling you now, I *will* hang up.' *How dare he? How dare he?*

'No, wait, Esme, please don't do that! You misunderstand. Hear me out, if you will. It's important.'

She sighed heavily. She was in no mood for this. 'Go on then.'

'Look, I'm making a complete and utter hash of this. I knew I would. So, please, will you just listen while I try to explain what happened?'

Even though he obviously couldn't see her, she nevertheless treated him to a despairing shrug. 'All right. Go on. I'll listen.'

And so, she did. She listened to him telling her that she had been right: without him realising what had been going on, he had been corralled into spending time with Caroline; that in her desire to present the Trevannions as beyond reproach, and thus protect Hedley's chances of being selected to stand at the forthcoming by-election, his mother had taken advantage of his confusion and heartbreak at being jilted to advance her own cause. He'd been so busy with his work, he said, and Caroline had played her part so perfectly, acting with such calmness and understanding, that he had failed to see what the pair of them had been up to.

At the other end of the line, Esme sat listening. None of what Richard was saying came as a surprise — that he should be telling her at all simply making her cross. Still, at least he was no longer throwing away his life on someone he didn't love.

'So, you see, Esme, you were right.'

'Hardly the point now,' she said bitterly. 'But thank you for bothering to tell me.'

'Dear God,' he said. 'I'm not telling you because you were right!' To Esme, he suddenly sounded as exasperated as she felt. 'I'm telling you because . . . well, because if you would still like us to try again, then nothing would make me happier.' Despite her desire to leap up from her chair and shout with joy, Esme remained perfectly still and forced herself to replay in her mind what he had just said. 'Esme, are you still there? Please God tell me you haven't hung up?'

'I'm still here,' she said, unable to prevent her lips from forming into a smile. 'So, what, precisely, is it that you're proposing — that we just pick up where we left off? That we set a new date for the wedding? That we take some time to start over and . . . well, what, exactly, is it that you envisage us doing?'

When, from the other end of the line there was only silence, she tried to swallow down her panic. *Please don't let him be having second thoughts.*

'I suppose, in an ideal world, I should like us to go back in time a few months and just . . . well, just start again from there as though none of this had happened. But you have your work now . . . and even just the fact that you are no longer in town would make that difficult . . .'

Work? He was worried about *her work*? Although he couldn't possibly know it, the unlikely timing of this couldn't *be* more opportune.

Circumspect, she reminded herself. *Be sure this is really what you want. Be sure you are prepared to make the necessary sacrifices — because it won't fall upon him to change his way of life but upon you to change yours.*

'Richard, the reason I ask what you are expecting us to do, is because appealing though it might seem, and the matter of my work aside, we can't wind back time. No one can do that. After all that's happened — especially to me, and none of which you yet know about — I've

378

changed. The work I've been doing has opened my eyes and made me see the world differently. I don't think it would be exaggerating to say that it has fundamentally altered who I am. In addition to that, a little while back I lost a dear friend, and that tragedy, too, has had a profound effect upon me, has put things into perspective and given me a better understanding of what's important in life.'

'Yes, I suppose it would have.' Suddenly, he didn't sound so bright. 'So, what are you saying, Esme? That you *don't* want us to try again?'

'God, no!' Clutching tightly to the receiver, she almost leapt from her chair at the thought. 'I most definitely *do* want us to. Look,' she said, struck by what seemed the obvious solution. 'Why don't we meet? I could take a couple of days off work and we could just spend some time together, see how it goes. Just because we can't go back in time, doesn't mean we can't go forward.'

'Do you think you could come up to town?' Now he sounded relieved — cautious, but relieved.

'I should think so, yes.'

'You could arrange it? Even with the travel restrictions and the diabolical state of the trains?'

'I should be able to. When were you thinking of?'

'Friday? Or is that too soon?'

'No,' she said, beaming to herself, 'Friday would be perfect.'

'Bring a bag. Stay the weekend. If I'm due to work, I'll wangle some leave. We'll spend a couple of days together.'

Her grin deepened further; the longer they continued talking, the less she felt able to contain her joy. 'Dare I ask where you intend for me to stay?'

'I'll leave that up to you. But you'd be welcome at the flat ... .'

With her free arm, she hugged herself. 'What time on Friday?'

'I'll try to be back there for six. But I'll leave a key next door with Mr Harris just in case, so arrive whenever you can.'

'All right. I'll see you on Friday then.'

'Friday, yes. But Esme — '

'Damn. Our three minutes are up.'

' — perhaps don't say anything to anyone else yet.'

'Oh, God, no. Absolutely. Not a word to a soul.'

'Well, goodnight then,' he said, the familiar tenderness back in his voice.

'Yes, goodnight, Richard. See you Friday.'

★ ★ ★

'So, what shall we do with the rest of the day then?'

In response to Richard's question, Esme pulled the sheet over her naked limbs and propped herself up on her elbow. 'More of what we were just doing would be nice.'

'Esme Pamela Diana Colborne!' he said, affecting outrage. 'Do you have *no* shame?'

Warm and relaxed, Esme grinned. 'Where you

are concerned, apparently not.'

'Personally,' he said, running the tips of his fingers over the top of her shoulder, 'I think this wanton behaviour from you is all just a ploy to get me hunting out that very expensive wedding ring I bought for you.'

She sat more upright. 'You still have it? You didn't return it and try to get your money back?'

His expression suggested he was genuinely affronted. 'Of course I still have it. And although perhaps I shouldn't admit to it just yet, yesterday morning, I even checked that I knew where it was.'

Oh, how she loved this dear man! And how foolish had she been! Were it not for her bullheadedness, she could have been here with him like this all along. 'And was it?' she asked, smiling at the way things were turning out. 'Where you thought it was?'

'Fortunately, yes.'

'Only, given how we've just spent the morning, I really do think that now you'll *have* to marry me.'

His expression straightening, Richard, too, sat upright. 'Are you saying . . . ?'

'I'm saying . . . I think we should go ahead and get married. But quietly, no fuss.'

'Seriously?'

'Seriously,' she said. 'The instant you came through that door yesterday evening, I knew it was what I wanted.'

His relief seemed almost tangible. 'Thank heavens for that.'

'As to how and when — '

'Well, what I should probably tell you — '

'Richard Trevannion, what have you done?' Although laughing as she said it, she nevertheless felt a prickle of panic. What *had* he done?

'I may or may not have spent my lunch hour finding out the earliest date we could be married . . .'

Speechless with surprise, she launched herself at him. 'You didn't!'

Disentangling himself from her embrace, he looked earnestly back at her. 'Don't get cross with me,' he pleaded, holding up his hands as though to protect himself, 'or accuse me of being presumptuous but, knowing the subject would come up — or, rather, *hoping* it would — I decided to establish how these things work.'

'And how do they work?'

'Well, if we're happy to be married by the superintendent registrar, rather than in church, we could do so on the twenty-seventh.'

'Of September?'

'Of this month, yes.'

'Golly.'

'Too soon?' he asked, brushing aside her hair from her face.

'Not soon enough!'

'Please, Esme, do let's be serious for a moment. First of all, do you still want us to be married?'

'Yes. Yes, yes, yes! Of course I do. Don't you?'

'I do, yes.'

'As long as you don't mind that I've changed,' she said, it seeming critical now, more than ever, that she be honest with him. 'The things I've

seen, the things I've done . . . they've made me
. . . well, they've made me grow up, I suppose.
Back in Clarence Square that night in May — '

'The night of the family dinner?'

She nodded. 'The night I shudder to recall
now, yes. Anyway, you asked me that night
whether I had any last-minute doubts. I seem to
remember I made light, but the truth was, I did
have doubts. Even before finding out about my
parents, I doubted that I could be good enough
for you. I felt panicked by the idea of having to
be perfect — '

'Esme, darling, there's no need to explain — '

'No,' she said. 'There is. I need you to know
that despite feeling giddy and in love, inside I
was terrified that I wouldn't live up to the
Trevannion standards. And then, when my
mother broke the news . . . '

'It was my fault,' Richard said. 'I rushed you
and I shouldn't have. Just because *I* felt certain, I
should never simply have assumed that you did
too.'

'Anyway,' she said, and exhaled a long sigh.
'What I'm trying to say is that although I had
qualms then, I don't now. Being without you
these last months has helped me to see what is
important . . . in particular to see that striving to
be perfect is a waste of time. No matter what we
might like to think, none of us is perfect. And so,
if you don't mind that I've become more certain
of my own mind . . . more assertive, I
suppose . . . '

Smiling back at her, Richard shook his head. 'I
don't.'

'And that I should want to keep working. Well, for now, at least . . . '

'I don't mind at all. In fact, the thought of my wife working for the good of the war would make me proud.'

But it wasn't just the act of working, she reminded herself; it was the secrecy attached to what she had done so far, if not to what she subsequently went on to do. After all, who knew what that might turn out to be? She had begun to hope she might continue to work for SOE, just not as a decoy; here now, with Richard, even just thinking about what she'd been doing in Brighton made her feel unclean.

'Perhaps more importantly,' she said, 'you won't mind that I might not be able to tell you about it?'

Still smiling, he shook his head. 'No.'

'And that no matter the work I might do in the future, I will never be able to discuss with you what I've been doing these last three months — that the Official Secrets Act will always trump our contract of marriage?'

Again, he smiled. 'I don't need to know what you've been doing. Besides, the same rules apply to me. I'm bound by the same restrictions.'

'And your parents?' she asked, sitting back and looking at him. All of a sudden, what had seemed simply a matter of setting a date with the registrar felt beset with hurdles — some of them rather thorny. 'It doesn't bother you what they will have to say on the matter? Because I don't think they are going to open their arms and welcome me back.'

'If they don't,' he said, 'well, that's down to them. It will make no difference to my desire to make you Mrs Richard Trevannion.'

'You're sure,' she said, matching his expression for earnestness. 'Only, family disagreements can be — '

'Esme, darling, this won't be the first time I've caused my parents to shake their heads in dismay or wring their hands in despair and question where my loyalties lie. And I somehow doubt it will be the last time, either. If it's a golden boy they want, they have Hedley — that burden being one I am more than happy to let him carry.'

Fine words, she thought, but she still needed to be sure. 'You're certain of that.'

'Certain,' he replied. 'Either they accept us as Mr and Mrs Richard Trevannion, or they don't. It really couldn't be simpler.'

'And we agree that we're going to do this without telling them — without telling anyone?' Gradually, she was lowering each of the hurdles to a more surmountable height or, at least, removing some of their thorns.

'What about Mrs Colborne? Won't she be put out?'

Esme shrugged. 'I should imagine she will be horribly put out, yes. And yet, when we tell her afterwards, I think she'll understand.'

'All right. Well, given all that's happened, then yes, I think it would be best not to say anything to anyone. As long as we have two witnesses, no one else need know.'

'Witnesses.' In a far corner of her mind, Esme

felt the stirrings of an idea.

'But we don't have to worry about that now. We can always drag someone off the street. People do that, or so I've heard.'

Despite knowing that he was joking, Esme shook her head. 'No,' she said, her idea exerting a tighter grip on her thoughts. 'No, I know the perfect couple . . .'

'I thought we weren't telling anyone . . .'

'We're not,' she said, lowering herself back to the pillow and pulling him down alongside her. 'The people I have in mind aren't just anyone. But, given their whereabouts, it's going to take some pulling off.'

Against her side, she felt him shrug. 'Then I'll leave it in your capable hands.'

'Good,' she said, convinced she would never be happier than she was at that moment. 'Then I think all that remains . . . ' Slipping from his embrace, she reached from the bed to her handbag and rummaged about inside. ' . . . is for me to start wearing this again.' Turning back to him, she held up her left hand, the diamond in her engagement ring glinting in the sunlight. 'If nothing else, it makes the fact that I'm here in your bed with you feel just that little bit less wanton.'

'Shame. I rather liked wanton.'

'Hm.'

Settling back against him, she let out a sigh. Lou had been right. Her seeming mound of confusion over who she really was had been merely a distraction. Colborne or Ward, the real issue was simply whether or not she still wanted to marry Richard.

And, yes, she might have taken a long and circuitous route to arrive at the answer to that question, but now she had. Now, she could stop worrying about who she was and what anyone would think of her; far more important than having been born Esme Ward and brought up as Esme Colborne — both matters in which she'd had no say — was what she chose to do with her life from hereon: building a life with Richard as Esme Trevannion.

September 1940

The little waiting room reeked of polish. As smells in public buildings went, it wasn't the worst, but it *was* pungent — especially, Esme thought, glancing about at the dark wooden furnishings, on an empty stomach. Not helping the situation was the fact that the closer it drew to eleven o'clock, the more Richard kept getting up and pacing about.

'Where did you say they're travelling from?' he asked, glancing yet again to his wristwatch.

'Windsor. As I told you not five minutes back, they were staying last night with Aunt Diana. And I know they arrived there because I telephoned to check.'

'Then you'd think they'd be here by now.'

Getting up from the chair where she'd been sitting for the last twenty minutes, she went to take Richard's hand. 'Darling,' she said pressing it between her own, 'they'll be here. If they were going to be late, they would have telephoned.'

In his dark navy suit, and with the immaculate Windsor knot of his patterned necktie setting off his astonishingly white shirt collar, he looked more like a Whitehall official than a groom, but she didn't mind; one way or another, even if they did have to drag two witnesses off the street, at eleven o'clock, they were getting married.

For her part, Esme had chosen to wear a tea-length dress of ivory Mikado silk, with a cinched-in waist and a pearl trim across the wide neckline. Seeing it in the window of a shop in Bond Street, she had marched straight in, tried it on and bought it there and then. Bridal, but without being too girly, and elegant in its simplicity, her only regret was that she could foresee no possible occasion in the future that would ever warrant the wearing of such a romantic dress.

Startled from her reflections by the opening of the door, she swivelled sharply towards it. They were here!

Sadly, it turned out to be the assistant registrar. Having glanced between them, he checked the chit of paper in his hand. 'Still not here yet?'

She shook her head. 'No, but I assure you they will be.'

The look he gave her was a weary one. 'Well, if they're not here in the next five minutes, you will have to decide whether you want to go ahead without them.'

'Let's go and wait in the lobby,' Esme said when the assistant registrar had left and closed the door behind him, the smell of the polish combined with hunger and the onset of her own panic now beginning to make her feel nauseous. 'I could do with breathing fresher air.'

With a single nod, Richard got to his feet, and together they stepped out into the foyer. But, no sooner had they done so than through the entrance doors burst Lou, pink-cheeked and breathless on the arm of a broad-shouldered man in military attire.

'Sorry! So terribly sorry, both of you . . . '

Exhaling with relief, Esme rushed the remaining few steps to greet her. 'Well, you certainly cut *that* fine!' she said, wrapping Lou in a light hug and kissing her cheek.

'Yes, so sorry. We took a wrong turn leaving Waterloo station.'

'Come on, then, both of you, quickly. The registrar's assistant has already warned us about holding things up. And trust me, I have absolutely no intention of missing my wedding for a second time!'

Acknowledgements

I should like to take this opportunity to acknowledge the role of the real 'decoy women' of World War II, whose lives were nowhere near as glamorous as I have portrayed, whose vital contributions to the war effort are little known, and whose sacrifices are rarely recognised.